Advance Praise for

The Cha-Cha Babes of Pelican Way

The Cha-Cha Babes of Pelican Way is a fast-paced romp of death, passion, and dark humor. Way too damn much fun!

— Jonathan Maberry, *New York Times* best-selling author of *Glimpse*

You will never look at the cha-cha or a fifty-five-plus gated community the same way again. This novel has suspense, murder, laughter, and twists and turns in the story until the very end. Find out about the close calls three friends have. How bad are they really?

— Gloria Mindock, author of *Whiteness of Bone,* editor and publisher for Çervana Barra Press

Frances Metzman has written a compelling, complex tale that blends retirement living with murder, romance, and friendship, reminding us of *The Golden Girls*. The novel is laced with humor, pathos, and sex. It also delves into the lives of three best friends who are residents of the retirement community and met during cha-cha lessons, highlighting their foibles and achievements as well as their entanglements and challenges—mental and physical illnesses, strained relationships with adult children, and second chances at love. *The Cha-Cha Babes of Pelican Way* has humor, darkness, and nobility throughout. A real page-turner!

—Janice Booker, journalist, teacher, author of *Philly Firsts: The Famous, Infamous, and Quirky of the City of Brotherly Love*, and former host of Philadelphia radio program *The Janice Booker Show*

Frances Metzman's fiction leaps with subtle humor and dynamic surrealism. Her characters enter your private study to partake in a bit of tea or to casually recount a bawdy joke—depending on mood. The American landscape filleted before you!

— Ray Greenblatt, teacher at Temple University–OLLI and reviewer for the John Updike Society and the Dylan Thomas Society

The Cha-Cha Babes of Pelican Way

A Novel

by Frances Metzman

**WILD
RIVER
BOOKS**

Published by Wild River Books
PO Box 672
Lambertville, NJ 08530
www.wildriverconsultingandpublishing.com

Distributed by Wild River Consulting & Publishing, LLC.

Design and composition by:
Tim Ogline / Ogline Design for Wild River Consulting & Publishing, LLC.

Publisher's Cataloging-In-Publication Data
Metzman, Frances
    The Cha-Cha Babes of Pelican Way

ISBN: 978-1-941948-06-4

Library of Congress Control Number: 2018934330

Printed in the United States of America

First Edition

For my children, Carla, Stephen, and Ross,
and my grandchildren, Zander and Zax.

And for Jay, of course.

Chapter 1

Celia

The piercing sound of the phone startled Celia Ewing awake. With a feeling of dread, she fumbled for her cell on the night table.

"Celia." A female voice squeaked like a trapped mouse.

"Marcy? What's going on?" Celia propped herself up on an elbow and checked the clock on her nightstand. It was nearly 3:00 a.m.

"Um, big problem here. I need help." Marcy's voice sounded squished.

Celia heard a wheezing intake of breath, and a guttural outtake. "Marcy, honey, should I call 911?"

"No, no. Please. Just get over here. Just ... but ..." Then a hissing sound. "Not home."

Celia rubbed her half-closed eyes, then blinked them wide open. "Where are you?"

"Get Deb. Come to Melvin's office. Door lock ... broken ... something blocking." Marcy started her sentences like a fully inflated balloon, slowly diminishing till the air rushed out in a big whoosh. "Both ... push door. Can't get up."

"Should I get help? A security guard? I don't think ..."

"No help, damn it! No outsiders. Don't think! Get here pronto."

Celia heard a loud grunt before Marcy hung up.

What in the world had Marcy gotten herself into, Celia wondered. This wasn't her beloved, vivacious friend's first call for help, but Marcy had never sounded this dire. Celia speed-dialed their friend Deb, jumped up, and switched on the light above her queen-sized bed. No answer from Deb, who suffered from full-blown rheumatoid arthritis and took sleeping pills every night. Deb and Marcy were the only good friends she'd made in Boca Pelicano Palms, Florida, the fifty-five-and-over retirement community where she'd moved two years ago. The longest street was Pelican Way, which they all lived on.

Struggling to organize her thoughts, Celia put on jeans and an oversized T-shirt. If the urgency in Marcy's voice hadn't terrified her, she would have laughed. Some of Marcy's past antics had caused eyes to roll among a small cluster of gossipy neighbors who had nothing better to do with their time than judge what people wore or said. She first met Marcy Worthmire and Deb Castor at a cha-cha dance lesson. They'd connected from the get-go, and what Celia loved most was their honesty and lack of pretense. Although their three personalities ran the spectrum from conventional to ornery to sexpot, her new friends had her back and she theirs.

When her husband, Gabe, had died three years ago, she had felt grief but also a rush of freedom that she'd rarely ever experienced. The village of Boca Pelicano Palms sat in the middle of the town of Boca Pelicano in Florida. The Sunshine State seemed to offer Celia a new life, but she soon realized she didn't fit in. But three months after arriving, she met Marcy and Deb. They became her village, her tribe, her family. She'd do anything for them, especially since they had saved her life. She didn't want to think about that near catastrophe now.

She left her apartment and started power walking along the outdoor block-long corridor. Once she reached the stairs, she'd still have to walk several minutes across the complex to Melvin's office at the clubhouse.

"My new friends are zany but are straight shooters and caring. I love them," Celia had explained to her daughter, Allison, during one of their many awkward calls.

"Zany? Does that mean loony tunes?" Allison didn't call again for two weeks.

At that first cha-cha lesson, Deb, the oldest of the three at seventy-one, wore an ill-fitting dress with an uneven hemline and splashed with magenta flowers over her skeletal body. Her rheumatoid arthritis had started in her forties and progressed over the years. Now it affected every joint and muscle in her body, except for her acerbic tongue. Her personality vacillated from cheeky to a bit hostile, and she seemed to have no filters, spouting just what was on her mind. In restaurants she absconded with sugar packets, ketchup bottles, and bread. Her attempts at knitting with gnarled fingers turned out lumpy, mish-mashed, lopsided scarves in colors that Marcy called vomit green and oily yellow. Still, the three of them always wore the scarves on cool nights. At those times, a smiling Deb never uttered a nasty word.

Celia's heart kicked up a notch faster as the panic in Marcy's voice echoed in her mind. She pressed Deb's number on her cell once again.

"Hulloo," Deb said in a sleepy voice.

"It's me. Marcy needs help. We can't call 911. Meet me at Melvin's office."

"Oh shit. She's at it again?"

"She sounds awful."

"On my way."

Tall, curvaceous Marcy—flamboyant and unapologetic—decked herself out in blinding, neon-colored skimpy skirts and low-cut chartreuse or orange blouses. At sixty-five, the same age as Celia, and in vibrant health, she sought out unattached men—on the premises or electronically—with a vengeance. Both Marcy and Deb, despite their different personalities, often joined Celia on jaunts to art galleries, theaters, or the orchestra.

As Celia crossed over the bridge that connected her building to the walkway leading to the clubhouse, she listened for the dreaded sirens that often fragmented the night air. Ambulances zipped in and out of retirement complexes as frequently as ice cream trucks drove around playgrounds. But only palm fronds rustled overhead, lit by a full moon silvering the surface of the reflecting pool, spouting a fountain of water at the center.

Celia recalled Marcy's last predicament. A few months ago, she had been caught, stark naked, with the gardener after a tryst in an isolated area near a brook along the golf course. An alligator had crawled out of the water, sending a naked Marcy and gardener into the clubhouse. Before that she got caught on the roof with the roofer. One more violation and the board of directors promised to evict her. Celia often wondered if Marcy got into trouble as a way to thumb her nose at the few mean spirited-people who tortured her with snippy remarks.

Celia entered the clubhouse that housed the community's offices and where they served the community meals, brought in entertainment, and hosted card clubs, movies, and speakers on health issues.

The kitchen and nurses' station were empty. When she reached Melvin's office, she saw Deb hobbling along the corridor, wearing a frayed sweater over her nightgown, her backless slippers flopping and her face grimacing with effort. Celia pushed against the door, but it wouldn't budge. "Marcy!" she called.

"Keep it down," Marcy's hoarse voice came from inside. "Push hard."

Celia looked at Deb. "Let's do it."

"Are you kidding?"

It seemed impossible to force the door open but Celia would never desert her dear friend. "Push as hard as you can."

Deb raised a tired, white eyebrow that blended with the pale skin of her creased forehead. She placed two palms against the door.

Celia braced her shoulder and thrust against the door. It moved a couple of inches. Then she used her foot and pressed with all her might as Deb flattened her back on the door and shoved. "On the count of three, give it all you have. One, two …"

The door opened enough for them to squeeze through. From the corner of her eye Celia saw that an overstuffed, worn-out chair had blocked the door. The air conditioning was turned down for the night, and the hot humid air in the small office smelled of Melvin's stale cherry pipe tobacco, the scent more like overripe, decaying fruit.

Befuddled, Celia saw Marcy prone on the desktop buried up to her neck under a huge white mound.

"Thank God you're here," Marcy rasped and raised her head an inch off the desk.

"Is that Melvin's bare butt? You guys look like a porno cartoon in a retirement magazine," Deb croaked.

Celia blinked hard. Marcy's body was obliterated by Melvin's overweight, blubbery frame. No surprise that they were stark naked.

Marcy's arms flailed. In one hand, she held a cell phone. Melvin's unmoving body drooped over the edge of the desktop, his legs dangling. "I managed to reach my handbag on the chair to get my cell, thankfully." She grunted. "My Melvy collapsed on top of me during … oh, you know why. I can't move." Her breath came in sluggish pulls. "We've got to help him."

"Do you think he's okay?" Celia didn't go any closer. "This is terrible."

"Poor Melvin fainted. Get him off … move him, so I can breathe," Marcy barked.

"How bad is he? Sorry I made a joke. Didn't know …" Deb's face morphed into alarm.

While Marcy pushed Melvin's shoulders, Celia tugged his calves, trying not to look at his nakedness. She avoided touching his wide, flat butt. The effort sent the lower half of his body hanging further over the desk. Marcy's arms and legs freed up, but her body remained imprisoned.

"I'm so sorry, Melvy honey," she crooned, tears streaking her cheeks. "You'll be okay."

"Stop," Celia said. Melvin's feet hung about a foot off the ground, and his head rested on Marcy's abdomen. "If we force him off he'll crash on the floor and maybe bash his head or something. They say never move an unconscious person." Celia had never been fond of the man, and tried to erase the vivid images of his nude body. "How are you now, sweetie?"

Marcy managed to choke out, "I can … breathe a little better.

Melvy, honey we'll get you to the doctor ASAP, and you'll be eating my brisket before you know it."

Deb clucked her tongue. "It's bad," she mumbled. "He's dead. Maybe a heart attack?"

Celia felt her stomach tighten hearing her thoughts voiced aloud.

"Melvin had diabetes but no heart problems," Marcy said, taking a deep breath.

Celia knew Deb was right but didn't want to give up hope. "Deb, call 911."

Celia noticed a small refrigerator in the corner. Something sugary for a diabetic in shock would help. She stepped over books, manila envelopes, metal file holders, paper clips, and a smattering of pens on the floor and pictured Melvin and Marcy sweeping everything off the desk in a fit of passion. Inside the refrigerator she saw a jar of honey and some orange juice.

"Maybe orange juice to get his sugar level up?" She held up the carton, forcing her voice to sound calm. Celia found a paper cup and poured juice into it.

"There's no point," Deb said. "I checked his breathing and pulse. Nothing."

Celia watched for the slightest movement. Nothing. "Where are the paramedics?"

Deb shrugged and her white eyebrows met over the bridge of her nose. "This is Florida. They're busy all night long."

Celia rubbed Melvin's cold, taut cheek with her hand. Nothing. "Oh God." She tried to find a pulse because Deb's fingers were often numb. But she found nothing.

Marcy gulped air. "Help him, please."

"He's gone," Deb whispered to Celia. "Marcy's in big trouble."

Celia squeezed her eyes shut for a moment and didn't disagree. She surveyed the scene. A frayed gray blanket cushioned Marcy's back, her eyes wide with fear as she kneaded Melvin's neck. "You feel so cold, Melvy, wake up." She pressed her fist to her mouth and gagged. "I might be sick."

Deb grabbed a wastebasket, removed Marcy's handbag from the chair, and replaced it with the can.

"Did this guy of yours take Viagra?" Deb squeaked.

"Not with me." Marcy wheezed. "Had a heart like a healthy ape."

"Deb, call 911 again." Celia saw a sheepish look on Deb's face. "Didn't you call?" Celia had both hands on Melvin's cold, waxy back to keep him steady. "God, please don't fall."

Deb grabbed her shoulder. "He's dead, Celia. We did all we could. Nothing left to do."

"Call anyway." Melvin slipped an inch and now teetered on the edge of the desk. Celia slapped both hands on his back, stopping the downward slide, and shuddered at the cold plastic feel of his skin.

Deb turned to Marcy and made a sarcastic face. "For God's sake, Marcy, why Melvin? You know Edith wants him back. She's got clout around here, and you've made her your sworn enemy."

"He begged her for a divorce before I arrived on the scene," Marcy snapped, a sob rising in her voice.

Deb looked away. "Okay, okay, but his office? Another public place."

"Stop squabbling and call an ambulance," Celia demanded, stamping her foot.

Deb walked to the other side of the room, her cell to her ear.

Marcy shook her hand. "I can't feel half my body."

"I'm thinking how to get him off without hurting either of you." Celia snuck a peek at Melvin's sunken, filmy fixed eyes.

"We can save him, right, Celia?" Marcy coughed, and took shallow breaths. She started pounding his back. "Wake up, you jerk, breathe."

"Stop, before he hits the ground." She grabbed Marcy's wrists, picturing his cracked skull bleeding on the washed-out blue tile floor—dead or not the vision made her shake.

"Listen, both of you," Deb took a deep breath. "I've seen lots of dead people. I'm telling you he's gone." She tented her hands under her chin, blinking hard. A tiny, earnest tear appeared in the corner of her eye.

"He can't be," Marcy said, flushing deep red and breaking into sobs. Celia braced herself against the desk to stop her trembling. Despite her dislike of the man, she never would have wished him ill.

Marcy, still sobbing, said, "I don't care how the medics find me. I love my Melvy."

Deb shook a gnarled finger at Marcy. "You know inappropriate behavior in public spaces is reason for eviction. That includes sex. You don't believe in a bedroom?" Deb scrunched her face. "When you and Melvin had sex in the clubhouse bathroom during the bridge tournament they heard you moaning in three counties. Now Edith is next in line to take over as president of the board and you're in deep shit."

The bluish color on his face was spreading to Melvin's neck, and Celia forced herself to look away. "Let the authorities handle it."

Marcy's shoulders jerked. "Celia's right," she whispered. "I'll have to take the flack."

Deb stared at Melvin's body. "Let's be practical."

"We wait till the ambulance gets here." Celia noticed Deb staring at the phone. "Damn it, you didn't call. Give me that phone."

Deb looked sheepish and kept the phone out of Celia's reach. "Can't we get her out and leave Melvin here? Then we'll call 911 anonymously and block our number."

"We have to call them now," Celia said with determination. "Call them."

"I mean, I'd have called 911 if he could be revived, of course! They'll want her off the premises right away. Where will she go? She's broke."

"God knows I don't want that," Celia said. "Even if we pry her out from under him they'll see a naked man on his desk who looks like he died in the throes of having sex."

Deb snorted. "Finding him here will open a beehive. Edith is still technically his wife and can demand an autopsy. If anything is out of whack, she'll jump all over Marcy. Bigger trouble."

"Oh Lord." Marcy fisted her hands. "I'm a goner."

Celia stomach turned cartwheels as she agonized about Marcy's predicament.

Deb looked up, her eyes brightening. "If we move him to his apartment it will look like he died of natural causes. He was about to go on an insulin pump for diabetes and oxygen for emphysema." Deb looked at Celia with pleading hound dog eyes. "Look, he didn't take care of himself." Deb snickered and said, almost to herself, "The pecker head saved Global HMO a ton of money for medical costs."

"That's a sick joke. Life isn't judged by cost," Celia said, suddenly cold and shivering.

"Sorry." Deb waved her hand as though erasing what she said. "Just trying to lighten things a bit."

"Moving a body is criminal." Celia said, glancing at Melvin's drooping body. The position looked painful. "We'll never get away with it."

Marcy gulped. "You're right but ..."

Celia kneaded her hands as she noted how much bluer Melvin's skin looked now.

"So?" Deb asked.

"Let me think." Celia's breathed in slowly just the way Marcy had taught her to do as her mind spun.

Chapter 2

Allison

"Apologize to Mom for being so abrupt with her," Allison said to the papers on her office desk. She tried to read them but they were a blur.

Allison knew why her mother agitated her so much. She hadn't been a big part of her life growing up, but right now, with all Thomas's problems, she didn't want to think about her past. Thomas, her husband of eight years, felt like he'd become part of her past because she'd just about decided to leave him. Out of a job, he still continued to gamble. He'd told her he was withdrawing money from his meager retirement plan to pay debts, but she'd have to go through all her records to see if he hadn't dipped into accounts, including their retirement monies. She worked so much overtime it had been impossible to find the time to do that. When she learned he cheated on her with one of the caregivers at the agency where she worked as an accountant, she should have left him, but she wasn't ready to admit failure. Her nursing background and an MBA in accounting had gotten her a better paying job, but it came with longer hours, leaving her husband to his own piss-poor devices. *Mom never liked Thomas, and she was right.* Although her mother never expressed her disdain, Allison sensed it but hesitated to give her mother the credit for pegging Thomas as a jerk. Immediately, Allison realized how immature that sounded.

Despite being a very smart woman, her mother had shied away from responsibility for years. Allison knew her mother loved her, but she'd changed a lot since her dad died. What upset her most was that her mom didn't appear to miss him.

She turned to the computer and opened a spreadsheet for payroll. Focusing was difficult. Instead she decided to send her mother an e-mail:

"Mom, I hope you're well. Sorry I cut you off when we last spoke a couple of weeks ago." It had been longer, but Allison softened the amount of time. "You didn't sound like yourself, but I'm glad you seem content with your life ..." Allison almost thought about adding, *unlike your severely depressed years during my childhood*, but didn't. Instead she continued, "... and glad you have new, ahem, zany friends. Love, Allison."

Allison hoped that pacified her mother. Their arguments threw her into a tizzy. It seemed that when they had ordinary conversations, bile rose in her throat—the old nasty past came cascading over Allison, and she inevitably lost control of her mouth. Oh, she had read the self-help books and had gone into group therapy, but her past, the present, and Thomas pushed her life into chaos.

She thought about how much she missed her father. The idea of death still puzzled her, even at thirty-three. So final. It had no sense of touch, sound, or sight. Poof, you're gone into thin air. The memories of him that had once been so vivid had started to dim. She forced herself to recall his image: balding, a bit of a potbelly, and the sleeves of his striped shirts always rolled up; his forehead furrowed, and a perpetual frown clouding his olive skin, but when he smiled he lit up the room.

She had always blamed her mother for his unhappiness.

He'd been the one to take her to the park, Girl Scouts, and then high school events. Father's Day without him just about knocked her out for days. If only she had Thomas to lean on even the tiniest bit. For once she didn't want to be the strong one as she'd had to be most of her adult life. As much as she'd loved her dad, when she moved to Kansas they'd drifted apart somewhat. She tried to keep up, but her problems with her marriage and his busy business schedule kept them from speaking as much. Lots of e-mails, but not enough face to face. And now he was gone.

Someone knocked on her door. "Come in."

The comptroller walked in with a five-inch stack of papers and set them on her desk. "Can you get this to me by five o'clock tomorrow?"

She was underpaid, overworked, and dealing with personal issues. But what did he care? She smiled through gritted teeth. After he left, she threw her pencil at the door.

Chapter 3

Celia

As Celia agonized about Marcy's situation, she recalled a brochure she had received three years ago, just after her husband, Gabe, had died. The brochure proclaimed the community of Boca Pelicano Palms a paradise on earth, and there were apartments available on Pelican Way.

They offered a range of care to the well seniors, which Celia was, to the seriously ill. Glossy pictures of tall palm trees and bougainvillea clinging to trellises hid what turned out to be five stark, square, five-story concrete apartment buildings. They did show streams flowing past high hedges, obscuring fifty townhouses with Spanish tiled roofs peeking out. She knew she couldn't afford to keep their big house on the South Shore of Long Island, and with the money she would get from the sale, Florida seemed a seductive choice.

Besides, her daughter lived in Kansas, enmeshed in a problematic marriage. Depression, on and off, had dogged Celia's teen years and her marriage. A lifelong habit of allowing herself to be told what to do had stifled her, but Florida beckoned as a way to start a new life. That thought bubbled through her like drinking champagne.

It turned into the best move she'd ever made when she met Marcy and Deb at a cha-cha lesson. She discovered that buoyant sensations could still be kicked off in her, like sunbeams warming every fiber of her being. The women became her best friends ever. And she stopped worrying about never getting Gabe's approval.

Now, watching Marcy's and Deb's anxious expressions, Celia recalled her resolve to never go back to being the obedient, compliant wife with scheduled meals and TV watching on the sofa with Gabe when he was home.

Deb cleared her throat and brought Celia up sharp. "If Melvin died in his own place there's no big hullabaloo. By God, if they did an autopsy on every old person who died in Florida, it'd cost as much as the national debt." Deb blew out a puff of air. "Do we want Marcy to be evicted and out on the street, broke and old?"

"What? I'm only fifty-five," Marcy huffed.

"More like sixty-five." Deb drew the number in the air.

"If anyone finds out that we moved a dead body we'll all go down," Celia said, her stomach wrenching. She agonized, but their friendship seemed more important right now.

"It's a no-brainer. They'll find him in bed and think he died in his sleep."

Marcy looked pitiful, one arm resting over her eyes, her enhanced breasts looking youthful, Melvin's head on her abdomen. "Oh God, I can't believe we're talking about Melvin … about his card not on the door."

Celia knew that everyone put a card on their door every morning to indicate all was okay. If the card didn't appear, then management checked on that resident. Would Deb's idea work?

"Look," Deb said. "Most people around here go to bed by nine and get up at five or six. I don't think anyone will see us if we bring Melvin back to his apartment."

Celia swallowed hard. She couldn't refuse. They'd all lose. A tiny patch of early light glimmered through the window. They were running out of time. "How can we transport him? He's over two hundred pounds."

"There's a wheelbarrow in the gardener's shed downstairs," Marcy said.

Deb gave Marcy a derisive glare. "You should know all about gardening tools."

Celia wagged her finger at Deb but smiled inside. "We won't be able to roll Melvin in that thing. You've got to lift the handles to move it." Celia rubbed her forehead. "What about your wheelchair, Deb? Haven't seen you use it in a long time. Do you still have it?"

"Yup. It's a strong one. It's just inside my door—it's unlocked."

"I'll get it," Celia said. "I'm hoping we can ease Melvin into it from his position. We'd never lift him off the floor." She looked around the room. "Clean up what you can, Deb."

Celia rushed out, glad they hadn't installed cameras in the corridors or elevators. The community boasted that there had never been a crime in their development to justify surveillance—till now.

She decided to walk the long route and avoid the elevators in case she met up with an insomniac. It was a ten-minute walk, but five minutes longer counting the several floors of steps. She'd duck into one of the numerous alcoves if she saw someone coming.

Her hands trembled. She'd hidden in a cocoon of safety all her life, accepting the suffocating protection of her parents and then Gabe. She was always down on herself. Celia had been a good mother to Allison when she was a little girl. They had done so many things together—going to the library, parks, and the merry-go-round in Central Park. But as Allison got older, raising her presented an increasing challenge. Gabe helped, but the truth was that Allison practically raised herself. She worked hard to repair their relationship. Now, in the space of a few seconds, she'd made a decision that might send her to jail. Though Marcy and Deb were family, it was still harrowing.

The endless bottles of pills she'd taken to stave off suffocating bouts of depression made her wince; her depression paralyzed her, forcing her into walking only in a straight line because a move off course made her anxious. Since her friends had saved her, she no longer took meds. But, after this, she wondered if their lives would change. Could they go back to their usual routine of dancing, going to the theater and art galleries, giving themselves up to abandon without fear of being hauled off for committing a crime? Would they become enslaved by fear?

On her trek to get Deb's wheelchair, Celia recalled how Marcy and Deb had saved her life. They'd begun dancing and attending art lectures, dramas, and even little theater Shakespearean plays. She'd already planned on teaching art to inner-city kids and getting back to her own art, making pottery.

She recalled the awful phone call from Allie who accused her of lying when she told her she'd given up antidepressants. Allie had been right, of course. Afterwards, she walked into the bathroom and stared at the last two plastic bottles of Xanax and Elavil on the sink. She filled a glass of water, then sat on the toilet seat, staring into space. *Allison is right. I should have fought back all those years. Did*

I need others to make my decisions so I had someone to blame? Celia dove further into the depths of a world saturated with gloom, tumbling into a lightless cave of sadness and regret. It didn't matter if she lived or died. Allie hated her. Her desire to live went out like a campfire doused with water.

She poured thirty pills onto the bathroom counter. Heart pounding, she held two pills in her hand. A knock on her door. *I won't answer.* The knocking escalated to pounding. The door slammed open, and a moment later, Marcy and Deb stood at the bathroom door, staring at her, clearly having used their emergency keys to get in. Celia wheeled on the toilet seat and a bunch of pills hit the tile floor, clicking and rolling across black and white tile.

"We knew something was wrong the way you've missed meals in the last four days." Marcy gently took her by the hand and led her to the couch. Deb followed.

They sat in silence for ten minutes. Celia saw tears running down Marcy's cheeks. Deb trembled and said, "Don't do this. We need you and so does your daughter."

And so, Celia didn't.

Chapter 4

Allison sat at her desk in her small home office just off the kitchen, still working away on her computer. She often brought work home in order to keep up with the busy pace of her office, and she found her mind slipping away from the pages on the screen.

Life in Florida and especially a community like Boca Pelicano Palms is so different from New York! Mother says all is fine, but it can be trying to change a lifestyle, especially at her age. Allison's concern centered on Celia's past history of dependence on controlled substances. Even though her mother claimed she'd gotten off of them, who knew. The woman might not realize that independence came with a price. And in her mother's case, it could mean letting her health go to hell. She said she was playing tennis and relearning the cha-cha, but the woman could trip and fall, break a hip, and then what? It had been so hard to get her to focus in the past and now she'd become an elderly dynamo.

Allison's nursing background always led her to the dark side. She knew it wasn't easy to get off of prescription pills once someone was addicted. *Why would she change? I've never seen her have a hobby or volunteer. When I was in high school, Dad was the parent I counted on.*

With a pang, Allison recalled a phone call after Celia had been in Florida for several months, one she always regretted.

"Allie," Celia had said, her voice tight. "I'm about to flush my antidepressants down the toilet. No more Xanax or Elavil. You're right to be angry. I'm making a new life."

"Mom, really?" Allison had snickered. "C'mon. Most addicts don't stop cold turkey. Remember why Daddy didn't invite you to go anywhere with us? He was afraid of your behavior. You always look dazed."

"I took those prescriptions stupidly, thinking I'd be a better parent, more alert ... wrong. I was very unhappy and it hurt my relationship with you."

"You always said we make our own happiness."

"I never followed my own advice. I was afraid fighting with your father would hurt you because you were so attached to him so ... I don't know ..."

A long pause. "It upsets me to hear about the new you. Where were you when I needed you as a child? Yes, you were there early on, but so many days I'd find you with the covers over your head." Allison paused again. "Hearing about the new you is stressing me out. I have a lot going on and this isn't helping. It's better if you let me call you instead."

Allison had hung up, knowing she'd hurt her mother. Then again, she should have to prove her sincerity about quitting the pills. That would need months of observation, something she had no time for.

Now the issues concerning her mother bubbled out of her, big bubbles that enclosed her head, leaving her breathless. Her large workload sat in front of her, as did Thomas's shenanigans. She had promised him that she would give him one more chance to stop gambling, cheating, and depleting their funds. But why one more chance? How many dozens had she given to him already?

She went back to her computer to finish organizing the payroll for newly hired caregivers. When she'd taken the job as an accountant she hadn't expected to give classes to caregivers for ill and elderly patients as well, but she didn't mind when they asked her to do it. It was part of her nursing job before getting her MBA. She enjoyed it. But they didn't compensate her for the extra work. Jobs were hard to come by in her town, so she didn't complain. She emphasized understanding patients' needs. Once, an elderly woman with a live-in caregiver almost died because she developed bedsores. She carefully instructed her classes to see it never happened on her watch.

Tapping her pencil on a legal pad, she wondered if Thomas might come through this time. After all, two weeks had passed and he'd been out each day looking for a job. Often he'd start dinner when he came home while she tried to catch up with work. If only one of the places where he'd applied would make him an offer, then she'd not ask for more.

Her phone buzzed with a new text message. She'd been expecting one from her boss but it was from Thomas. He said he'd be home a little late as he was being interviewed after working hours and then needed to pick up steaks for dinner. *Would he only be a little late or out all night at a high-stakes poker game, or with a prostitute?* He'd told her sex with a prostitute wasn't cheating because there was no emotional involvement. Shit to that. She had come within an inch of walking out when he'd begged and pleaded for her to stay, saying he'd change.

Allison tried to turn back to her work but a heavy cloud settled on her shoulders. She was desperate for things to be different this time around. They just *had* to be. *Oh please, Thomas, don't make me leave.*

Chapter 5

Celia

Celia returned with the wheelchair to find Deb hovering over Marcy, patting her hand. She and Melvin were in the same positions. Most items from the floor were on a nearby table.

"We need antibacterial wipes and latex gloves," Celia said.

"Why?"

"To remove all traces of our DNA on Melvin, especially yours," Celia said, nodding to Marcy. "We can't do the whole office, but we need to cover our fingerprints, just in case. I've watched enough detective shows to know that."

"Can you please hurry? I'm so numb."

Celia thought for a moment. "I'll try the infirmary." Celia hurried down the corridor. As she neared the infirmary she heard a creaking sound, and a figure emerged from behind one of the columns just outside the kitchen. Celia pressed her back against the wall.

"Oh my God." The woman stopped suddenly and some liquid splashed over the edge of the glass she held. "Geez, you scared the hell out of me."

"So sorry. I didn't expect …"

"I didn't think anyone came out this late." The woman balanced the glass. "I came for warm milk for my patient. Helps her sleep. I'm her caregiver. My name is Vanessa."

"Hi," Celia said her voice quavering. "Going to the infirmary. I cut my finger."

"Want me to take a look at it?" The woman approached.

Celia put her hand behind her back and raised her voice a half octave in an attempt to disguise it. "No, no. I'm fine. Just need Neosporin and a Band-Aid." The woman stood in dim lighting, but Celia thought she looked like Penélope Cruz, just as stunning but taller and with dark, luxurious wavy hair. Celia positioned herself in the darkest part of the hallway. "Well, thanks and good night."

"Uh, what's your name?"

Celia waved. "Good night."

"Nighty-night," the woman sing-songed and hurried away.

Celia's hands shook. People didn't wander around the clubhouse in the middle of the night for a little cut. It had to seem odd to Vanessa. She opened the door to the infirmary, which luckily was unlocked. Inside, she found latex gloves and antibacterial wipes and hurried back to the office.

The few papers left on the office floor made crinkling sounds as she stepped over them. "I bumped into a caregiver by the name of Vanessa. I gave her a lame excuse for being there. She was quite striking. God, I hope she didn't see me clearly. I stood in the dark so maybe she didn't see my face—I hope." Celia heaved out a shaky breath.

"Ahh," Marcy said. "She takes care of a sick woman in the apartment next to me. Vanessa Cordova is her full name."

Deb patted Celia's back. "Don't be paranoid. She doesn't know we're in here."

Marcy rolled her head to one side. "I'm dying. Get moving, and don't hurt my Melvy."

Wearing latex gloves, they got to work, swabbing Melvin from his head down his back to his toes. Then they bent down to maneuver around to get the front of his legs up to his crotch.

"Yuck. I'm not scrubbing his penis. You get to do that when we free you up," Deb said to Marcy. "You know that part of male anatomy pretty well."

"For heaven's sake ..." Marcy scrunched her face in disgust. "Get it done."

"We've got to move fast." Celia bit her lip, looked away, bunched up a two-inch wad of antibacterial wipes, and finished the job as fast as she could.

"Do we put him into the wheelchair naked?" Deb asked with an anxious expression.

"I don't see how we can dress him," Celia said. "We'll just throw a blanket over him."

Celia moved the wheelchair between Melvin's drooping legs and put the brakes on. She positioned Deb to tug Melvin's legs and Marcy to push his shoulders. Celia stood behind the chair to steady it.

"On the count of three, ease him down." *What in the world are we doing? Suppose he falls to the floor. Then we'll have to call for help and explain the wheelchair, disarray, naked bodies, and whatnot. Lord help us.*

Marcy pressed down on his shoulders; Deb tugged his legs. In slow motion Melvin's body began slipping in the general direction of the wheelchair, and Celia held tight to the handles, her feet against the wheels. Terror detonated in her chest, knowing that at any second the top weight of Melvin's body would plunge him downward at full speed. She released the brake and jumped the chair forward as Melvin plummeted into the seat. She gripped the handles, steadied it, and snapped the brakes back on. Deb and Celia shoved him upright, both grunting with the strain.

Then Celia and Deb helped Marcy off the desk. Wobbling, Marcy pressed one arm across her breasts and the other over her bikini-waxed pelvis.

"Hey," Deb said. "You displayed that body enough not to be modest."

Marcy pursed her lips. "Shush." She grabbed her skimpy black shorts and bright red halter top off the floor and put them on as Celia quickly swabbed Melvin's chest, neck, arms, and face with the wipes. "Oh God. Thank you so much, ladies."

Celia was wondering how Marcy survived Melvin's weight on her slender body when she noticed it was five a.m. "Put the items back on the desk as best you can." She grabbed the gray bristly blanket that had been under Marcy on the desk, snapped it open, and threw it over Melvin, glad not to see his nakedness.

Marcy replaced the desk items—trays of paper, pencil and pen holders, and a lamp. Tears streamed down Marcy's face when she found Melvin's New York Yankees baseball cap and gently placed it on his head. It hit Celia with the force of a rocket that she'd just wrestled with a dead body.

I wish to hell we knew what we were doing.

Exhausted, Celia folded Melvin's arms on his lap, tightened the blanket around his neck, and pulled the peak of the cap down over his face. They'd reached the point of no return. Celia froze.

"He just looks like he had too much to drink," Deb said. "Let's go. I'm pooped."

Celia took hold of the wheelchair handles and commanded her legs to move. At first, she stepped gingerly as though walking through a minefield. She usually admired Marcy's risk-taking, but this monkey business had gone too far. They checked the darkened hallway and wheeled the squeaky chair, all three wincing at the noise. As they passed the kitchen entrance, a dim light was on.

As Celia picked up the pace, a stretched shadow lunged forward along the floor in front of them. It reminded Celia of an elongated, skeletal runway model. Vanessa appeared in the doorway. "Is everything all right?" she asked squinting into the darkened hallway. "Need help?"

Oh shit. Celia gasped and huddled in the darkness over the handlebars to appear smaller and faceless. Deb and Marcy turned their backs to Vanessa and shoved the chair forward

"Just a friend who drank too much," Celia said in a high-pitched voice. The chair rolled quickly as they pushed. Vanessa seemed composed. Celia's body shook as she took bigger steps. *Did Vanessa come back out of curiosity or did she really need something from the kitchen?* Celia swiveled her head for a quick look and saw Vanessa, wearing a jacket over pajamas, watching them.

"You okay, Marcy?" Celia asked.

"I'm scared out of my wits. What do you think that woman saw?"

"Not much," Deb said. "We were in the dark."

They quickened their pace.

"I feel so sad for my Melvy." Marcy's shoulders drooped. "Celia, do you think it was my fault?" She cried softly.

"It's no one's fault," Celia said, her body still buzzing from the scare. "Melvin could have had a heart attack at any time." She turned her head and looked at Deb. "Are you okay?"

"Yeah. I'm just worried about the elevator and the wandering insomniacs around here."

They'd already crossed the first-floor connecting bridge to Melvin's building. His apartment was on the fourth floor. There were steep ramps connecting the floors, but she knew it would be easier and faster to take the elevator. "We have to risk taking the elevator. And remember, keep the latex gloves on your hands," Celia said, wondering if someone else inside of her was giving directions. They headed towards the elevator.

"We're the Marx brothers," Deb said, her laugh lines deepening with a goofy grin.

"No jokes. I'm kinda worried Vanessa might tail us," Celia said.

"She believed us. Look around."

Celia turned in all directions and saw nothing. Her fears felt like icicles inside her, but she knew why she had conceded to this crime. *They'd do it for me. Move your ass, woman. My friends saved my life, now I'll help save them.*

The elevator doors squealed opened and they hustled inside. Just as the elevator began moving up, the cage jerked to a stop. Celia pressed the button several times. Nothing.

"Damn it to hell," Deb said. "This old firetrap's been acting up."

"Why now?" Celia looked skyward, her heart slamming in her chest.

"Don't hit the emergency button for help," Marcy groaned. "But if we wait much longer, Melvin will … will, oh God, I hate to say, he'll start smelling. We're gonna be arrested."

"Calm down," Celia said in a tight voice. She jabbed the button again. Then, with a mighty groan, the elevator started moving again. They breathed a collective sigh. Sweat dripped from Celia's forehead into her eyes, despite the cool night. She pictured herself in jail, eating stale bread and showering with other inmates. *Not funny.*

Once off the elevator, they pushed the chair a short distance until they reached Melvin's apartment door. "The key?" Celia asked, holding out her hand.

"Oh shit. I remember that he left them in the office desk drawer."

"Go get them and come back right away." Celia looked around for a place to hide as Marcy hustled away.

"The laundry room," Celia said. "No one is supposed to use the machines overnight."

"Are we going to do laundry?" Deb asked, dazed.

"No, we're moving Melvin. Remember?" Celia rubbed Deb's cheek.

Deb's non-expressive face suddenly burst into recognition. "Right." They moved down the corridor, the wheels clacking. Celia walked on tiptoe as though that would stop the noise. She glanced at Melvin, slack-jawed with his eyes open, and shivered. Inside the dark, dank room, the strong smell of lint and soap seemed pleasant and clean— too clean for their errand.

"Shhh. Don't make any noise," Celia whispered.

Just then the door opened. A stooped, elderly woman rolling a cart stood in the entrance, the palest of morning light spreading across the floor.

"You can't come in," Celia yelled from a dark corner. "I'm here to see you don't use the machines until eight a.m. People are complaining about noise. Read the note on the door."

"Who the hell put you in charge?" the woman asked as she shaded her eyes in an attempt to peer into the darkened room.

"I'll report you. You'll be fined," Celia said, using her harshest tone.

"Laundry room Nazi." The woman stepped outside and slammed the door. Celia leaned her back against the damp wall and wiped sweat from her forehead with her sleeve.

A minute later, Deb cracked the door. "Marcy's coming." They wheeled him to his apartment.

Inside Melvin's living room they saw newspapers and golf magazines lining the cocktail table and on the floor in front of a worn yellow lounge chair. They quickly went down a hall that connected to each room until they reached the bedroom. The smell from a pile of dirty laundry near the bedroom door made Celia flinch. Marcy and Deb held their noses.

"No wonder he never had me come here," Marcy said, cringing.

Celia wheeled Melvin to the edge of his low platform bed and tugged the blanket off. "Again, on the count of three," Celia whispered as though someone might hear them. They began the ferocious lifting of the back of the wheelchair and managed to toss the upper portion of his body on the bed. Celia pointed to his legs and they tugged hard until they rested on the mattress.

"This is not a job for old women, or young ones for that matter," Celia muttered. Then they backed out of the room, pulling the wheelchair along.

"Shame we didn't finish what we started." Marcy said, the pang of loss etched on her face, her eyes half-closed.

"When you do sex therapy again, make sure they have healthy hearts," Deb said.

"Stop. We've still got work to do," Celia said.

As they hurried back down the hallway toward the living room, Celia stopped short when she noticed the medicine chest in the bathroom was open. On the shelf, she saw a large assortment of pills, including insulin and wrapped hypodermic needles. She peered at one medicine bottle and picked it up. "Did you say Melvin never took Viagra?"

"Yes, why?" Marcy asked.

"This bottle has a handwritten label that says Viagra, but has no doctor or pharmacy name. It's almost empty. Maybe he got it online. I see the bluish pill, but there's something else in there," Celia said, putting the bottle back and looking through the shelves.

"He didn't need Viagra with me!" Marcy puffed her chest out.

Deb rolled her eyes. "They all take it, dopey. C'mon, we have to have to get out of here."

"Wait," Celia said. "There's a bottle with the same kind of handwritten label that says oxycodone. Was Melvin in pain?"

"Complained about his back sometimes."

"Strong stuff. Did he have a drug habit?"

Marcy giggled. "Melvin? He hardly drank. No way. Let's go."

Marcy wiped Melvin's keys and left them on a table. The front door locked automatically behind them.

"Melvin died of natural causes," Marcy said, her voice a squeak. Deb and Marcy removed the latex gloves. Celia noticed she'd already stuffed hers in a pocket. When had she removed them? Before she touched the bottles? There was no going back—the keys were inside; the door was locked. *Shit.*

The three women huddled in an alcove of the hallway. It was six a.m.

"We have to act as though we're shocked at Melvin's death and be careful what we say," Celia cautioned. "When they tell us he died, we act grief stricken."

Marcy's shoulders shook, and she sniffled. "I won't have to fake my grief."

Fatigue coursed through Celia. Covering their tracks had caught up to her. She hugged both women. "We have to stick together."

"Thanks so much." Marcy shook her head. "I love you guys. I'm falling off my feet."

"Well, stay in an upright position," Deb said. "You're safer."

Arm in arm they walked together until Marcy waved goodbye, taking the stairs to her apartment. Celia, pushing the wheelchair, walked Deb to her third-floor apartment then took the elevator to the fourth. The doors opened and Celia stumbled out.

A hot dry fatigue overwhelmed her as she placed one foot, heavy as a pile of bricks, in front of the other and trudged down the outdoor corridor. On the horizon, pale streaks of orangey clouds cut across a brightening, streaked sky. She loved to watch dawn break, but now felt numb with fear, sadness for Melvin, and pity for Marcy.

Plodding along, she reached her condo door. Celia tried inserting the key. It didn't fit. Her mouth went dry. Then she realized she was trying to insert it backwards. "Damn," she muttered. From behind her, an unmistakable, nasal voice startled her.

"Up early, aren't you?" Edith Onstader said.

Celia swiveled and saw Edith approaching her. She looked like an innocent grandmotherly type: short white-blonde hair, nose drooped to just above her upper lip, mouth a bit caved in, and blue eyes as pale as an icicle. A sad twist to Edith's thin lips gave the appearance of a person about to cry.

She'd heard that even four years after Melvin had moved out, Edith stalked him, knocking on his door in the middle of the night and calling incessantly. Edith then went gunning for people who defied her rules. Celia gave Edith a curt nod.

As Celia fumbled with her keys, she heard another voice say, "Hello."

Trailing just behind Edith, Celia recognized the woman she'd bumped into coming from the kitchen. She rocked back on her heels. "I … like … walking early in the morning when it's still cool." Celia worried that her breathless voice revealed her nervousness. Her knees turned to liquid.

"I'm Vanessa. I'm a caregiver," the woman said, extending her hand sincerely with no telltale signs of recognizing her. "Edith is introducing me to a potential client."

"Julia's okay. Just a little weak. Vanessa's advising me," Edith snapped. Her voice had a commanding edge as she turned toward Vanessa. "Right, Missy?"

Celia almost expected Vanessa to salute and felt sorry for her. Vanessa gave a weak smile, but her lips seemed stuck on her teeth.

Then Vanessa moved closer to Celia. "Do I know you?"

Celia clutched her doorknob. *Shit.* "Uh, no. We've never met." She turned sideways.

Vanessa narrowed her eyes. "Guess not."

"You seem upset," Edith said with a phony smile.

Celia hid her agitation. "Tired from walking."

"You look disheveled. Getting lessons from your friend Marcy?"

"You have no right to judge people," Celia said, noticing Vanessa staring at them.

Edith couldn't have known about Melvin, but seeing Vanessa tagging along caused a lump in her throat. Celia finally got her key into the lock. "And isn't it pretty early to be visiting people, Edith?"

"Julia called to say she's dizzy. We're on our way to see her."

Celia opened the door, trying to keep her trembling fingers hidden.

"Nice meeting you," Vanessa said.

She turned but saw no malice on her face. A peek at Edith's smirk just before she shut the door chilled Celia. If questions surfaced about Melvin's death, Edith might interrogate Vanessa about whether she'd seen anything. And Vanessa might put two and two together and put Celia wandering outside around the time of Melvin's death.

Chapter 6

Celia

After a very long, hot shower, Celia threw the clothing she'd worn into a trashcan and dropped into bed. She couldn't sleep and wondered if nights would be like this from now on— plagued by memories of Melvin's chilling blue pallor and utter stillness. There were no second chances with death. Her teeth chattered.

In her head she heard Melvin bragging about how women adored him, his manly strength, his high intelligence, and how he did his own legal briefs when suing companies. He claimed to have a degree from a non-accredited law school. But his repertoire of corny jokes and an impressive amount of volunteer work at a local nursing home redeemed him. Deb's take on his altruism was that he volunteered in order to score with women. The rumor was the nursing homes were beehives of sexual activity. Marcy joked about offering her services to the men in nursing homes and then deducting the time from her taxes as a charitable donation.

Melvin had been one of several deaths that had occurred in Boca Pelicano Palms since she'd moved. Of course they were oldsters with multiple illnesses, but although she hadn't counted them, the numbers seemed a bit out of whack, even for a retirement community.

Until now, with the exception of her late husband, Gabe, death had existed in the abstract. With her health in tip-top shape, she sometimes forgot her body's age. But with deaths occurring around her, it started to hit home. Each death resounded like a bell, reminding her of her own mortality. She felt grateful she wasn't on the obituary list—yet.

Weary but wired, she rose from bed and paced around her two-bedroom, one-and-a-half bath unit. She disliked her kitschy furnishings, but had taken the apartment fully outfitted with fake wicker furniture, lamps shaped like palm trees, and numerous abalone shell candy dishes, planning to refurnish it later. It would do for now. Funds were low. She stopped and sat down.

Celia embraced her new life of sunshine, palm trees, year-round tennis, and new friends, but was taken aback by the alligators in human form like Edith and company. Her new best friends gave her sustenance and good laughs—until now. Would they be haunted by tonight?

Celia tended to be obsessive about what made her anxious—unusual noises in the night, shadows, and driving over bridges. When Gabe died, she forced herself to drive over the Brooklyn Bridge, huddling over the steering wheel going twenty miles an hour, horns blaring behind her. She'd begun to fight her fears, but they paled in the light of what she had done tonight. *Funny that bravery arises first from love and second from necessity.*

What would Allison, with her high standards and ethics, think of what she'd done? Her daughter helped and nurtured people even now as an accountant. In the summers of her college years, she had gone to remote areas of developing countries to help. She'd be appalled. Maybe she'd even think about turning her in to the police.

Celia vowed to not let this one awful night ruin all she had gained. After the move to Florida, she'd floundered for a while. Then she answered a note on the community bulletin board, posted by Marcy. "Guys, gals, all you old buggers," it had said, "Get your booties moving and learn how to cha-cha. For those who know the dance, come over to the community room and let's boogie. Even those who don't can watch, sing, clap hands, or holler." Celia knew the basic steps and not much beyond that. Still, she answered the ad with a resounding yes.

That handwritten note changed her life. The hour and a half of that first cha-cha lesson welcomed her into a new world. Could happiness be so simple?

When Celia had first stepped into the white square community room with a fifty-inch flat screen TV, chairs lined up against the wall, and dance steps drawn in chalk on the concrete floor, she saw two women in the middle of the room talking excitedly. One, a curly-haired, pretty redhead, looked very trendy with hot pink short shorts, a green low-cut cotton shirt, and spike heels. Her animated expression made the room sizzle. Her nametag read "Marcy."

The other woman, whose nametag read "Deb," was slim and slightly bent over. She wore a long, flowered dress, and her hands, gnarled with what looked like arthritis, held several CDs. "I hate this song," she said, tossing a CD into the trash. "That's the one my ex loved."

"Hey, pretty lady," Marcy had cooed, looking in Celia's direction. "Come for a cha-cha lesson?"

Marcy wide grin relaxed her. Celia nodded.

"Dancing opens you up and cleanses your soul." Marcy tugged at the hem of her shorts as she wiggled her hips. "My style of teaching is very spiritual."

"Forget spiritual," Deb had yelled over her shoulder. "Get on with it. Teach the steps."

Spiritual, thought Celia, enchanted. And she had said, "Amen. I came to shake my booty, learn the steps, and find my soul at the same time."

They all laughed as Marcy put on a CD. Celia stiffened her back, waiting to start.

Marcy fell to her knees, shoving and pushing Celia's feet to the outlined steps on the floor. "Now, pretty lady, this is your right foot and that's your left. Got it?"

Celia then grabbed Marcy's hand and helped her up. "We're too old to get on our knees."

"Speak for yourself, young lady." Marcy waggled her shoulders.

"She spends a lot of time in that position," Deb snickered.

Celia laughed despite the shock. These two outrageous women awakened a long-dormant part of her brain, the one that sent waves of life and comfort sailing through her body with belly laughs and a feeling of well-being. The sensation of thumbing one's nose at expectations of behavior sent shimmers of pleasure inside of her.

"You goof." Deb pointed at the floor and shuffled her feet. "These steps are too basic. When I taught the cha-cha we got right into it, no preliminaries. As a professional, I taught a lot of celebrities in LA. Movie studios hired me."

Deb pointed to a picture of a beautiful, exotic young woman on a corner table with flawless, pale skin. Her braided black hair tugged at her temples, enhancing her high cheekbones and large, round, dark brown eyes. She wore a golden sequined dress that hugged her slim hips and full breasts. "Yup, that's me at twenty," Deb said. "Now I'm about to turn seventy." Her deeply wrinkled face seemed older, as though illness had wreaked havoc on her appearance. "Then I met my bum husband who insisted we leave LA and live in Florida. I think he was jealous of my meeting interesting people." Deb looked at her feet.

"What's your secret to the dance?" Celia broke in, trying to bring Deb back to a festive mood. Sunshine flooded the room through a bank of wide windows. Celia already loved these enchanting ladies, especially after having come up against an unwelcoming clique of women when she had first moved in.

Deb threw her head back but couldn't get it beyond her shoulder line. She grimaced in pain for a moment. "Make eye contact, head erect—be bold. Feel the thrill of the rhythm. You interact with a partner intimately. It's not like these kids today who jump around and don't know they're dancing with another person."

Celia gave Deb a thumb's up as she caught a whiff of Marcy's perfume—it smelled foreign, heady and French.

"I beg to differ," Marcy said in huff. "First learn the structure and then improvise later."

Celia experimented with a few steps, not favoring one theory over the other. They both made sense.

Deb shrugged her shoulders to the music and shuffled her feet. "Two-three. Forward and backward. Too bad I can't dance like I used to with this rheumatoid arthritis," she said. Celia noted that Deb worked her back straight in increments, like doing scales on a piano. She struck a sensual dance pose. Her footwork was much more complex than Marcy's as she did a fast mambo despite wincing in pain. Celia tried to follow, stumbled, and left Deb to finish with an exuberant foot stomp.

"I'm not a professional like this woman here," Marcy said, dripping sarcasm. "But we're here to have fun and connect our bodies to our minds."

"Well, I like both of your minds," Celia said, getting into the sway of the music.

Marcy snapped her fingers. "I like you. You've got potential."

"That's all? Just potential?"

"I don't want it to go to your head. Truth is you've got the looks and the stuff."

"You mean for an old lady I'm not half bad?"

"Right. You look as though you sailed through life, like good dancing."

"Actually, mostly a bumpy ride. I didn't do much with my life," Celia said.

Marcy got a faraway look. Deb high-stepped now.

"This dancing looks like pure fun," Celia continued. She put her arms out for the women to join her as the music tickled along her spine. Deb stood at Celia's back, putting her hands on either side of Celia's hips, tugging right then left, in time to the rhythm. Marcy, a bit shaky in her spike heels, led the way for Celia to follow.

The first line of a new Spanish song played. "That means, Love beats working," Deb quipped.

They moved in sync, laughing. Marcy made up words to the music. "*Sí,* I'm working for love," she mimicked. They laughed harder then took positions side by side and held hands while Celia forgot everything else but her feet and a delicious floating sensation. The brief glaze of sorrow that had overcome the women a moment ago disappeared when they began dancing in unison.

"Two-three forward, then one-two-three back in place,"

Marcy said, guiding Celia's arm with a firm grip. "Then the same going back."

Deb offered constant critique, which Marcy ignored, and soon Celia got the rhythm and her feet began finding the right steps. A few more miscues, but she managed to get back on track each time. She gave herself up to the rhythm, her neck stiff, calf muscles taut, feet slapping the floor flat-footed. A sense of freedom enveloped her.

"Who needs a man to dance with?" Deb shouted. "Look at us! We're terrific."

"Oh, it's good to have a man, but I'll admit they're just icing on the cake. Girlfriends first," Marcy said, swinging her hips while keeping her upper torso straight. Deb gave her an approving nod.

Celia strode on a cushion of air, her body finding its own momentum. She'd stopped concentrating on her feet and all of her worked in harmony. The music zinged through her body. The outside world didn't exist.

Although the dance was intended as a seduction—the man and woman flirting, tossing heads, touching, pushing away, moving close—on another level it allowed a woman to be audacious without caring about judgment. Celia realized the dancing needn't only be about seduction and control, but that it could also be about wholeness, trusting each other, trusting her movements and the space she created with others.

Just then the door slammed and the dancing stopped. Celia saw Edith, the grumpy woman who was the apparent leader of the clique that had rejected her. What was she doing here? She hardly seemed the type to dance, let alone cha-cha. A chill went through the room as Edith silently entered the fray.

"Did you get permission to use this room?" Edith demanded.

"I thought residents could use it whenever it was empty." Marcy did a rhythmic shuffle.

"You have to sign up for it, make sure it's not already reserved. Where is your head? I saw your ad and figured you'd ignore the rules."

"I'll apply at the office, thank you," Marcy shouted as she turned up the music and swayed. Celia hated that Edith had broken their magical spell, giving off her angry vibes like eruptions of boiling hot lava, something she'd spent too many years running from. Celia joined Marcy and Deb.

"Try it," Marcy said in a welcoming voice, pointing to the lines on the floor.

"You think you know everything?" Edith sneered. "Maybe you have Melvin, but he'll come back to me." Edith plodded towards the door. "What else do you intend to use this room for, Marcy? You do have a sullied reputation, you know."

"We're here strictly to dance," Marcy said, swaying to the music again. "Dance or go."

"Who do you think you're talking to? No wonder your kids won't have anything to do with you." Edith marched out.

"Goodbye, bitch." Although Marcy's voice sounded indifferent, her body stiffened as though shot through with arrows.

Celia saw Marcy's face crumble, as did her own heart. She put her hands on Marcy's shoulders. "I get it. My daughter and I have a tough relationship. I wasn't there for her as I should have been when she was young. We don't talk as much as I'd like. When we do, she's short with me."

Marcy went into spasms of sobbing. "I left my kids for twelve years to go to a spiritual ashram to follow a guru I was in love with. My husband verbally abused me, but what I did was unforgiveable."

"You're a different person now. I promise you they'll come back." Celia chided herself for blurting that out, but Edith had ripped Marcy's skin off.

When Marcy caught her breath, she tossed her hair over her shoulder, put on a forced smile, and said, "Let's dance. At least I have that, and Melvin, until he gets tired of me."

The women picked up where they left off, clearing out Edith's toxins. By the end of the session, Celia had connected with the two women by sheer enthusiasm and a shared, palpable, underlying pain. An invisible contract for a lifetime of friendship was signed.

Over time, Deb and Marcy helped her to stop playing the victim, to take responsibility rather than being ruled by a sense of inadequacy. These women lifted her from the murky waters of her past—a past filled with endless bottles of antidepressants to stave off suffocating bouts of depression. She'd felt like she was on a rollercoaster downward—till now.

A door slamming next door shook Celia out of her reverie. Exhaustion overtook her, and she went back to her bedroom and fell into bed. The last images she saw before falling asleep were of Melvin and Edith—not what she had expected to deal with in her golden years.

Chapter 7

Celia

After four hours of fitful sleep, Celia rose, changed her bed linens for the second time that week, did the wash, and dusted the entire apartment. Then she showered again and dressed in a pair of black slacks and a white top. She called Deb first.

"Remember, when we go for lunch, act surprised when they do a speech for Melvin. Sure as hell they've found him by now when they didn't see his card on the door."

"I feel bad that he died, but I disliked the mean-spirited dog," Deb said. "Did you know Melvin and Edith reported Mr. Angstrom to the condo association for sitting in his wheelchair in front of his building, waving to neighbors? The poor guy had a stroke, but they made him go inside because they said he 'blighted the neighborhood.' He died shortly after."

Celia bit her lip. "That's awful."

"So, I won't pretend that I liked him."

"Well, forget your personal feelings." Celia paused. "I bumped into Edith and that caregiver after our, uh, incident. It made me so nervous I nearly fainted. Vanessa thought I looked familiar then backed off."

"See? She doesn't recognize you. Don't get yourself in a knot."

After they hung up Celia called Marcy, who sounded like she'd been crying. "I miss that old bastard. He was good to me."

"I'm sorry, darlin'. It's going to be tough going for a while, but we have to be realistic." Celia brought Marcy up to speed. "They know we usually do lunch and dinner. Edith and her cronies are always at lunch, too."

"Can't face the bitch. I'm off the wall," Marcy wailed.

"I know you don't have to pretend to be heartbroken." After Celia hung up she worried about her own reaction when they gave a brief eulogy for Melvin, as they always did when someone died. For ten minutes she sat, trying to take deep breaths, drumming her fingers on a table. With fifteen minutes until lunchtime, she mustered up a false bravado and left.

She followed the pebbled paths, lined with red flowering bushes and evenly spaced palm trees, greeting residents she saw with a smile although she didn't know most of them. Passing the signature piece of landscaping that defined most gated enclaves—a fountain spouting a tower of water in the middle of a large manmade pond—she spied a pair of white egrets with their long, gently curving necks. They usually gave her a peaceful feeling, but not today.

With a headache pulsing in her temples, she pictured the police waiting at the clubhouse to arrest them. Celia thought maybe they should just jump in the car and pull a Thelma and Louise. Make a getaway. Celia bent over the reflecting pool outside the clubhouse and saw her tired face, eyes glazed with tension. She continued on, rolling her shoulders to loosen her stiff gait. Her spine felt replaced by a metal pole.

Stopping short of the entrance, she prepared herself to face Edith. Still, she had no regrets about moving to Florida even now, recalling the marketing promises of the brochure: "A beautiful new life awaits you in Florida." And while she hadn't exactly found paradise, she had found two new friends who made her belly laugh from deep in her gut—healing laughter she'd rarely indulged in when she lived with Gabe.

Early on she'd hidden under the wings of her parents who made decisions for her. She was an only child who'd had few friends and read every day after school, and this created shyness to the point where she'd been unable to look people in the eye.

"Sweetie, you don't have to go to the class party, you know," her mother would coo. "You can stay home and help me cook your father's favorite dinner." These two sentences formed a template her mother used over the years for any social events she deemed Celia too shy to attend—a classmate's birthday party, the prom, social gatherings.

Upon reaching college, Celia had pushed herself to strike up acquaintances and go to campus parties that she didn't enjoy. Sometimes she'd be drowning in pain with a migraine but went to an event anyway, forcing herself to be social. That's how she'd met Stanton Mortinson, her first real boyfriend. They began a relationship, first as friends and soon as lovers. They confided in each other almost from the start. She told him she was an introvert, and he said he had an emotionally bereft childhood. That resonated with her.

"My parents loved to party," he'd told her. "I'd have five different babysitters in five nights." The other two nights when his parents were home, they caught up on sleep.

But after graduation he moved to California, and so began the demise of their relationship. The letters and phone calls dwindled to a dribble and then ended after a year. Though she tried hard to keep up their connection, he stopped responding. It crushed her.

After college, Celia got a job creating public relations pamphlets for an art museum. Working in a dim, windowless cinder block basement office echoed how she felt. She liked her job but didn't seek a social life. Each of the two men in her dating life ended nastily—one after four months and another after six months. Then she met Gabe at age twenty-eight. He worked for a company that supplied hardware and came in one day to deliver special hooks for paintings.

Gabe wooed her with romantic dinners and with flowers, from roses to calla lilies. Although the romantic element waned a tad over time, she grew closer to him. They married two years after they met and Celia had Allison two years later. During the first year of marriage, Gabe started his own hardware business. Retreating into Gabe's circle of protection came easily, and she pushed aside any resentment. Now she hated her past cowardice.

Glancing at her watch, she saw she had five minutes left before lunch began. Her eyes flickered over thick, perfect blades of grass and her mind wandered to the cha-cha lessons. After Edith had the sign for lessons taken down, the women snuck into the community room in the early evening and continued dancing by themselves. Those times infused her with pleasure, injected her with new life. Swaying to a cha-cha rhythm, in sync with another person, she exploded with internal combustion, feeling a high no medication could imitate. Her soul soared until her spirit hovered just above her body, watching the slow realignment of her moods from bleak to upbeat. Sometimes, the next day her muscles pleasurably ached.

When Allison was thirteen, Celia had tried to teach her some dance steps. She had put on cha-cha music, wrapped an arm around Allie's waist, and said, "It's like this, Allie: forward one-two, then in place one-two-three, and repeat it going backward." She knew minor basic steps and her stiff legs moved awkwardly, but she'd always loved the Latin music.

A jittery Allison had seemed like she wanted to jump ship, but Celia tightened her grip on her daughter. Soon Allison's feet found the rhythm as Celia began loosening. Though their movements were jerky, Allison's enjoyment radiated all over her face. She bobbed her head to the beat.

After ten minutes, Gabe poked his head in and beckoned to Allison. She bolted. "Dad's taking me to the city."

"Allie," Celia had called out. "Let's finish."

Celia opened her mouth to further protest but Gabe snorted, "Don't you want your daughter to go out with her dad to the Big Apple for culture? You're stunting her mental growth with crappy dancing."

Celia clamped her mouth shut, refusing to argue in front of Allison.

Allison looked up at Gabe with adoring eyes and they were off, leaving Celia behind. Gabe had been taking charge of Allison's upbringing for a while. It pained Celia. She felt Allie slipping away.

Allison and Celia had had fun times together. Celia's medication had been working well for a number of years, and she'd felt strong and confident enough to take her daughter to Central Park once a month starting when she was eight. They strolled along the pathways to the lake and fed the ducks breadcrumbs. She recalled holding her daughter's small, soft hand and laughing together as they meandered down Fifth Avenue, gazing in the store windows. Celia began adding excursions like the Bronx Zoo, the children's theater, and the ballet.

As Allison's twelfth birthday neared, they returned home aglow from a children's play, *Peter Pan*. Gabe began his inquisition, wanting to know what they did down to the last detail. He hadn't shown a lot of interest in parenting until that point. Allison was usually in bed by the time he came home from work. Celia suspected he'd grown jealous of their relationship but said nothing.

He started demanding that mother and daughter not go into the city by themselves—it was too dangerous. He formed a gun with his hand. "What if anything happened? You wouldn't know what to do if trouble hit you in the face," he'd said.

She winced when she remembered that she'd accepted his demands without a fight, allowing herself to be taken out of the equation. Two weeks later he started taking Allison into Manhattan himself. Hurt at not being included, she tried inviting herself along. Gabe shrugged and told her next time. There wasn't a next time.

She never objected to the expensive gifts Gabe gave Allison, not even when he gave her a sports car for high school graduation, claiming she deserved it because of all her community work. Celia applauded Allison. It didn't matter if they scrimped to make their only child happy. But having to view her family as if she were a stranger peering in from the outside pushed Celia into a void filled with glass splinters. Family events for her played out from a distance, like watching a foreign language movie with no subtitles. Celia's heart felt porous, like an icy wind blew through it every time she thought about Allison pulling away from her. She had failed as a mother and depression had taken hold once again.

This new adventurous life in Florida trumped her old one of loneliness and denial. She'd been able to slowly begin to trust herself and develop some confidence. Not one serious bout of depression had occurred since her new friends saved her life.

Overshadowing this was the thought: *But you broke the law. A man is dead and you messed with his body.*

Deb and Marcy arrived, and the three women stood together outside the clubhouse, steeling themselves to make their first appearance among the community members since they'd snuck Melvin back to his condo.

Marcy tugged at the short green skirt that rode high on her shapely thighs. She had thin white skin that flushed deep red when upset. Her wild tendrils, dyed bright red, brushed her large breasts. Just before leaving her family, she'd had breast implants, thinking the procedure might improve her marriage. It didn't.

"Nice mourning outfit for Melvin," Deb said.

"Hold off on the teasing," Celia said.

"You said to be my usual self, and hide my distress," Marcy said. "For cripes sake, this is me. I've been worked up since last night. I couldn't sleep a wink."

"Ladies, let's keep it together," Celia said. The two others nodded, and together they walked into the clubhouse lobby, which was decorated with fake columns and six life-sized plaster statues of Venus embedded in white alcoves. The dining room had bare white walls, white tiled flooring, and French doors opening to a wide concrete terrace that had a view of the gardens. Twenty round tables of assorted sizes—accommodating four, eight, or ten people—filled the large communal room, and each was draped in a crisp mauve tablecloth and decorated with a small vase of yellow daisies.

The three women sat at a small table in the middle of the room, and Celia found herself fidgeting in her chair. Her stomach clenched as Edith stepped up to a podium with a microphone.

"I have a sad announcement. My dear husband, Melvin, passed sometime during the night and we want to honor him," Edith said in her nasal, flattened-vowel accent. "A man admirable in his devotion to humankind, who sought to help others."

"No, he can't be dead!" Marcy shrieked, shooting out of her chair. People turned to look at her. She put her hands over her mouth and sat down again.

"Have respect, you ..." Edith sputtered, her face blood red. "He was my husband."

Celia held Marcy's hand and squeezed as Marcy seemed about to speak. Deb fiddled with the tablecloth.

Edith glanced at her group. "He was good to all and would give you the shirt off his back," she droned on in a monotone. "My best friend is gone." Edith lowered her head.

"He took his shirt off his back only to seduce someone," Deb whispered.

Celia put her finger to her lips.

"And," Edith looked up, "in the face of this tragedy and the loss of our great leader, the board of directors voted me the president in his place. And I thank the residents for their vote of confidence."

"Confident you're a tight ass," Deb whispered again. "Who voted her in?"

There was a smattering of applause, mostly from Edith's cronies. Celia noticed a good bit of eye rolling, murmurs, and soft groans rippling through the rest of the audience.

Edith asked everyone to bow their heads in silent prayer. Celia's eyes filled with tears as she silently apologized to Melvin for moving his body and hoped he found a place to rest in the great beyond. When heads rose, people began to eat. Celia wasn't hungry, but Deb left for the buffet. Marcy sat, looking crushed as Celia hugged her.

Celia saw Edith's friends staring at them from their table. *Oh shit.* Edith's crew of eight female friends were almost indistinguishable from each other. They all had short, dull, dyed blonde hair that was almost white, slashes of blood-red lipstick, and streaks of rouge against pale dry skin. Celia didn't care how they looked but resented how they treated Marcy. From the corner of her eye, Celia noticed Edith walking in her direction. As Celia started to fold and refold her napkin, she refused to turn around, but felt a pinch on her arm from Marcy.

Edith stood behind them. "I called the police because Melvin's death was suspicious." Her voice whined like an out-of-tune violin. "They found antidepressants and Viagra with no doctor's name. He never needed that with me. Someone gave them to him. Who do you think?" From the corner of her eye, Celia saw Edith bending over Marcy's head. "Melvin was found nude, and he might have had a woman over during the night."

Celia tightened her hands until her knuckles turned white. She turned to stare at Edith. "Why are you telling us?"

"Marcy here was more than chummy with Melvin."

"He was the love of my life," Marcy spat, as tears rolled down her cheeks. "And he certainly didn't need Viagra or any drugs with me."

Edith had a smug smile on her lips. "As the new president of the board of directors, I'm pressing to get this investigated. I'm guessing some hussy gave him Viagra, and it killed him."

"Are you the FBI or what? Let's go," Marcy said, her face white as she jumped up. Celia followed her lead and the two hurried to the buffet table before Edith could respond. Celia grabbed Deb's arm.

Deb dropped her plate filled with a burger and French fries as they practically dragged her out.

"What the hell is this about?" Deb asked as they left the building. "I didn't eat."

"Edith's on our case about Melvin," Celia said. "We had to get out of there."

Marcy had an innocent look, but her eyes blurred. "Sometimes what people think of me does hurt. I'm a good person, aren't I?" Marcy's shoulders shook. "Right, Celia? Right, Deb?"

Celia sensed a volcano about to erupt. "Right, and you're certainly not boring like Edith."

Marcy gave a tiny grin while tears flowed down her cheeks. Celia had never seen her so shaken except when the subject of her children came up. Celia hugged Marcy close to her as she recalled the story Marcy had confessed after a couple of glasses of wine. The horrible abuse she had suffered as a child, the beatings, living in terror of what was next. Celia suspected that Marcy felt unworthy and that she left her husband and children to follow the guru to an ashram because of it.

Celia knew her daughter would not approve of Marcy's flamboyance or see her profound inner pain. Most people only saw her over-the-top personality. Still, it seemed awful for her kids, now adults, to cut their mother out of their lives. *If I found a way to contact her children without Marcy knowing, I'd beg them to try to reconcile.*

"You visit sick people and help them get out for walks and shopping," Deb said soothingly, patting Marcy's back. "You even buy groceries for them out of your own pocket."

"I do, don't I?" Marcy lifted her head. The tears had stopped, but her body still trembled.

"You do it because you truly want to help." Celia held both of her friend's hands in hers until Marcy's tremors eased. "Now remember, we can't talk with anyone about Melvin," Celia whispered.

Her two friends nodded vigorously.

Celia felt dread creep up her neck. Why did Melvin have the blue pills in his medicine cabinet? Where did he get them?

Chapter 8

Celia

They stood outside the clubhouse in the glaring sunlight, and Celia felt her headache worsen. Flashes of light in her eyes, a head-smashing pain that tore through her ears and skull—these symptoms usually happened when she was worried or tense. She called these migraines her prison. Blinking rapidly she led the women to a quiet area in the shade of a grove of palm trees and rubbed her forehead. "It really is a shame about poor Melvin."

Deb widened her bloodshot eyes. "I hate to speak poorly of the dead, but like a lot of people, he had a habit of suing—like faking slip and fall accidents in supermarkets. He was a half-cocked lawyer himself, and he was suing Global HMO, the company where my son is CFO. He claimed they made him sick by not sending him to a specialist quick enough."

"But wasn't he already ill when he moved here?" Celia asked.

Deb twisted her lips. "He didn't take care of his diabetes. Then when he's really sick and he needs more serious medical help, healthcare costs and frivolous lawsuits skyrocket. Melvin had larceny in his heart."

"You're talking out of your hat," Marcy said in a shrill voice.

"Michael gives me the lowdown on his company. When people

sue, the company usually pays them off rather than have a long, drawn-out court case. The HMO is growing by leaps and bounds across the country. Melvin and others see deep pockets."

Marcy pouted.

"Ladies. Let's stick to issues," Celia said, clapping her hands hard once. "We need a game plan. I'm thinking we might participate in more activities around here, become part of the gang, blend in."

"Marcy has lots of activities on the premises and Melvin was just one of them," Deb said.

"I resent that, you mean old grouch. Everyone thinks I love barhopping and flirting," Marcy said, looking remorseful. She grabbed Celia's hand. "That's not really me. Once I met Melvin, my life changed. You have to believe that I miss the jerk."

"I believe you," Celia said, returning the firm grip. "He loved you, I'm sure."

"Celia, you'd believe in Santa Claus. I could probably sell you Miami Beach."

Marcy held up her hand, showing a small sapphire ring on her finger. "He gave me this."

Deb raised her eyebrow. "We know, but are you sure he didn't lift it from a nursing home while he was visiting?"

"C'mon. That's uncalled for," Celia chided Deb.

"Oh, I'm just kidding," Deb said. "We need a laugh."

Whenever Deb's teasing left the realm of amusing and entered the sphere of mean, Celia felt a sharp pang in her stomach. It triggered festering scars left from Gabe's scathing comments to her: "You were so pretty when I first met you—not that you've aged badly, just that you were prettier." Or, "Stop this depression stuff. You're just begging for attention." *Poof to you, Gabe. I'm free.*

Celia forced herself to push down the icy fear in her chest. "We're the amazing cha-cha babes who live on Pelican Way. We dance till we drop or they haul us off to jail. Do they dance in prison?"

She reached for her friends' hands and led them through cha-cha steps. Marcy sang in a lovely lilting voice a song by Chelo called "Angelina."

Celia threw her head back, the muscles in her neck straining, her headache easing. Amazingly, Deb's body straightened in slow increments as she danced, and a youthful aura glowed about her face. They stamped feet in precision. Celia heard Marcy's singing as though she had a full orchestra behind her. As she raised her face to the sun, she closed her eyes and the world dissipated into the rays embracing her. Forward, backward, her feet slid or thumped with each beat, her calves tightening, pleasant currents zapping to her belly. The dance ruled her body and all disturbing thoughts floated away into the clouds. Marcy stopped singing and Deb finished by wiggling her butt before returning to her stooped position.

Then Celia noticed Edith and her group glaring at them just twenty feet away. "Oh shit," Celia whispered. "The devil strikes again."

"I heard that, you, you … irreverent bitches. You are all going to hell," Edith shrilled.

"I'll meet you there." Marcy stuck her tongue out.

Edith's presence sent Celia into turmoil. Celia's head hammered as she hustled them away until the group was out of sight. She rubbed her temples. Despite having known each other for two years, it felt like she, Marcy, and Deb had been friends for a lifetime. They shared common bonds. Celia recognized vulnerabilities that resonated in all of them, like their struggles in connecting with their adult children and finally trying to grow up themselves. Marcy tried to contact her kids in vain, and Deb shadowed her son like a hawk circling prey. Sometimes when Celia's mind drifted, she had the vague sense she'd never borne a child, then the sudden recollection that she'd had Allison caught her by surprise.

She so wanted Allison's approval. A therapist once told Celia that wanting your child's approval puts your kid on edge. That might be the case, but she'd accept just being liked and respected. Maybe a little forgiveness for her past actions? But Celia knew her behavior had done enough damage as to be unforgiveable.

And now, for the first time, it struck Celia that none of them had a successful romantic relationship. Deb and Marcy were both divorced, and Celia herself had lived for years in an unhappy marriage before being widowed. The three of them, feeling bereft, had constructed a family of their own. That gave Celia a warm feeling despite her chilled skin.

"I've been thinking about our game plan," Marcy said, her eyes glinting.

"More trouble?" Deb asked.

"Let's go out tonight, hit some high spots, as though nothing happened. Make everyone think Melvin and I weren't that close."

Celia shook her head. "It doesn't seem right, going out so soon after his dying."

"Hey," Deb said, tugging Celia's sleeve. "Marcy's right for a change. It isn't her style to sit around looking sad. That would arouse even more suspicion."

Celia heard Gabe's voice saying, "Three old crows hitting the bar scene is not a pretty sight." That stuck with her.

"You have two choices," Marcy said with emphasis. "Go with us, or stay here and bump into the likes of Edith."

Celia raised one finger. "One bar. No hopping. My head is killing me."

They decided on a time and went their separate ways.

"Be right out," Deb called from the bedroom when Celia stepped in.

Celia picked up stretched-out sweaters and T-shirts from the floor and hung them in Deb's closet. It was hard for Deb to reach the clothes bar. She recalled the picture of Deb as a stunning young woman and her own early years. *Who we are today is the sum of reaching goals like education, career, marriage, and children alongside unfulfilled desires, lack of self-awareness, and life's profound disappointments.* Florida teemed with crotchety old people. Had they given up on fun? Was the past too burdensome?

Deb pranced as best she could, swirling the skirt of a sky-blue designer dress from the sixties that she'd bought at a vintage shop. It hung at the waist, and the neckline sagged. Some of the powder sprinkled on her face collected in wrinkles and her red lipstick bled into the vertical creases above her top lip. But she walked a bit straighter and kept her gnarled hands at her sides.

The extra efforts Deb made in dressing touched Celia. She'd never thought much about aging and assumed she'd live out her future married, with an adult child and slightly shaky finances. Now she doubted her life had played out. She saw a small envelope of time left to have new experiences—taking up pottery, dancing the cha-cha, and, taking a cue from her daughter, helping disadvantaged people. There was so much she could do. But she and her daughter seemed to be skidding on ice towards unknowable futures. She shook her head, pushed away dark thoughts, and linked her arm through Deb's, forcing a smile. They headed out to meet Marcy.

Celia squared her shoulders as the three women walked through the parking lot to the waiting cab. Along the way, they encountered Edith and her group. Their stares were like knives at their backs, but Celia tried to keep a spring in her gait. *Why should I let Edith intimidate me? Oh, but I do let her.*

Chapter 9

Allison

Allison faced Thomas. "Did you get the job?"

"Not yet." He pulled off his windbreaker and threw it on a worn mid-century modern chair in their meagerly furnished living room. Allison had shopped for sofas and chairs at Goodwill. And even if her furniture looked tired and sad, it did have style.

"Did you even go to the interview?"

"Of course. I have a second one in two days. What's for dinner?"

Another phantom second interview? "It's ten o'clock. There's chili in the fridge."

"Hey, mind warming it up?"

"Yes, I do." Allison swiveled the squeaky chair back to face some papers on her desk. After a while she heard the ding of the microwave. She looked through the numbers, pushing buttons on a calculator.

Thomas stood next to her, his fork making clicking noises as he swept the chili into his mouth. She looked up and for a moment recognized the man she'd fallen so hard for. He was tall and handsome, with black hair, a Roman nose, and piercing blue eyes. He was able to chat in a way that made people think he was so interested in their lives, even though he'd tell Allison afterward that their conversations were boring. There were dark rings around his eyes. *No wonder. Out late, sleeping in and happy to have me slaving away.*

"How's your mom?" He set the plate at the edge of her desk on top of papers.

Too tired to argue with him, she didn't answer.

"Hey," he tugged her ear, "I asked about your mom."

"She's fine."

"Does she like Florida?"

She sat up straight. "You never ask about her. What's with you?"

"Maybe we can take a vacation in Florida."

"Hmmm. Yes, you certainly need a rest. Are you interested in the casinos, by any chance?"

"Could always do that. I'm on to a betting method that's sure-fire." He sat in a chair and put a leg up on the armrest. "It's not about the cards. To win you have to know how to bet. It's kind of like managing a tough job."

"So, where's the money you're managing, huh?" Allison swiveled her chair to face him. The squeak came out like a shriek. "You're a total ass. It's called gambling for a reason. People have no idea what the outcome will be." She pointed her finger at him. "Admit it. You're addicted, just like my mother was addicted to pills. I don't care what you use to give yourself a high, you're still an addict."

He stood and stretched. "I don't know what the hell you're talking about. I do it for recreation. It's not anything to get ruffled about." He raised a thick black eyebrow. "Hey, come to bed. We can solve all our problems there, sweetie." He took a step toward her.

She held a hand out to stop him. "I don't want to make love to an addict." She narrowed her eyes. "As you are." She turned back to her papers. "I'm going through all of our accounts right now. I hope I don't find anything missing."

She heard his feet shuffling to the stairs. "Why should you? I'm off to bed. Come up soon."

"I'll sleep on the sofa," she muttered.

She saw he'd only gone halfway up the stairs. He looked forlorn. "Can't we work things out?"

She heard a plaintive note in his voice and thought he meant it. Her chest squeezed. If only they could. Maybe. After everything was looked at ... maybe a chance? She'd only just started. Maybe it was just her paranoia kicking in and it wasn't as bad as she thought. Maybe they had a shot.

Chapter 10

Celia

The three women arrived at a trendy, busy, neon-lighted street in Delandra. The cab dropped them off at Fritzy's Rendezvous, where the mature set paraded in all modes of dress. Women of a certain age sashayed in short-shorts with mesh stockings, skirts of varying lengths or tight pants, and thick makeup. Men wore jeans, slacks, leather jackets, or colorful sweaters. Lots of the trendier-dressed folks obviously had undergone cosmetic surgery, teeth whitening, Botox, and hair extensions.

Celia felt the need to boost Deb's ego. "You look great tonight, Deb," she said.

Deb smiled. "Thanks."

"And I look like chopped liver?" Marcy said, flouncing her short turquoise and yellow skirt as she made a full turn. "Come on. Tell me I look great."

"You look fabulous as always," Celia said.

Fritzy's Rendezvous had a big dance floor and a live band that played oldies from the fifties, sixties, and seventies. Memories of dancing to those old songs—"La Bamba," "Rock Around The Clock," "Only You"—squashed Celia's embarrassment over spending the evening at a bar.

The song "Hound Dog" by Elvis was playing as they entered, and couples did the twist on the shiny oak dance floor. The women sat at the bar; Marcy ordered a vodka martini, Celia got a glass of chardonnay, and Deb got a merlot. Behind the bar, the liquor bottles sat on backlit glass shelves, and the mirrored walls sparkled as they reflected the dancing crowd back at Celia. She had the sensation that she was looking through a crystal wine decanter.

"To Melvin," Marcy said, raising her glass. "May he rest in peace." She looked lost.

Celia knew Marcy's occasional unfocused tendencies came from her childhood. Her brutal father had once dragged her down the steps, breaking her femur and nose—not the only time he'd been so violent. One therapist diagnosed her with post-traumatic stress disorder. It tore Celia apart to watch Marcy live by impulse, running in frenetic circles trying to escape ugly memories.

"We have to tread carefully from now on," Celia said. "I can't say that enough."

As they sipped their drinks, a tall man approached. His open-necked shirt was unbuttoned to the top of his belly bulge, which strained against his pants, and he wore two thick gold chains around his neck. Wisps of thin white hair were combed over his bald pate.

"Would you like to dance?" he asked Marcy, keeping his eyes focused on her breasts.

A dazzling smile lit up Marcy's face and she jumped off the stool, her stiletto heels clacking on the hardwood floor. On the dance floor, he started flailing his arms as Marcy appeared to dance by herself.

"He dresses like it's still the 1970s and can't dance worth shit." Deb eased off the barstool, straightened up, and did a few steps. "He won't be able to do a cha-cha, that's for sure."

Celia still marveled at Deb's transitioning from a slightly bent-over oldster to an upright woman who moved with grace and danced to perfection.

"You see," Deb said, "you swing your hips but keep the upper torso rigid. That's one thing Marcy knows how to do." She stopped and leaned against the barstool. "Whew."

Celia helped Deb back on the stool. "You are really good."

"Shoulda seen me in my heyday." She pointed to the dance floor. "No talking, just sexy looks, whirling around, head back, locking eyes." Deb flung her arms up.

"The cha-cha is deeper than most dances, spiritual in a way." Celia held her hand out. "It's like something you feel in your bones, like, uh, meeting your own soul." She waved her hand. "I'm being silly."

"Why are you always downing yourself? You're so clever. Look at how you handled the, er, um ..." Deb whispered, "the Melvin thing."

"I don't know where that came from. I can't even decide on what to make for dinner."

"You need to see yourself like we see you: confident, rational, and intelligent."

Celia furrowed her brow. "Wish I could."

Pinching her chin, Deb looked reflective. "Time for change. I'm over the hill, but not you." Deb smacked her palm on the counter. "Ouch," she said, laughing.

Celia rubbed Deb's hand. "That guy with Marcy never even said hello to us."

"Not when Marcy's around. He's old, but cleavage wins hands down," Deb said.

"You can't tell me these old buggers are mesmerized by a little show of boob? They can see naked women on TV, movies, on-line—wherever."

"They're obsessed with tits and want to nurse forever." Deb scrutinized Celia as though looking at her for the first time. "Speaking of ways to attract men, you lose. You're wearing a black shroud like the grim reaper. You're a beautiful lady with a great complexion—just a few character wrinkles and big green eyes. Why cover that great body with that shapeless outfit?"

"Gabe said that women who dressed, you know, suggestively to get male attention were vulgar." She sighed. "Besides, isn't inner beauty more important?"

"Ha, ha, ha," Deb roared. "Inner beauty is a load of crap to most guys."

Deb looked around then reached into her large bag, which was littered with crumbs, and pulled out a wrapped sandwich that Celia recognized had come off the clubhouse buffet.

"Men want sex and a woman who doesn't say much but gazes at him adoringly." She offered half the sandwich to Celia.

Celia refused but caught the bartender's dirty look. "They might as well get a blow-up doll if that's all they want. I'm sure you're not speaking about most men."

Deb bit into the sandwich and chomped away. "Wrong. How about the women's magazines when we were young?" She lowered her voice comically to sound like a man. "Be demure in the parlor, a dynamo in the kitchen, and great in bed. And don't tell him you can do math."

"Maybe we need a Woodstock in Boca Pelicano Palms with all the women who live on Pelican Way."

"Forget that. Concentrate on yourself. You got it so flaunt it. Your sweet hubby might as well have wrapped you in a woolen blanket and stowed you in the basement."

"He was controlling," Celia said. "And a bad business man. I'm not flush with cash." Celia flipped her wrist. "I looked at his books and they confused me." Her eyes fluttered as she swiped a finger across the cold condensation of her glass. "Gabe worked hard, traveled to housewares shows but never took me along. He said I'd be bored. I didn't argue." She puckered her lips. "He cared about me, but I have to admit that I love my freedom." Celia felt a twinge of guilt.

Gabe had left her just enough money to live on without luxuries. His hardware store had grossed $1.4 million or more each of the last ten years, but he had complained about increasing expenses. Celia asked him to retire and buy a small condo in Manhattan so they could travel—do things. "Impossible," he'd shouted. "Money doesn't grow on trees. I'll always have to work."

She shopped sales and bought food bargains to keep expenses down. Now, her present kitchen, with its pressboard cabinets painted with faux maple graining, didn't please the eye. At one point, after moving to Florida, she'd looked for a job but no one would hire her. She felt sure that age and being out of the job market for so long were the reasons.

"Phooey on marriage," Deb said, taking a gulp of wine. "My husband told me to let my hair go gray and picked out frumpy clothes for me. Then this fifty-five-year-old creep up and leaves me for a buxom, dark-haired beauty who was thirty years old. He got a facelift and hair implants. I think she saw that his wallet was bigger than his penis."

Celia giggled. "How did he meet her?"

"She went from job to job, making a play for the married bosses. She'd flatter them and give good sex, but only my schmuck fell for it."

Celia winced, knowing that after fifteen years the divorce still pained Deb like a fresh wound. Maybe that's why she clung to her son for dear life. "You sure didn't deserve that, but you're better off without him."

"Damn straight."

"Most men are more mature than that." Celia twirled her stemmed glass.

Deb laughed harshly. "You've been sleeping under a rock. Even smart guys fall for women who act like they adore them."

"It's hard to believe that men could fall for that baloney."

"Believe it." Deb ordered another round of drinks. "I'm alone but happy in my misery. Besides, I had enough sex in my marriage to last a lifetime."

"Gabe lost interest in sex about fifteen years after we married. I always had a fantasy it got better with age, kind of like good wine," Celia said, smiling although gloom settled over her.

Marcy waved from the dance floor where she and Mr. Disco Nights were doing a slow dance to "My Funny Valentine." Throughout her marriage, she'd envied couples who looked in love, walking together and holding hands, or talking animatedly to each other in restaurants like they shared exciting secrets. She'd yearned for the same thing with Gabe. But, she told herself, everyone had some problems, even those seemingly happy couples. True to his word, Gabe worked until the day he had a stroke.

Marcy came stumbling back, very shaky on her spike heels, her face scarlet.

"Where's your guy?" Deb asked.

"That macho pig asked me step outside so he could fondle my boobs."

"What?" Celia asked, startled.

"Yup, a half-assed booty call. Makes me miss Melvin more." Marcy puckered her lips.

"You won't be a virgin for the rest of your life. That's a given." Deb laughed.

Celia nudged Deb's arm to ease up.

"Maybe if you had a boyfriend you wouldn't be so feisty." Marcy rearranged her plunging neckline, making it more revealing, and, with her hands, raised her breasts up from the bottom, creating a swell of bare flesh protruding over the top.

"We've got to get a boyfriend for Celia." Deb chucked her bumpy finger under Celia's chin. "Look at that shayna punim! Is that not a gorgeous face for an old cocker?"

"Don't exaggerate." Celia laughed.

"Whatcha looking for in a guy?" Marcy asked.

"Oh … I guess … hmm … a man who is sensitive and shows his feminine side." Celia knew she sounded cliché, but it was true. "Someone to dance and laugh with."

That brought to mind her lover from college, Stanton. He'd once brought a boom box to the beach and they tried to do a cha-cha. After a while they tripped and fell in the hot sand of hills and valleys, tangled together and hysterical with laughter.

When they'd met, they were both naïve and virgins, so he bought a sex manual, *The Joy of Sex,* scandalous for its time. They'd wrapped the manual in brown paper and sat on the grassy quadrangle, reading and giggling. She could still smell the sweet, dense fragrance of newly mowed grass, hear the crinkle of the paper book cover, and feel the light pinch he'd give her thigh at the sexiest parts.

They were dead broke and ate pasta with sauces made from packets of ketchup, mustard, sugar, and butter they took from the cafeteria. They went on picnics and drank jug wine. Everything had tasted delicious. She confided in him that, despite her love of art, especially pottery, she felt she lacked talent. Stanton believed in her abilities, but she pursued an art history degree instead.

After graduating engineering school, he moved to California and eventually stopped writing. She thought about him for years. When Gabe died, she Googled him and found out he was living in Florida in a retirement community. That led her to Boca Pelicano Palms, a neighboring community. She often puzzled over why she'd moved so close to him. *He dumped me, after all.*

Marcy, who'd been chatting with Deb, broke Celia's spell when she said, "I'm tired. Let's go home."

"That's a first," Deb said. "You always want to go home last."

"None of us has slept much, and our nerves are raw," Celia said, fisting her hands.

As they headed towards the exit, Celia caught a glimpse of someone who looked familiar—the way he shifted his left shoulder upward, the slightly uptilted nose in profile. Celia's heart pounded. *Geez Louise. He looks like Stanton! Could it be …? Nah.* The person got lost in the crowd and Celia headed into a taxi with her friends. She figured her imagination was playing tricks on her after two glasses of wine and thinking about him while being sleep deprived. Anyway, if he frequented places like this, was he like the creepy guy who'd danced with Marcy? Was it possible he'd turned out to be a dud?

In her last letter to Stanton she'd written, "I suppose we're star-crossed lovers." No answer. That wretched sentence made her sad for a long time.

She broke from her reverie and tuned in to the heated conversation between Marcy and Deb sitting in the back of the taxi. She hadn't been following their discussion.

"No, I won't leave Michael alone. He should be married, having babies," Deb yelled. "The end."

Marcy looked irritated and a heavy silence filled the car.

The taxi pulled into their development and stopped to let them out. Sprinklers splashed and watered the lush manicured lawns and tidy greenery. Celia noticed an unfamiliar black Lincoln Continental just behind them. Oddly, no one got out of the car. She brushed it off. How could she be wondering about running into Stanton? Or who drove what car? She and her friends might wind up in jail.

When Celia entered her apartment, she saw the message light on her phone blinking and Allison's number on the caller ID. Allison hadn't responded to her last call. She pressed the message button. "Just calling you back."

As always, she speed-dialed her daughter with some trepidation.

"Hello," Allison said, a faraway sound like a lonely foghorn in her voice.

"Allie, how are you?"

After a long hesitation she said, "I'm fine, Mom. How are you?"

"I'm good." Celia nearly shouted that neither of them was fine. "Sure you're all right?"

"Just touching base."

Celia tried a lighthearted tone. "So, how's work?"

"Fine. What are you up to, Mom?" A viselike tightness gripped Allison's voice.

Celia didn't like that edge. It meant trouble. "Oh, a bunch of stuff around here." *Lord, may you never find out.*

"Your message said you're getting back to tennis? And I assume a little canasta or bridge?" Before Celia could reply, Allison hurriedly said, "I'm really sorry, but I'm in the midst of calculations. How about I call you later."

"Can I call you?"

"Wait for me to call, please."

Celia hunched her shoulders forward. "Hold on. I know you and Thomas are in a tough place. Can you tell me what you plan to do?"

"You really can't help right now. I'll keep you up to date."

Celia heard Allison breathing hard. "Allie? You can always come here till you sort things out."

"I can't talk about it right now." A click, then the dial tone.

Allie's voice haunted her. She wanted to hug her daughter and tell her everything would be all right, but that was foolish. No one knew if that could be said for either one of them.

Chapter 11

Allison hung up the phone, feeling guilty about how she'd treated her mother, but most of her memories of the woman were not pretty. As a child, she saw her mother spending half her life in bed popping pills. No one could fill the huge gap of being bereft of a mother. There were some happy times, like her mom taking her to the park and the zoo, walks in the city, and how she made an effort to read to her. She remembered with a razor-sharp imagery when her mother taught her the cha-cha. But starting in her early teenage years, something in her mother had shifted and her father had stepped in, making up for her mother's crappy parenting. *Why couldn't Thomas be more like Dad?*

Allison had looked through the bank statements again and again as though rereading them would bring back the money Thomas had taken. Rage boiled within her. Her husband would never change his ways. *That's it.* She'd give her notice at work. Slapping the check stubs on her desk, she went to her closet. Shifting hangers back and forth, she chose work-appropriate dresses and business suits and picked out skirts and tops to go with the suit jackets. As for date outfits? Not a chance. No more romance for her.

I thought being married to smart, handsome Thomas would end my unhappiness. Wrong. Although he'd had a good computer job early on, after three years he started going to work late and taking days off to play high-stakes poker games that ended at sunset. He'd been fired. He'd told her he approached gambling like a career by managing his betting. Ha! Where were those winnings? She plopped on the bed, staring at his pillow. When they'd first married, there were many nights of pleasure as Thomas, a gentle, sweet lover, talked about a happy future. But soon, he'd stopped coming home many nights.

No more playing nursemaid, no more being the nurturer. He'd robbed her of something more valuable than money—her energy and optimism. But where to go? Immediately her mother's place in Florida came to mind. If she stayed at her mother's for a while, she could find a good job and save enough for her own apartment. And Florida sounded nice with its mild winters, but it was hard to imagine staying with her mother.

Maybe I should give her another chance. She rubs me the wrong way, but to her credit, she is trying to reach out. I regret shutting her down. I'm a nurse by training, damn it, and supposed to be helping people heal.

"I wasn't a drug addict. I needed medication for depression," her mother often insisted. *Even now she says she kicked the habit. Should I trust that?* Old memories and flickering images, like an old black and white movie, shimmered through her mind. One rose to the top. When Allison was eight years old and opened the door to her mother's bedroom during a bad spell, it became obvious that Celia could hardly raise her head off the pillow. Allison stood at the foot of the bed shaking, thinking her mother had died. Finally, Celia pushed herself out of bed and read a book to her. Sometimes she'd managed to pull herself together, but despite that, Allison always knew something was terribly wrong.

The front door swung open. Allison started. Thomas edged in, carrying a huge bundle of roses. "For my rose." He held out the bouquet and tried to put it into Allison's arms. She backed away.

"Darling, these are for you. I hit it big this morning and decided to register as a gambler. I'm good. I can do this as a profession. I'm learning to count cards."

Allison started to walk away and then wheeled around on her heel. "If you're so good, where is the money from our accounts?"

"Ah, that was an investment in me. I am going to return every cent." He put his hand over his heart. "I swear."

"And what about the prostitutes?"

"That's a figment of your imagination."

"I saw the checks for the massage parlors."

He stamped his foot. "You know I have a bad back." He chuckled. "I might even be able to deduct those massages on income tax now that I'm going pro."

The words she had to say stuck in her throat. Allison swallowed hard. "I'm leaving, Thomas."

He stepped in front of her, his face horrified. "You can't. I love you. I need you."

"You need a doormat." She tried to sidestep him. He blocked her way.

"Please." He got down on one knee. "I've been awful, but I'll make it up to you. I can do it. I'll get a job."

"Do it on your own. I can't take any more."

He put his hands over his face. "Don't say that."

She resisted with all her might the urge to take him into her arms and forgive him. She'd seen him like this before. Then she went upstairs.

Moving in with her mother while she got a fresh start seemed to be the most reasonable approach since she had no money to her name. Her mother had invited her, after all. Earlier at work she'd sifted through a number of want ads in the vicinity of the town of Boca Pelicano and found one from Global HMO. Their Well Services caregiver division needed a senior accountant with a healthcare background. Made to order. She was to contact Michael Castor, CFO. Tomorrow she'd apply. Then she'd get her affairs in order and get a plane ticket.

She sighed, pulled a suitcase from the closet, and started to fold her clothing into it.

Tears flowed over her cheeks, dripping onto a skirt. *Florida, here I come.*

Chapter 12

Celia

In the afternoon, Marcy arrived to meet Celia for a walk. Celia sometimes wondered if Marcy slept in heels. At least today she wore sandals more suited to walking.

They strolled around a manmade lake on the perimeter of the perfectly manicured grounds that boasted a carpet of thick-bladed green grass, rustling palms, rooted branches of huge banyan trees, and colorful bursts of flowers that cascaded from scattered pockets of gardens. They passed rows of magenta bougainvillea climbing white trellises between a couple of dozen ranch-style villas. The square four-story buildings were connected by bridges, with a separate two-story building housing those needing more nursing help.

Marcy seemed quieter than usual. Celia admired Marcy's gutsy openness and her philosophy that anything goes as long as no one gets hurt. But when she pushed the boundaries too far, she only hurt herself. Celia blamed jealousy as the reason Edith and her cronies constantly gossiped about Marcy.

"It doesn't matter how they talk about you, good or bad, they're still talking about you," Marcy had said many times. But Celia didn't buy into her friend's indifference. Gossip about Marcy's naked escapade with the gardener and the alligator had escalated into an orgy.

Macy picked up the pace. "I hear Edith is still carping about Melvin's death," she finally croaked. "My words of wisdom for you? Get a beau, screw the living daylights out of him, and let them know."

Celia laughed. "Sex doesn't cure everything." She tossed a small stone into the lake.

"It's that or drink and smoke pot." Marcy winked. "Join us sometime?"

"Before I muddle my brain, I need to examine my crappy past behavior."

"None of us needs to change. We're all perfectly fine as we are."

"I'm speaking for myself," Celia said, throwing another stone in the lake, watching it skim the surface for a couple of feet before sinking. "I'm determined to stop being so passive." She thought of something she'd been meaning to tell her friends. "I enrolled in a pottery class."

Marcy got her usual faraway look then snapped back into focus. "That sounds nice. For me, I hope to find a relationship as good as the one I had with Melvin."

Celia hunkered down and dipped her hands in the lake, the cool, silky water rippling through her fingers, thinking about how the theme of so many poems, songs, and novels was a desperate need to find and keep love, or else the pain that came from losing it. Why do relationships often fail, she wondered. Notions of love were shaped, more or less, by books, movies, magazines, and, of course, one's parents. Crap, they were all doomed.

Marcy walked with Celia back to her apartment. Once inside,

Marcy said, "I have something for you to read. Just came across it." She pulled a tattered yellowed paper from her pocket.

Celia settled into the pillows on the sofa and took the folded paper. The print was from an old-fashioned typewriter. "What is this?"

"I was sixteen and this beautiful olive-skinned Brazilian woman moved in next door. She was around forty. I thought she was ancient but I adored her. She taught me the cha-cha." Marcy shrugged. "She gave me her cha-cha rules and said to me, 'No matter where you go, learn these rules of cha-cha. You can use them all through your life.'" Marcy sighed and looked down. "Eight months later she moved away in the middle of the night. I was crushed."

Celia reached for her reading glasses and put them on.

"Don't ask why I kept them, but I thought you might want to see them. You can toss them if you want. There're just a bunch of silly rules from an irresponsible woman. Gotta go."

Marcy waved and left.

Celia flattened the yellowed paper on her coffee table and read aloud:

RULES OF CHA-CHA

TRUST YOURSELF. BE YOUR OWN BEST FRIEND.

LEARN YOUR STEPS. DISCIPLINE LIBERATES.

IMPROVISE. THE DANCE IS A PALETTE TO EXPLORE THE UNFAMILIAR.

CREATE YOUR OWN INNER RECEPTIVE SPACE. IT ALLOWS FOR HEALING.

DON'T DROWN IN THE PAST. STAY IN THE MOMENT.

EMBRACE YOUR MISSTEPS. THEY ARE THE KEY TO DISCOVERING YOUR INNER SOUL.

DON'T BE AFRAID OF RESISTANCE. IT OPENS NEW HORIZONS.

IT IS DANGEROUS TO FEAR RISK. WE MAY NEVER KNOW JOY.

JUDGMENTS IMMOBILIZE THE MIND. THEY LIMIT FREEDOM OF CHOICE.

FINALLY, BE A LITTLE BAD. THE KIND OF BAD THAT ENHANCES LIFE.

Without warning, Celia began to sob, putting her hand over her mouth to muffle the sound. These rules spoke to her, with their message of living life to its fullest, something that Celia had avoided like the plague.

Celia thought of herself and her friends and her daughter. Marcy, estranged from her children who she left because she fell for the guru. Deb, still surrounded by toxic air from her bitter divorce. Allison, struggling in the wake of her father's death and saddled with an unsupportive husband. Could following the rules of cha-cha help them? How?

Chapter 13

Celia

Celia and Marcy mingled with a crowd of about fifty people in the lobby of the funeral home. They looked around for Deb.

"Wasn't Melvin the most gentlemanly man?" Celia did a double take as she heard Deb's voice. "Everyone loved him," she went on.

Celia smiled. Why not be heard in public idealizing the departed in a masterful work of fiction? A woman standing next to Deb joined in, speaking of Melvin in reverential tones. One would think he'd saved the world from extinction. Melvin the hound dog was emerging as a statesman.

Hustling her friends into a pew in the chapel, Celia sat on the edge of the bristly velour seat. She peered into the coffin, noting that Melvin looked almost handsome, a tribute to the skills of the cosmetician. He wore a navy-blue suit, a white shirt, and an elegant aquamarine paisley tie. A vein pulsed on her neck as she thought about how they'd moved his body. She looked away.

Edith and her friends hustled into the row of seats in front of the coffin and turned to give them imperious stares. *Terrorists, all.*

Marcy dug her fingers into Celia's knee, and she winced in pain. Celia removed Marcy's clawed hand and made a motion for her to calm down.

Inefficient air conditioners circulated humid air. Celia leaned back, trying one of the meditation practices Marcy had taught her, but her mind wandered. This was her seventh funeral in the last three months. She'd known both Mr. Angstrom and Melvin better than the other five. Celia shivered, aware that she had to get used to death, which came with the territory of aging, but still, seven people seemed a bit excessive for a community of just four hundred people.

When the service ended, the pallbearers carried the coffin to the hearse for the private burial, only for the immediate family. Celia, Deb, and Marcy held hands. Celia's heart swelled, knowing that they were of one mind.

Marcy drove fast on the highway to the funeral luncheon at Melvin's son's house. Melvin's children were from his first marriage before Edith. "That Edith is talking through her butt. There won't be an investigation. I'm … friendly with the vice president of the condo association …"

"Is friendly a code word for screwing?" Deb asked.

Marcy made an aggrieved huffing noise. "Lyle told me Melvy bragged about taking Viagra. He couldn't stand to be 'im-po-tent,' as Lyle called it. He also told Edith, and she said I fed it to him. You can get Viagra anywhere, like aspirin." She paused. "Pshaw. I doubt he took it with me."

Deb opened her mouth to retort, but Celia elbowed her in the ribs and cut her off. "I still worry about what we did."

Marcy glanced at Celia in the rearview mirror and said, "Oh Lord."

"It's going to be fine," Deb said, sounding strained.

They arrived at a low-slung, one-story all glass and stucco house. It seemed that everyone who could walk, limp, or crawl had showed up. Funerals offered good food and booze and made for a great social outing in their community. Five women lined up behind them, each clutching a casserole dish.

"Aha," Deb exclaimed, once inside. "The casserole brigade is looking for available men."

"They came to help," Celia said.

"Nah." Deb rubbed the large joints in her hands. "Women show up at mourners' luncheons when they smell a new widower—or, if a man dies, they go after his buddies."

Marcy nodded. "Invites galore for dinner, then tell him he's wonderful, and next thing they're an item. It's kind of an Olympic sport."

"Oh please. Most of us are here to mourn, I would hope." Celia rolled her eyes.

Deb stepped up to the table filled with five chicken casseroles, platters of cold cuts, and bowls of potato and macaroni salads. Most of the men seemed more interested in heaping food on their plates than meeting women. Deb opened her large purse, revealing a Tupperware container inside.

"This is not the place to steal food," Marcy said.

"If we don't take it home it will go to waste. It's conservation."

"I'll pretend we're not together," Celia said, nibbling on a cucumber sandwich and looked away as Deb began loading her container with sandwiches. Celia watched Marcy corner Lyle. He seemed receptive as she leaned her body close to him.

Julia, Edith's best friend, slowly approached Celia. She had dark circles under her eyes and her hands trembled. Her gait had become tentative and shuffling. Celia was surprised to see the changes in the woman and wondered if Vanessa had become her caregiver.

"She's heading for the Alzheimer's unit soon," Deb whispered.

"Hello," Julia said. She had an unwashed odor, smelling of sweat.

"Julia, how are you?" Celia asked.

"I'm fine." Julia seemed to look right through Celia. "Are you Vanessa?"

Just then Edith walked up to them. "Julia, sweetie. Come with me."

Deb stopped foraging and stared.

"At least Edith is kind to her." A vise squeezed Celia's chest. "I don't want to face Melvin's family. Let's go."

As they headed out, they grabbed Marcy, who stood fast at first then relented.

Once they stepped outside, a familiar voice lilted, "Hi, ladies." Celia stiffened as Vanessa approached, a look of concern on her face. "I'm a bit late, but Edith wanted me at the mourners' luncheon. So tragic."

Marcy raised an eyebrow at Celia and Deb. "We're all devastated."

Vanessa turned to Celia. "I heard you play tennis, Celia. I'm always looking for a partner. How about a doubles game sometime?"

Celia had to think fast. "I'm rusty, and I'm sure you're busy with work."

"I can play in my off-hours."

Suppose I say the wrong thing when we're together?

"Stay away from the handsome white-haired guy inside. Name's Lyle," Marcy said, an overly sugary smile on her lips. "He's the only one without a gut, and reserved for me."

Vanessa opened her mouth to speak, but Deb interrupted her. "You don't want an old fart like Lyle anyway. I've got just the man for you. Interested?"

Although Vanessa looked surprised, she said, "Well, I am single, but I don't know ..."

"My son, Michael, is CFO of Global HMO," Deb said, then added, with a flourish, "It's one of the biggest health outfits around here—and growing across the country."

Vanessa's casual demeanor snapped into military attentiveness. "What a coincidence. I've done caregiving work for them."

"Go to Starbucks on Lewis Street at 8:30 a.m. He's there every morning for coffee. He'd love to get married and have kids real soon. But don't tell him I said so."

"Whoa." Vanessa looked taken aback then smiled. "Don't put the cart before the horse."

Celia shook her head over Deb's lack of boundaries.

Vanessa looked like she was casting around for a change of subject. "It's a crime that such a kind, sweet man like Melvin died."

Celia's radar snapped on. *Crime? Funny word choice.* "How did you know him?"

"He had trouble with his insulin. I got him to the right doctor and worked with him on his diabetes." Vanessa leaned closer like they were all coconspirators. "Melvin's kids demanded an autopsy, that's why no one was allowed at the cemetery—just a service and no burial. They think it's foul play because he died of a heart attack and didn't have a bad heart. A jilted girlfriend doing him in is the rumor." Vanessa stared at Marcy. "Edith is bugging the police about it because Melvin was about to reconcile with her."

Celia knees buckled, but she caught herself. Marcy looked away.

"Silly rumormongering from a bunch of old biddies with boring lives," Marcy said, thrusting her hip out and placing a fist on it. Her voice had a quavering, high-pitched tone.

Vanessa looked askance at Marcy. "You and Melvin were an item."

"That old weasel? Just friends." Marcy gave Celia an imploring look.

"He was everyone's friend, very social," Celia jumped in.

Vanessa lowered her head with a forlorn expression. "Life takes you by surprise." She looked at each woman slowly before handing Celia her card. "Please call me. I'm serious about tennis." She scrutinized Celia's face. "You sure do look familiar."

Before Celia could respond, Edith stepped out the door and, ignoring everyone, sidled up to Vanessa. "Melvin's kids are waiting. Hurry."

Vanessa waved then bounded up the steps and into the house with Edith behind her.

"What the hell are Melvin's kids doing with Vanessa?" Marcy asked in a tight voice.

"Don't make a big deal out of it. And if she says she thinks she knows you, Celia, just tell her she saw you around the tennis courts," Deb said.

Marcy pointed her finger at Deb. "And you want to match her up with your son?"

"My son's a catch!"

"Damn." Celia gritted her teeth.

It was four in the afternoon by time the women got back to their complex from the luncheon. They had spoken little on the drive home. After parking the car, they all agreed that they didn't want to be alone. Deb and Marcy gave each other a quick glance and Celia knew it meant they'd be smoking pot. *Hmmm, this might be the perfect time to finally indulge.* "I'm in," she said. A look of delight crossed the other two women's faces.

"Great." Marcy scampered ahead while Celia kept step with Deb's slower pace. When they arrived at Marcy's apartment she opened the door a crack and Deb entered. The dense, sweetish scent of pot surrounded Celia in a haze of smoke and froze her to the spot.

Celia hesitated. She replayed Gabe's sermonizing on the evils of pot when, years ago at a neighborhood party, weed got passed around and she had indulged. *Nuts to you, Gabe!* "Bring it on, ladies." She rubbed her hands together.

Marcy pulled her inside. "You'll get me arrested—there's smoke pouring out." She locked the door and motioned for Celia to sit next to Deb on the faded blue couch. Taking a towel from her shoulder, she stuffed it at the bottom of the door. "You're gonna be so relaxed."

"I'm high just inhaling the smoke."

"This is good shit for the heebie-jeebies," Marcy said in her Brooklyn accent. Wisps of smoke rose from a fat joint in an ashtray, curling up the sheer white curtains covering the window. Marcy picked up the joint and puffed deeply.

Celia bit her lip. "I don't like that Vanessa is so cozy with Melvin's kids. It's strange."

"She's a hard-working woman. Get off her case," Deb insisted.

"I think she just dangled us on a string." Marcy held her breath before letting the smoke out. Her eyelids drooped over her eyes, which were as blue and serene as a cloudless summer sky.

Marcy handed the joint to Celia as the smoke twirled around her fingers. "The list of people we need to worry about are Edith and her cronies, Vanessa, and now maybe Melvin's children. Even though Edith's their stepmother, they seem to take her word as gospel."

"Smoke, Celia," Deb said. "It'll bring back the color in your cheeks."

Celia inhaled deeply then coughed. "We've got to keep our stories straight."

"Later," Deb said, then took two long drags. "Enjoy the moment. This is my survival kit for old age." Her voice became raspier with each puff.

"Where do you get this stuff, Marcy?"

"It's Tijuana Gold, the best. I buy it at the news shop across the way." She closed her eyes. "The best time to smoke weed is when you're getting it on with a guy."

Celia grinned, wondering if pot would have made Gabe sexier. She had a mild high and her troubled thoughts receded. The room shimmered with a silver hue and Marcy's numerous knick-knacks glowed; two brass lamps washed a pale, yellow light over a cocoa-colored wall where a series of ten-inch-high naked male figures filled a wall of shelves. Several porcelain winged angels hung on strings from the ceiling, their innocent faces oblivious to the antics below. In the corner sat a three-foot-high statue of Buddha.

The traditional Florida white-tiled floors seemed to float in the air. Giddy, Celia wallowed in the pleasure of feeling liberated. She took the roach from Marcy, giggling at nothing in particular. The others joined in. Marcy rolled another joint. Celia kicked off her shoes and sank back into the couch, her body relaxing as though a tight rope had been loosened inside her spine. She felt like a scarecrow blowing in the wind. Celia searched for a phrase that she'd heard long ago. "Don't bogart that joint."

"Our kids should see us now," Deb said.

Time stretched out for Celia as though all the clocks had melted and a day was as long as a week. Her daughter would be outraged. She recalled the time seventeen-year-old Allison came home from school ranting about her best friend smoking weed, then dropped her.

"Florida is boring," Marcy blurted out. They howled. Celia didn't know why she found that funny. She didn't care.

"I can't imagine you being bored," Deb said. "You are a sex queen. Life is never dull for you." Deb's mouth crinkled into a sardonic smile.

Marcy said, haughtily, "I'm discriminating and always faithful to whoever I date."

"Looks like Lyle is next. You don't let grass grow on your woo-woo," Deb said.

All three women howled again. Celia knew Deb's hard-edged humor covered up a lot of disappointment. Deb sometimes joked that her ex should remarry her because she'd done so well in the divorce settlement and he'd always wanted to marry a rich woman. In reality, his leaving had imploded her life. She blamed her ex for Michael's teenage distress, years of anguish when Deb had had to run to school often because Michael got into a fistfight or set fires in the bathroom. Celia knew it must have been hard for her to raise Michael alone during those tumultuous years, and she was gratified that Deb's son was now a success.

"I was intimate with only one man in the ashram." Marcy brushed her wild red curls back over her shoulder. "We abstained. It was a rule meant for residents to be celibate so you could feel at one with your soul without interference from the body."

Deb gave Marcy a piercing look. "The guru interfered with your body all right."

"I did abstain … for two weeks." She stared at her hands. "We had a good relationship for years until he stole from the till," she said, with a caustic smile. "He disappeared. I'm sure he beat it to Rishikesh in India."

"It's too bad you gave up your kids for that loser," Deb said.

The mood in the room shifted and grew heavier, and Marcy looked stricken. Celia reached over and grasped her hand. "You're amazing to be so honest about yourself. Not many people are."

Marcy held up the joint. "This helps loosen the tongue."

"I have a confession." Celia meant to bring an upbeat mood back, but she heard her words echoing as though from a mountaintop. "You know that my husband wasn't very, uh, adventurous in bed." His rejection of her still had the power to cut through her, and she took a breath to steady herself. "I yearned for him to want me so much, be my soul mate." Celia's throat grew tight.

"So, what's the confession?" Deb asked, twirling a finger to get on with it. "Don't do your usual dawdling."

"Okay, okay. I often fantasized about having sex with my college boyfriend, Stanton … like when Gabe and I were intimate." Celia looked down.

The sound of loud laughter jarred her. Both women were laughing hysterically.

"What?"

"Pshaw," Marcie sputtered. "We all fantasize about other men during sex, girl."

"If Gabe had known, he'd call me a … you know, a slut." She waved her hand in the liquefied air.

"At our ages, being called a slut is a compliment," Marcy said. "Tell us more about Stanton. Forget crabby old Gabe."

Celia sat forward, looking at both women, and said, "Stanton and I made beautiful love together. I had more orgasms in the three years we were lovers than in all the years of my marriage. We'd talk about living together after college. We were so in sync. And then … bam. He dumped me." She cleared her throat. "As a matter of fact, I know he lives in Braxton Square."

Marcy sat upright, eyes wide. "That's practically next door. Hot damn. Look him up, even though he was a jerk for letting you go." She flopped back in her seat.

"Maybe I'm only remembering the good parts." Celia felt lightheaded and thought she could fly, just like her tongue was doing. "I did better. I got you two."

"Look him up," Deb said. "Don't wimp out like you always do."

Celia shook her head. "What if he's married?"

"Maybe he's a widower." Deb sat at the edge of her chair. "You know why women live longer than men? God wanted to give married women a long rest." Deb grinned. "Maybe it was a blessing my husband dumped me. So much tension—maybe that's why Michael is afraid to get married."

"Remember when you fixed Michael up with that woman at the nail salon?" Marcy giggled.

"She was pretty and a doctor back in Russia," Deb insisted.

"Doctor my ass. Her father was Russian Mafia and insisted that your son marry his daughter and give her a green card. Michael squeaked out of that one by the skin of his teeth."

"Do you have sweets?" Celia asked loudly.

"We've got the munchies," Marcy said, speaking in slow motion. She opened a drawer and removed a golden box. She opened it and offered it to the women.

Deb took two chocolate buttercream candies and stuffed them in her mouth. "This has to be more fun than sex," Deb said.

"That's questionable," Marcy said.

Somewhere deep in Celia's underbelly something familiar yet foreign stirred as she imagined having sex with a man who would be like the old Stanton, willing to listen and respond, a man who would pass by and ruffle her hair, sit close to her on the sofa. *Oh, the marijuana is killing me.* Startled by a loud noise, she turned to see that Deb was snoring, her chin resting on her chest. "I guess I'd better take her home."

"Okay," Marcy said, closing her eyes, curling up in her chair, and nodding off herself.

Celia thought for a moment, then decided not to half drag Deb home. She raised Deb's legs onto the couch, took a silky green quilt from the back of the couch, and tucked it around her. Tiptoeing out, she hurried back to her apartment. On her way, she remembered one of the cha-cha rules that Marcy had given her. TRUST YOURSELF. BE YOUR OWN BEST FRIEND.

Deb's right. I am a wimp. Can I be my own best friend? How?

Chapter 14

Celia

Invigorated from a good night's rest, Celia skipped from cocktail table to end tables, swiping each one with a feather duster. A sharp banging at the door stopped her and she opened it, Deb and Marcy rushing in.

"John Rappan dropped dead at the pool," Deb said in a loud voice. Celia gasped.

"Another one who didn't take care of himself," Deb huffed. "Took all the leftover fries and bacon from the hot table and smoked cigars. Made himself sick. My son's company spends millions on brochures to educate these dumbheads to live better. Do they listen?"

"But he didn't have a bad heart, as far as I knew," Marcy said. "I think he had lupus."

"Oh, you know a lot about him. Did him, too?" Deb asked, dripping sarcasm.

"Absolutely not, big mouth. He was gross and I was loyal to Melvin."

"Quiet! A man just died. What a shame," Celia said.

"There she goes all soft again. He's the one who asked to see your financial statement when you first moved in." Deb sat down at a kitchen table.

"Well, I made a mistake inviting him to dinner."

"He invited himself," Deb laughed. "Remember he told you ... um," Deb tapped her forehead. "Oh yeah. He blasted atheists and agnostics and said they deserved to go to hell."

"Well, he was nasty. He said he was taking Viagra and did I want to ..." She made a disgusted face. "Yuck."

"That's not the issue," Marcy shouted. "Listen, Edith's spreading rumors that you were dating John Rappan. She's agitating for them to do an autopsy."

Celia rubbed her forehead. "That's ridiculous. Why would she say that? I had coffee with him twice at the clubhouse because I bumped into him and then dinner at my place once."

"She probably wants to make a case against us. She's spreading rumors that a woman gave Melvin Viagra and pain pills, implying me, because no doctor's name was on the bottles. She found them when she was cleaning out his apartment. She's getting Melvin's children all riled up, called the cops, and is insinuating someone did it deliberately—as in murder. He still hasn't had a proper burial because of the autopsy."

"Can they do autopsies just like that?" Celia asked.

"They do if the family makes a case." Marcy shrugged and then took some leftover soup from Celia's refrigerator and put it in the microwave. "Let's eat. Trouble makes me hungry." She set three places at the table and dished out the soup.

Celia lifted her spoon and set it back down again. "I'm a champ at ignoring problems, but here it is in a nutshell: I might be accused of causing John's demise, and you causing Melvin's. We did commit a crime when we moved Melvin, and Vanessa might know more than she lets on." Celia thumped her elbow on the table and set her chin in her raised palm. "How did all this come down so fast?"

"Let's all just take it easy," Deb said, slurping her soup.

Celia stared into space. "I hear Vanessa took care of Rappan, too, when he went through a bad patch."

"Sweet Jesus," Marcy said. "That woman gets around."

"Not as much as you, sweet pea," Deb said.

Marcy glared at Deb and then began clearing the dishes.

"Rappan's death makes number eight in three months that I know about." Celia briefly considered looking up the death statistics in their community compared to the surrounding areas, but she told herself not to be silly.

Deb pinched her chin. "Hope I'm not next on the grim reaper's list."

Marcy giggled. "Curmudgeons like you don't die. They just aggravate everyone else to death."

"No more talk of death," Celia said, shuddering.

"I've got just the cure," Marcy said, her eyes widening and glinting like crystal. She pulled a joint out of her pocket, and the three women breathed a communal sigh.

The next morning, Celia stared at the red glare of the clock numbers with stinging eyes. Five a.m. and a night of insomnia. She shivered as her bare feet landed on the cool, glazed white tile that reminded her of the slick ice rinks up north. In Florida, hot days with cool, pleasant nights were the norm in wintertime.

Celia went to pick up her newspaper, the still-dark morning shrouding her. Light from inside reflected on something lying on the newspaper. She jumped back then carefully stepped closer. A bloodied animal? Not an animal. She used the edge of the newspaper to flip the hairy thing over. It was a toupee covered in something glossy and red that looked like ketchup and had a large note on the side with bold lettering:

Move out!

No signature. A surge of anger tightened her throat as the smell of mildewed synthetic material wafted upward. "Is this mangy thing Edith's stupid version of a horse head on my pillow?" she muttered. She grabbed a plastic bag and swept the toupee into it.

She did laundry, dried and folded it. Then she showered, dressed, and took a deep breath before power walking to the clubhouse at lunchtime. As she marched to Edith's table, the eight women stopped chattering and looked down at their plates— all except Edith.

"Well, which one of you did it?" She glowered at Edith.

"I don't know what you're talking about," Edith said with a sarcastic smile.

"Edith, I understand your late husband had several toupees." She took a deep breath to steady herself. "I feel awful about Melvin and John Rappan, but why are you spreading rumors? I didn't date John."

Edith stood. "John told me he visited Pelican Way a lot, but you wanted to keep it quiet." Her lips trembled. "And how dare you stroll around here like you're better than everyone else?"

"I was shut out by all of you after I made every attempt to be friendly. Why can't you live and let live?" Celia asked.

"There are rules and regulations around here."

"Your standards of right and wrong?" Celia tapped her temple. "Let's see: Invade people's privacy, gossip, conform to rigid made-up rules, and issue unreasonable demands." Celia's stomach cramped. "Look, let's try to be civil."

Celia noticed Edith glance at her friend Julia as though they shared a secret. "You're so politically correct," Edith said snidely as she sat back down. "And very condescending."

That description of herself stung Celia, but she bit her tongue to keep from weeping. "Let's just try to accept our differences and get on with it. We're too old to waste good energy."

Edith snickered. "You're no goody-two-shoes, and I'm going to get to the bottom of Melvin's and John's deaths." Edith's eyes swept over the group of women and they nodded in return.

Celia simmered with anger. "In that case …" Reaching into the plastic bag she carried, she removed the musty-smelling toupee and threw it on the table. It landed in   cold gazpacho soup. She snapped back in her chair as red liquid and bits of cucumber splashed the front of her blue flowered dress. Celia walked away as calmly as she could, her insides vibrating.

For a few days, Celia stayed in her condo, forgoing her allotted two meals a day. Marcy and Deb showed up in the dining room a few times, mostly to hear the gossip, but ate most meals with Celia. They reported to Celia that the unofficial reason for John's death was a heart attack, but his kids managed to convince officials to do an autopsy. No results yet.

Cabin fever hit. Enough, Celia thought, and began walking the grounds again only to find that several people she passed stared at her. Finally, when she saw a person whispering behind her hand to a friend, she returned home. She called Marcy and Deb to come over.

Together they sat down around the living room and Celia pressed her forehead into her hands. "They think I'm a murderer."

Marcy gently lifted her head with an anguished expression. "You know you're not."

"What's wrong? You look scared."

Marcy looked up at the ceiling. "Ah, there's some buzz around the place. You know how these places operate ..." Marcy's sentence faded. She didn't make eye contact.

"What is it, for heaven's sake?" Celia demanded.

"Melvin's family got the okay on their petition for an autopsy ASAP," Deb said.

Celia folded her hands on the table. The vague possibility was turning into a reality. "Do you think drugs killed Melvin?"

"Maybe," Deb said.

"What if any of my hair ended up on his body?" Marcy moaned. "Melvin ran his hands through my hair." She slung back her red curls with two hands, as though keeping them safe. "They'll say I murdered him." She jumped up and paced.

Celia felt like she'd swallowed glass splinters. Have we slipped up on anything that could show up on DNA examinations, she wondered? *Probably.*

The next day, Celia awoke to a loud knocking at her door. She threw on her robe, then peered through the peephole. When she saw two police officers, she thumped her back against the wall as though she could hide. *What in the world do they want?* The knocking thudded louder.

She had no place to run so she turned the knob and opened the door a crack. A large, imposing police officer stood there, his mature brown face deeply wrinkled and covered with a five o'clock shadow of white bristly whiskers. Just behind him was a tall, slim woman wearing a light blue pantsuit with epaulets on the shoulders. She had bags under her eyes, sharp cheekbones, and puffs of white hair. They looked about the same age, older than the average police officer. An article Celia had read said the depressed job market had driven young people out of the state in droves. Budget cuts had forced the county to fill some police positions with retirees who worked part time, drew lower salaries, and had no benefits, to the county's advantage.

Blood rushed to Celia's head. "Can I help you?" she asked in a tight, high voice.

The policeman kept his arm extended on the door and pushed. "We need to ask you some questions about John Rappan. I'm Officer Ronald Johnson and this is Detective Dawkins. Can we come in?"

"You're practically in already," Celia mumbled, leading them to the sofa and two chairs in the living room. Her heart pounded against her ribs. The policeman sat on the sofa, lowering his big bulk with difficulty, while Detective Dawkins stood nearby. "Go ahead." Celia tightened her arms across her chest.

"Okay, madam. John Rappan died on the premises of Boca Pelicano Palms on …" Officer Johnson checked a notepad. "January 10. Did you two date?"

"Definitely not." Celia grabbed the material of her robe around her throat.

"Six women who live here corroborated that you in fact were a couple."

Edith's cronies. "Maybe I saw him three times over a two-year period."

Johnson cleared his throat. "Mr. Rappan died of an apparent heart attack even though he was never diagnosed with a bad heart." He paused.

"They can come out of the blue at this age," Celia said, clutching the neck of her robe. The detective seemed to study the room. She sidled up to the wicker bookcase and ran her finger over a line of books, then picked up a picture of Allison and put it down.

Please, let him have died of natural causes.

"His family ordered an autopsy, but you might know that. We have preliminary toxicology reports."

Celia repressed a yelp. *He's going to deliver bad news by the looks of it. Shit.*

The officer gave a wry smile. He placed his top teeth over his bottom lip. "We need to know if, um, you've had an intimate relationship with Mr. Rappan."

Celia was outraged. "Are you asking if we slept together? Hell no."

"Okay, Ms. Ewing. I understand, but it's our job to inform you that your friend showed overdoses of antidepressants and oxycodone and the medical examiner is leaning toward homicide. There is less of a possibility of suicide because why would your friend go to the pool after ingesting all those pills if he intended to kill himself?"

"He wasn't my friend. Don't you get it?"

Johnson looked at Dawkins with a skeptical expression. "Are you sure you didn't date him?" Dawkins asked in a deep, scratchy smoker's voice as she strode over to Johnson's side. "When we get older we tend to be forget …"

"Of course I'm sure." Celia had never heard her voice so tightly knotted.

The officer squinted at his notes. He looked up. Dawkins sat down, hands on her knees. Celia thought these two resembled the Keystone Cops from the old silent film comedies, but they still had police authority.

Detective Dawkins stared at Celia. "Did you help administer Rappan's meds?"

"No way. I hardly ever saw him."

Johnson scrutinized her in a way that made her fidget. He squinted. "If you remember something later on, you'd best call us." He handed her a card.

Celia bit her lip.

Johnson nodded to Dawkins, stood, and put his hat on. Celia faced him, tightening the belt to her robe.

Officer Johnson scratched his chin with the side of the pen, making an abrasive noise, then turned to Celia. "We might need to come back."

Celia let out a whoosh of air and wrote her number on the officer's pad that he extended to her, trying hard to steady her hand. "Call first next time." She hoped never to see them again.

"By the way," Dawkins said. "We're waiting for the other autopsy report on the gentleman Marcy Worth …" she checked the pad. "Wothermire dated Melvin …"

"Goodbye," she whooshed out. She ushered them out the door quickly then stood facing the empty room, embracing the silence, as though ear-splitting hours of noise had suddenly stopped.

Steadying herself, Celia realized she needed to talk to Marcy. She couldn't care less how many sexual encounters Marcy had, but she hoped John Rappan wasn't one of them. That could really be big trouble if Melvin's toxicology reports said the same thing. Marcy had denied seeing Rappan, but Celia needed to be sure. She remembered Marcy was playing bridge that day and headed out to find her in the card room.

Celia spotted Marcy sitting at a table across the room with two other women and Lyle. As Celia walked in their directions, she heard Lyle say, "Opening bid?"

"Tricks," Marcy said, keeping her eyes on the cards.

"Exposed hand," Lyle quipped, his lips pressed together.

"Entry," she said, tossing her hair back and staring at him.

"Entry squeeze," Lyle said, sucking in a deep breath.

"Zones."

"Erogenous zones?" Lyle guffawed.

"This is wrong," Marcy said flatly. "We're still mourning Melvin."

"Play," one of the women said, unsmiling. "This is a serious game, not a porno."

Lyle chortled. "We heard that someone gave Melvin oxycodone. I see Edith at the resident board meetings and she's raising hell. She's claiming people are being poisoned. Some families of folks who died recently are demanding disinterring them and doing autopsies."

Celia stopped in her tracks halfway to the table.

"Hey, Lyle," the other woman piped up. "Watch out. Marcy might be the one."

"How dare you," Marcy shouted.

Celia hurried and lunged forward, grabbed Marcy's arm, and hustled her out to a quiet place.

"Damn jealous cats," Marcy sputtered.

"Listen. The police showed up on my doorstep and said John Rappan's early reports show he was loaded with antidepressants and oxycodone. Edith is pointing them in our direction—they implied I dated him for a long time."

"This is crazy!"

Celia felt her muscles loosen. "What the hell is going on?"

Marcy cocked her head. "Hmm. Didn't Vanessa care for both Melvin and John?"

"Yes. That's why I ran over." Celia spun around and said to the air, "And here I thought I'd just be having nice clean fun in this last stage of my life."

Chapter 15

Celia

For the rest of the day Celia paced her apartment. Everything felt desperate, from her tired-looking apartment to the idea of lunch at the clubhouse. She had no appetite and moved in slow motion. Depression rose slowly inside her body, clinging to every fiber on its way to her brain. She likened it to swimming against the tide, being sucked into a spiral down to the bottom of a lightless ocean, a soundless suffocation.

If she allowed herself to drop into that tiny room deep within herself, windowless and airless, thoughts spinning in a never-ending hamster wheel, she knew she'd never return. She recalled her psychiatrist's words: *Think of yourself as a rehabilitated heroin addict. Kick the drug habit.* So, with all her might, she tried calming her clogged head.

Her breathing became labored. She decided to distract herself with one of her art books and pulled *World of Matisse, 1869–1954* from her shelf. She blew lightly over the glossy colorful cover and raised a small puff of dust. The cover painting, "Woman with a Hat," had originally met with derisive anger from Parisians. The face was green, yellow, pink, and red and the clothes, orange, blue, violet, and purple. Such wild colorations introduced a new concept of painting. Celia also recalled how Marcel Duchamp, a Dadaist, had scandalized audiences with his "Nude Descending a Staircase," which looked more like abstract shapes than anything real. These painters had dared to breach the status quo of what people expected. But like any art form they had to know how to do realistic art first, needing to master fundamentals before breaking out with new ideas. It reminded her of the cha-cha rule: LEARN YOUR STEPS. DISCIPLINE LIBERATES. Right now, she had to think like those artists who broke through the status quo and were liberated.

As she paged through the book, John Rappan's face flashed in her mind. Why did he overdose? Elderly people often swallowed dozens of pills a day, and some took them improperly. If that were the case it wouldn't raise a ruckus, but families were alerting the police. *Problem is even if there is reason for suspicion, the finger is pointing at us. Damned Edith.*

Celia couldn't reach Marcy so she headed to Deb's. She needed to discuss Rappan's overdose and the suspicions raised over Melvin's death. She knocked on Deb's door until Deb appeared, wearing a T-shirt that read "I'd Rather be Fishing" and shorts with a stretched-out elastic waistband she kept tugging up. Her white socks sagged, touching the buckles of her sandals. She narrowed her eyes. "Are you all right, Celia?"

"No. The worst thing that had ever happened to me before all this was getting a parking ticket. We need to talk. Can we take a walk?"

"Sure, if you can keep up with me." Deb chuckled at her own joke.

As they made their way around the grounds, Celia told Deb more about the police interview while accommodating Deb's slow gait. "They scared me half to death. What really freaked me out were the rumors I dated Rappan and was intimate with him. God forbid."

"I bet these people made a mistake taking pills. They get goofy and overdose. Michael's HMO sends caregivers to homes to teach people the proper way to take meds. They show them how to exercise and eat right because they want to keep people from getting sick." Deb looked at Celia and grinned. "At least they don't have to educate us on family planning." They both giggled. "I hope this scares Ms. Hotpants to slow down. Edith is watching."

"Hey, at least one of us is out there living it up."

"I'm cooped up in this mangled body." Deb sounded gloomy. "At least Michael is a big blessing, helping me shop and getting to doctor's appointments."

"He takes good care of you and comes often. I envy that. I wish Allie and I connected better." Celia reflected for a moment on herself and her friends and their relationships with their children, realizing that none of them was truly ideal. Marcy used sex to numb the pain of being estranged from her children; Deb hid her anguish behind abrasive jokes and an obsessive fixation on her son's life. She herself had always been in denial of the damage her depression had caused on her relationship with Allie, so she'd buried herself and fantasized about a man she'd dated in college. *Pathetic.*

"On the bright side, nothing's come up about Melvin that indicts us," Deb said, bringing Celia back from her thoughts.

Celia raised an eyebrow. "Ever the optimist. The police mentioned it as they left."

"Forget about that for a minute." Her wrinkles broke up as she grinned. "Good news."

"I need good news."

"Michael and Vanessa got together." Deb showed Celia a clear photo of a woman sitting at a window table in Starbucks across from a man with a sculpted, handsome profile. He wore a gleaming white shirt, his long sleeves rolled up above his elbows, exposing strong forearms.

"Your son and Vanessa. You took this?"

Deb looked away, pointing. "Look, an egret."

"Give it up, Deb."

Deb sighed. "Fine. I took the picture from my car, with my zoom."

"Geez. Why in the world do you follow Michael? It's so intrusive."

Deb cringed. "You know his father was practically nonexistent even when we were still together. He was a good kid until he hit his teens—you know, suspended and what not. He finally calmed down and got a scholarship to Duke. I kept my fingers crossed till he finished." Deb blinked hard. "I can't shake an old habit of watching out for him."

As a teenager, Allison had a fresh mouth with her, but never turned it on Gabe, friends, or teachers. But stalking one's child? Out of the question. "It helps when teens are rebellious at an early age. They get it out of their system. Later in life can be troublesome." Celia frowned. "But you must stop following him."

"What harm is there?"

"It's bonkers and he'd be plenty pissed if he found out."

Deb flicked her fingers, dismissing Celia's remark. "Hey, if she's nice, let them get married. I want grandkids." Deb hitched up her loose shorts.

"I must admit, she seems compassionate to her patients, but ..."

"No buts." Deb removed her house key from a chain around her neck as they reached her apartment. She started to unlock the door when a slender handsome man, dressed in a dark gray business suit and a yellow silk tie, stepped up to them. He put his hand on Deb's shoulder. His wavy black hair, cropped to cling halfway down his neck in a coifed manner, was gray at the temples. His demeanor looked carefully orchestrated, more New York than Florida. He exuded confidence and his wide smile spun the air around him, welcoming all to hop on for a fun ride.

"Michael!" Deb cooed.

"Hi, Mom." His voice had a pleasant deep-throated lilt. He waved to Celia.

Deb hugged him around his waist. Celia noted that Deb looked like a just-hatched baby bird, her delicate bones protruding against her blue-veined wrinkly skin. There was a strong resemblance between mother and son in the robin's-egg blue eyes and long, sharp noses. Michael, about five feet ten, seemed to fill a bigger space. His strong jaw, also inherited from his mother, gave his face authority.

Deb turned to Celia. "Here's my CFO sonny boy."

"Mom, stop." He held out his hand. "Good to see you again, Celia."

"Hi, Michael." His long-fingered, smooth hand gave her a no-grip handshake. She found that younger men did that to older women, thinking they might break a finger if they gripped too hard. Deb always spoke about Michael's busy, stressed life, but he exuded the poise of a man who enjoyed himself.

Michael smiled and raised an eyebrow. "I have no doubt my mom asked if you know any available women to introduce to her socially inept son." He turned to his mother. "Mom, I met a terrific woman. You can quit your antics now."

"What antics? I don't do anything." Deb straightened her neck. "Tell me about her."

"This woman walked into Starbucks recently. We made eye contact and bammo."

"Oh yes?" Deb asked innocently. "What's her name?"

"Vanessa. It turns out she works for our company." Michael put his arm around his mother's shoulders. "Most of her clients are here in Boca Pelicano Palms and many are on your street." He gave Celia a knowing wink.

"That's wonderful, Michael," Deb said. "When can I meet her?"

Michael's head snapped back. "Soon. I'll call you later." He bent over, kissed Deb on the cheek, and gave her an envelope and a small paper bag. He waved to Celia and walked away.

Celia watched his well-tailored back retreating. *He's devoted to his mother. Despite her meddling, she did something right. Unlike me.* Celia swallowed a lump in her throat and blinked away a tear.

Celia strolled over to the tennis courts, hoping her note seeking a doubles game had gotten a response. It hadn't, although most courts emptied out in midafternoon, the hottest time of the day, when the direct sunlight and high humidity knocked your breath away.

Inside the pro shop, Celia was browsing through the racks of tennis outfits when Vanessa tapped her on the shoulder. Celia felt walloped, like recognizing a face from a most-wanted notice in the post office.

Vanessa's full blood-red lips grinned broadly as she held a tennis skirt over her flat belly. "How's it going?"

"Fine, fine."

She put the skirt back on the rack. "Things are slow. I have a

woman named Sadie part time. I took care of Olivia, but she died."
She sighed sadly. "I get close to my clients, then poof! They die."

Turning sharply, Celia bumped the rack, rattling it. *She's so
nonchalant about death.* Olivia had lived next door to Marcy. "Um,
what did Olivia die of?"

Vanessa looked taken aback. "You know, the usual—old age. She
was very ill and on oxygen."

"Who else did you work for?"

"A nice man, Mr. Angstrom. The association made him stop
sitting outside in his wheelchair." She crossed her arms angrily over
her chest. "The rule is no decorations outside of your house. A human
is a decoration? He died soon after."

Celia did some quick arithmetic in her head. By her count, the
number of residents who had died in the last three months was up to
nine that she knew of. How many had been Vanessa's patients? *Please
don't let anything be amiss with Melvin's autopsy. It might jog Vanessa's
memory of encountering us in a dark corridor.*

Vanessa kept talking as she perused the rack once again.
"I welcome complicated cases. I love helping. And my patients give
me the wisdom of the elderly. It helps get me through."

That kind of talk made Celia jittery. Did she really mean that?
Was it to cover a dark side? "Um, where did you live before?"

Vanessa removed a white tennis skirt on a hanger. "I lived abroad
for a few years, mostly Spain, and lost time to develop a career."
Vanessa scrutinized Celia. "Do you know Lila Donaldson?"

"I've chatted with her from time to time."

Vanessa's smile widened. "Well Services is giving me a job
with her. She's the aunt of the CEO of Well Services, Brady
Shirkson."

"That's nice," Celia said. "But I've got to go. It was a pleasure seeing you again, Vanessa. And good luck."

"Want to play tennis soon?" Vanessa looked eager. "I've seen you play. You're good."

Was she being watched? "I'll give you a call." She hurried out.

A part of her admired Vanessa, a single woman who approached life with bravado and compassion while struggling to earn a living. But if she knew something about that fateful night—what then?

Chapter 16

Celia

Later that evening, Celia sat and dissected her conversation with Vanessa, looking for hints she recognized her; missed dashes, commas, or exclamation points. She found nothing out of the ordinary. Getting up, she poured a little schnapps, and for the next twenty minutes folded the clean clothes in her basket to perfection until she had a regiment of neat fabric rectangles on her dining room table. She placed everything in its place in her dresser and closet and decided that any suspicions she had about Vanessa were nonsense. Vanessa worked for a reputable company who had vetted her. They'd never hire someone with a spotty record.

As she returned the clothes basket to its place, the doorbell rang, and she started. It was 11 p.m. and most everyone in the community was asleep. What could be wrong now? She looked through the peephole then pulled the door open.

There stood Allison, gripping a suitcase. Celia's stomach flip-flopped. She'd last seen her daughter three years ago. Now Allison had a sullen expression, the one permanently engraved on her face starting in her teenage years. Celia knew why she looked so grim.

"You came!" Celia said, opening the door wide and ushering her in.

"I've left Thomas for good, Mom."

The women hugged stiffly. Celia knew that Allison gave leeway for blunders in relationships, but once she decided to end things, she didn't look back.

As Allison set her suitcase down, Celia whisked her schnapps glass discreetly into the sink.

Allison's oval face looked paler and thinner. The determined set of her delicate jaw and her narrowed green eyes told Celia her daughter wasn't all that happy to be here. Allison sat at the edge of the blue and white flowered chintz sofa, her hands tightly clasped.

"I'll make tea," Celia said, heating the kettle. Her galley kitchen opened into the living room and she stole a glance back at Allison.

"Thanks." Allison's eyes looked like two grenades with the pin pulled, detonating, splintering. "I left a message on your voicemail as soon as I landed."

"Oh, I've been out and didn't play messages. No problem. You can come at any time of day or night. It's okay."

"It's a lot to put on you."

"Sweetheart, your problems are mine, too." Celia meant it and stood still, fearing any movement would stop the conversation.

"How did Thomas react?" Celia knew he wouldn't want to give up easy street and have to go back to work.

"Not good. When Thomas saw I meant to leave he went ballistic, shouting, screaming, pushing me around, blocking my way." She went on to explain how she managed to run out with her suitcase and take an Uber to the airport.

Celia gasped. "Did he hurt you?"

"No, not actually. I did worry he might." Allison massaged her neck with a pained expression.

A few minutes later, Celia set two filled teacups on the coffee table. "You can talk to me, honey. I'm here to listen."

"Later, if you don't mind." Allison's face seemed bruised, although there wasn't a visible mark. "I'd like to just hang out for a while. I had to get away so I decided on Florida. It's as good a place as any."

"You're welcome to stay here, but as a thirty-three-year-old they won't let you stay long. Damn rules of retirement communities."

Allison stood up. "I'm not living here permanently. We'd wind up killing each other."

Celia bit her tongue. Could they ever communicate without opening old wounds? "Sorry, I know you're not staying forever." The thick air rolled over Celia and she blurted out, "Why are you mad at me all the time?"

"Not on my agenda right now, Mom. Give me a break."

"Can't we be peaceful and pleasant?"

Allison grunted. "I think you know why I'm resentful. Let's leave it at that."

"Ouch."

"Okay, in a nutshell, Dad took me out for fun times and to my activities while you stayed home to brood."

Brood? "I admit that I wimped out on you." Depression had often ripped her willpower to shreds. She chided herself for being gutless and making a mess of Allison's childhood. "Do you remember when we went to the playground and the park? And you loved helping me cook."

For a split second Celia saw a faraway look of pleasure overtake

Allison's face. Then she made a weary gesture with her hands. "I have to figure out my future, not the past. I can find a hotel."

"Please, I'll stop. Stay."

"I'll find a job, get my life back on track, and get my own place." There was a long pause. "Thomas lost all of our savings gambling. He also cheated on me." Allison covered her face with her hands for a moment. "So, why did I stay?" She looked up at Celia. "Thomas kept promising to change, and I bought into his bullshit."

Celia winced, feeling her daughter's pain. She hugged her daughter. "I'm so sorry."

Allison put her head on Celia's shoulder for a moment. Then she moved back. "You never liked Thomas. You were right. I became the nagging mother, and he was the little boy who always got into trouble. I would save him and we'd start the cycle all over again."

"You can't take responsibility. Stealing your hard-earned money is terrible, and cheating is horrible."

"The nurse in me thought I could make him better," Allison said, running her fingers through her long wavy chestnut-colored hair, tugging at the ends like an exclamation mark. She blinked hard as though fighting back tears. Allison, who had always had an aura of strength even as a teenager, now looked so vulnerable.

Not knowing how to comfort her daughter, Celia said, "Would you want to do hands-on nursing?"

"Mother," Allison said curtly, "I got my MBA with a major in accounting four years ago. That and my healthcare background got mc better paying administrative jobs. Why do you forget what I do?" Allison fisted her hands.

Celia gulped. "I had a senior moment." It struck Celia that

a strange thing happened to her in the company of her adult child—a kind of disconnect from rational thought. She dumbed down. Their unresolved problems sometimes opened a crater that she filled with silly chatter.

Then Celia had an idea. "My friend, Deb Castor, has a son, Michael. He's CFO of Global HMO and Well Services, their caregiver division. Do you want me to contact him?"

Allison widened her eyes. "What a coincidence. Well Services is on my list for interviews. I can handle it."

"I'd be happy to put in a good word."

"My résumé reads well." Allison's lips looked as though they'd been tied with string.

Celia winced at the snip but decided to ignore it. "How about a grilled cheese sandwich?"

"Good old Mom—food cures all." Allison appeared to study Celia. "You have activities and friends. Don't stop anything on my account. I mean it."

"I'm here for you."

"I know you are. I really appreciate it." Allison sucked in a deep breath. "I haven't always been nice ..."

Celia saw sincerity in Allie's softened expression. "Don't worry about that. You're not wrong. I was a big jerk."

Allison shook her head. "I've given myself six months. If I get a good job, I'll stay in Florida. If I don't, I'll leave."

"I hope you stay." Celia prayed for a chance to establish a loving relationship with Allison, recapturing the compressed, precious minutes of joy when Allison was a preteen and Celia taught her the cha-cha. She needed permission to stop her emotional suicide over past mistakes and reassure her daughter that she would never again hit such a low that she wanted to kill herself. "I'm sorry the guest room is tacky." She pointed down the hall.

"It doesn't matter." Allison looked around. "If Daddy had lived … it's so sad he's gone. I miss him."

"Your dad was a comfort to everyone." *Except for me.*

"So true." Allison's voice grew quiet. Then she yawned.

Allison gave Celia a sweet-sad smile that was reminiscent of the stunning young lady Allison once was, with high cheekbones, a straight, short nose, and a pointed chin—the beauty she might still be if she could find some peace. "I love you." If only she could wrap her love for Allison in a package and gift it to her.

"I love you, too, Mom." Allison looked away as though the admission made her a tad uncomfortable. "Remember, I insist you keep your usual schedule."

It occurred to Celia that Allison thought she played bingo, bridge, and spent hours on end shopping. *If you only knew that I've learned to talk dirty, go to bars, and smoke pot. To add to that I was interrogated by the police and disposed of a dead body.* "I hang out a lot with my friends. We've even learned the cha-cha all over again. Remember when I tried to teach you?"

Allison looked surprised. "Yes, I remember. I wasn't very nice, was I?"

"You were young and kids are embarrassed when parents sing or dance."

"I have to admit, I kind of enjoyed that dance and moving to the Latin rhythms."

"Really?" Celia started doing the basic steps, clapping her hands to the rhythm. "Me too."

Allison followed, smiling for the first time since she arrived. They danced for a minute, but, as though an alarm had sounded, Allison stopped. "You're a good dancer, Mom."

The small glimmer of hope caused Celia to stammer, "Well, uh, it's good exercise when you get older."

Allison looked closely at her mother. "But what you do here is kind of mellow, right?" Allison put her hand on Celia's shoulder, exerting a little pressure.

Mellow? Celia realized that Allison needed to cling to an image of her as a woman aging appropriately. "That's me, mellow and boring." She patted Allison's hand still resting on her shoulder. It sent waves of warmth through her body.

Allison raised an eyebrow. "Maybe you do need to get out more, like volunteering. You're smart enough to be a docent in an art museum."

"Good idea." *I can do that between police interrogations.*

Allison walked toward the hallway carrying her suitcase and Celia trailed behind. Her love for Allison came with a thick coating of anxiety. Allie might get a firsthand look at her mother's new life while visiting. *Not much good would come out of that.*

Chapter 17

Allison

In the guest room, Allison agreed that the tired-looking room needed a good coat of paint. She touched the worn, prickly wicker headboard, smelling a faint whiff of Florida humidity that bred mildew through the thickest walls. She turned on a glass lamp filled with seashells standing on the night table. "This is so Florida," she muttered aloud, smiling. *What is my mother doing with the money she inherited from Dad? Too cheap to spend it?*

The thought of money reminded her of how Thomas had cleaned her out. Early in her marriage, she had adored Thomas, loved how he used to touch her so gently. She could talk to him like a friend, tell him about how her mother used prescription meds. He'd listen and whisper, "God, I understand, and our love will wipe those memories away." His pained expression during those times had dissolved the profound aching deep inside her.

Allison unpacked, organizing the drawers as she went along—underwear neatly laid out in a top drawer, polos and camisoles in the next. She knew her housekeeping habits resembled her finicky mother's. A shudder snaked down her back.

Coming to Florida was madness, but her only choice. Trying to change Thomas had drained her blood and organs until only dried-up bones remained. Her own insecurities drove her to be The Lady of Perpetual Male Cons. Some other weasel, before Thomas, had her waiting on him hand and foot. She'd turned into an enabler of machismo despite thinking of herself as a modern woman. There would be no more rescuing others—she needed to rescue herself.

Outside the window palm fronds rasped together in the warm breeze, and the moonbeams wavered like silver ribbons on the surface of a stream. The semitropical climate appealed to her after those brutal winters in Kansas, weather she'd always associate with Thomas.

Even now as an adult, Allison still awoke many mornings in a twilight zone, thinking about what places her dad would be taking her to that day. Within seconds, the realization of his death would strike with head-hammering pain. Allison rebuked herself for not going after a man like her father. He always praised whatever she did: ballet: academics, creative writing, volunteering in nursing homes, and advocating for the needy. But look where it had landed her.

At sixty-five her mom looked good. And now there seemed to be an inkling of gutsiness she'd never seen before. Her mother's revelation that she was dancing at her age seemed like a foolish, pitiful attempt to capture an earlier era. But she did look alert.

But could her mother truly have changed? Had she really stopped using those pills? Allison closed her eyes, recalling the numerous times she'd run home from high school in a panic, fearing her mother had died from an overdose, or the times she peered through the keyhole to her bedroom to see if the blanket moved so she knew her mother still breathed. She wished she could apply a welding tool to her memory bank and cut out those hazardous, painful memories.

Perhaps she resented her mother for past mistakes, but seeing her gave a dash of stability to her own tumultuous life. She hoped her mother might become more of what she needed: someone to rely on. Although Allison had already contacted Well Services for an interview, maybe her mother's connection could help. Then again, her ineptness might be a detriment. Thinking along those lines gave Allison a profound sense of sadness. Her mother did seem somewhat changed, more upbeat, compassionate and concerned with what happened to her. We might not like each other, but we do have love, she thought.

Exhausted, Allison lay down in bed and dozed off.

Chapter 18

Celia

Celia resisted an urge to cook something just to keep busy. Although thrilled to see Allison, she guarded against letting too much of the new, more assertive Celia show. She saw how Allison clung to an image of a happy connection to her father that Celia thought of as more enchanted than real. She and Gabe had hurt Allie, but she hoped Allie had come to her senses about the men she chose. Maybe the rules of cha-cha would help. But coming from her mom ... yikes.

As long as Allison was unhappy Celia could not be content. On her way to bed, Celia checked in on Allison, who slept soundly on her back, barefoot and fully dressed. A clenching ache gripped her as she covered her sleeping daughter. She thought about the rules of cha-cha, which seemed increasingly relevant, especially the one that said: DON'T DROWN IN THE PAST. STAY IN THE MOMENT. Would she ever get unstuck from the swamp she'd been mired in?

In the morning, Celia found Allison sitting at the breakfast table, texting on her smart phone. Next to her was the list of interviews she'd compiled.

"Would you like coffee, honey?"

Allison looked up, smiled, and nodded before returning to her phone. "Be finished in a minute, Mom."

This seemed like an opportunity to show her the rules of cha-cha before she started a new job. She hoped Allison might find them helpful as she had. After setting the coffee brewing, she took them from a drawer filled with tape, dozens of pens, scratch pads, and scissors.

When Allison put her phone down, Celia flattened the sheet of paper next to her on the kitchen table. "I want to show you something," she said somewhat tentatively.

"Rules of cha-cha?" Allison gave Celia a disdainful stare. "Not now. I just set up an interview this afternoon with Michael Castor. He needs an accountant with a healthcare background. Fits me to a T."

"I'm glad you called him." Disappointed, Celia put the rules aside. She held a drop of hope Allison would read the rules first. It might even help with a new job.

Allison wrinkled her brow. "I just got a text from a caregiver who works mainly in this development. Vanessa Cordova. Do you know her?"

Celia flinched. "I met her recently. She's about your age." She cleared her throat. "Why did she text you? How did she get your number?"

Allison shrugged. "She must have gotten it from Michael Castor. She said she reports to the CEO, Brady Shirkson. Apparently, he'll be at the meeting briefly and she wants to give me a head's up that might be helpful. It's unusual, but I'll take any help to get this plum job."

Celia went to the refrigerator, her knees wobbly. "Toast?" Her voice croaked.

"No thanks. I'll grab a bite with Vanessa." Allison's cell phone rang. She checked it and shut off the ringer, her face flushed. "It's Thomas."

"If he's harassing you we can take out a restraining order."

Allison gave Celia a look that shouted *Keep out of it*. After a quick check in a mirror, she hurried to the door, tugged her skirt— just the way she always did before going on a date—and rushed out. Celia reached her arms out as though to embrace the swirl of air Allison left behind.

Celia picked up the rules, stared at the paper, and read them again.

TRUST YOURSELF. BE YOUR OWN BEST FRIEND.
I'm trying.

LEARN YOUR STEPS. DISCIPLINE LIBERATES.
That I've enjoyed.

IMPROVISE. THE DANCE IS A PALETTE TO EXPLORE THE UNFAMILIAR.
Like theater, art galleries, and getting back to pottery! That's what I see for myself.

CREATE YOUR OWN INNER RECEPTIVE SPACE. IT ALLOWS FOR HEALING.
I wish I could.

DON'T DROWN IN THE PAST. STAY IN THE MOMENT.
Tough one.

EMBRACE YOUR MISSTEPS. THEY ARE THE KEY TO DISCOVERING YOUR INNER SOUL.
When will I ever be able to do this?

DON'T BE AFRAID OF RESISTANCE. IT OPENS
NEW HORIZONS.
Did make a tiny start with this one.

IT IS DANGEROUS TO FEAR RISK. WE MAY
NEVER KNOW JOY.
Took some risks but still waiting for the joy.

JUDGMENTS IMMOBILIZE THE MIND. THEY
LIMIT FREEDOM OF CHOICE.
That includes not judging myself.

BE A LITTLE BAD. THE KIND OF BAD THAT
ENHANCES LIFE.
I'm waiting and hoping to be brave enough to do this.

She stuck the paper back in the drawer. Enough. She needed to clear her head with a walk. Here it was, January, and it was eighty-five degrees already. Striding past bursts of red, yellow, and purple flowers in formal arrangements calmed her a bit, but worry snipped at her.

Allison's meeting Vanessa? That mystery woman comes out of nowhere. But Celia thought that if she knew anything she'd have turned them in by now. Maybe Vanessa could help Allie get the job.

Celia walked for an hour and stopped at the clubhouse to check the bulletin board. Off to the side of the building about fifteen yards away she saw Edith talking to the two officers who had come to her condo.

Celia headed home, her heart pounding, hoping they hadn't seen her.

Later that day, a voicemail from a stranger invited her to play doubles. She'd gotten her name from the tennis pro. Celia's spirits lifted. Just what she needed. She got ready and hurried over. There she found Vanessa practicing with two women.

Vanessa caught her eye and waved. "When I heard your name, I told the nice ladies you were my partner."

I'm stuck. Celia walked stiffly to her side of the court.

Vanessa grinned and said, "I had a lovely breakfast with your daughter. She got the job."

"Great." Celia's excitement over playing tennis was tempered by this woman's nerviness. "And how were you involved?"

"I try to meet up with new candidates, mostly caregivers, and I was happy to help someone who seemed a perfect fit."

Who set up a caregiver to interview someone as advanced as Allie? And Lord, is that Joy perfume she's wearing to play tennis? It costs $700 an ounce! How can a working woman afford it?

The two women they were playing came to the net. Deeply tanned and heavily Botoxed, from afar they seemed to be in their mid-forties. Up close Celia noticed softening jawlines at odds with their smooth foreheads. They were most likely in their late fifties to mid-sixties. "I'm Suzy from Teaneck," said the taller woman, who had a solid, slim build, a form-fitting Nike tennis dress, and a flowing blonde ponytail.

"And I'm Dolores from the same place." Dolores had an athletic build that looked like it came from rigorous workouts with a personal trainer.

Vanessa tapped her racket as Celia introduced herself. "Let's go. I only have a two-hour break before I go to my next patient."

One of the rules of cha-cha struck her: LEARN YOUR STEPS. DISCIPLINE LIBERATES. Vanessa's agile body moved effortlessly.

Playing with Vanessa pressured Celia to stretch to her highest level. The sun beat down through the vibrant blue cloudless sky. *Think perfect swing.*

Vanessa's serve was weak but she ran to the net several times, smashing the ball down the middle and making excellent cross-court forehand shots. Awkward at first, Celia thought of another cha-cha rule: TRUST YOURSELF. BE YOUR OWN BEST FRIEND. Energy coursed through her. She decided to play like she danced. At forty/love, Celia's and Vanessa's favor, Vanessa aimed a hit with precision to win the game.

Backhands were Celia's weakness, but not her serves. She threw a high ball toss and slammed her racket against it as her arm arced down. The solid, rhythmic thwack told her she'd succeeded in slicing the ball into a savage spin, and she watched it hit the ground, twirling out of Dolores's range. But on Celia's next serve Dolores returned it down the line making the point.

When Suzy served, Celia sliced a short shot under the ball to make it drop just over the net. The play became heated and competitive as they went back and forth, but she and Vanessa won the set, six games to two. They stopped for water. Celia wanted to chat with the women, but Vanessa cornered her.

"Allie is a quality person; and that ex of hers—what a loser." Vanessa's mouth curled in a sympathetic frown.

"Agreed," Celia replied, surprised. She knew Allison to be tight-lipped, especially with strangers, but she'd apparently opened up to this woman. Why? There was something magnetic about Vanessa, but why had this young, talented, and beautiful woman gone into a career that was a barrier to meeting people her own age and that would probably never pay well?

Back in the game, Celia put those thoughts out of her mind. A lob came over and Celia smashed it out of anyone's reach. Vanessa gave Celia a victory salute. The temperature inched toward ninety. Celia felt dizzy, the heat sapping her energy, but they won the first three games. In the fourth game, at fifteen-fifteen, Suzy and Dolores figured out Celia's backhand weakness and played to it. Vanessa poached the next three shots in Celia's territory. Feeling like a spectator, Celia watched Vanessa play the geometry of the game and had the sensation she was now competing with her partner. They won the set by a bagel—six/love.

"Hey, ladies. That was fun but we're exhausted from the heat," Suzy shouted. "Let's call it a day."

Vanessa probably scared them! Celia walked across the pebbly court surface, feeling the stones rub against the soles of her tennis shoes. After swiping her shoes on the stationary brush, they stepped under a canopy into the shade. The back of Celia's tennis shirt was soaked with perspiration. Sweat glistened on Vanessa's upper lip. The scent of Joy perfume mixed with clean sweat wafted around Celia, not unpleasantly. Vanessa put her hand on Celia's arm as though sensing her unease. She thought Vanessa resembled a tall matador, with her compact, graceful frame, and Celia pictured her in the bullring. She was mystified that this intrusive woman had charmed her Allie.

"Well, I've got to be going," Celia said.

Vanessa pressed Celia's arm more firmly. "Let's play again sometime. I can help bring up your backhand. We'll be the dynamic duo."

The offer appealed, but a stern inner voice admonished Celia to keep her distance. Vanessa seemed to have the ability of a psychologist who convinced people to give up secrets. Hadn't Allison? "I'll check my schedule."

"It would cheer me up to play again. One of my patients, Sadie, died of a stroke," Vanessa said, her face drooping.

"I'm so sorry." Another death? That made ten.

"Thankfully I got the job with Lila Donaldson, but her COPD is worse. She can't go ten steps without a walker and uses oxygen at night." She flicked her wrist. "I need more work."

Stop buying Joy perfume. "Shame about Lila's health. Nice lady."

"She might improve with more meds and equipment. Brady Shirkson got me that job."

Shirkson, the CEO. Vanessa went right to the top with the tenacity of a football player running for a touchdown, just like she played tennis. Would she do the same for Allie?

"I have another patient, Julia Collier, Edith's friend. She's got mild Alzheimer's." Vanessa tapped her forehead. "I met Julia the morning I first bumped into you." She narrowed her dark eyes. "I'd swear I'd seen you before that morning."

Although there wasn't anything threatening in Vanessa's expression, Celia held her breath as the sweat on her arms chilled despite the steaming sun. "Err, how long have you been playing tennis?"

"I learned tennis in high school, in the suburbs of Detroit," Vanessa said. "I've not played in years. I went to college but dropped out. Lack of money. Knocked around, then backpacked through Europe for three years on a shoestring until I decided to be a caregiver. I studied hard and got licensed." Suddenly Vanessa gripped Celia's shoulder, startling her. "God put me on this path to help people. Nothing else matters."

Celia pulled away from her grip, and Vanessa's eyes flickered.

"Sorry if I scared you. I'm very passionate about my job." She lowered her head and removed her peaked hat from her head, her brown hair falling over her forehead and around her face. "Anyway, if you hear of anyone who needs help, let me know." She made an exaggerated buttoning motion over her lips. "Please be sure to mention my skills and discretion." She narrowed her eyes then swirled around to leave.

Celia took a step back, wondering if Vanessa was trying to tell her something. If she was, it couldn't be good.

Chapter 19

Allison

Vanessa pulled her old Honda into valet parking on Jackson Boulevard with a sharp squeal of her brakes. She and Allison stepped out.

The parking attendant jumped into the front seat. "Good evening, Miss Vanessa."

"Hi, Larry. You're good?" Vanessa gave him a flirty wink.

"Yup. I'll park your car where you can get out real easy."

Vanessa nodded and handed the kid a five-dollar bill. The two women made their way into the restaurant and headed to the bar. "Can't wait till I get my new car. It's in the works."

"Great." From what Allison saw, Vanessa's income could barely keep a roof over her head. *Is she kept? Is it an inheritance?*

"You'll head up the ladder fast. You're a quick study. Michael Castor thought you were perfect for the job."

"You helped hugely. When Mr. Shirkson asked what I thought about Well Services, I remembered what you told me to say." Allison straightened her back and said in her most business-like voice, "Well Services is vital in providing services to the elderly, the sick, and the disabled no matter the cost. Actually, I believe it, but he seemed delighted."

"Celebration time."

The bartender came over as soon as he spotted Vanessa. "How's my gorgeous Vanessa?" he asked, grinning. "What's your poison, ladies?"

"Your house white, please," Allison said.

Vanessa flourished her hand. "We'll have two glasses of Spanish Verdejo." The bartender raised an eyebrow.

"Whoa. I'm keeping expenses low," Allison said. "My soon-to-be ex drained our accounts."

"What a shit. I usually order big only when some guy is paying, but this is a special occasion. Tonight is on me."

"I should pay for you," Allison protested as the bartender went to retrieve the bottle.

"Nah, you got the job on your own. I just nudged it along."

"How did you learn so much about Well Services while being out in the field?"

"It's called survival. Chutzpah. I got a foot in the door and then pushed it wide open."

"Good for you." Allison admired Vanessa, especially her smarts, but would have liked knowing, step by step, how she did it. She'd tapped into the politics of Well Services, which had become a giant in its field in just twelve years. And being sexy wasn't enough.

The drinks arrived and the women clinked glasses.

"Michael went gaga over your résumé, and your good looks don't hurt. Don't let anyone kid you on that score. Sometimes it's all we have," Vanessa said with authority.

Allison cocked her head. "You knew I got the job fifteen minutes after the interview ended. How?"

"I stopped by Michael's office on my way to visit Brady Shirkson."

Allison felt her jaw drop. "How do you get to know the CEO?"

"Oh, I made sure I met him and asked him how to move up the pecking order pronto. I pulled the lost little girl card, and honestly, I did need advice. He acted the caring boss and told me keep my nose to the grindstone and he'd check my evaluations each month." Vanessa laughed and turned to the side, crossing her long, shapely legs. "I went into overdrive during that time. But I don't have talent like you, knowing the healthcare field and accounting. You use both sides of your brain."

"Oh, but it takes real skill to handle patients like you do. People can get ornery when they're sick. You damn well understand the psychology."

The band played an oldie, "Every Breath You Take," and Vanessa's tall, slim body swayed. Allison was reminded of a slender but sturdy oak tree. She owned whatever space she occupied. "What's your background?"

"Brady listened to my tale of woe from my childhood. I'm a product of poverty and let him know. It's a sad story but got his attention." A deep crease appeared in her forehead. "My background had to be good for something."

Allison saw pain in that expression. "Instead of going to human resources, she goes right to the CEO." Allison spoke to an imaginary person in front of her then turned to Vanessa. "And the boss gives you career counseling? I'm sticking with you, woman."

Allison's phone rang, and her gut clenched as she answered. "Thomas, stop calling me. I'm not coming back." She listened for several seconds then said, "It's over." She hung up. "Damn him. I want to end this as simply as possible. I tried to help, but sometimes I feel a little guilty for giving up."

"You seem like the mothering type to grown men, which is a no-no for career women."

"Can I buy you lovely ladies a drink?" a man's voice asked behind them.

Vanessa let out a squeal. "Oh Brady. I didn't know you'd be here tonight. What a delicious surprise." She tapped his chest with her index finger.

Shocked, Allison had the feeling that Shirkson knew just where Vanessa would be this evening.

He stiffened into a formal pose and turned to Allison. "Michael made an excellent decision. Welcome to Well Services. Impressive résumé."

Allison found that Shirkson's large physical presence and aura sucked up all the air in the room, yet this imposing man became almost childlike in Vanessa's company, practically shuffling his feet.

"Bartender, champagne for the ladies. The best in the house on my tab." He moved closer to Vanessa, who looked up at him with undisguised, raw admiration.

"Did I get that promotion?"

Brady looked sly. "Maybe."

"I got it?"

"Yes, you did. You've done a great job with patients and taken the extra courses. Now you'll train caregivers in CPR, and teach them how to do Activities of Daily Living."

Vanessa hopped off her seat and threw her arms around Brady's big torso. It lasted longer than a business-like hug. "I can't thank you enough. But can I still do in-home care?" She let go but remained at his side. "I really love doing that."

"Sure. The new job is about fifteen hours a week. We'd also like you to spot check on the caregivers in patients' homes to see that all is going well, work out small problems. Don't overdo it though." He winked.

"Does that include the certified nursing aides?"

"Hmm." He rubbed his chin. "Let's see how you do. That's a big category and includes social workers and hospice workers. That's the next step up."

"Fair enough. I'm so excited," Vanessa cooed.

"It's a win-win. The patients regain health and stay at home as long as possible. Any HMO wants to avoid people going down-hill. We're a company with a heart. The average life span in a nursing home is only two to three years. It's too institutional and demoralizing."

"Brady, you are a doll. And Allison is my new bestie."

"You two enjoy your celebrations. I'm headed home. Early riser."

Vanessa gave him a seductive smile. "Good night. Thanks again."

After he left, Allison said, "He seems really smitten with you."

"I want to take him seriously, but I worry that he's just a flirt. He's been divorced three times." Vanessa laughed. "I like him. That promotion amped up my affection." She held her fist up in a victory salute.

The bartender came over and handed them both flutes filled with champagne, then placed the bottle nearby in an ice bucket. Vanessa downed her glass quickly. "Congrats to both of us." She filled her glass again. "Chug-a-lug and then time to go," she told Allison as she wiped the bottom of the half-filled bottle with a napkin and put it in her purse.

Allison tensed. "Are you all right to drive?"

Vanessa shrugged. "You can drive."

The valet brought the car around and helped a giggling Vanessa into the passenger seat as Allison hopped in. *Why did she help me? Maybe she just needs a female friend. Well, so do I!*

Chapter 20

Celia

"Melvin's toxicology showed he had lethal doses of antidepressants and fentanyl in his body," Marcy said in a rush of words over the phone. "Lyle said Edith is making accusations, claiming that I deliberately overdosed him."

"We've got to put a stop to this," Celia responded, pressing the receiver to her ear.

"The worst part is that Edith had told Lyle that around twenty people had died of heart attacks in the last six months who didn't have heart issues," Marcy said. "Edith is goading the families to have a meeting and see what they can do. She's on a rampage."

That's it, Celia told herself after Marcy hung up. No more pussyfooting. She searched the internet for information on the implications of obstructing justice. She'd put this off too long. Her hand froze over the keyboard as she read aloud: "The acts by which justice is obstructed and if the intent is meant to delay or prevent informing the authorities of a criminal act." In Florida specifically, things like depriving someone of help by not calling 911 or interfering with an investigation were felonies punishable by jail time ranging from a few months to up to fifteen years. Drops of sweat gathered at Celia's temples.

Next she looked up legal fees, but most sites were law firms and wanted you to contact them directly. She read what private people involved had to say and the consensus was that a person accused of obstructing justice or any type of criminal infraction of the law paid a private attorney an average upfront retainer of thirty to fifty thousand dollars. To make matters worse, every time a lawyer went to court, approximately three thousand dollars or more had to be paid, plus an assortment of costs for preliminary court dates and hiring experts. Homicide charges shot higher. Celia slammed her computer shut and breathed quickly.

She realized she had a tad too much money for a court-appointed lawyer and not nearly enough to pay for a private one. Would she have to spend all of her assets, maybe even lose her apartment? With a trembling finger she pressed Marcy's number again. "Are you all right to talk?"

"Yeah. I took one or two tokes. Shoot."

"I had a bit of a scary afternoon yesterday with Vanessa. You won't believe what happened."

"Oh no. How bad is a bit?" Marcy asked in a near whisper.

"First off, I played tennis doubles with Vanessa, and man, was she aggressive."

"Ah, that doesn't sound too bad." Marcy sounded shaky.

"Hold on! After the game, she told me that in her job she knew how to be discreet and gave me this awful stare."

"Discreet? What did she mean by that? Is she inferring she saw us with a dead body and won't tell—does she want something from us?"

"Don't know." Celia inhaled and exhaled, whimpering. "I also saw Edith talking to the police officers who'd come to interview me."

Marcy made a loud clucking noise. "Oh my God, we're going to jail."

"I checked out the consequences of obstruction of justice. It's bad and expensive." Celia rubbed her forehead with her fist. "Why don't we just go to the police? I'm tired of losing sleep over this."

"Are you crazy?" Marcy yelled. Celia held the phone away from her ear. "You might as well send us straight to prison without passing go." She heaved out a huge breath. "Cops are probably watching us."

Celia remembered seeing the black Continental when they were coming back from Fritzy's, and the more she thought about it the more she was certain she'd seen it again since then without it really registering. *Don't get nuts. Big black cars are all over the place.*

She heard Marcy gulping back tears. "I can't afford a criminal attorney. And what about Deb?"

Celia tried to stay composed. "Listen, I did the numbers and you'll qualify for a public defender. I don't. This will bankrupt me if it explodes. We have to tell Deb what's going on."

"What with all of her ailments—arthritis, high blood pressure—and all the meds she takes, God knows what it'll do to her. And she's terrified of upsetting Michael." Marcy's voice rose an octave higher. "Please! Don't call the cops. We'll get through this."

The panicked lump in Celia's throat kept her silent for a moment. Marcy's emotions had reached a fever pitch and Deb would need delicate handling. "Okay. Let me talk to Deb myself."

"What if that Vanessa blackmails us?" Marcy words sounded choked.

"Then for sure we go to the authorities," Celia said with a sigh. "They'll want to know why we waited so long. We can only hope they believe us."

Before calling Deb, Celia went out to get some air. She wandered towards the fountain, organizing all the facts in her head.

Marcy lived hand-to-mouth with just Social Security, so she'd qualify for a public defender. Deb at least had Michael to fall back on. Celia herself still had mortgage payments, taxes, car repairs, medical supplement insurance, and insurances for seemingly everything else. Where would she and Allie live if her condo went into foreclosure? Allie needed help until she got back on her feet. Her heart pounded, making her dizzy. She sat on a bench.

She looked up and saw Vanessa walking along a path, her hand under the arm of a shuffling Julia. "Sweetie," she was saying, "it's all right. Walking is good for you. I won't let you fall."

Julia, her expression totally blank, nodded in agreement.

Allison had mentioned Vanessa's excellent reputation in caring for patients. Still, Celia wondered what game she was really playing. Celia had the sensation that if she moved a millimeter she'd be blown to bits.

When she got home, Celia called Deb about the possibility of getting legal advice.

"Bull. No one has proof we were anywhere near Melvin that night," Deb said firmly.

"It might have been dark, but Vanessa can put it together. A guy in a wheelchair, head hanging low on his chest, and three women pushing him away from his office?"

"It's her word against ours."

"But there's been a preliminary toxicology report on Melvin and it looks bad for us."

"That doesn't mean we have anything to do with Melvin's drug addiction, and that's what it has to be." Deb's voice wobbled.

"We can go on pretending everything is fine if you want. Just in case, I think we need a strategy that includes legal advice. We can't trust Edith or Vanessa."

"Don't you think you're overreacting?"

"Maybe, maybe not."

"Ach, when I see Michael I'll burst into tears. He's due here now to fix a cabinet door in my kitchen. He's my sun, moon, and stars. I can't disappoint him."

"Do your best to stay calm." Celia worried about Deb's occasional bouts of zoning out. She might slip and say something inappropriate.

"All right, but you have to understand that my son's job was on the line once and now he's back on track. I can't do this to him. I'd kill myself first if I thought it would keep him safe."

Celia's heart jumped as she remembered her own close call with the pills and how her friends had rushed to her side. "Stop. Don't talk foolishness."

"I'm not talking foolishness. What's the point of going on?"

Deb hung up. Celia called Marcy and quickly filled her in. "Meet me at Deb's right away!" She flew out the door.

She banged on Deb's door, breathing hard from the five-minute run. The door opened and she saw clothing strewn on the floor, sofa, and chairs.

"Got you here in a hurry."

Celia's legs wobbled in relief. "You are a madwoman. Just don't talk about killing yourself again."

"I'm here," Marcy shouted, thrusting the door open. She wore a filmy pink nightie with a low-cut bodice and ruffles at the bottom.

A thin scarf hung from one shoulder. "Thank the Lord you didn't hurt yourself." She grasped Deb's hand. "What were you thinking, idiot?"

"I'm not going anywhere." Deb kicked the sweaters to the side and put a CD called *Cuban Fantasy* into the Bose all-in-one player that Michael had given her. "Let's dance. We need to lose ourselves."

Celia scuffled her feet in preparation. "I'm ready." Clapping one-two, one-two-three, she tossed her head to the side as the great Cuban singer Celia Cruz's voice filled the room. Celia felt proud to have the same name. She swayed to the music and hopped to the beat.

Marcy stepped in, catching Celia's movement with precision and soon Deb joined in.

"Two, three, cha-cha-cha," Celia sang.

"Olé," Marcy hollered with gusto.

Celia put her hands out to steady Deb when she faltered. Deb hadn't done that before. They danced for the next fifteen minutes, thrusting their heads back and moving in unison. Celia let the music possess her, rid her mind of everything but the music, arching her back and clapping. Suddenly, Deb plopped into a chair laden with threadbare skirts. "That's it."

"What are you doing with all these old clothes that you don't even wear?" Marcy squealed as she rotated and danced in sync with her back to Celia.

"I love them. They're from my dance-teaching days."

"They are insanely old, as old as you."

"I'm not that old," Deb laughed.

Hands overhead, Celia clapped her hands in time to the rhythm like a flamenco dancer, thigh muscles rippling.

When the CD ended, Celia and Marcy sat down on the floor and leaned against the sofa. "Can we help put everything back?"

"Oh no. I'm sleeping on these tonight. Don't touch anything."

"That's …" Marcy started to say, but Celia raised her eyebrow to keep her quiet.

"Just don't sleep on the floor. Put them on your bed."

The odd moments when Deb went off the grid were more disturbing now. Celia knew Deb had to take a lot of medications and wondered if she was having trouble keeping them all straight. Was she taking too much of one, or not enough of another? If this kept up, she'd need to talk to Michael. Celia waved goodbye and trekked home, at a much slower pace this time.

When she got home she went into the kitchen and scrambled three eggs. Just as she started to eat, the phone rang. It was Sam Loftus, her accountant. She had always liked him, and now his voice sounded tense. "I finally finished your husband's books."

"Good. Those numbers were like schools of fish swimming by. I wondered why it wasn't on the computer."

"His bookkeeper wanted to do it the old-fashioned way, and against my advice. Gabe was in favor."

Celia vaguely remembered the woman, tucked back in Gabe's office. "I can't figure out how Gabe made a lot of money yet here I am scraping to get by. You were his buddy. Did he have setbacks I didn't know about or what?"

An interminable silence followed.

"Uh … Gabe uh … well. The benefits the bookkeeper, Marilyn Fisherbach, received might have set Gabe back a bit."

"What? I know his employees all received similar salaries. Why would she be responsible for such big expenses?" Celia's head started to pound.

Sam spoke delicately. "It seems that Gabe paid her rent for about twenty years and she got bonuses beyond what any other employee received. Big bonuses. I'm sorry ..."

"Why did he ...?" Another pointed silence made lights flash in front of Celia's eyes. "Oh my God. She was his mistress."

"Well, um. Yes."

"You knew? Why didn't you tell me? Never mind. Wives are supposed to know. I was the fool that didn't." Celia swung her free hand as she stammered. "She was a bleached-blonde chubby younger woman who had cleavage up to her chin?"

"That's the one. Now, understand that she didn't hold a candle to you."

"What does it matter? She got all the goodies."

He cleared his throat. "I'm so sorry, Celia."

It sounds like condolences. In a way, it is. Celia hung up and recalled Deb's bitter voice describing her philandering husband, never dreaming it could have happened to her too. And to think she told her friends that her marriage might not be the best but that Gabe was very loyal to her. How many times had she tried to get close to him, and how many times had he rejected her? She sat down heavily as the room spun. "Fisherbach only wanted your money, you jackass, and she got it big time!"

Her stomach roiled and the next thing she knew she was sobbing and vomiting into the toilet. When she finally stood upright, she wondered how she had been so stupid. All the red flags had been there and she'd simply flicked them away like annoying mosquitoes. Gabe had worked late three nights a week, but she was forbidden to call him, and he'd convinced her not to travel with him because she'd be bored. Bored? Had *she* been with him? Who was this man?

Had she given him incentive to have an affair? No, she argued with herself. Why hadn't she been willing to face the truth? Ahh, she thought. Because then she'd have had to make decisions.

Around ten-thirty, she heard Allison come in and softly call her name from outside her closed bedroom door. She didn't answer. When Allison finished in the bathroom, Celia heard the door to the guest room close. A tomb-like silence fell over the apartment and she stared at the ceiling. A massive headache sliced through her head, unsettled every bone in her body, begging for relief. Even her gums ached.

One of the cha-cha rules said: CREATE YOUR OWN INNER RECEPTIVE SPACE. IT ALLOWS FOR HEALING.

Celia had mourned her marriage for so many years. Now she needed to figure out how to heal.

Chapter 21

Allison

In the morning, Allison stood at the kitchen counter making coffee. Her mother came shuffling in, wearing an untied pale pink robe that hung from her shoulders. She stood like a robot, watching the carafe fill with the black liquid. When it stopped, she poured a cup and sat at the table. Allison watched her set the cup down and stare out the open kitchen window as though unseeing. A soft, warm breeze flowed in and Allison watched her mother duck as though the air scorched her skin.

"Morning," Allison said. Her mother hardly stirred. Allison poured herself a cup of coffee and sat across from her mother.

Celia seemed to drag herself back from wherever her mind had just been. "Hi, honey. Tell me about your new job."

"Geez. Where do I start? Vanessa clued me in on the inner sanctum of hierarchy and personalities at Well Services. She's very chummy with the CEO, Brady Shirkson." Allison wrinkled her nose. Was her mother listening? "Michael hired me on the spot. He seems very nice. And sophisticated. Vanessa was a big help."

"I'm so happy for you, sweetie."

Her mother's response sounded remote. *Was she back on pills?*

"Isn't it out of kilter for a caregiver like Vanessa to be hobnobbing with the CEO?" Celia went on, sipping her coffee.

Allison bristled. It was just like her mother to immediately be suspicious of her good fortune. "Look, she's ambitious. Why are you so judgmental, and snobby to boot?"

"You're right. I just saw a pushy side of her that, uh … annoyed me."

Allison stood. "Are we talking about me or Vanessa here?" Her tone was icy.

"Sorry. I'm really interested in hearing about you." Celia's voice quavered. "Please."

"Okay." Allison took a deep breath. "I'm senior accountant of the in-home healthcare division." Allison looked askance at Celia.

"Wow. Impressive! Go on, Allie." Celia flexed her hand as though asking for more information.

Allison raised her eyebrow, but her mother sounded sincere. "There's budgeting, accounting, payments, purchasing, and collections." Allison took a deep breath as though coming up from under water. "Oh, and payroll, too."

"Wow. That's a lot."

"They've moved Vanessa up a slot, giving her more responsibilities, but I'll keep an eye on her since I have the nursing background."

"They're giving you huge responsibilities for someone so young. Smart of them to see how talented and clever you are." Despite her mother's encouraging words, Allison noticed that she looked pale and shaky.

"It's a dream job and pays well. You know, poor organization can break a company. They have to maximize the revenue coming from home care workers, but they seem to overspend. Well Services has had setbacks, but I'm determined to set them on a steadier economical track."

Butterflies started up in Allison's stomach as she thought about what faced her. She had to get over her fear of failing.

"There's no question you can do it. Do you get involved with in-home patients?"

"Well, I might oversee a few supervisors, just to check up because of my nursing background. We work with all ages but mostly with the frail elderly like the older residents in this development." Allison waved her hand toward the window as though taking in the whole community, then wrinkled her nose. "I've got Dad's organizational skills."

"Guess you got lucky there."

Allison saw her mother's face tightening like someone had turned a screw at the back of her neck. "Are you all right, Mother?"

"Fine. Just my allergies." Celia coughed.

Allison popped two slices of wheat bread into the toaster. "One or two for you?"

"No thanks. Not much of an appetite this morning."

Allison squinted at her. "If I didn't know better, I'd say you look hungover from a big night out on the town."

"I wish. I just didn't sleep well."

"Find activities that keep you sharp and tire you out by bedtime."

Celia gave Allison a strained smile. "I registered for a pottery class."

As Allison got a dish for her toast, she noticed that all the mugs on her mother's cabinet shelves were lined up with the handles facing the same way. Her cream-colored dishes were stacked according to size, and alongside them, sparkling glasses marched in orderly rows. Her mother's penchant for neatness had always been in stark contrast to the chaotic tribulations in her life. Allison didn't like how she looked right now.

Allison spread the toast with butter that melted and puddled in crevices.

Celia folded her hands. "Michael Castor is nice and polite. I only met him a few times. His mother, Deb, is dying for him to get married."

"I wouldn't think he needed help at age forty-two."

"He doesn't, but she's dying for grandchildren. She's a little goofy, but a goodhearted and a generous spirit. Well, at least his company does good things with all the sick people in these developments." Celia puckered her mouth. "But there are too many deaths here, if you ask me."

"It comes with the territory." Allison looked at Celia sadly and noticed her coffee had gone cold. "Are you worried about dying?" Allison blurted out. She guessed she feared her mother dying herself.

"Not really. It's just that all these deaths are starting to spook me out."

"It's natural for a community of older people. Many have been sick for a long time. Look, it's not a college dorm around here." Allison waved her hand as though dismissing the topic. "Anyway, there are bigger issues waiting for me at work. The other supervisor left after embezzling big money."

"They're lucky to have someone as ethical as you." Celia reached over and squeezed Allison's hand. "This job is a great way to start a new life."

"I miss Daddy and wish I could tell him my news."

Allison saw her mother flinch. She looked defenseless. *It must be hard for her to be a widow.* It pained Allison, who wanted with all her heart for her mother to be in a better place.

Chapter 22

Celia

Celia looked around for what else she might clean. Her back tightened like a kettledrum. The place glittered, yet she longed to break everything and start over.

Then she stalked her prey, a framed picture of Gabe from two years before he died. She glared at it then threw it across the room, making a dent in the wall. She called Marcy and Deb and asked them to meet her at her apartment right away.

The women were there within five minutes. Marcy put her hand on Celia's forehead as though feeling for fever. "Are you all right?"

"My entire marriage was a sham," she blurted out, her body shaking. "I found out from my accountant that Gabe cheated on me for years with an employee. She got tons of money from him while I lived like a pauper."

"A mistress?" Deb put her hand on Celia's shoulder. "Oh shit. Welcome to the club, or should I say unwelcome. It's not where you want to be."

"Okay, listen up, girl." Marcy moved closer to Celia and wrapped an arm around her. "The money thing sucks and let me give some advice about what we do in that case. In the short run, part of the cure is to get a fabulous lover and every morning thank the spirits that you're alive and Gabe isn't." Marcy put her hands on Celia's cheeks and forced her to look her in the eyes. "You're going to make up for lost time, get out there, and have wild sex. Orgasms are as necessary as taking vitamins. And once you've done that, we'll figure out the next step."

"What?" Celia laughed in spite of herself. "Wild sex? I'm too old for that."

"Nonsense. I told you before that vaginas tend to dry out like old figs, but all you need is a special cream to lubricate your woo-woo. If you do that, you'll have an orgasm as good as you did at twenty-five."

"She's the expert," Deb snorted.

"Sex education for older women doesn't come from frumpy, uptight male gynecologists," Marcy said, pressing her lips together. "They don't think we do it. Now you listen up. We get tighter down there so if you get a man with a small weenie, not to worry. With us older gals, he's in demand. If they're too big, it hurts. When I told the gardener that his little thingie was the greatest, he was in heaven." Marcy's face was animated. "And then he died a week later."

"At least he didn't die in your bed on top of you," Deb cracked.

Celia gave a half-smothered laugh. "I'm talking about my lousy husband having had a long-term affair, and you're talking penis sizes."

"It's better than losing sleep over the bums," Deb said.

Marcy leaned closer. "You need to prepare for the onslaught of men you're about to attract. You see, darling, you haven't been giving out the right vibes." Marcy gently tugged on Celia's mock turtleneck shirt. "Get rid of these nun's outfits and show some skin. Give them the devilish sparkle in your eyes you get when you cha-cha. Remember, if a man can dance, drive at night, and get an erection, he's like gold. Two out of three isn't bad either."

For a moment Celia let her mind wander and imagined a man who attracted her, embracing her waist, his smooth fingers caressing her neck, roving down her arm to rest on her hips as they did a seductive cha-cha. He'd give off the smell of lemony cologne.

Marcy went to Celia's fridge and found a bottle of white wine. "Let's cha-cha," she shouted, putting on Masala's "Mi Son Entero." "Fuck Gabe. And may his mistress age like a wizened old bitch."

They toasted each other. Celia laughed as tears ran down her cheeks. "Be my friends always!"

"Olé," Deb shouted as she clapped, one-two, one-two-three in time to the music.

As they danced Celia lost herself in a fast-moving fluffy cloud with not a dark one in sight. Her back muscles rippled, shoulders moving forward and back to the beat, her arms bent, elbows leading the way.

"No pity parties for us," Celia said, pushing a loose lock of hair behind her ear and doing a side step.

"There are men like your husband who could only get it on with a hussy." Marcy hummed the Latin tune as they moved in sync. "I have an idea."

"Uh oh." Deb rolled her head side to side. "Another sex lesson."

"I think you should confront that bitch."

That idea stung Celia as she stepped lightly, spinning and returning to her steps. She wondered if she had the nerve to face Gabe's mistress, and what she would say. Why prolong the misery. Cha-cha-ing would put her out of her mind forever.

Celia felt a whoosh of dizziness as she turned on the ball of her foot. Her vision blurred as she whirled. *Adios, Gabe.* She moved faster and faster, noticing Marcy and Deb had stopped. Still she kept dancing.

"Let's get some air," Marcy said, bringing Celia to a stop and handing her a glass of wine. "Sip first, then we'll take a walk." Then Marcy and Deb led Celia outside, each one taking an arm.

The slightly cool breeze felt refreshing. "Want to see the play *Tribes*? It's due here in a month," Celia said, feeling a sudden desperate need to keep busy, plan ahead. "We can do other things in the meantime."

"I'm in," Deb said.

"Hey, I'd rather see a revival of *Phantom*, but I'll see *Tribes*," Marcy said.

Celia rejoiced that they were making plans together and avoiding talk of Gabe. She needed time to cast his spirit out of her soul.

They'd just reached the entrance to Boca Pelicano Palms when an ambulance siren sounded as it careened to a stop.

"The medics are going into Lila Donaldson's house," Celia said, clutching her chest. "I hope she's all right. She has some kind of lung disease and needs oxygen." Celia suddenly remembered that Lila was Vanessa's patient

Marcy frowned. "Female vultures will soon be swooping in to console Curtis Donaldson."

"I saw you drop off a dish at their house," Deb said. "She's not even dead yet."

Marcy tossed her head back. "You old pervert, watching the buildings like Edith. Get a life. That poor man had no food in the house and Lila was on liquids." Marcy stuck her tongue out at Deb and wrinkled her nose. "I do the same for women. Do you do anything to help people?"

"I do. You're not the only one."

Celia tsked-tsked.

Two EMTs came out wheeling Lila on a stretcher, her husband hobbling behind. Celia started to turn away out of respect when she saw Vanessa trailing them, carrying a large paper bag. Maybe it was Lila's toiletries for the hospital.

Vanessa nodded to Celia. Another EMT rushing behind Vanessa bumped her arm and the bag fell, spilling out dozens of medicine bottles. She scooped them into the bag and walked away, acting as if nothing had happened.

"Whew," Marcy said. "I thought caregivers keep lists of meds! What's with taking a bag? You think she doesn't expect Lila back home? Or she might be stealing them."

Celia held her finger up to tell Marcy and Deb to wait then slipped away, trying to see where Vanessa headed. She caught sight of her getting into a black Lincoln Continental. Someone with a hoodie pulled over their face sat in the passenger seat.

Blood rushed to Celia's head. She hurried back to Marcy and Deb. "Something is weird. Vanessa dropped the pills into the lap of a suspicious companion. Plus, her car looks like the one that I swear has been following me." Celia pressed her hand to her chest.

"Come on. There are thousands of black cars in Florida," Deb said.

"What puzzles me is the person waiting in that car. Vanessa was on duty. Who waits for hours in a hot car?" The hairs on Celia's arms stood up. "I couldn't tell if it was a man or woman with that hoodie."

Marcy gritted her teeth and began pacing. "Maybe that's her contact to sell the meds."

"How would she know Lila won't be back home to need them?"

"Michael said she's excellent and compassionate," Deb said,

her voice like a tight spool of wire. "He wouldn't hire anyone questionable."

Vanessa's clever and a charmer. Celia went through a mental checklist of those who'd died under Vanessa's care that she knew about: Mr. Angstrom the stroke victim; Marcy's neighbor, Olivia; Melvin; Sadie; and John Rappan. There were others she heard about. And what about those she didn't hear of? "Seems a lot of people have died under Vanessa's watch."

"I wouldn't overthink it, Celia. She works with sick people. And we're old enough to die, kiddo," Deb said.

"Stop intimidating Celia," Marcy said. "Let her think."

"You're too prickly to get along with kind people like Vanessa," Deb shot back.

"Not prickly of recent times." Marcy smirked.

"Right. You're sex deprived so you're inventing murder mysteries," Deb snorted.

Celia wondered if Vanessa killed her very ill patients in order to ease their pain. Mercy killings were still murder. But it couldn't be—it was too bizarre.

"Go home, Marcy. Lila's husband needs another casserole," Deb said.

Marcy smacked her fist on her hip. "Just what I had in mind, Deborah."

Chapter 23

Celia

When Celia entered the clubhouse dining room, the first thing she noticed was that Edith and Julia were not at their usual table with their four cohorts who clustered together like a bunch of cackling gossips. Celia gave them a big smile, her new approach to making friends with the enemy. In return, she got icy stares.

Marcy and Deb, who were nearly finished eating, waved her over to their table. Celia dropped into a chair.

"How do you feel?" Marcy asked. "You look pale, knocked out."

Deb touched Celia's shoulder.

"I'll be okay," Celia managed. "Restless sleep. Let's talk about other things."

"Suits me fine," Marcy said. "Tell Deb what you told me about Michael."

Celia gave Marcy a narrow-eyed stare. "Not now."

"You can't hide it," Marcy said, turning to Deb. "Michael and Vanessa aren't an item anymore. She's dating Brady Shirkson."

She looked at Celia, her eyes asking for confirmation. Celia nodded.

Deb blinked hard as though someone had tossed sand in her

eyes. Then after a minute of silence she brightened and gave Celia a coy glance. "Your daughter will be available soon."

Uh oh, we're stepping into alligator-infested waters. "Don't go there," Celia said. "My daughter doesn't date anyone at work."

Deb slouched in her seat. "Why the hell not? Especially my son. He's a catch."

"She's not even divorced yet. She'd probably scratch Michael's eyes out." This was an exaggeration Celia hoped was effective.

"So he'll be blind. He can get a seeing-eye dog, he'll have a nice, steady girlfriend. You and I can be co-mothers-in-law." She gently nudged Celia in the ribs.

"Come on, Deb," Celia said. "We can't push adult children."

Deb grunted. "We have to interfere sometimes. We know what's best for them."

"All right, you two," Marcy said. "More to the point—what should we do Saturday? Any ideas?"

Deb shrugged. "You're both going to services at the synagogue with me. We all need to ask for forgiveness."

"None of us are religious," Celia said. "I don't even go to church."

"Deb doesn't go to pray," Marcy said in a huff. "She started something new just last week. She goes for a free Oneg Shabbat luncheon right after Shabbat services." Marcy gave Deb a hopeless glance.

"You didn't mind going along, checking for single men." Deb wagged her finger.

Marcy flicked her hand in Deb's direction. "Deb skips the ceremony and goes right to the buffet." She shook her head.

"It's the best place to get pickled herring, smoked salmon, and whitefish salad here." Deb closed her eyes and licked her lips. "It makes my mouth water just thinking about it."

"I'm spending time with Allie," Celia said. "I haven't seen her all week."

As they rose to leave, Celia heard a man calling her name. She scanned the tables for the male voice that softly whistled a tad when he said his S's.

The voice triggered her memory. Looking behind she saw the handsome face stamped within a somewhat craggier, older outline. He walked toward her. "Celia, it's me, Stanton."

He gave her a brief, friendly hug. "Stanton?" *Hallelujah.* "What a surprise." She found herself back in college again, naked, his full lips on her breasts. She tried to regain her composure. "You live in Florida?"

"Yup. For nearly ten years. My wife and I needed to escape the harsh Minnesota winters. We were only here five years when she passed on." He clasped his hands.

Celia felt shame for being glad his wife was dead. She tried to make an appropriately sad face.

"Where are you living?" he asked.

"Right here in this development. I'm on Pelican Way."

His eyes took her in top to bottom. "I recognized you right away." Holding on to her wrists, he raised her arms outward. "You look great. Are you taking fountain of youth pills?"

"Thanks, but the lighting in here isn't very good." The past thundered around her, kicking up blinding dust. What had happened the last night they spent together, more than half a lifetime ago? She shivered, remembering his hands on her naked back, their teary goodbye. After picnicking at the beach, they'd returned to the musty, salt-smelling motel room and lay on the tattered blanket, making love to the sound of waves crashing on the beach. Afterwards they'd clung to each other, promising that they would see each other soon.

Her knees weakened, and she grasped the back of a chair. Back then neither embarrassment nor modesty entered any part of their relationship. His touch, the sound of his voice had electrified her and still did. She hoped her facial expressions weren't giving her away.

His once dark blonde hair was now a shock of white. Strands brushed his lined forehead, and his wiry torso had thickened. Crow's feet surrounded his clear brown eyes that once had seen every inch of her young, naked body. Hollow cheeks had once dominated his thin, haunted face. Now he glowed, robust and confident. Although his chin sagged a bit, he still retained strong facial angles. His incisors overlapped neighboring teeth, those very same teeth that once lightly grazed her belly. *Stop!* Celia gulped and introduced him to her friends. She almost snickered thinking about two old fogeys trying to get that back.

"Is your husband with you?"

Celia detected the tiniest wavering in Stanton's question. "He passed away."

"Oh, I'm sorry."

A tinny voice sounded from behind Stanton. The floor seemed to shake beneath her as Edith came up from behind him and took his arm. She had dyed her short, straight hair black. Instead of her usual outfit of jeans with an elastic waistband, she wore a crisp, sparkling white short golf skirt and red jersey shirt.

"Edith, this is Celia. Celia and I go way back," he said.

Be friendly. "Hello, Edith," Celia said in a sweet tone.

"We know each other," Edith said in a razor-edged voice.

Stanton looked confused. "But you said you never heard of her."

"Her last name wasn't familiar. Several women named Celia live here," Edith stammered.

He took a step closer to Celia. "If I'd known you were here, I'd have looked you up. Edith and I often play golf in my community. Luckily, I got her to play on your course today." He stared at Celia, looking wistful. "It's been so long."

Celia noticed Marcy and Deb watching the scene with amused concentration.

"I'm his girlfriend," Edith said, showing her small, sharp teeth.

Celia noted Stanton's surprised expression. Deb and Marcy coughed, a sound that covered up a soft tittering.

"Edith and I are good friends," he said, emphasizing the word "friends." "We met when she came to my wife's funeral. She knew Ada from high school but the girls lost track of each other over the years." He gave a loopy but sad grin. "She helped me when I was at a low point."

"How nice." Celia heard soft snickering behind her. She was sure Edith had lied about knowing Ada. It was a hoax that many single women pulled by scanning obituaries, looking for fresh widowers.

Stanton looked uneasy in the total silence that followed. Edith tugged his arm. "Let's go. Can't be late for tee off."

"I hope to see you around, Celia," Stanton said.

"Sure," she replied.

"Time to go," Edith said, taking his arm.

Stanton pulled away from her, leaned over, and kissed Celia on the cheek. "It's so good to see you. Hope to catch up soon. What's your married name?"

"Ewing," Marcy yelped.

He smiled and quick-stepped to catch up to Edith.

Celia pressed her fingers to her burning cheek where he had kissed her, watching Stanton's back recede.

"He's the one, isn't he?" Marcy asked as soon as the pair walked out.

Celia nodded.

"Go after him," Marcy demanded. "He said Edith and he were only friends."

"No way. He broke my heart, you know."

"You were kids, you idiot."

Celia gave a bittersweet smile and said, "When it comes to men and my dormant libido, I'm lost." Still, she was glad she'd worn a flattering turquoise tunic top over black slacks.

"Libidos never quit with the right partner," Marcy said.

"It looks like every man is the right partner for you, Marcy," Deb said.

"Shush your mouth." Marcy tapped her fingers on Deb's arm. "He stared at you with desire in his eyes, the way every woman wants to be looked at."

"Well, Edith thinks they're an item," Celia said.

"Baloney," Marcy said. "He's in great shape, no potbelly or hair growing out of his nose and ears. He can get your number online."

"He is a good-looking guy," Deb said.

"If he calls, fine. If not …" Memories had hovered in the back of her mind throughout her marriage, periodically giving her attacks of guilt. Now the truth hit her full force: Gabe had blamed her for the failure of their marriage in order to alleviate his own guilt for cheating on her. She wanted Stanton to call her, but worried about being careful what she wished for. She didn't want to be hurt again.

As the three women moved to leave, Vanessa walked toward them, holding Julia by the hand. Julia shuffled, her face blank.

"Say hello to the ladies, Julia," Vanessa said in a singsong voice.

"Hello," Julia said in a monotone. "Can we go?"

"In a minute." Vanessa turned to them.

"How's Lila?" Celia asked.

"She's still in the hospital, poor thing. I'm taking care of Curtis, her husband." Vanessa looked at Celia. "Your daughter is great company, but she's all work. She needs more play time, and I'm going to be her social director."

"Thanks for watching out for her." Celia forced herself to smile, her jaw aching along with her head.

"My pleasure. Bye." Vanessa led Julia away.

"Well," Marcy sputtered. "She's moving into everyone's lives."

Having thought that herself, Celia still felt a jolt hearing it aloud.

Chapter 24

Vanessa stood in front of Allison's desk, checking work orders. "I just got two more clients in Boca Pelicano Palms in the nick of time. The raise for my promotion isn't putting me in luxury. And you know I like that good life." She grinned.

"Obviously they must like the job you do." Allison gave her questioning glance. "Do you think it's too much?"

"I've worked three jobs during lean times. This is a piece of cake." Vanessa flexed her smooth biceps with a grin.

"Ready for your first class in CPR today?"

"Yup. I'm prepared."

Allison handed Vanessa a list of state regulations. "You'll need to know these, especially when you start training other caregivers."

"Thanks."

"Michael is sending a sandwich over so I can work through lunch. They're huge. Want to split it?"

"Sure." Vanessa raised her eyebrow. "Did your mom tell you that Michael's mother tried to set us up? We kind of knew each other and had a good laugh. Besides, Brady's more my style. He loves to indulge me." She wrinkled her nose. "Looks like Michael wants to indulge you."

Allison cracked a nervous laugh. "He sends food out of guilt because my work load is over the top."

"Ha." She gave Allison a knowing grin. "Michael said you're holding this place up single handed and saving his ass."

Allison loved that her work was being recognized. "Nah. I'm putting Band-Aids on their bleeding inefficient system for now."

"How would your economies work?"

"Glad you asked. For one thing, when any department hits ten percent–plus in savings above their last year's budget, they get half of what they save as a bonus." Allison's spirits rose as she thought about all of her ideas to boost profits. "It's an incentive to watch the spending."

"I've been telling the execs how smart you are."

Allison noticed that Vanessa wore a large emerald on her ring finger. She also wore a gorgeous green silk dress that matched her emerald. She wasn't kidding when she said she had expensive taste. But she was easy to talk to and fun.

"Although I love having patients, I was conflicted about my promotion and worried about enough time for hands-on care. But it's working. Brady wanted me to be a full supervisor, but Michael talked him into taking it in slow increments. I'm not sure how I feel. Pay would have been better, but I love doing in-home care."

"Might be a good idea to ease into a supervisory position."

"Maybe. Augh, men making decisions for us. Truth is, I'd miss the patients. Lots of caregivers don't want the really sick ones and it's a crying shame." Vanessa pouted. "I keep thinking I'll get them to jump out of bed and be healthy again. I know it's silly, but it's not just a job for me." Vanessa pulled up a chair beside the desk. "Let's have girl talk. Flirt with Michael. He's a catch."

"I like him as a person, but I'm still going through a divorce."

"You'll be mad for him soon, if you aren't already now."

"I do have a crush on him, but so does everyone else."

"See, told you so. He's a hunk, but not a run-around."

A knock sounded on the door and Allison shouted, "Come in." A young man set a brown paper bag on the desk and left. Allison removed a huge corned beef sandwich wrapped in wax paper, large containers of coleslaw and potato salad, and paper plates and plastic forks.

"Wow, this is a feast for ten people."

"Michael knows I'll take home leftovers," Allison said. "I can hardly shut the fridge at my mother's." The room filled with the scent of garlic, pickling spices, and peppery, dark red corned beef. Her mouth watered. She'd missed breakfast.

Vanessa helped dish out the food. "Want to go out tomorrow night?"

"I really need to work, unfortunately."

"All work and no play will kill you. We could go to happy hour at Charlie's over on Glades. It's not far from your mother's place."

"Sorry. Between work and looking at apartments, I'm swamped. My mom still thinks I'm a teenager and we have issues from way back."

"I'm sure she did the best she could." Vanessa took a bite of sour pickle. "My mom died of cancer when I was twelve and my dad died recently. Maybe I went into healthcare thinking, unconsciously, that I'm bringing my mom back. At least you had a mom growing up."

Allison mulled over how she'd feel if her mother died. She knew in an instant she'd be crushed, despite all their fights. "It's complicated. She suffered from depression and took lots of meds." Allison stopped, surprised at her own candidness. The image of her mother lying in bed, covers halfway over her face, flashed in her mind. "She does seem better since coming to Florida."

"I won't pry. When you're ready to let it all out, I'm here to listen."

Allison glided her fingers across the waxy paper and placed half a sandwich on each plate. "In Kansas, what they called corned beef was like beef jerky rehydrated."

"I first tasted corned beef when I came to community college in Florida." Vanessa chewed slowly, clearly savoring the food.

"I should have the divorce papers within a couple of weeks," Allison blurted out.

"Good. That creepy cheater."

"That's one of his better qualities."

Vanessa laughed. "I totally get it. When I got my associate's degree and went to work as an accountant, I met a dark-haired charmer and we got engaged. He turned out to be a con man who ripped me off big time. I thought my life was over at age twenty-five, but I recovered. That's when I took off for Europe."

"That's a bitch. How'd you get here?"

"I heard there were plenty of jobs and got my training around here. But I'm tired of hustling for a buck. Now I want a rich older guy. I don't want to work forever. Just set me up in a great apartment and adore me." She smirked.

Allison didn't judge her for turning love into a business arrangement. "I still fantasize about finding true love, whatever that is." She took a small bite of her sandwich.

Vanessa crossed her legs. She wore sandals with delicate rhinestones sprinkled across the tops, like a bridge to a happy place. "Rich or poor, marriages usually go sour, so the man I marry might as well be rich." Vanessa's face took on a sardonic expression. "Look at us. We both loved bad boys and got the crap kicked out of us. We're fed bullshit from magazines, movies, and romance books—be feminine and nurturing and we'll live happily ever after." She rolled her eyes. "C'mon."

Allison stared at Vanessa. "You're right but maybe …"

"Looking for true love in all the wrong places. Come with me to Charlie's. Work and apartments will be waiting for you."

Allison considered for a moment. "Ah, the hell with it. You've got a date." She smiled.

Vanessa threw her head back, long curls swaying, and giggled. "Listen, Allie, we might have grown up differently, but we've got lots in common."

"You're right. We both want to better ourselves, even if we go about it differently, and we've been hurt by love."

Vanessa stood, dumped her empty plate in the trashcan, and waved her work assignment sheet in the air. "Got to go. I'll pick you up at seven." She hurried out the door.

Allison sat back and slowly finished eating, feeling a sense of relief at opening up to Vanessa. She had found a friend.

Chapter 25

Celia

Celia watched the instructor with trepidation as she kneaded a three-pound mound of clay, squeezing all the air bubbles out. The instructor was a little wisp of a woman, covered in clay dust, her white hair awry and her upper arms punctuated by muscles that had clearly developed over years of centering clay. She gave detailed instructions to six waiting women.

Having taken a pottery class at college, Celia found she could make a ragged plate and nothing more, although she liked the feel of cool, damp clay in her hands. In love with painting, she pursued that genre until she declared herself a mediocre artist and switched to art history. Now she'd promised herself to succeed at making pottery, to stick with it, like she'd done with the cha-cha. Aiming to produce a brightly colored vase to cheer up her apartment, she furrowed her brow. Deep inside she felt a burning in her belly for success so she could exorcise the old demons of failure.

The instructor dropped a sponge in a pan of water, set it on the side of an electric pottery wheel, picked up the blob of clay, and smacked it down in the middle of a round wooden bat that sat on the wheel. With the flick of a switch she sent the wheel spinning. "Start."

Celia's heart thudded with anticipation as each student was expected to sit at the wheel, attempting to duplicate what the teacher had said. The first two students centered the clay but as they tried to raise it into a shape it collapsed.

Then Celia sat, hands shaky. *Don't fail.* She went through all the motions of getting air bubbles out of three pounds of clay, then stared at the mound, daring it to defeat her. The wheel spun. Celia planted her open hands on the sides of the blob, pushing hard to center. Her muscles burned. It wobbled until it rotated smoothly in a balanced ball, the musty clay smell wafting upwards. As it spun in Celia's hands it felt like she touched Mother Earth.

"Good," said the instructor. "It's hard to center a big blob of clay." She dipped the sponge in water and squeezed it on top of Celia's hands and over the clay. "Now for the finessing."

Don't fail. Celia rested her hands on the spinning mound. Head down, she pressed her thumbs into the top. What she did seemed like the steps in cha-cha, moving to the rhythm. Forcing her thumbs into the top to depress the clay, she made an opening, leaving half an inch on the bottom for the floor of the vase. Four deft fingers pressed the clay's outsides as thumbs pressed against the middle of the well, forcing the well to widen.

She slowly began lifting the sides. Every now and then, she paused to dip the sponge and wet the rotating pot. Slowly, she thinned the wall and raised the sides to a ten-inch height. A round-bottomed vase took shape. She slowed the wheel with her foot on the pedal and with a long, pointed stick cut the excess clay away at the bottom. She stopped and ran a wire through the bottom of the vase to unstick it. Looking up, she saw all the women smiling at her. Joy!

"Okay. Good work for a first one." The instructor flipped her head to the side, checking all around. "Once it dries to what we call leather dry, you can cut in designs. Then fire it once, decorate it with glaze, then fire it again. Congrats. You're off to the races."

Celia's heart soared as she got up and went to wash her hands. At the sink, she did a few tiny cha-cha steps, two-three, one-two-three. She recalled how long ago Stanton had encouraged her to do her own art and told her he saw amazing promise. She'd had no confidence and over the years Gabe reinforced her no-talent notion by saying she didn't have what it took. Now she stood up straight and puffed her chest out, knowing she could do this. *Screw you, Gabe.*

Celia washed up, took off her apron, combed her hair, and left to meet Deb and Marcy at an art lecture.

Celia drove to the university, where she was due to meet Marcy and Deb. In the lecture hall, still flying high from her success, Celia sat next to Marcy and looked around at the half-filled room, catching a whiff of mustiness. Dampness invaded most interiors of southern Florida as humidity plugged into every inch of air during the hot summer season, and the smell lingered year-round. The scent of old leather and dried flowers mingling with mildew produced a not unpleasant tang on her tongue. If they chose an official fragrance for a state this would be Florida's brand.

She had been attending art history lectures here before Melvin died but stopped when they'd gotten tangled in this mess. The last lecture she'd attended had been about Édouard Manet. She'd especially loved his painting "Absinthe Drinker" and found it interesting that his subjects were unusual for his era, depicting modern life of late nineteenth-century Paris with its beggars, singers, gypsies, and people from all walks of life.

The lecturer, a professor of art history at the university, looked the part of a Southern gentleman: white goatee, mustache, thin gray hair parted in the middle, and a shiny black three-piece suit. When he emphasized a point about an artist, he would tap his fist against his chest.

"Oddly enough," the professor pontificated, "although Degas declared his celibacy, he painted nude women, many dancers, laundresses, and women of the working class performing tasks of their trade. He was known as reclusive."

"He couldn't stay away from painting the beautiful female form." Marcy jiggled her shoulders.

Celia never tired of hearing about an artist's life: what influenced them to become artists, the tenor of the times, and how their particular styles evolved. She loosened her hands from the worn, prickly armrests and watched Marcy and Deb looking enthralled.

Degas studied and painted dancers in rehearsals, the whirling motions made on graceful pointe and quiet meditative poses that highlighted their isolation and feeling of aloneness. She related to the forlorn sensations he evoked. An invisible force whisked Celia through the canvas into the interior of the paintings. She became a ballerina, standing sad and isolated from the world.

On the screen now was a painting, "The Dance Class." The professor declared this to be Degas's most famous work and smacked his chest.

"The prof is going to knock himself out," Deb said. Someone behind them shushed her.

When the lecture ended, Marcy said, wistfully, "That was beautiful."

They walked out into the bright sunshine. "Now I can catch me a professor or doctor since I can talk art now," Marcy joked, wagging her finger.

The late afternoon air held a hot, damp heaviness. They strolled past stores selling expensive Hawaiian print shirts, Lily Pulitzer dresses, and reproduction antiques.

Celia noticed a large black Continental slowly roll past them. "I think that car is following us." Celia blinked hard.

"You're imagining things," Marcy said. "You think every black car that passes is out to get us."

"Well, Marcy, you put crazy ideas in her head. No wonder she's scared," Deb sputtered.

Celia wanted to believe she only imagined it—so much.

When Celia got home, she found Stanton waiting outside her apartment complex. He wore a crisp yellow shirt, opened at the neck to reveal a puff of white chest hair. His smile was wide and enveloping.

"I was hoping I'd bump into you."

"On your way to see Edith?"

"Matter of fact, yes. We have a Scrabble game. There are two more ladies."

"How nice. I'm sorry I have to rush." She tried to duck around him but he stood in her way.

"A little chat won't hurt. What have you been up to?"

Maybe he was right—a little chat wouldn't hurt. "Tried

my hand with pottery today. It was my first time in years, and I loved it."

He beamed. "I always said you have talent. Would you show it to me when it's fired?"

"It's not that good."

"I don't believe it. I'd love to have coffee with you sometime, you know ... catch up."

His smile warmed then stung her. He'd broken off with her all those years ago and now he wanted to chat? "Edith won't like that." She tried to pass and he stepped in her path again.

"Look, if you don't want me bothering you, I understand, but Edith is not my girlfriend. I thought you got that message." He clucked his tongue. "Look. I know she had no idea who my wife was when she showed up at the funeral luncheon. She wanted to meet the new widower. I felt sorry for her, but needed company too. I told her from the get-go we weren't an item."

She raised her eyebrow in surprise. "You knew she was from the casserole brigade?"

"From the get-go." He laughed. "Don't you want to cook me a brisket? All the other ladies do."

His laugh was infectious and when she caught her breath she said, "Hell no." She moved to the side and he turned in her direction.

"Good. I hate brisket." He half-smiled. "There were other casseroles left at my door, but Edith's tasted the best." He laughed. "To tell the truth, the other dishes had no cards, and I suspect Edith removed them. Why don't women realize that most men aren't worth all that effort, including me?"

"Women can be much too forgiving."

There was a long pause. "Fine. So ... uh, would you like to meet up sometime? That is, if you don't have a significant other."

"Um ..." She wasn't sure she should do this.

"Oops. There's that famous hesitation. You're busy?"

"Oh, I mean I don't have a significant other."

"All right. How about coffee with me tomorrow afternoon?"

"Well, I ..." She thought back to how he loved running his hands over her body, commenting on the baby-soft smoothness of her skin. Now sags trailed along that road. She'd never live up to his memories. She studied the sweet expression, the eager look in his eyes. No, she thought. I'm free and don't want that again. Especially with a man who disappeared on me years ago. She scratched an imaginary itch on her neck as she tried to think of a smart remark.

"Uh, Celia ... what do you think? Yes or no?"

"I'll check my schedule. Call me," she said, and pushed her elevator button. He waved and walked away. Clearly, her response hadn't pleased him. He wouldn't call. *That's that then. What have I done?*

Chapter 26

Allison

Allison hurried down the long corridor that led to Michael Castor's unassuming, rather shabby office. She found it odd that the CFO of such a large corporation that took in most of Florida and new affiliates across the country didn't have a luxurious office like Brady did.

Shirkson's office had burnished mahogany furniture and a wall of floor-to-ceiling windows with a nice view of the downtown skyline. The room where Michael worked had the same drab look as the squat, square building in which the company was housed. Most of the offices in their building had glaring fluorescent light fixtures and foam drop-ceiling tiles. Some of the tiles were even stained with rust spots from old roof leaks. Like many of the other offices, Michael's window shades were worn, his view blocked by a neighboring brick building, and his desk and sofa a bit battered. Allison thought about the profit and loss statement she'd just been reviewing. Just when they caught a break, something pushed them into the loss column where they now were. She thought again of Brady's palatial office. If she were in charge …

At first, she and Michael had met once a day for work-related items. He always gave her his undivided attention, and almost from the beginning she felt a sizzle between them that seemed to grow each day. She started taking advantage of every legitimate reason to meet: working on budget cuts, salary changes, numbers of new hires, which employees to let go. He'd agreed to her suggestions to cut the number of social events and parties and to freeze salaries for everyone, including the top level of executives. When her attraction to him seemed to get the better of her, she resorted to e-mail. After a day or two of electronic communication, he would encourage her to come in person, saying they got more done that way.

Sometimes he touched the top of her arm when he wanted to emphasize her talents in management. At first, he looked away but soon he looked right at her, his sky-blue eyes lingering a few moments longer than need be. She didn't know if that was just his way of working with employees or if he felt the same excitement she did. When he suggested she hire an assistant, she refused, claiming it was too costly. But secretly, she wanted him to depend on her alone.

Whenever she entered his office she'd notice his white shirtsleeves rolled up to his elbows. She often focused on his bare arms, longing to run her fingers along his tanned skin. It scared her to think that her feelings might become even more powerful. *Whew!*

Allison knocked on Michael's door, her equilibrium quivering as waves of electricity shot through her body when he called for her to enter. She wondered if he felt it too.

He sat at his scratched wooden desk, tapping his fingers on a stack of papers. "Take a look at these," he said.

She saw printed blocks of numbers. "Where did these come from?"

"They're from the embezzler who did the accounting before you came." He stared into space. "She was so nice and such a whiz." He grimaced. "And she whizzed us out of lot of cash. We're still trying to determine how much. Can you take a careful look at them?"

"Did she get indicted?"

"We pressed charges but she didn't appear at the arraignment. They have a warrant for her arrest."

Allison stood beside Michael's chair and inhaled the scent of his musky cologne. She felt a tingling in the pit of her stomach as she bent over and the numbers came back into focus. Shrugging she said, "These need decoding. How about I start tomorrow?"

"Thanks. Sorry to saddle you with this. When do you think you can finish?"

"Um, I'd have to take a hard look. Three days maybe?" Her voice quivered as she thumbed through the papers.

"Good. Just let me know." He sat up straight, turning toward her. His eyebrows furrowed. "Let me ask you something."

His look startled her, and she caught her breath for a moment. During his long pause, he seemed to be assessing her. "Do you get out at all? I mean like for fun."

She gave him a dubious glance. "Hardly with this workload."

He swiped his hands under each eye and grinned. "I feel so guilty. But you should get out more."

"My social life wasn't in the job description." She laughed with him.

He leaned toward her with a mock sigh. "I don't want your health to deteriorate. Then you'll need a caregiver from our company."

"Well, you'll be glad to hear that Vanessa invited me to Charlie's tonight."

His face brightened. "Hey, why don't I take both you hard-working gals out? I promise to get you back early."

She managed a nervous laugh. "I guess you need to make sure we're back at our desks on time."

He smiled. "Absolutely. Consider me your designated driver so you can have that extra drink. Just let me know the time." He pulled a mock-serious face. "But for now, back to work."

Allison playfully saluted him. "Yes sir."

He turned back to his computer, and she picked up the papers from his desk. As she turned to leave, she stole a final glance and felt her heart flutter faster.

Chapter 27

Celia

At the Pelican Retreat Coffee Shop, Stanton set two lattes on a small table then held the chair out for Celia. She smiled at such a traditional gesture in a place where they sold fancy overpriced coffees to patrons typing on laptops, their smartphones chiming with new messages.

Stanton looked closely at her for a moment before picking up his cup. "I almost didn't call, you know. You seemed sort of, I don't know, not very eager to see me."

"I'm glad you called. Truth is, I was feeling overwhelmed at seeing you again after so many years."

"I understand." He paused and looked around. "This is sure different from the coffee shops we went to when we were young. Remember those?" he asked. "Couldn't have been more than fifty cents a cup."

For an instant, the young Stanton sat in front of her. "I only remember the ones where hippies hung out, singing folk songs by Joni Mitchell."

Stanton pretended to strum a guitar. "We belted those songs out too."

He still has that cute way of puffing a short whistle when he says an S. She leaned back and pulled her hand away from his.

"To think that when we were dating, there were still phone booths and rotary phones. I was introduced to the computer rudiments in engineering school. They were these humongous towers, what they called mainframes." He laughed. "Hell, Dick Tracy had a phone wristwatch and everyone laughed, but now they're for real."

"You picked a good major."

"Yeah. Knocked around for quite a while, after we, uh, parted ways. California was opening up for engineers. Computers became my focus and the rest, as they say, is history."

Sitting here, the idea that he dumped her opened the wound as though it just happened. She would have moved to California had he asked—but he never did, and then it ended. She blinked hard. "Why did you stop writing to me?"

"Whew. That dirty look you're giving me." He jerked his head back as though anticipating a punch. "I fell into a funk. I didn't know what I wanted to do. Dragging you into my misery didn't seem fair."

She gave him a piercing stare. He shifted in his seat and looked away. *Good. Be uncomfortable.* "Bull," she said finally. "We talked about our miserable upbringings and swore we'd never do that to our children. Remember?"

"But we were so young, worrying about our futures ..."

Celia smacked her fist on the table and he jumped. "I don't buy that crap about floundering." She felt her face grow hot with anger. "Why didn't you ever write to ask how I felt? You dropped me like a hot potato."

He paled. "Look, I really missed you and wanted to be with you, but I was also immature and wrapped up in myself." His voice lowered to a near whisper. "Not one woman measured up to you."

"I would have been with you if only you asked." Celia harrumphed.

"But you were too busy dating other women."

He let out a burst of air. "I didn't date right away. By the time I started dating I thought you'd lost interest in me."

"That is the lamest excuse I've ever heard. You're putting this on me?"

"Whoa." Stanton held out his hands as though to stop her barrage. "I worked hard to get over you. I guess my wife had to take the brunt of my immaturity, but I grew up over the years." He stared at her. "Listen, it was so long ago. We were both so young. Can we forgive and forget past mistakes?"

"That remains to be seen."

"Tell me what you did after we, uh … what kind of work did you do and all that?"

She got a perverse pleasure from watching him squirm, shocking herself. She'd promised that if she saw him again, she'd pretend she didn't care a whit.

She sucked in a breath. "I worked in a museum writing promotional brochures about artists and upcoming exhibitions. I loved interviewing artists to get their take on what their art meant to them, what they were trying to achieve, questions like that. I went to exhibitions in Manhattan and met interesting people, got into discussions about the art scene." *Take that, Stanton. I had fun without you.* Celia pressed her lips together. "I stopped when I got married."

"Wow. That sounds terrific. Why didn't you keep working after marriage?"

"My husband wanted me to stop, and I became a full-fledged suburban housewife. I guess I wanted to be protected."

"Well, you seem the same upbeat person I knew in college."

She gave a noncommittal smile.

He tipped his head and stared at her. "Maybe you're a tad grumpier." He quickly grinned. "Just kidding." He patted her tight fists, and she had to admit his big hands felt good on her skin.

"It's true. Call it grumpy or whatever you want."

He waved his hands as though to erase his words. "So, you gave up your fabulous job for your marriage. Go on."

Memories of her marriage flashed through her mind. Those lovely first ten years—rose petals on the bed, iced champagne. When it stopped there were stone-cold silent breakfasts in the mornings, sporadic and perfunctory sex. "It was fine. Let's not talk about the past. It happened a hundred years ago."

"Well, it doesn't seem like a hundred years ago. You look so good—hardly a worry line on your beautiful face."

Celia tried to gauge how much to tell him without it getting sticky. "Good genes."

He looked away. "I don't mean to pry."

Celia stared at her hands. "Maybe when I know the new Stanton better, if we get to that point, we'll talk more. I'm still a work in progress." She sat up straight in the chair. "I try to live in the present."

"Fair enough."

The door opened, and a soft, warm breeze wafted in, but when she saw Edith and Julia approaching their table, a cold chill ran through her bones.

"Hello, Stanton," Edith said. She turned to Celia and gave her a frosty nod.

"Hey there," Stanton stood and motioned for them to sit down at their table.

What was he thinking, inviting them to sit down? She wondered what Edith might have told Stanton behind her back.

When she looked up, Edith was staring at her with narrowed eyes, but Julia looked to be in la-la land. Celia pushed her chair back and rose, her body shaking with annoyance.

"Where …?" Stanton wrinkled his brow the way he used to when he'd screwed up.

"Nice to see you, Stanton."

"Uh, I'll call you. Okay?" he asked, wrinkling his forehead deeper.

"Sure." By the hard, determined expression on Edith's face, Celia figured she'd never hear from him again. Which was probably all for the best.

Her life was topsy-turvy: Allison's arrival, Stanton reappearing, uncertainty about who knew of their involvement with Melvin, the visit from the police, learning of Gabe's infidelity, worries about Vanessa, and the strange black car she was sure was tailing her. Not to mention the rumor that there were numerous heart attack deaths of people who had no heart disease history. She'd just heard that Curtis Donaldson, Lila's husband, had had a heart attack and it didn't look like he was going to make it.

Celia stepped out of the café. At the curb, a black Lincoln Continental sat idling. She walked closer and made out the back of an older, gray-headed person sitting inside, unsure if it was a man or woman. Binoculars and a takeout coffee sat on the dashboard. Just as she approached the driver's side, the person sped off.

Who was this person? She was certain now that she was being followed.

Chapter 28

Allison

At Charlie's, Michael sat with Allison. Vanessa danced a rhumba with a young man who wore hip-hugging jeans, a white silk shirt, and a diamond earring in his left ear with a matching pinkie ring. Vanessa's tight jeans, white blouse, and necklace strung with small rubies gave the impression that she and her partner had planned parallel outfits. Though strangers, the two moved on the dance floor in unison, keeping constant eye contact. Allison couldn't help being impressed that two perfect strangers could move their feet in the same perfect patterns. The man did complex, flamenco-like steps and damn if Vanessa didn't follow. When his body floated into withering, seductive motions, Vanessa glided into the positions like they'd practiced for months. Well, Vanessa *had* lived in Spain.

The Latin band played dated music—cha-cha, rhumba, merengue—yet it impressed Allison that so many younger people on the floor improvised on the traditional steps with fresh, timeless performances, their bodies shaking, bumping, and sometimes seemingly soaring. Allison felt like a child staring at a candy counter. "The dancing is remarkable."

"Three guys asked you, so why are you still here?" Michael teased.

She frowned and squirmed in her seat. "It's been so long, I'd trip over my own feet."

"Are you upset about anything?"

"I'm okay." The vodka martini stung pleasantly on its way down and started lifting her mood as she sipped it. "I'm trying to get on with my new life. My soon-to-be ex is harassing me, and I just want to end it fast. No fuss, no muss."

"I'm sorry about that." He gave her an impish smile. "I'm kind of looking to make changes in my life too. Work is making me as dull as a well-worn copper penny. I keep telling myself there is life out there, yet ..." He looked at her with a raised eyebrow. "We both deserve to be happy, don't we?"

His piercing look made her feel like she was staring right into the sun. She turned her head away. "Not sure what happy is." She tightened her clasped hands, fingernails digging into her palms. She wanted to pinch herself to make sure she wasn't dreaming, sitting next to the man who stirred her like no one else ever had.

Vanessa returned from the dance floor and broke the spell. "Am I interrupting," she said, with a coy smile that implied she hoped she had.

"You dance like you've done it all your life, Vanessa."

"I just love it. And that guy can move." Vanessa drew the corners of her lips up. "I just followed."

"Don't be so modest. You're really good," Allison said.

Vanessa sat, took a long swig of her cocktail, and glanced at Michael over the top of the glass. "Do you dance?"

Michael laughed and pointed at his knees. "I have not an iota of rhythm in this sad body."

Vanessa poked Michael in the ribs. "The management at Global HMO and Well Services is loaded with white bread men who can't dance."

"It's mandatory they don't dance. Work or die," Michael said, ordering another round.

As Allison sipped her drink, she realized that Michael was looking intently at her. Although her insides spun in delight, she shifted on her barstool and turned her head so that he gazed at her profile.

Vanessa placed her elbow on the bar and rested her cheek on her hand, staring down intently at the highly polished black marble bar top. Then she tapped the bar top with her knuckles. "I know we're here for pleasure and not business, but I work hard. I could use a better raise, sir."

Allison couldn't help thinking about her new car, Joy perfume, and expensive clothing. She probably needed the money to support her lifestyle. But she had to admit that through sheer will and wit Vanessa sure got the top brass to pull for her.

"You're good at what you do, and showing promise with your new responsibilities." Michael shifted and draped an arm over the back of Allison's seat. "I'll think about it, and Brady will have to give final approval. I'll talk to him."

Vanessa smiled and blew him a kiss. "My hero. Thanks a million."

His gaze hadn't wavered from Allison. In the low light of the bar, his face looked softer and less harried, like a charcoal portrait with smudged edges. Her heart pounded.

After a moment, Michael signaled the bartender for the bill. "Well, lovely ladies, sadly it's time for me to depart. I've got a meeting bright and early at seven tomorrow, and I'm driving you both home."

"Allison and I will take an Uber," said Vanessa "You go so we can have girl talk."

Allison's spirits fell as Michael paid the bill and said goodbye.

While Vanessa kept chatting, Allison wondered what Michael had meant by all the looks he'd given her. Or had they all been in her imagination?

"Hey, are you listening or are you daydreaming about Michael?" Vanessa giggled.

Allison snapped back to reality. "Am I that transparent?"

"Lady, a three-year-old could tell you're in deep."

"I won't deny it. He's such a, I don't know, a good guy? He wasn't even upset when you asked for a raise. In fact, bringing it up now was not an appropriate time, I'd think. But you went ahead and he didn't miss a beat. Good for you."

"You gotta take the bull by the horns. Literally. If I see a chance, I go for it."

"My mother said you were aggressive in tennis. I told her if you were a guy you'd be a hero for being so competitive. You've come a long way, sister."

"You bet your sweet ass. I try to reach for the brass ring. Brady taught me that."

"I think you have Brady's attention. I'm sure that raise is coming."

Vanessa ordered another round of drinks. "I think you should ask for a raise, too."

"I'm paid pretty well, better than in Kansas."

"Screw Kansas. This is a company that needs what you have. Don't be a wimp."

"Yeah. Sometimes I remind myself of my mom—I mean, the old mom. I'm not sure where this new mom is coming from. I kinda respect how she's grown. I really try hard to get close to her, then something happens and old wounds are opened." She sighed. "But I act like a brat."

"I really like your mom. She's got the grit of a much younger person, and she's a damned good tennis player."

"Ha. She hardly played tennis that I remember. She must have honed her skills here." Allison swiveled in her seat to face Vanessa and raised both eyebrows. "What do you think of her personality?"

Vanessa looked away and took a long sip of her drink. "Geez, I don't know her well enough to make a judgment. She's seems fine, with a zest for life, I guess."

Something about Vanessa's shaky response disturbed Allison. "Is there something you're not telling me?"

"Shit no. Hey, it's late. Let's go."

The women were quiet on the way home in the Uber. Allison had an inkling Vanessa held something back in her opinion of her mother, but didn't want to press her. Maybe sometime down the line she might get it out of her.

Chapter 29

Celia

Four days had gone by and Celia hadn't heard from Stanton. She'd almost called him several times, but had stopped herself. She wasn't quite ready to forgive him for how he'd tossed her away so many years ago and the incident at the café didn't win him any points. Yet she found herself wanting to talk to him again.

The next time she found herself reaching for the phone, she called Deb instead. "Hey, Deb. How're you doing?"

"Do you really want to hear that I ache all over? Can't get my ass in gear until around noon, tired all the time, and hate all the people around here except for you and Marcy?"

"Nope, already know all that."

"So, don't ask, Ms. Politically Correct. What's up?"

"Eh, the other day I saw someone in a black car who had your hairstyle and a pair of binoculars on the dash. I didn't know if you were following your son again." She took a breath. "But then I couldn't tell if it was a man or a woman."

Deb sounded exasperated. "Are you saying I look more like a man than a woman?"

"I only saw the back of a head. You're avoiding answering my question about following your son."

"C'mon. I haven't done that since you yelled at me. Not even been in a black car. Hey, did you hear about Curtis?"

"What?"

"He finally kicked the bucket. Off to join Lila, I suppose."

"Deb! Have some respect for the dead!"

Celia heard her phone beep. Stanton was calling. "Deb, I have to go, I'll call you back." She clicked to the other line.

"Hi, Celia. It's Stanton. Been a few days, hasn't it?"

The familiar voice filled her with trepidation. "Yes, it has been," Celia said dryly. "Did you enjoy Edith's company after I left?"

"Cut it out. She's been a good friend to me."

"You didn't have to invite her to sit with us."

"It would have been rude not to. Besides, you did catch me by surprise with some of the things we talked about." He sighed.

"Stanton, I'm not the same person I used to be. The young Celia doesn't exist anymore. I'm more outspoken. I enjoy not answering to anyone."

"I'm different too, I hope. But I'd like to see you again. When can we do that?"

Celia was silent. "Let me think about it. I'll get back to you." She struggled whether to say what popped into her head. *Say it anyway.* "Will you be inviting Edith?" She expected him to hang up on her with that one.

He snorted. "Boy, you're relentless. Meet me at Gunger's tomorrow. You know, the place on Glades with the best pastries. Edith never goes there because she had a fight with the manager."

"I know Gunger's."

"We can meet for tea, pastries, and conversation. Just the two of us."

He's making amends. Good. "Well, okay, but I can't meet you till five. I've got a pottery class."

"That's fine. You'll have to tell me all about it."

"See you then." Celia hung up. As she dialed Deb back, a small smile crossed her face.

The scent of sugar and yeast perfumed the air of the tiny, rustic coffee shop, layered with the fragrances of strawberry, blueberry, and cherry. Celia took a bite from a flaky, crisp elephant's ear, still warm from the oven.

"Delicious," Stanton said.

"I love this place." She chewed slowly, savoring the pastry melting on her tongue. She rarely indulged in late-afternoon sweets. Stanton held his coffee mug to his lips, eying her. *I bet he's having second thoughts.* "What's up with you?"

"I guess I owe you an explanation for not calling sooner. For one thing, you just up and walked out. And then Edith told me some weird things, so it made me nervous."

Celia felt her hackles rise. "Exactly what is she spreading now? E-coli? Malaria?"

He laughed. "Almost as bad. Well ... I didn't want to get involved. Then I thought, a quiet, humdrum life is overrated. I've been there and—borrrring. Now, from what Edith's saying you're in a bit of trouble. I thought it might be easier to discuss it in person."

Oh shit. "It's nothing I can't handle."

"Is that so?"

"You know, Edith is a rumormonger."

"Well, she's nothing you can't handle." He grinned.

Celia forced her voice to stay light. "What did she say, just out of curiosity?"

"Something about her estranged husband dying mysteriously. She talked Melvin's kids into getting an autopsy based on the fact he had a heart attack with no previous diagnosis of heart disease. She said your friend Marcy is involved."

"My friend was his girlfriend, that's all. What else?"

"And she also said you had a boyfriend, John, who died under the same mysterious circumstances." He cleared his throat. "I know it's a bunch of hokum. Edith can be paranoid."

She exhaled impatiently. "I didn't date the man. He was rude and vulgar. And you believed her? You didn't think to ask me?"

"No. I guess she exaggerated, that's why I called you." He shook his head and held out his hand. "Enough of Edith. I feel like our talk the other day got interrupted just as we were starting to make some headway, and I want to be honest about my marriage. Do you mind?"

"Go ahead." Celia bit her tongue though she still fumed about Edith.

"I was never really happy. Don't get me wrong, my wife was a good person, but I took the easy route. It was time to get married and Ada offered stability." He seemed to be prodding himself to continue. "Conflicts at work I can handle, but what I mean is … you know, the emotional stuff? As you saw when push came to shove I wasn't so good with that."

Sounds familiar. "Relationships can be damn messy."

"Oh yeah. By the time I hit on a career in computer engineering and got married, we were both older so kids weren't in the equation. I loved Ada as a good friend. She was a homebody who liked reading or watching TV. I thought when I retired and we came to Florida it would be different. But then Ada got sick, and I took care of her for the last three years of her life."

Celia felt sorry for him, but admired his dedication to her. She thought it unlikely Gabe would have done the same for her and felt a pang of sadness.

"It was awful. I felt guilty because I began to think about other women from my past—well, to be exact, you." He pressed his lips together and looked away, his face flushing like a sudden rush of wind had singed his skin. "Is this inappropriate?"

Her own face felt hot. Unsteadily she said, "Well, yes—no. Go ahead."

"I thought I'd never see you again, but I never let go of the … uh, I don't know what to call it … a fantasy maybe." He shook his head and a strand of white hair fell over his eyebrow. He brushed it back with his hand. "Ada never knew."

She felt a tinge of joy at the thought that he had suffered over his decision to drop her.

"My wife stuck by me in hard times and went along with a … a kind of unwritten rule to avoid arguing. So, it was a flat monotonous ride that was mostly my fault." He widened his eyes. "I had a yen to travel to places like Tahiti, Bali, Africa, maybe even scuba dive. Ada told me to go by myself, but I knew it would hurt her if I went alone. Instead, for an outlet, I began welding scraps of metal and calling it sculpture. It's fun." He grinned. "In the back of my head I think you influenced me."

"Wow," Celia said, breathing in deep as though she'd held her breath the whole time he spoke. "I hardly think of myself as an inspiration." She shook her head. "A computer person who also creates art? Right brain, left brain."

"It took me a long time to grow up. I dated women I knew I couldn't marry. Guess I was afraid of commitment. That is, until Ada. And she was a safe, unchallenging choice." He furrowed his brow and gave her a questioning look. "I just thought of this. Maybe I distanced myself from you for the same reason—fear of commitment. You think?"

"Don't ask me. I hardly know you now."

He gave a rueful smile. "Back then I put my all into work."

Celia narrowed her eyes at him.

"Okay, I know what you're thinking. I got consumed by work to keep from dealing with, you know, stuff. All the feelings I didn't know what to do with." He shook his head. "I'm exhausted. You go now."

Well, he's been pretty open with me, so what the hell. "I, like you, always avoided confrontation. I wanted to do exciting things, but Gabe made the decisions. I should have showed some spunk, taken some chances. Instead I kept it all inside but harbored resentment. It was my own fault for going along, maybe even encouraging it. I took the easy route."

"You certainly seem confident now."

"I'm working on it, trying to make sensible decisions that I never faced before. I should have insisted on being more equal in my marriage." She hesitated. He looked attentive. "I was a bad example for my daughter. I, well … I had bad bouts of depression."

Was she scaring him? And why should she care? She had Marcy and Deb, who accepted her unconditionally, warts and all. Like everyone else, she'd had problems in her life. So what?

"I'm not that much in touch with my inner self like you are, Celia."

"Is digging into yourself scary to you?" She gave him a tight-lipped smile.

"Used to be. Now, maybe, somewhat intriguing."

She remembered how she'd drifted through so much of her life in a bubble, her feelings numb. "Well, I used to be a hollow shell of a human. Never again."

"How do you change that?"

He caught her off guard, but it was a damn good question. "It's about embracing the struggle, being honest with myself, examining my flaws. I've made lots of mistakes and went back in time to find out what makes me tick, what shaped me and brought me to this moment. It's like an archeological dig. You sift through sand and stone for weeks, months, even years and then find a little treasure. That treasure is an insight into myself."

"Give me a for-instance."

"Oh, for heaven's … okay. My parents instilled a terror of the outside world. I bought into that fear and married a man who continued to control my life. I was climbing out of that shell in college but fell back after you … disappeared. So, no more depending on others to make me happy. No way. We make our own happiness."

"Could you teach me?"

"I'm not your therapist. You deal with that yourself."

"Ouch. I get it, but can you say it nicer?"

She glared at him. "Don't depend on women to do your work."

"Not even Edith?" He covered his face with his hands as though ducking a punch.

Celia smiled. "No, especially not Edith."

"Listen, in my opinion, Edith is jealous and carrying a vendetta against you and your lady friends. I tried to talk her out of it, but she gets upset whenever I mention you."

"I can't imagine why she'd be jealous of me." *More likely she's jealous of Marcy and her freewheeling lifestyle.* "Edith plans her life like a robot. That's fine, but she wants everyone to be like her."

"Uh oh. I agree, but I can't insult her by telling her that."

"Man up, for heaven's sake."

He jerked his head back. "Geez. This new Celia. You do say it like it is."

"Is that too much for you?" Celia moved her empty plate to the side and rapped her knuckles on the table.

He gritted his teeth with mock horror. "I need time to absorb all this. On a lighter note, tell me how you like living in a retirement village. I love having golf and tennis on the premises, and warm weather all year."

"The weather is a bonus." She put her finger to her cheek. "Let's see. I enjoy the lectures on the latest medical studies, politics, and world news. Also, the author readings. I even like the C-class renditions of older musicals like *South Pacific*. But on the flip side, there are small cliques of people who do everything together. Independent thinkers sometimes get cut out."

"Hey, don't forget all the medical complaints," Stanton said. "At breakfast someone showed me his bunions and told me every detail about his bowel irregularity. Didn't eat much that morning."

"Yuck! Here's one for you: I was stopped by a man who wanted to show me his insulin pump, privately."

"That's a new come-on line for the elderly. Instead of do you want to see my etchings, it's do you want to see my surgery scars?" Stanton chuckled. "Men like that are usually looking for a woman to take care of him."

Celia felt propelled back in time to their college days, their conversations pinging and veering like beads dropped on a sheet of glass a handful at a time.

Stanton drained his coffee cup and smiled at her. "Can we get together again soon? I miss, you know, banter." There was a brief dubious flicker at the corners of his mouth.

Celia nearly blurted out a yes but stopped herself. "Let's think about it. I've been busy lately. Life's gotten complicated. My daughter moved in with me while going through a divorce, among other things." Celia pursed her lips. "Do you even like the new me?"

"I think it needs some getting used to, kind of … I don't know." His cheeks reddened.

"Like an acquired taste." They both laughed, but a heaviness squeezed her chest. *Can one go home again to that old magic?*

"I enjoy talking to you." He rubbed his jaw. "Even if you've unraveled me." He held his hands out like a referee. "In a nice way, like the good part of my past is being wrenched into the present."

"Are you sure the wrenching isn't your arthritis acting up?"

"You still have that dry sense of humor I loved so much." He lightly touched the back of her hand.

Celia hurriedly got up. "Well, let's call it a day." Celia wanted to leave before she got herself into trouble.

They made small talk as Stanton drove her home. When he pulled up into Celia's parking lot, she extended her hand.

"No kiss?" he asked sheepishly.

"We're not back in college." Celia turned her head in a flirty way. "This is all new, don't you think?"

He kissed her hand, leaving a tingling sensation on her skin. She pulled away and got out of the car fast. They had spent three hours talking and the time had flown. Now, for the first time that day, she felt the gnawing of hunger pangs.

Inside her condo, she reheated some leftover vegetable soup, eating it slowly as she recalled pieces of their conversation. *Acquired taste indeed.* No doubt he'd tire of the new Celia, she was sure of it. She cleaned up the kitchen, showered, and slipped into her pajamas. Before getting into bed, she danced a cha-cha without music, spinning and turning, hearing the notes in her head. She found herself buoyed, soaring out of her world into one with no problems. Or did Stanton's interest in her induce this euphoria? Nope, it had to be the dance. One of the cha-cha rules hit her. IMPROVISE. THE DANCE IS A PALETTE TO EXPLORE THE UNFAMILIAR. More and more, the cha-cha rules were impacting her life big time.

In bed, she picked up *Selected Stories* by Alice Munro from her night table. She snuggled under the covers, eager to get back to the book. Stanton was merely an outing, but this book was like an old friend. She loved Munro's writing, the way she took a small incident or an ordinary person and revealed, layer by layer, the depths of intelligence, behavior, and feelings in people. It reminded her of college when she and Stanton struggled to make sense of who they were. Today he seemed to be struggling to get back to that and found it to be a plus.

The phone rang. She sat up, frightened at getting a call at ten o'clock. "Not another Marcy emergency," she mumbled, but saw Stanton's number.

"Haven't seen you for a long time. Hope it's not too late."

"I don't get calls this late." *Except when I need to move a dead man.* She thumped her head back into the pillow.

"Sorry, but I felt an urgency to call you."

She sighed. "What about?"

"I went over our conversation in my head. I want to …"

"You want a philosophical discussion now? I'm in bed with my favorite author. Go to sleep."

"Who's in bed with you?"

"Alice Munro, that's who."

"Oh, I've heard of her. She won the Nobel Prize for literature."

Good for you. "She did and is a terrific writer. I'll talk to you tomorrow."

"Just this, and I'll go quietly into the night. Observe the beginnings of a new me by joining me for dinner Saturday at Chez Pierre? Seven-thirty."

"Chez Pierre? What, no early bird special? Does that mean we're going steady?"

"In these parts, when you go out to a candlelit full-priced dinner it means you're engaged." He let out a nervous guffaw. "I can always sit and complain about aches and pains if you'd prefer."

"It's a start."

"So, you accept my invitation? I don't have to call back tomorrow for an answer?"

His voice, filled with eager anticipation, made her lightheaded. She remembered his different tones of voice: the urgency when he was expounding on liberal causes, the soft caress of his whispering, "I love you," when making love. For a moment she was ready to accept. But there was nothing worse than an old fool. "I … I'll have to think about it. Call me tomorrow."

She hung up and fell back against her pillow, feeling wrung out. *What's wrong with me?*

Celia awoke at seven a.m. with something gnawing urgently at her. She brushed her teeth three times then circled the phone, checking her watch until it hit eight o'clock, a decent time to call Marcy. "Listen," she said as soon as her friend picked up.

"What's up? Am I in trouble?"

During the night certain thoughts, other than Stanton, had niggled her. "Hear me out. Lila Donaldson died recently and then her husband had a fatal heart attack a few days later. Both were Vanessa's patients. Now she's caring for Julia, who has Alzheimer's, and I don't know who else. What if something happens to them too? And what about the others Lyle told you about? This is creeping me out. Do we have an angel of mercy here?"

There was a long silence before Marcy spoke. "Mercy my ass. Vanessa—and I think she's the one—can't decide who lives and who dies. It set me on edge when Vanessa dropped that bag of pills after they took Lila to the hospital. Caregivers make a list. I'd bet she didn't expect Lila to live and was stealing them. They've got a high street value with this opioid crisis now."

"That would be heartless. It's hard for me to believe."

"Should we talk to Deb?" Marcy asked.

"I don't want to upset her, but I had to tell you. Let's just keep an eye on things. It could be coincidence, right?"

"Could be. But I didn't like that one from the minute I laid eyes on her." Marcy snorted. "That car you keep seeing … it's probably Vanessa."

"What do we do?" Celia drummed her fingers on the table.

"For now, you should see Stanton, keep doing the cha-cha, and enjoy life."

Celia thought back to the late-night phone call from Stanton and told Marcy about the conversation.

"Oh, I'd love it if someone took me to Chez Pierre!"

"Well, I'm not sure if I'm going to accept."

Celia heard Marcy exhale impatiently, like fire spouted from her nose. "Are you crazy?"

"We have a loaded history and he dumped me. We've each got baggage," Celia fretted.

"Pssh, baggage! Who doesn't? This is your second chance to see how things go. Who cares what happened when you were twenty-one. If you don't give it a whirl, you'll have regrets all of your life, wondering what could have been."

Celia agreed reluctantly. "I'll see you later." She hung and stared into space as though an answer were written there.

The phone rang. She jumped. The caller ID said it was Stanton. "Hello?" She heard the tremble in her voice and cleared her throat to steady herself.

There was silence and then she said again, "Hello?"

"Celia. I don't want to play games. I'll just be direct. Will you please go out with me to Chez Pierre? We're too old to do the wait-and-see game."

Celia clamped her lips. At the very least she'd have some fun rather than thinking about all the mysterious deaths taking place in her community.

"Celia?" Stanton's voice broke into her thoughts. "I'm waiting. Yes or no?"

She took a breath. "Yes. Just this once."

Chapter 30

Allison

Allison went looking for her mother and found her standing in front of her open closet. Clothes were strewn all over the floor.

She stepped over a pile of skirts and shook her head. "What are you doing?"

"Cleaning out my closet."

She picked up a black turtleneck. "Didn't Daddy buy you this?"

"Yup." Celia kept dumping clothes on the floor.

"Don't you have any sentimental feelings about any of it?" She picked up a gray shirt.

"Nope. They're dumpy and from another time in my life." Celia seemed unnerved but didn't stop. She continued to throw half her wardrobe on the floor. "New life, new clothes."

"Isn't this a bit callous? Dad bought clothes that were you. He only died three years ago."

"These are clothes for up North, not Florida." She turned to look at Allison. "Here it is winter, sunny and eighty-five degrees. These clothes don't suit me."

"Florida has some chilly nights."

Celia waved her arm over the piles. "Black, brown, olive, high necks, long sleeves. Are these the right clothes to dance the cha-cha?" She giggled.

Allison felt her hackles rise. Who *was* this woman? *She's trying to preserve her youth.* "You want to be a cliché with short sundresses and a flower in your hair? I know you weren't happily married to Daddy, but it seems insulting to dishonor his memory."

"Excuse me," Celia said. "Let's make a promise to not interfere in each other's lives."

"I need my own apartment, that's for sure." Allison crossed her arms over her chest. "I'll be out of your hair in no time, don't worry."

Celia grabbed Allison's hand. "Oh, I'm not chasing you out. Please understand that I'm just beginning to breathe. I've paid my price, and dearly, to your dad's memory."

Allison bristled again. "What does that mean?" *Does she have a guy she wants to impress with new clothing at her age?* Allison had to admit that although her father was a great parent, he did hem her mother in and didn't help her during bad episodes. Now she didn't want to give in and didn't know why. "Dad had no choice but to take over when you withdrew." Allison picked up a handful of sweaters and dropped them. "I don't give a damn. Toss them all."

Celia started stuffing the clothes into large plastic bags. "Help me bag this to donate to Goodwill, Allie."

"I've got some papers to fill out to finalize the divorce." Allison went to her room, tired of fighting. First Thomas, now her mom. She tried to decipher what her mother meant by saying she'd paid dearly. What had come over her? Maybe it was those new friends of hers. Bad influences. Was she in a second childhood?

Allison looked in her closet, mostly empty except for business clothes, but she reached up to a high shelf and brought down a box.

Opening it, she held up a black slip of a dress that she'd recently purchased—beyond what she could afford, but it was lovely. Michael had asked her out on the pretext of awarding her a dinner for keeping her nose to the grindstone. Excellent work, he'd told her.

"Um, uh," he'd stuttered just before asking her. He had looked past her, tapping a pencil on his desk, looking like a kid who had just batted a ball through a neighbor's window. "Dress up. I want to show you how much I appreciate what you've done in such a short time."

Yes! She whipped the dress against her body and loved the soft, fluttery feel of the silk. Too dressy? The hell with it. She wanted to look smashing.

She'd wavered about whether to tell her mother or not. In the end, she thought it too complicated. Knowing Deb's history about her son was the main reason. And she'd told her mother she didn't date people from work. All this secrecy made her feel a tad guilty. Her mother had been good to her and she'd been bitchy. She needed to stop being so ornery.

She folded the dress carefully with tissue in between the creases and placed it in her work messenger bag. She planned to shower and change at the gym in their building. She added her curling iron, spikey black shoes, and a teddy, although sex was out of the question at this point. Her breath quickened at the thought. It was going to be a special night regardless.

Chapter 31

Celia

As Celia bagged up the clothes, she hoped getting rid of them would deaden Gabe's voice in her head, admonishing and scolding. Allison had hurried out, looking huffy and annoyed. Celia looked for a dress to wear on her date with Stanton and realized she was coming up empty. In desperation, she called Marcy.

"You gotta help me. I finally made a date with Stanton for dinner at Chez Pierre and have nothing to wear."

Marcy squealed with delight. "This is no happy hour special. We're doing it up big."

"I need something that's less frumpy than my usual wardrobe, but I don't want to look slutty," she warned Marcy.

"At our age slutty is a compliment." She let out a yelp of glee. "I'll call Deb. Leave it to us. You got the makings of a stunner. Gun the engine."

An hour later, the three women entered an expensive, trendy boutique dress store, House of Beauty. Celia had never dared enter before. She knew Marcy frequented the store without buying. She'd see the trend and head to a discount shop. Marcy called for the manager and with head held high struck a model's pose.

"Hello, madame, welcome back. Can I help you?" The manager spoke in a pleasant tone, but raised a skeptical eyebrow.

"This woman wants a dramatic but subtly sexy dress. With that fabulous body, she'll be a walking advertisement for House of Beauty for the … mature set." Marcy pointed to Celia's small waist and raised her mid-calf skirt to show her shapely legs. Celia pushed her hand away. Marcy put her hand under Celia's chin and tipped her face up. "See what I mean?"

Embarrassed, Celia glanced up at the huge glistening chandelier and the pale gray walls. Her feet sank into the thickest beige carpet she'd ever stepped upon.

"Indeed. I have some special dresses that will be perfect for her … excellent body type." The manager walked into the back and returned with garments draped over her arm.

Lord, I'm a body type? Celia viewed and refused a half dozen dresses she thought would barely cover her butt.

When the woman held up a knee-length, V-necked halter dress in fire engine red, Celia at first thought it was a lovely slip. The saleswoman tilted her head. "I sold one like this in another color to a young woman yesterday morning, but I think it's ageless for a woman with the right body type."

Marcy and Deb approved. "That's the one," Marcy said. "I can see it on you now."

Celia tried it on and thought it was beautiful but much too youthful—and rather expensive. Outside of the dressing room, she felt almost naked.

Her friends and the manager squealed and giggled.

"You look gorgeous!" Deb shouted.

Marcy tugged the neckline and pinched the material at her hip.

"You look like you were poured into this."

Celia blushed. "I don't know … I feel like I'm not wearing anything at all. It's too young."

"Aren't you always saying you don't want to act age appropriate?" Deb said. "Get the dress. Treat yourself."

Celia finally agreed to buy it. Despite how unlike her usual style it was, she agreed that dress was lovely and fit well. Marcy threw in a red thong and lacy bra, insisting on them over Celia's protests. Celia had to ask herself if she'd been living in a cave all these years.

When they left the store Celia said, "I can't believe I'm going to wear a dress that's barely a handkerchief. This is my first date in nearly forty years. Any advice?"

"With that dress, you don't have to say a word." Deb winked.

"Look at him adoringly and tell him he's brilliant," Marcy said. "Men like that best of all, maybe even more than sex."

Celia laughed. "Forget it. If I don't think he's that great, I'm not going to pretend."

"That's how my schmuck got roped in," Deb said.

Marcy rubbed her hands together. "Now let's beautify you so you'll look enchanting in the moonlight streaming through his bedroom window."

"I don't intend to hop into bed anytime soon." Celia was certain that if they ever got to that point it would be a fiasco.

"Never you mind. Let's get you a cut and color so we can get rid of that bun on your head," Marcy said, leading the way. "It looks like an old librarian did your hair."

Just as they turned a corner, Celia dropped her shopping bag. As she bent to pick it up, she saw a black Continental pull up in front of the dress shop. A pair of long legs with defined calf muscles stepped out as the chauffeur opened the door. The woman had a coiffed hairstyle and wore what looked like a Versace designer suit that Celia had seen in a fashion magazine and carried a Louis Vuitton handbag. With a start, Celia recognized her—Vanessa! Taking her friends by the elbows, she hustled them out of view, wondering how a struggling caregiver, hungry for work, had that kind of money—and a chauffeur to boot. Could that car be the one that followed her? Safely out of view, Celia straightened and pointed. "Vanessa just stepped out of that car looking awfully snazzy."

The women peeked around the corner, then at each other.

Marcy clicked her tongue. "It's obvious. Someone is keeping her. And then she acts like she needs money?" She clicked her tongue again.

"I wonder if that's the car I've been seeing," Celia said, still reeling. "I wonder …"

"Let's not think about that now. Right now you have more pressing things to worry about, like your hair." Marcy steered them towards the salon, and Celia tried to shake the image of the black car from her head.

Chapter 32

Allison

Looking around at the elegant, multi-chandeliered restaurant, Allison waited for Michael to return from the men's room. They had already decided on drinks and food. He had told her earlier in the day where they were going. Her eyes darted around, taking in the tall magenta ceilings and the walls papered in pale pink silk. On each table a vase held yellow, white, and red roses. The sizzle she felt around Michael in the office shot up several notches in this intimate, romantic setting. Her heart thudded hard. She was sure everyone in the place could hear it.

She admitted to working very hard, but this seemed over the top, and it really looked as though they were on a date. The office was a rumor mill, and though Vanessa said that Michael had a reputation as a serial dater, Allison figured he could temporarily fill the relentless loneliness that dogged her. She knew this wasn't the best reasoning and that dating her boss could blow up in her face. If things didn't work out, she could be out on the street looking for a new job before she knew it. Even so, she couldn't resist him.

Allison sat up straighter in her chair as she watched Michael approach from the men's room. Although he never bragged about his wealth, he gave the impression of someone who put giant companies together and merged billion-dollar firms every day. Yet he always treated all his employees with respect. When he gave orders, it was always with a please and thank you. If he barked a directive, he quickly apologized. She loved that about him.

Before taking his seat across from her, he brushed her bare shoulder with a finger. She swallowed hard at the exhilaration that charged through her. As he unbuttoned his jacket and adjusted his red silk tie, his eyes never wavered from her face. He took out his cell and shut it off. "That's it for tonight."

Allison held his gaze. His face had hard square contours with a high forehead, rounded cheekbones, a long slightly wide nose, and a full mouth. His forehead protruded over his deep-set, sky blue eyes, and a small bump on his nose made him look even more rugged and handsome.

His eyes often flickered as though his mind raced with thousands of details. But now, sitting across from her, his expression warmed, and his eyes stayed focused on her. She adjusted the halter strap on her low-cut black dress, trying to make the neckline a little less revealing.

He watched her with a mixture of teasing and desire. "Don't bother fussing with that dress. It looks more than fine."

Allison gave him an apologetic smile and they fell into an uneasy silence.

"Do you like living in Florida?" he finally asked.

"I love my job, in case you didn't notice, but Florida is a bit of a cultural wasteland. I know there are a few good museums and a couple of theaters that sell out fast. But good off-Broadway drama, excellent theater, music, and foreign movies ... it's like they barred everything at the border as dangerous to the environment."

He smiled. "I agree, but there are great things around that you have to dig for. Yeah, the roads are congested, and it is cement city with all the developments and strip malls, but I can show you more exotic and beautiful places." He dipped his head to look directly in her eyes. "Are you planning to stay in Florida?"

Allison looked around at the brass sconces that threw a soft light on the silk pastel walls, making them look edible. "I'm staying as long as your budget allows."

He raised an eyebrow. "We'll be on an even keel soon with the efficiencies you've put in place. Those budget cuts are beginning to work. Keeping your job is a given."

"Looks like I'm sticking around then."

"Tell me about yourself," Michael said, as the waiter brought them each a dirty vodka martini. "What were you like as a kid?"

Her stomach sank. This was not a subject she liked, but she figured his mother had her eccentricities, so she may as well go ahead. "I had an odd upbringing." He dipped his head toward her with unwavering eyes, encouraging her to go on.

"I love my mother, but she is a somewhat of a goofball. I think she's trying to act young in her old age." She sighed. "She suffered from depression and wasn't there for me when I needed her, and we don't relate well."

"On the flip side, my mother hovers over me like an FBI agent on a case," Michael complained.

"I don't know which is worse?" Allison forced a laugh.

The corners of Michael's mouth turned down. "Well, then again, she had to put up with a lot of my crap when I was a teenager. And underneath that brash exterior, she is a kind soul."

"Does your mother know you're not in high school anymore?"

"Don't think so." They both laughed. "On your résumé it said you took lots of sciences and got a nursing degree before you got your MBA in accounting. Tell me about that."

"I wanted to go to med school, but my dad's business was rocky and he couldn't afford it." She looked troubled. "I have to say my mom went to bat for me on that one, but my dad was adamant that I couldn't go. I met my husband, Thomas, after I finished my MBA." She glanced over Michael's shoulder. "He ended up cheating on me and stealing our savings." She shivered slightly. "It's still so raw."

"I've never been married." He looked at her intensely. "It sounds trite, but I never found the right person."

"Is there such a thing?"

"I hope so," Michael said. "My parents divorced when I was a teen and my dad wasn't around much, before or after the divorce. My mother is dying to get me married off and have grandkids. I sometimes see her car around our building."

Allison raised her eyebrows at him. "I'd freak out if my mother did that." She sipped her cocktail. "I know Deb tried to fix you up with Vanessa."

He smiled but his eyes darkened. "I pretended we were dating to get my mom off my back. A little while later I told her we broke up and that Vanessa and Brady are an item."

She looked askance. "I hope it works out for them."

A flicker of exasperation crossed his face. "He falls in love fast. And he has three divorces to prove it. Let's hope he gets it right with Vanessa."

"I've met your mother and Marcy, but I haven't gotten to know them," Allison said.

"They're pretty lively gals. My mom is a bit feisty." His mouth twisted in a wry grin. "For one, the three have had some battles with the community hotshots who torture them. Apparently they recently went to a pick-up bar for the Social Security set." He leaned forward and lowered his voice in a mocking tone. "Marcy's supposed to be a sexpot and apparently she gets around."

Allison choked on a sip of her drink and held her napkin to her mouth, coughing. "That'll never be my mother!"

"Hey, you never know. There are some pretty saucy seniors out there." He grinned.

She chuckled. "Maybe I ought to go on the prowl in nursing homes."

He waggled his eyebrows and twirled a non-existent moustache. "Maybe I can do something about upping the pace of your social life."

"Uh oh," she said.

"I can't believe I haven't told you that you look gorgeous," Michael said, reaching over. His hand hovered over hers, but then he drew away. "Oops. I could get sued for sexual harassment."

"Weren't we just discussing the new software for assignments?" she teased.

He laughed as the waiter set down their dinners—Chilean sea bass crusted in herbs and baked with a creamy wine sauce for Allison, and lamb chops for Michael.

Michael cut into a chop as she speared flakes of fish into her mouth. The delicious tastes of cream and sage coated her tongue.

He leaned forward, his lips curling playfully. "Think we might go out again?"

"Don't push it. We haven't even finished this date." The martini was making her bold.

"I've sworn never to date staff, but you're different. I can't resist you."

She broke away from his intense stare with great effort. "Dating you is risky. If we got even a little serious and broke up, I'd have to quit just as I was getting on my feet."

"Don't make any decisions now. Let me show you the sights. South Beach is fun and Coconut Grove is artsy. The Keys are gorgeous. Been to Key West yet?"

"No."

He looked appalled. "What? You haven't been to Key West to see Hemingway's home and the gathering at the harbor that happens at sunset." He cradled her hands in both of his. "I can't wait to take you."

Allison took a sharp breath, trying to still her nerves. "Okay, but we have to keep it uncomplicated and unserious. I mean really light."

"Romance light?"

"Yeah. Exactly." She didn't mean it, but hoped her face didn't give her away.

He smiled as he sat back and eyed her as though considering his next statement with care. "I'll go out on a limb. I've fantasized about seeing you sitting across from me like this ever since you arrived."

She'd never had trouble finding the right words. Now sentences formed in her head but she couldn't get them past her lips. She loudly cleared her throat. "Well, I knew from the get-go that this was a date. It didn't stop me, did it?"

The laugh lines around his mouth deepened with his grin.

Allison paused. "I have to say my romantic chemistry has always led me astray."

"Let's not overthink this. We'll go with the flow."

They finished the meal, and she folded her hands to keep from touching him. Glancing away to avoid the intensity in his eyes, she saw a sight that startled her. She watched a slim, petite woman, wearing a red low-cut dress, glide across the room. The dress was a duplicate of her black one. She slumped in her chair. The glamorous woman was her mother! The silk material clung to her mother's narrow hips, accenting her small waist and full breasts. A fit, good-looking white-haired man walked behind her.

"Oh my God." Allison slid her chair over until Michael's body blocked the view. "It's my mother out on a date."

Michael followed the direction of Allison's eyes. "She sure looks beautiful. I'd ask her out," he teased.

"Not funny. I don't want her to see me."

Celia and the man sat at a table across the room, her mother's back to Allison. Most days her mother wore little makeup and tied her long hair into a bun. Now her chestnut locks brushed her shoulders in smooth waves. *Chestnut?*

"Can we get out of here? I hate seeing her like this. She should still be grieving for my father."

"Hey, my mother told me it's been three years. Give her a break," he snapped. "Do we really need to leave now?"

Annoyed at the sound of irritation in his voice, she insisted, "Yes, now."

Michael called for the check and paid. The only way out forced Allison to walk near her mother's table. As she hustled to leave, she turned her head away from the table as they passed.

"Allie, is that you?" Celia stood and put her arms out. "I didn't expect to see you here."

Allison forced herself to turn around and hug her mother. "I didn't expect to see you here either, Mother," she almost growled.

"Nice dress. A little short for you though, don't you think?" she whispered in her mother's ear.

Celia took a step back as though struck. Jerkily she turned to the man, who stood. "This is Stanton, my old college friend. He lives in Florida now."

Allison nodded. "Nice meeting you." She turned to leave, but Michael stopped her and stepped out where Celia could see him. She looked shocked.

"How are you, Celia?" Michael asked. "You look lovely. It's good seeing you again."

"I'm … I'm just fine. Uh, join us for a drink?" Celia's face flushed.

"Thank you, but we were just leaving. Got to be up early in the morning." Michael forced a laugh, then reached out and shook Stanton's hand. "Nice meeting you." He turned to Celia. "A pleasure to see you, Celia. Don't let us keep you from your dinner."

Celia stood there, looking stunned as they walked away.

They slipped out the front door and waited for the valet to bring Michael's car. "Are you okay?" he asked Allison softly.

"I think so. My mom looks better than I do." She gave him a crooked smile.

He stood back and scrutinized her from head to toe. "She looked lovely, but it's not possible she looked better than you."

"She looked so, so … stylish."

"She needs a life." He chided her gently, like a child.

"Please. I know, but I can't get used to the route she's gone."

He held up his hands in a surrendering gesture. "Change is inevitable."

Her fists, balled up tight since leaving the restaurant, were numb.

She uncurled them and shook them out, wanting to lean her head against his shoulder but resisting.

The attendant opened the passenger door of Michael's late-model dark green Jaguar for Allison. Michael gave him a ten-dollar bill, and the guy beamed.

Michael slid into the driver's seat. "I've been itching to take a long drive along the coast for weeks. Would you like to do that now? I think you could use the fresh air."

Her insides squeezed. She didn't trust herself in her current mood. Seeing her mother out with another man had made her miss her father so much. He always knew what to do in a crisis. Finally she said, "Can I take a rain check? I'm apartment hunting tomorrow."

"No problem, as long as the rain check is for next Saturday night."

Allison felt her shoulders relax slightly out of their tight position. "Sounds good."

Chapter 33

Celia

"That was awkward," Celia said to Stanton. "I bump into my daughter on a date with her boss while I'm on a date wearing the same dress. She'll say I'm inappropriate."

"Don't be ridiculous. You're the most beautiful woman here. Never mind age."

"She's not over the death of her father," Celia fretted. "Seeing me with you must have upset her."

"She'll get there and appreciate how much you love her. Relax and try to enjoy our evening."

"You're right," Celia said, smoothing her napkin back over her lap. Unexpectedly encountering her daughter made her think of the cha-cha rule: DON'T BE AFRAID OF RESISTANCE. IT OPENS NEW HORIZONS. *That's the way to go, but it sure isn't easy.*

Stanton studied the wine list and mentioned ordering a Château Grand Moulin wine. He turned and gave Celia an approving gaze.

Although she enjoyed the look on his face, she fidgeted in her chair and traced her finger over the design carved on the thick handle of her sterling silver fork. She thought he looked so handsome in a navy blazer and gray slacks. "That wine sounds so elegant. I'm used to ten-dollar bottles of Chardonnay."

"I don't have a sophisticated palate, but I Googled it, trying to impress you." His tone grew more serious, almost sheepish. "You were always a beauty, but …" he squinted at her, "well, how should I say it … you've grown into your beauty with grace, is what I mean."

Celia blushed. "That's poetic. I've become a graceful old lady."

He cocked his head and seemed to study her. "You look sad."

"I am a bit. Maybe just confused. Do you mind if we skip dinner here and take a walk? We're so close to the ocean."

"Does that mean the engagement is off?" He grimaced.

"Yes, for at least twenty years. We'll go to the same nursing home and get engaged there."

He signaled to the waiter and apologized. He said Celia didn't feel well and they had to leave.

They left the restaurant, walked two blocks to the beach, and Celia removed her shoes and carried them as she stepped on the sand. "Oh, the sand is still warm. My feet hurt from those heels. Ahh, this feels so good."

Stanton did the same and they walked down to the water's edge. The half-moon lit up segments of high waves foaming at the top and then crashing into the vast sea. A fickle moon lit up new waves, replacing those that disappeared. So many stars appeared and melted into each other like a creamy dessert. The warm, packed sand caressed her feet, sending comforting hints to her spine to relax, like the sizzling signals her body received to dance with joy to Latin music. They walked without speaking. Then Stanton took her hand. She liked the feel of his leathery skin against her palm.

Celia stopped, dug her toes into the wet, hard sand, and said, "Remember how we found the least expensive bottles of wine when we were young? I was such a cheap date." She wanted to bite her tongue. Drinking vinegary wine in her dorm room while soup heated on a hot plate was a memory that twanged in her mind like soft musical passages fingered on a harp.

"It's unbelievable that we're here, huh?" He caught her eye and grinned.

"Yes, it is." She glanced at his incredulous expression and felt in the moment as ocean breezes caressed her cheeks. No yesterday and no tomorrow. Only now.

"Celia, over the years, I thought about getting in touch with you, just as an old friend, but I worried about how you would react. And your husband."

Stanton mentioning Gabe made it feel like her husband's ghost had pulled up right alongside her. *Go away, you hypocritical old lecher.* "You sensed right. He'd probably say that it's improper to get phone calls from an old boyfriend."

"I'm prying into your private life again. I apologize."

"It's all right." She took a deep breath, let it out slowly, then forced a crooked smile and continued walking.

"Ada ..." he started.

She remembered another cha-cha rule—DON'T DROWN IN THE PAST. STAY IN THE MOMENT—and interrupted him. "No more talking about the past."

Stanton paused thoughtfully. "Tell me about pottery class."

"Ha. I made what might resemble a vase, but I know I can do more."

"I recall you were upset with the pottery wheel back in college."

"Yup. But no collapses this time. I can wind up making Picasso-like plates that will sell for a million dollars." She laughed.

"I'll be your agent for fifteen percent." He puckered his lips. "Did I hurt your artistic sensibilities, talking about commerce?"

"Not at all. Artists have a right to make money, and smart ones know the power of promoting their work. Or, as they say now, branding."

They swayed their hands back and forth as they trailed along. Celia felt like a kid again.

"What else are you up to besides pottery?"

She deeply inhaled the brininess of the ocean, heard the waves crash as tension eased out of her body. "Some tennis." Light-headed, Celia skipped along. Stanton laughed and tried to follow, but he mostly hopped.

Her head felt soothed and buoyant as though her body rode the waves without a care in the world.

Stanton looked at her expectantly. "Tell me more."

"I spend lots of time with my two dearest friends, Marcy and Deb. We come from different backgrounds, but accept each other as we are. We enjoy theater, art museums, and even a happy hour now and again." Warmth flooded her. "They're like family."

"I'd like to be a fly on that wall." Stanton raised his eyebrows playfully.

Celia gave him a sideways glance. "You'd be bored for most of it." *Except when we're moving dead bodies and smoking pot.* Her silky dress, damp from the humidity, clung to her body. "What about you?"

"Mostly I do computer forensics and information security."

"Computer forensics? What's that?"

"I don't want to sound like a geek even if I am one. It's like a detective uncovering different layers of information contained in computers. I gather and preserve evidence from computers for investigation and analysis. Government and police authorities need it and it's vital for many court cases. Sometimes it's tedious, but it's good when you find what you're looking for." Stanton took off his jacket and slung it over his shoulder. They walked slowly now.

"Is that similar to hackers? I've heard hackers teach government agencies how to do what they did illegally and end up getting well paid, with our tax dollars to boot."

Stanton's deep belly laugh filled the space between them, enveloping her. "You got it right. I'm one of the few who never went to jail."

"Are you retired?"

"I still do consults, but pick and choose only the most interesting jobs." His lowered his head. "Sometimes I feel guilty about enjoying things without Ada."

"Ada would probably want you to go on with your life and do something new."

He grinned, deepening his laugh lines as the moon outlined his face with its bluish light. "You're kinda new." He seemed to study her face. "I decided that I like this new you."

"Too bad if you didn't." Celia pressed her forearm to his as she suggested they return. She imagined time passing between them like pages in a book, each page turning as they spoke, bringing them to the present moment. A craving for him ignited in her, and she cursed herself for her desire.

"Being here has a surreal quality to it," Celia said. "We're like subjects in a Dali painting. I feel like his melting clock." She brushed her finger along the soft cotton of his shirt. *Say it.* Celia peered at him. "I think there's a new, stable dimension to you now. You used to be all over the map in college."

"Wow! Are you really giving me a compliment?" He raised his fist triumphantly and hopped in place, kicking up sand. "If I heard right, it's the first one since we met here in Florida."

"It might be the last." *Especially if you turn out to be a player.*

Stanton pretended to take a knife out of his chest. "Ouch. That hurt."

"I'm just wary. I don't want to be disappointed again."

"I'm not going to defend myself." His words held a hint of annoyance. "What happened to the new assertive Celia who's willing to take risks?"

"Depends on how risky." She flipped her hair back.

"I think the new you says we're in the last roundup and can't waste time with outdated standards." His grin beamed stronger than the moon. "Celia. I'm interested in everything about you. Your mind and opinions and activities and … you." He ran his finger gently up her forearm.

At his touch, her whole body grew warm, and the air between them shimmied with heat.

"Can we get some of what we once had back?" he asked softly.

His words knocked the breath out of her. "I'm … I'm not sure."

He lifted her arm and kissed the crook of her elbow. His firm lips jolted her. "Still butter soft."

Celia's quick shallow breathing left her struggling for air. She tugged her arm away. "Stanton, I'm not ready for this kind of intimacy now. I need to straighten things out in my mind."

He grimaced and walked along, slumping his shoulders forward. "Yeow."

Celia looked up at the sky

"Do you think I'm inept?" he asked.

Celia smiled. "You're a friend of Edith's. Need I say more?" She instantly regretted her words.

"That's not fair," he said with a steel edge. "Why can't you let it go?"

"It's scary that you'd befriend a woman like that." They had almost reached the main road. Celia quickened her steps.

"You're being ridiculous."

"Is it ridiculous that you dumped me when we had such a great thing going?"

He squeezed his eyes shut. "You've got to drop all this shit about the past. It's useless."

No one is telling me what to do ever again. "I've had enough of men not taking responsibility for their behavior—you, my husband, Allie's ex."

He narrowed his eyes. "I just wanted to have a nice time with you."

"Well, the real world has a way of creeping in. We didn't start with a clean slate."

"Why not? I'm willing to."

"You weren't the one who was devastated."

"I had plenty of hard times. My marriage was a mistake, we never had kids. I spent a lot of time floundering careerwise and ended up with a sick wife. You're not the only one whose life kicked their butt. Now will you drop it?"

"The only thing I'll drop is you. Don't worry. I'll get a taxi." Celia hurried off the beach, her vision blurred by tears. She waved at a passing cab. Stanton ran behind her but stopped and turned away.

What just happened? Things were going great and then bam. I faced my past and that unleashed a deluge of anger. In a flash, it occurred to her that the decades-old pain at being dumped by the man she loved always reared its ugly head. She was certain she'd never hear from him again. It ended before it began.

Celia was still upset as the cab drove through the gates of her development, and when she noticed a black Lincoln Continental sedan, her heart banged in her chest. It looked like the same car she was sure had been following her. She tried to calm down, reminding herself that many of her fellow residents used these hired cars to get around instead of taxis. *It's just a coincidence—right?*

As they came into full view of the car, Celia asked her driver to slow down. To her surprise, Vanessa stepped out of the passenger side and a woman she didn't recognize followed. Vanessa hitched up a large backpack, looked behind her, and walked up a lane leading to a building she realized Marcy lived in. Melvin had lived there too.

The cab made a sharp turn around the corner and Celia lost sight of them. After she paid the driver, she snuck back to get another look, but the black car was gone. Her knees felt shaky. What was in the backpack? Who was the other woman? She went toward the elevator to see if they were still around but saw no trace of them. She wanted to call Marcy, both about seeing Vanessa and to get some consolation after her terrible date, but it was already so late. She went home, not bothering to check if Allison was home, threw herself on her bed dry-eyed, and stared at the ceiling, her stomach clenched.

Chapter 34

Allison

Allison arrived forty-five minutes late to her first office party, which was celebrating the retirement of a senior vice president. Gatherings with higher-ups were held in better-furnished, renovated rooms, but this was taking place in the cavernous, dingy basement. Despite their budget crunch, Brady requested that they hold parties often to encourage good office morale.

It was a lovely evening with a cool breeze, and she wanted to be outside. She girded herself. It tired her brain to make small talk, ask about spouses, listen to cutesy stories about kids, and look at pictures.

But everything seemed to be falling into place workwise. Michael seemed to have forgotten the nasty little scene she'd created at Chez Pierre. Thomas agreed to settle the divorce, and with her salary above the going rate, she'd signed a lease just that morning for a spacious apartment in a nice building with a doorman. She had a beautiful view of the rising sun and a brush stroke of ocean. Even better, she was out of her mother's place at last.

She swept past tables scattered with empty beer bottles and paper plates heaped with chicken wing bones and pizza crusts. Three middle management guys who ogled her when she went to the galley kitchen now waved politely. They always teased her about how she needed to smile to brighten their dull surroundings. Slipping past them, she saw Vanessa navigating through the crowd and felt relief. She hurried over to her, watching as she introduced field workers and caregivers to office staff, greeting them all warmly and hugging a few. She sure knew how to work a crowd. Allison thought she should be a social director.

Vanessa beamed when she spotted Allison and introduced her to the two people standing closest to her. "Allison, meet Barbara Shuster, head of pharmacy in our mail-in division. And this is Wayne Showder, assistant head of pharmacy. I consult with them for meds for my patients. They're wonderful, always going beyond the call of duty. Barbara even made an emergency home call with me last night when a patient mixed up her meds and didn't know what to take."

"I'm impressed." Allison gave her warmest smile and once again thought how Vanessa enchanted people she might need. She envied her friend's easy social graces and smarts.

Wayne began passing around baby pictures when Allison saw Brady and Michael, both tieless and in shirtsleeves, circulating through the crowd, shaking hands and greeting employees. Brady, a big bear of a man with a commanding presence, had a flushed, beefy face. Tiers of flesh pressed against his expensive, custom-made sparkling white shirt with his initials on the cuffs. His laugh rang with forced jolliness, reminiscent of a mall Santa Claus. Allison knew that Michael did most of Brady's job while the CEO got all the credit. On a rare occasion, Michael issued a clenched-teeth complaint, but accepted the situation for the most part.

When Brady and Michael approached them, Allison sensed a playful jumpiness in Vanessa, like a little kid testing out a trampoline.

Brady cleared his throat. "Vanessa gets excellent reports from the field supervisor on her caregiving and her classes got off to a great start. Now," he cleared his throat. "The classes, uh, CPR?" He glanced at Vanessa who affirmed with a tiny nod. "There's a break coming up for a couple of months and she'd liked to continue coming in-house." His eyes skirted Allison and came to rest on Vanessa. "She wants to work with her good friend … you, Allison."

With every bit of strength, Allison kept her head from snapping back.

"Nah. You just wanted to keep me in-house, silly," Vanessa cooed. Her piercing green eyes focused on Brady.

Michael's mouth lifted the tiniest bit in a skittish smile. The hairs on the back of Allison's neck stood up.

"You're overworked, Allison. Vanessa can assist you in the office." Brady brushed Vanessa's bare upper arm with a finger as she stared up at him worshipfully. "She'll be a great asset to you, Allison," Brady went on, never looking away from Vanessa's face. "You know, she has some accounting experience."

Allison gave a stiff smile. She didn't blame Vanessa, who gave her a guilt-tinged sweet grimace, for using her connections to move up the ladder, but why hadn't anyone told her? Allison glanced at the bar, craving a slug of vodka.

Michael gave a lame grin. "You'll just bring her up to speed. She really wants to work with you."

Among all her other tasks, she had to prepare for a major auditing because of the past embezzlement. And now this. *Damn you, Michael, you owed me a head's up.*

Brady had saved Michael's butt over the embezzlement when the board of directors complained Michael should have been more attentive. Since then Michael had a strong sense of loyalty to Brady.

But Allison knew that spotting embezzlers involved heavy-duty forensic accounting. She'd spent a good bit of time delving into the figures he'd given her and had some information for him.

Vanessa leaned her body ever so slightly against Brady.

"Vanessa can do long division in her head. You should see her in the boutiques, calculating prices." Brady guffawed and patted Vanessa's arm. "We have a potential contract with Blue Cross Blue Shield and she's helped analyze the profit margin, so make use of her skills."

I'm sure those weren't the skills you concentrated on, Mr. Shirkson. The contract numbers should have been run by me.

Vanessa gave a slightly uncomfortable toothy smile, like a model in a toothpaste ad. "It'll be such fun to work with Allison. I admire you so much."

Allison turned to Vanessa. "And I'm happy to have you on board, Vanessa." The tightness in her throat made her voice hoarse.

"Let's circulate now," Brady said, guiding Vanessa with his arm under her elbow. Though Brady had a folksy attitude with staff, the crowd quieted and parted as they passed.

Michael gave an apologetic shrug and said in a strained voice, "Brady's decision, not mine. He asked me to keep it quiet until he made the announcement."

"Hold up, Michael." Allison spoke in a flat, soft voice, keeping a neutral expression so that no one saw her anger. "I admire Vanessa, but I don't have the time to train anyone. It's not fair that I'm being railroaded."

Michael splayed his hands helplessly in front of him. "Brady's smitten. He's thinking with his you-know-what. I'm totally uninvolved in this one. Sorry."

"I don't want bad feelings. Now there's tension because no one told me."

"If she's not working out, I'll talk to Brady." He scanned the room. "Got to circulate."

Allison walked to the bar and ordered a vodka on the rocks.

"Hi, boss." Vanessa sidled up to Allison, grimacing. "I take it by your expression that no one told you. I apologize. I left it up to them."

Allison thought Vanessa seemed sincere. "Good thing you're my friend. I'm a little miffed."

"Whatever you want me to do, consider it done. You'll never have to tell me a second time. I'll only be part time and I'm a quick study."

I hope so. "I know you're one hell of a bright woman." Allison took a long sip of her drink, positive that Vanessa had her sights set on becoming Brady's fourth wife. Vanessa wore a short strapless hot pink dress. Her outfit, showing off her long legs and full cleavage, seemed more appropriate for making a grand entrance at an upscale nightclub.

"Will you stop in-home caregiving?"

Vanessa pouted. "I'm still going to have patients. Don't want to give that up." She shrugged. "Maybe Brady didn't do me a favor with all that work." Vanessa raised her eyebrows. "Just kidding. I'm getting a much-needed big raise."

"After I show you the ropes you might not like it."

Vanessa gave Allison's cheek a light pinch. "I'll never be as good as you. Look how you got good contracts for maintenance, electricians, and all that waste cutting. I want to move up, but never over your head."

Allison felt a tad calmer. "Approach the new job like you did working with patients and you'll be fine. Brady can spot talent."

Vanessa sipped her wine. "I have to say, I'm falling in love with Brady."

"Wow. Great." *Is she telling the truth?*

"And here's something else you need to know." She bumped Allison's hip with her own. "Michael is falling hard for you. And don't ask how I know, but I do." She gave a firm nod.

It felt like Vanessa shot an arrow into her fluttering heart. Did Michael confide in Vanessa?

"Look, let's get out of here. I've got a yen for cosmos and the best ones are down the street at Bar 33. I'm going to say goodbye to Brady. Meet in fifteen?"

The room now smelled of beer and sweat, and Allison's head was still reeling from the surprise dumped on her. "You're on."

Allison saw Michael nearby, grinning at her. He must have noticed the girl talk. After giving Michael the slightest nod, he mouthed, "Saturday night?" She motioned for him to call with her thumb at her ear and pinkie at the corner of her lips. Allison began to think Vanessa's cavalier approach to dating had merit.

A ruckus erupted near one of the exits. A man stood at the threshold of the door and screamed into the room, "You're all God damned liars! Liars, you hear me? Crooks! You'll be sorry!" The room went quiet as everyone turned to stare. Michael sprang into a run after the man as he fled out the door. Brady pulled out his cell and dialed 911.

"What's going on? Is Michael all right?" Allison pressed her fist to her mouth.

Brady had gone pale. "That's the husband of the woman who

embezzled. Yes, hello, we need the police here," he said into his phone, turning away to give the address to the dispatcher.

Allison was stunned. Why had Michael endangered himself by chasing him? She ran to the door but the corridor was empty. *Oh my God.*

Michael and Brady huddled with a police officer who jotted notes as two other cops spoke to witnesses. The man, Richard Hartner, had gotten away.

Michael broke away from the officer and told Allison he and Brady had to go to the station to bring a restraining order against Hartner and file more reports. He told her he'd see her tomorrow.

After assuring herself that he was fine, Allison finally headed out of the building with Vanessa. They headed for Bar 33, where they sank into padded bar seats and quickly ordered cosmos. The lights were dim, which helped soothe Allison's headache.

"What the hell is going on with that nutcase?" Allison asked.

"The kook insists he's innocent. He probably helped his wife embezzle and is furious he might be indicted, too. There's an ongoing investigation. He's guilty as sin."

"I'm thankful Michael came back in one piece." Allison shuddered. "I saw the embezzlement numbers. Got to say, it was clever of her, or them."

"Oh, what did you find?"

Allison shifted in her seat. "Can't say till I talk to Michael. Sorry." She drummed her fingers on the base of her glass.

"Brady said the scam happened under everyone's nose. That's why he didn't let Michael take the fall." Vanessa took a long sip of her drink and looked up at the ceiling, eyes wide open. "Ahh, this is much better than that watered-down office vodka."

The cranberry juice in the lemony vodka cocktail puckered her tongue. "These drinks are great." Allison ran her hand over the supple brown leather edge of the bar and inhaled the aromatic alcohol that infused the air with an astringent scent. The drink soothed her frazzled nerves.

"Well, you should get a good night's rest in your new apartment. Can't wait to see it."

"It's really nice. My mother seemed unhappy, but I think deep down she liked my moving out. After all, I did tear into her place like a tornado." Allison took a few more sips.

Vanessa ordered two more drinks but Allison shook her head. "No more for me."

"Don't worry. Brady left his limo for us down the street and is paying the tab so drink up, kiddo. Don't worry about your car. He'll send the limo to pick you up in the morning."

"Pays to be pals with the CEO," Allison said.

The bartender gave Vanessa a sly wink when he delivered the drinks. Allison sipped the extra strong drink with caution while Vanessa gulped it.

"Slow down, these are strong," Allison cautioned.

"Sometimes I worry I might turn into a drunk like my dad. Most times he was a nice drunk but every so often … watch out. Good thing he wasn't around much."

Allison felt her forehead prickle. "Oh, I'm sorry."

"I left home at seventeen and never went back, not even when he died recently. Couldn't get away fast enough from that scuzzy neighborhood."

"God, it must have been awful. You raised yourself." Allison gave her a sad glance.

"Worse, after my mom died, a couple of guys who knew a twelve-year-old was home alone most of the time dropped by—a lot." Vanessa's lips trembled. "Need I say more?"

Allison shook her head, feeling sick to her stomach. "Goddamn bastards. But you climbed out of that. Amazing."

Vanessa put her hand over her eyes. "I got straight A's in high school and got a college scholarship. I took mostly accounting classes and enjoyed them but I needed to work to live. So my grades dropped and I lost the scholarship after two years." A silence fell over them.

Accounting? Allison stayed silent so Vanessa could choose to continue or not.

"I got lucky and found an entry-level job as a junior accountant that had some teeth. They wanted me to move up, and said they'd pay for me to finish college."

Again, Vanessa seemed to swallow her words as they touched her lips, and Allison sensed something deeper was coming.

"On the way up the ladder ..." Vanessa twiddled the stem of her empty glass then ordered a third round, which Allison refused. She'd hardly touched the second one.

Vanessa's face collapsed and Allison said, "Stop if it's too painful."

Vanessa's body swayed. "It's great to talk to a girlfriend you trust. So, this bad guy came into my life ..." She stopped. "So stupid ... he drained me of ... everything ..."

Allison gently put her hand on Vanessa's forearm. "I had a sheltered life and look where it got me. A husband who cheated and robbed me blind." A freeing sensation opened up Allison's chest. It felt good to talk to Vanessa.

Dry-eyed, Vanessa gave a harsh laugh. "Sister, I got you beat when you talk about vulnerable. I was gaga over this guy. I'd do anything he asked. That was my downfall and why I got waylaid." She twiddled her fingers in the air like walking down stairs.

Allison girded for what could be worse.

"He was the accounting supervisor. I was twenty and he was eight years older. He talked about marrying, kids, you know, the good life. Right?" Vanessa gave a dismissive flick of her wrist. "Wrong. We spent foolishly and got up to our necks in debt. He showed me how to steal company money and said that by the time they found out we'd be far away." Her words slurred.

"Oh shit. I'm so sorry." Allison clutched Vanessa's upper arm to keep her from tipping in the seat.

"Yup, I got caught, and the bastard took off leaving me, as they say, holding the bag. I spent three years in Allenwood Prison, not Spain. I lied. I knew I needed a trade because no one would hire me for accounting jobs, so I took up caregiving." Her lips trembled again. "Brady is the only person who would give me another shot at peeking at numbers."

Allison swallowed hard, her eyes blurred with tears. "You don't have to tell me more."

Vanessa put both elbows on the bar and rested her chin in her palms. "I'm sorry I wasn't straight with you, boss, but it's hard to tell anyone I was a felon." She lifted her sagging head.

"I admire you. Hell. I'd have slipped into the gutter if it happened to me." *How easily we needy women are influenced by men.* "But how did you get licensed with a felony?"

"I was able to file petitions to get my records sealed after five years. It was a bitch, but the prosecutor didn't object because … um, first offense, age, and mitigr ... oops, mitigating circumstances. Then a terrific pro bono lawyer convinced the court to seal the records, and I don't have to say I have a prison record." She hiccupped. "But records can be unsealed if I have another offense. That will never happen." Vanessa thumped her hand over her heart.

"I hope you and Brady work out."

Vanessa raised her head and flipped her hair back. "Pretty lucky. He's a great guy. I told Brady and Michael about prison," she chirped. "I kinda played down the charges." She grinned and suddenly looked frightened. "Oh, you can't tell anyone else."

"Never." She helped Vanessa off the seat. She had underestimated this valiant woman. No doubt she deserved another chance. "Let's go." Allison felt unsteady herself and forced herself to walk slowly.

They stepped out into a hot vacuum of humidity, somewhat unseasonable for winter. Allison waved to the chauffeur leaning against the limo. Vanessa's head wobbled and her knees buckled as the chauffeur put Vanessa's other arm around his shoulder.

Vanessa slumped into the back seat of the limo, her eyes closed. Allison cried in silence for both of them.

Chapter 35

Celia

"I've been reading up on how to be charming," Stanton said to Celia. They sat together at Tato's, an upscale restaurant. He cut into his steak.

Celia pierced her fork into a tender scallop and swished it around the miso-ginger sauce. "So, where's the charm?" she teased.

The evening at the beach had been disconcerting for both of them. Their walk along the ocean surf had been pleasant until she freaked out, the world crashing into dust around her feet. After he called to apologize, she regretted taking it out on him, but he wasn't a total innocent.

He'd waited five days to call her. When he did he had said, "I've been thinking long and hard. What a jerk I was to you after college. There are no excuses for my behavior. I was simply a selfish narcissist."

Celia thought him brave to admit his mistake, but she knew she harbored some bad emotions still. She'd accepted his date with caution, open to giving him a second chance.

He raised an eyebrow at her as he chewed. "I've been charming! Didn't you notice I opened the passenger door for you when I picked you up?"

"Too easy. What other tricks did you learn?"

He stuck his lower lip out and pretended to sulk.

She ate her scallops, enjoying the taste of the ginger on her tongue. "You've got to go deeper to impress me. Bah to chivalrous gestures." She pointed to his chest. "In there is where it counts. So what other self-improvements have you made?"

He snapped his fingers. "I've been practicing the cha-cha."

She laughed. "Now you're on track."

"I feel the rhythm through my body. It makes me happy, and I feel young again." He raised his arms above his head and pretended to play castanets.

Celia laughed. "Wow. You get it."

"I'm getting hotter, huh?"

"I wouldn't say hotter, but you've moved up a notch."

"Harumph."

He looks so earnest. Tell him. What harm would it do? "Listen, I have a confession to make." He looked at her expectantly as she took a breath. "I knew you lived next to Boca Pelicano Palms before I moved."

His eyes opened wide. "What? Really? Why didn't you contact me?"

She sat back and took a sip of wine, forcing herself not to squirm. *Why did I say that?*

He looked petulant. "Celia, am I a disappointment?"

She put her elbow on the table and rested her cheek in her hand. "No. I mean, well, part of you is the good old Stanton, but the other part I don't know yet."

He turned his face to show his profile and raised his shoulders like a Shakespearian actor. "Now?"

"A bit more intriguing."

"I'm too pushy, right?"

Celia took a deep breath and nearly forgot to exhale. "I'm not the same person."

Stanton smiled. "So you have a few wrinkles. I have an arthritic back and I've lost two inches."

Despite herself, Celia giggled like a silly schoolgirl and slid down in her seat.

Stanton flushed. "Oh my God. I mean in height."

"That's what I thought you meant. Just pulling your chain."

He reached out and held her hand. Her insides liquefied at his gentle touch. "If you stick with me, you'll see real change ... trust me."

She realized that Gabe's rejection of her had cramped her heart inside a tiny cage that kept most people out, even her daughter. Once again she thought of a cha-cha rule: IT IS DANGEROUS TO FEAR RISK. WE MAY NEVER KNOW JOY.

It was time for her to take a risk so she could know joy—maybe if only to capture a fragment of what they once shared. "Call the waiter," Celia said, her voice quavering slightly. "Tell him we have a party to go to, and we have to leave now."

He looked confused. "Where's the party?"

She looked him straight in the eye. "Your place."

Stanton's hand shot in the air, calling for the waiter.

As soon as he paid the bill, they hurried outside to the car. Celia and Stanton both reached for the door handle on the passenger side to open it. He gripped her hand and held it tight against his chest. She returned the pressure for a moment then jumped into the seat.

"If you're planning on seducing me," Stanton said, driving at a fast clip, "you'll get no resistance."

Her clammy hands gripped the edge of the seat. She smiled but heard her heart hammering in her ears as if the car were an echo chamber. Would he compare her older body to the firm, smooth one of a bygone era? She hoped her new underwear might divert his attention from her wrinkles. *I'm going to bed with a forty-year-old fantasy. Can this end well?*

The five-story stucco buildings, streets, and landscaping of Stanton's development were nearly similar to those along Pelican Way. She noticed subtle differences like greener, more manicured foliage and inside corridors carpeted with Berber. The beige walls seemed freshly painted.

Stanton foraged in his pockets and came up empty handed. "I forgot my keys, I was so excited about tonight," he said, tapping his forehead. "I can picture them on the kitchen counter. But never fear!" He reached into his pants pocket and pulled out his credit card. He jiggled it in the doorjamb for a few seconds until there was a click and the door opened. "Locks around here are flimsy. We depend on security at the gate to keep strangers out."

"My place too," Celia said, looking around approvingly at Stanton's solid black leather furniture, chrome bookcases, and slim, unadorned floor lamps. Compared to all the pastel chintz sofas, wicker furniture, and seashell lamps, this looked more like Manhattan digs than a Florida retirement community. The strong masculine room pleased her.

Celia kicked off her stiletto heels and sat down, massaging her feet. "These heels are the worst for old feet."

"Let me help you," he said, and to her surprise, he kneeled on the floor and took one foot in his hand, massaging tentatively at first, then kneading and pressing more deeply.

Celia closed her eyes, the sensation—both relaxing and erotic—sending electric shocks to the pit of her stomach. She wanted to run her hands through his hair. "Thank you. That felt wonderful."

Stanton crossed to the stereo cabinet and rummaged through a handful of CDs. "I've got lots of tunes here we used to enjoy," he said, passing her the discs. The Monkees, Marvin Gaye, and The Beatles.

"Play this track," she said, tapping a case with her finger, and a moment later, the opening notes of "With a Little Help From My Friends" filled the room.

"How about a dance, Ms. Celia?" He held out his hand.

"I'm barefoot." *Oh God, I'll have two left feet.*

Stanton took his shoes off. "So am I. I'm not as smooth. My balance can be off. We'll go slow."

Stepping into Stanton's outstretched arms, she recalled hearing the song long ago in a dilapidated motel room that Stanton had sprayed with his aftershave cologne to cover the musty smell. He'd transformed the ratty room by hanging red, white, and blue balloons all over.

Now he ran his hand down her back. She tensed.

"Sorry, it's just that your body feels exactly the same as I recall." He stepped back, holding her arms and looking into her eyes.

She chided herself to not resist. *Give in to the moment.* She relaxed and snuggled against him. She sang along and giggled in the midst of the line. "In fact, I get a lot of help from my friends." Her body tingled from the allure of dancing and she floated around the room, dancing on the balls of her feet and feeling light as air.

"My thanks to your friends." He tightened his arm around her waist and did some whirls. Celia followed and thought they fit together perfectly. When he did an old-fashioned dip, his fingers touched the back of her neck and he kissed the base of her throat. Celia's body turned molten and she wrapped her arms around his shoulders as he whipped her upright and they stood facing each other, still holding on tight.

"You're a good dancer," she said in a hoarse whisper. Caught between wanting him and anxious about the next possible step, she decided to change the pace. "And now for a cha-cha."

He gave a resigned shrug. "I warn you I'm still a klutz."

"I told you, cha-cha turns people into good friends and they dance on clouds." She found a CD by the Buena Vista Social Club and put it on. As the music thumped rhythmically, she recalled their attempt at cha-cha in college. "I remember when we first tried this."

He squeezed his eyes shut. "Tonight is better—special."

DON'T BE AFRAID OF RESISTANCE. IT OPENS NEW HORIZONS. She repeated the rule aloud, and he looked at her quizzically. "Follow me," she said. Holding each of his hands in hers, she moved at a slow pace, leading him through the basics. When he got the rhythm, they went faster. He placed his hands on her hips, stared into her eyes, and they moved as one. She made up another rule of her own: *Make a safe place and trust. One night might be all there is. Trust him for tonight.* In a happy place, she realized the rules provoked her to think.

When they stopped, Stanton stepped back and exaggeratedly wiped his brow. "Whew! I'm worn out."

"Me too." They plopped on his sofa.

"You're fun. You know that?"

"Glad you appreciate me. As well you should," she teased.

"I love being with you now as much as I did back then. More maybe."

She outlined his lips with her fingertip. He kissed her softly and then again, each kiss lingering longer than the last. She pressed against him. The trembling in his body kept in time with hers. "I feel like a scared virgin," she admitted.

"Me too. That would make us the oldest virgins anywhere," he said.

She chuckled, then gave him an exaggerated sultry look. Laughing, Stanton led Celia toward the open bedroom door, and, at the threshold, gave her a deep kiss that sent tingles from her underbelly to her toes. When he stepped back, his face soft and glowing, he stumbled and fought to right herself. "Balance is off."

"It must be the sizzle of kissing me."

"Clearly!" He took her in his arms. "I felt kaboom go off in my head."

She pulled closer to him. They stood still as he traced her lips with the tip of his tongue. Her body turned to warm liquid; his mouth tasted like a sweet treat she didn't want to finish. When he pressed his mouth harder against hers, she couldn't tell where his lips began and hers ended.

Stanton whisked her the short distance to his bed. "It's been so long for both of us. What do I do now?"

She didn't hesitate turning her back to him. He unzipped her dress, helping her step out of it. His breath caught and she silently thanked Marcy for insisting she buy the red thong and matching lacy bra.

He turned her around. "As much as I want to see you nude, I don't want you to take these off yet." He pressed his lips together and nodded approval, looking at her for so long she flushed. Then, slowly, he twirled her around twice. He trailed his finger down her cleavage. When his hands grasped her hips she stepped close to him.

He undid her bra and slipped it off. As he helped her remove the thong, he gave a soft whistle. "What were you thinking when you talked about being decrepit? You're magnificent and your breasts are beautiful."

"Thank God you didn't call them perky." They both laughed.

"They are lovely." He stared with longing.

She tugged at his shirt and he quickly took his clothes off. Celia felt as though time had stopped. His wiry, subtly muscled body was nearly unchanged except for some thickening and loosening of flesh around his middle and his gray chest hair. She wanted to get lost in his body and stay there forever. He pressed each of her fingers to his lips, then knelt on the floor and ran his tongue along her waist to her navel. It was an ecstatic sensation her body remembered as though it had only just happened yesterday.

As he moved his face to her inner thighs, she swayed her hips and threw her head back, biting the inside of her cheek. After a long while, she gently lifted his head. "It's really you, Stanton."

"Thank God it's me and you didn't find some other old goat." He stood and directed her hand to his erection that curved against his stomach.

She knelt this time and took him in her mouth. He grasped her hair and moved his hands to caress her cheeks. His body gently followed her movements as he moaned softly. Then lifting her up, they moved toward the bed and fell onto the soft mattress, wrapped in each other's arms. His skin gave off the scent of pears and soap. She inhaled deeply, filling herself up with his presence. Time stopped.

He trailed his tongue over her shoulders, down her side. Celia guided his hand to her breast, and Stanton kissed her erect nipples. Her breath quickened.

"I don't move as fast as I used to."

Celia smiled. "Slow is good."

He laughed then trailed a line of kisses from her cleavage to her navel. Wrapping her legs around his waist, she discovered, to her delight, she'd become wet. Some hormones were still pumping.

With gentleness, he penetrated her, and she had momentary pain. He stopped. The man could always read her signals, both physical and emotional.

"Am I hurting you?"

"Go easy," she whispered, hoping the lubricant Marcy had recommended helped.

The pain quickly disappeared, and they soon fell into a throbbing rhythm. The outside world shut down, her thoughts dissolved, and nothing existed but their bodies coming together and the sensation of electric currents zapping through her body. He pressed his lips on hers, his tongue whirling her desire into yearning. She tensed as she fell into an ecstatic vortex, a cry catching in her throat. Light exploded in her head and waves of pleasure coursed through her. Stanton's moaning soon followed.

After a few minutes, she drifted back into awareness and the ticking of a clock as she pressed her cheek to Stanton's chest, listening to his heart thudding. She raised her head and looked into his eyes, knowing her own expression mirrored his incredulous look. "You're still a terrific lover."

"Not bad for being out of practice, huh." He whistled softly. "And you're sexier and more exciting than ever," he said. He sighed and pinched her cheek, looking pleased.

"And you didn't die on me," she murmured, then clapped a hand over her mouth. It had just popped out.

"What? You expected me to die from rapture?" he cried. "What a way to go."

She hid her face in his chest. "We're ancient. Remember, either one of us could have a heart attack from all that excitement."

"I promise to do mouth to mouth to revive you, and you can do the same for me."

Celia felt an uproariously joyful sensation coursing through her body. She began to laugh hysterically. She was high on Stanton.

"What's so funny?" he asked, looking puzzled.

"Life is good." Celia couldn't stop laughing long enough to tell him she was over Gabe and all the pain he'd caused her. It didn't matter anymore if Gabe had loved that woman or not. He was a prisoner of his own making, just as she had been. She spent years seeking intimacy and he seeking the affection and adoration of his mistress. It made her think of another cha-cha rule: JUDGMENTS IMMOBILIZE THE MIND. THEY LIMIT FREEDOM OF CHOICE.

Even if it didn't work out with Stanton, she had her life back—almost. She had to be the one who made herself happy. From now on she determined to go day to day and not worry. Hopefully Stanton would prove she could trust him again, but for now, her friends remained the trusted ones in her life. In this delicious moment, police visits, criminal actions, her daughter's divorce, and all her other worries soared into a faraway place. Right now she didn't care a whit about the maybes.

Stanton snuggled close and drifted off to sleep, but Celia remained awake and unmoving, turning things over and over in her mind until she too fell asleep.

Celia's cell phone jolted her awake and she found herself in Stanton's arms. The clock said twelve forty-five. "I'm not going to answer."

"As much as I hate to say this, you should. Didn't you say Deb wasn't well?"

"Right." Celia jumped out of bed and put on the shirt Stanton offered her and walked into the living room. Marcy's number flashed on the screen. Celia's heart pounded. She knew it had to be an emergency for her to be calling now. "Hello?"

"I'm so sorry to bother you, Celia."

"You wouldn't call if it wasn't important. What's wrong?" Celia bit her lip.

"I'm beside myself. I found out the police are into a serious investigation of several deaths because more toxicology reports are available. The families of about twenty people that Lyle told me about have been meeting, with Edith leading them. Most of the half dozen or so autopsies where a patient had no diagnosis of heart problems or depression showed they all had very high levels of antidepressants and oxycodone."

"What! How did they all get so much?"

"Don't know, but in cases like Melvin, they had no label or doctor's names on the bottles. Edith's telling people it could have been put in their food."

Celia lowered her voice. "Are they saying for sure that it's murder?" She pressed her knuckles to her chin.

"That's what Lyle thinks. They'll come straight for us because he also heard …" Marcy's hyperventilating sounded like a stick scraping wire mesh. "I don't know how to tell you."

"Spit it out."

"Someone reported that we were seen wheeling Melvin out of the office the night he died. Vanessa has to be the one."

Celia's body went cold. "Oh Christ. Maybe she's trying to throw this on us because she's in the line of fire." Celia cringed and tried to compose herself. Now it seemed likely someone followed her in that black car. Queasy, she collapsed into a chair. "Did Melvin seem strange to you that night?"

"He was a little groggy and mumbled a bit and said he'd had a few glasses of wine." Marcy's raspy breathing became louder. "We can't protect Deb from this."

A long silence filled Celia with dread.

Celia pressed her hand to her chest. Had she removed her fingerprints from the bottle in Melvin's medicine chest? "I'll be back home soon." She hung up and heard the pit-pat of slippers on the tiled floor, a gentle sweet sound compared to the thunderous catastrophe swirling at home. Stanton entered, wearing a robe. "Everything all right?"

She forced herself to stand. "I have to go now. I'll explain later."

"Anything I can do to help?"

His concern touched her, but she couldn't tell him now. "No, but thanks."

"Okay, but please tell me about it when you can. I don't want to hear about it from Edith."

Her patience at the edge, she trembled. "Just don't listen to anything she says."

She refused to let him drive her, so he called a taxi. When it arrived he kissed her deeply. The outside world blanked out for a few moments before reality set in again. He promised to call her soon, but she wasn't sure he should. So much faced her, and she worried about dragging him into it. But then again, she'd never thought she'd experience such intimacy with a man again. She would see where things went.

The taxi stopped at the entrance of the community and waited for the electronic barrier to go up. One lane away on the exit side, Celia saw Michael leaning his head out of his car window, chatting and laughing with the guard. Why was he here so late? For a second she worried something had happened to Deb, but he wouldn't be so jolly if it had. Perhaps he'd been watching a movie with her, as he sometimes did.

The taxi went slowly along Pelican Way and dropped her off in front of her building. She hustled to the elevator. When she opened her door, Marcy jumped in front of her. She'd let herself in.

"What the hell are we going to do? I'm ready to cut my wrists," Marcy said. She began pacing back and forth, then stopped. "But first tell me what happened with Stanton."

Celia threw her arms up in the air. "Get your priorities straight." The euphoric high she'd felt just a short while ago had gone. "I might have left fingerprints on the bottle of Viagra in Melvin's medicine chest. The police might dust it for prints now. I hope someone like Edith ruined them rummaging around."

"Good Lord." Marcy covered her mouth with her hand. "This only gets worse."

"We have to tell Deb we've been outed," Celia said. "No doubt the police will come calling soon. We have to be prepared."

"How the hell do we prepare?"

"We don't speak to the police without a lawyer. Don't showboat."

"Me?" Marcy gave her an innocent look.

"No more putting off lawyers. I checked online about determining time of death. There's usually a wide spread and possibly it will include the time we got him back to his apartment. As for the fingerprints? I say I visited Melvin for a rendezvous, and he showed me the bottle. I can say I didn't tell the police because I was embarrassed." Celia pressed her hands to her face. "I don't know what else to do."

"Jesus. This is a damned mess. I'm scared out of my wits."

Celia felt as though she'd walked into a lightless, airless room and had trouble breathing. "It's late. I'm exhausted. Let's meet again in the morning." She had no idea what to tell Stanton. For sure he'd never want to see her again.

Chapter 36

Celia

Celia and Marcy, who continually tapped her hand on her thigh, were finishing their morning walk. They'd discussed Vanessa's implication until Marcy interrupted. "Tell me what happened with you and Stanton. Give me something fun to think about."

Reluctantly at first, Celia gave Marcy the outline—how they'd danced together, how he'd undressed her, how they'd made love. Marcy's mood perked up immensely.

"Did you wear the fancy underwear I picked out for you?" Marcy's eyes were wide.

"I did. He loved it."

Marcy squealed delightedly and clapped her hands. "I bet you looked like a knock out. So … how'd it go?"

Celia recalled Stanton's lips trailing over her back. "Amazing. I was like a teenager with raging hormones. It's odd, but good sex made me feel like I'm twenty."

"I knew it!"

"I can only compare it to good wine that improves with age. We weren't groping like we did in college. This time, it was sweeter. I was plenty nervous though, but he put me at ease." Celia swiped the air as though about to draw the scene from last night. "That is, until this crisis. This might kill my sex life if it doesn't kill me first."

"Argh. I'm living vicariously through you."

"I made a mistake getting so cozy so fast. When the news breaks about this Melvin business, Stanton will be on the first train out, and he's too friendly with Edith. She gossips about us to him." She sighed deeply as they reached the end of their walk and prepared to part ways for their own apartments. "Am I overreacting?"

"I don't know. If he's a good guy ..." Marcy put her hand gently on Celia's forearm. "You don't have to make any decisions now. Just take things one day at a time. We haven't been doing the cha-cha so you might as well substitute sex." She threw a shoulder forward. "Not bad."

Celia rolled her eyes. "I'll see you later."

She entered her apartment. Speaking with Marcy, hearing it spelled out, riddled her with anxiety again. She reached up and touched her shoulder-length hair and for a moment wondered why it wasn't still tied in a bun. Was she losing her mind? She decided to channel her nervousness into action and called Deb, telling her why she had to contact a lawyer right away.

"We'll be all right," Deb said. She sounded distracted and foggy.

Shocked at Deb's nonchalance, Celia wondered if her friend's sleeping pills kept her sedated or muddled during the day. "Has Michael found you a lawyer?"

"Don't worry. This is a ruse to scare us."

Celia wondered if Deb understood the gravity of the situation. She forced herself to stay patient, kept her voice calm. "Deb, this is probably turning into a formal police matter. You'll be questioned by them."

"We didn't do anything bad." Deb yawned loudly. "I'm sleepy. I think I'm going to take a nap."

Damn. Those pills must really have quite an effect. "All right. Take care."

Celia hung up, concerned. Deb had never seemed so out of it before. She decided to check back in later with her friend and see if the damaging information might sink in better.

She was supposed to have a tennis lesson with one of the pros but decided she was in no mood to play. When she called to cancel, she got no answer and decided to walk down to the courts to do it in person. She would turn tail if she saw any sign of Vanessa.

Most people in the community must have heard the rumors by now, so when she passed a few residents, she looked down at the cobblestone pathway or mumbled good morning.

Hurrying down the pathway between the courts, she heard the solid thwack of racquets smacking tennis balls and the yelps after a good play. The sun's heat made her weak and she wanted a cool shower.

She noticed a couple up ahead, an older man and a younger woman, not unusual in Florida. Celia stopped dead in her tracks. Vanessa was walking with Stanton, who leaned over and whispered something to her, and she bent over with laugher. Celia's heart leaped into her throat and she quickly turned in the other direction and hurried back home. Why was Stanton with Vanessa? What the hell was going on?

A message awaited her on her machine when she got home—a deep female smoker's voice. "Ms. Ewing, this is Detective Dawkins calling. Just wanted to speak to you about some issues. Please call me at the station. Thanks."

"Oh God, not her again," Celia moaned.

In bed, Celia pulled the covers over her head and rolled into a ball. Accusations of murder, obstructing justice, Stanton and Vanessa, and now the police again—it felt like a monsoon. She clung to her pillow as though it could keep her from drowning. With her misgivings about Vanessa, the fact that she'd befriended her daughter when Allison needed it most put Celia in a bind. Clearly she was the one who pointed the finger at them.

She recalled her friends' voices when she'd last hit bottom and was about to commit suicide, urging her to fight back. Her body shook violently as she fought against the feeling of being locked in a lightless room of depression.

After twenty minutes her tremors subsided and she tried to force her body to relax. She eventually rose. The inadequate air conditioning left her feeling clammy and sweaty. She greedily drank down a tall glass of water, then tried reaching Marcy and Deb. They needed to know about the call from Detective Dawkins, but neither answered.

The image of Stanton whispering into Vanessa's ear as they strolled kept coming back. They'd seemed so friendly—Celia had no idea they knew each other so well. The pleasure she'd shared with Stanton just the night before seemed a lifetime away.

Whom could she trust? Just about everyone was suspect when it came to the unusual number of deaths and now the disturbing autopsies. Stanton and Vanessa, looking like long-lost friends. Edith's riling up people might be a sign of a guilty person trying to throw suspicion on others. Her friends both visited sick, infirm residents often, although she saw no possible motive for them to harm anyone. Maybe they did the wrong thing, but killing? No way. Her head was growing muddled trying to make connections. She dialed Stanton's cell.

When he answered, she almost barked, "I saw you walking with Vanessa Cordova."

"Sure." A long silence. "Why didn't you say hello?"

"I was in a hurry," she said tightly.

"You sound ... kind of strange. What's this about, really?"

"How do you know her?"

"She was Ada's caregiver for the last few months of her life." He went quiet. "You aren't implying ...? There was nothing between us." His voice grew agitated. "Look at the age difference. She called out of the blue to catch up."

Celia tried to speak but words failed her.

"Does any of this have anything to do with why you left in a hurry last night?"

Celia cleared her throat. "In a way." She teetered between not knowing if she could trust him and wanting to confide in him. She had to give him some explanation, but decided to make it scant. "A man died and the family requested an autopsy before his burial." She tripped over her next words. "They suspected foul play."

"Oh, they think foul play on an old man." Stanton laughed. "That's silly."

"The man was Marcy's boyfriend. She was the last one to see him alive."

"And?"

"Well, we ... that is Deb and I, along with Marcy ... if he was murdered, we are implicated by association. None of us had anything to do with his death, but Vanessa is friendly with the man's family,

266 THE CHA-CHA BABES OF PELICAN WAY

as is Edith. Edith bamboozled them into getting an autopsy along with autopsies on a few other residents who died, but only to put us in a bad light." It had come out. Celia felt both relieved and worried.

"That is really nasty, but you three have to be innocent." He gave a short burst of laughter. "Three older," he cleared his throat, "but charming women have no motive to kill someone's beau." Stanton got quiet. "Just don't push me away again, Celia. Please."

"I don't trust Vanessa." Celia bit her lip until she tasted a trickle of metallic blood. "You should dump me and run."

"I like you being a little batty. Look, if you want, I won't respond if she calls again." After a long pause he said, "Is there more to this that you're not telling me?"

Why aren't you flying away like a normal person? "Um, my biggest dilemma is that my daughter will be mortified if we're charged."

"Why on earth would they charge you? We're all too tired to commit felonies and too old to get arrested," Stanton said, laughing.

"I've got to go."

"I have an idea. You need to get out and have some fun. How about going to the Boca Pelicano Art Museum at Mintnershine Shores tomorrow?" She heard the liveliness in his voice. "I need you to lead me through the Degas exhibition. What do you say?"

Her toes curled. She needed to be careful around him and not reveal too much, but she wanted to be back in his arms. "Sounds good."

Later that day, Celia and Deb sat in Marcy's apartment. The strong smell of Marcy's heady French perfume mingled with the fragrances of vanilla, marijuana, and melted butter. Marcy set out a plate of freshly baked chocolate chip cookies, and Celia noticed two new cherubic angels hung from the ceiling, each holding a piece of paper. When Celia looked more closely, she saw that the papers had the names of Marcy's children written on them, and she turned away as her throat tightened.

The three women were meeting to discuss strategy in handling a possible visit from the police.

Celia placed her cup in the saucer, her trembling hand spilling some liquid over the side. "I've avoided calling that detective back but can't for much longer."

Marcy finished eating a cookie and handed a few to Deb. "So you don't sneak them."

They laughed, but it was forced and nothing like the belly-shaking cathartic laughs they usually shared.

Marcy frowned. "It had to be Vanessa who turned us in. Curtis suddenly dropped dead just a few days after his wife died. Poor Lila." Marcy wrung her hands. "Who's next?" She looked at Celia and then Deb. "One of us?"

The air in the room suddenly seemed heavy to Celia. "Let's have a minute of quiet for those who died."

Deb lowered her head with the others, but then popped up. "Lila died in the hospital of natural causes." She looked at Marcy. "You look for trouble when you don't have a boyfriend."

"Shush," Celia said.

"We don't know what Lila died of, actually," Marcy said out of the side of her mouth as though by speaking that way it didn't interfere with the moment of silence.

"Quiet," Celia said louder.

After thirty seconds, Celia picked her head up. "Just for kicks, let's Google Vanessa and see what we can find." Celia pointed to Marcy's desk. "I see your computer is on."

"Of course it's on," Deb said. "On a dating site, most likely."

Celia pressed a finger to her lip to shush Deb. "I'm looking for gaps in her stories," Celia said. "She knocked around Europe for several years, came back, and went from job to job. I want to see if her background checks out with what she's said."

Marcy and Deb peered at the screen over Celia's shoulder.

Celia searched for Vanessa Cordova on Google. She came upon a page with Vanessa's name and clicked in to her website. The page told of her travels across the country from age twenty to twenty-three and included a picture of her in a gown, standing in a model-like pose. "People can fudge on social media. Now we get serious."

Then Celia did a search on all public information. The results offered a for-pay site that would give them a complete background check. Celia used her credit card, typed in Vanessa's name, and waited. Among the results were an obituary for her mother, Marie, who had died when Vanessa was twelve, and her father's more recent obituary. "So far, it isn't out of whack," Celia said. She scrolled down.

Marcy gripped Celia's shoulder. "It says her father's last name is Dostandov, and it doesn't say there's a stepfather or that Vanessa was married."

Scrolling further, Celia saw that she had spent two years at a local college until age nineteen. "She told me she backpacked in Europe for three to four years." Celia moved the mouse yet again. "She worked as an accountant at Massinger Inc. in Orlando for four years. She never mentioned that firm or that she was an accountant. So there's a gap in time from when she stopped working at Massinger and came to Florida. That's about seven years. Somewhere in that time or after she trained for two years to get her caregiver license and has been working at Well Services for four years."

Marcy bent her head to the screen and puckered her mouth. "We're getting somewhere."

"I'll search for public information on any legal issues she was involved in."

Deb and Marcy watched Celia's fingers fly. First she tried Vanessa Cordova. Nothing. Then she tried Vanessa Dostandov and dropped her hands on her lap. "It says no adult criminal record." Celia felt somewhat dismayed. She'd been sure something would turn up. She dabbed at the sweat on her upper lip. "I wonder why she's not doing accounting now."

"She's a bad egg," Marcy hissed. "Lot of loose ends, yet she's only about thirty-four."

"It doesn't make her a murderer," Deb said.

"You have to tell your son about this," Marcy said, shaking a finger at Deb.

"So there's a gap for a few years? Michael says she's licensed. He wouldn't hire someone who's not trustworthy." Deb jutted her chin out defiantly. "So that's that."

With a sinking feeling in her stomach, Celia had to admit that Deb had a good point. Or did she? She looked at the computer in awe. Although she'd been doing research and reading Dummy books for a few years, she still marveled at it like a miracle. What else would it tell her? Goosebumps tingled her arms. Maybe something she might fear hearing.

Chapter 37

Celia

Stanton stood close to Celia as they admired the Degas bronze statue titled "Little Dancer of Fourteen Years." They were at the museum and Celia lifted her hands, palms up in awe of the beauty around her. "This sculpture is so elegant. The child is pensive, standing still, watchful and positioned like a ballet dancer." Celia looked at the sculpture from all angles.

"I see what you mean," Stanton said, cocking his head as he scrutinized the piece.

She had always loved the grace of the classic ballet dancer. "It's tense and calming at the same time." She gave him a devilish smile. "But do you think she could do a cha-cha?"

"Not like we can." He shuffled his feet in abbreviated steps.

Celia took his hands in hers and moved them to his rhythm—bringing one arm forward, to show which foot to move, and one back. Two people nearby stared at them.

They giggled and moved on. Celia was having a good time, but the nagging shadow of Stanton's chumminess with Vanessa darkened the corners of her mind. The police must have questioned Vanessa because of her involvement in Melvin's medical care.

"You seem so far away all of a sudden." Stanton cupped her cheeks, and her face burned. He peered at her. "Are you thinking back to when you did studio art yourself? You were good."

"I didn't think so." She smiled. "I tried the visual arts before switching to art history." She looked up at him from lidded eyes. "You were there for me. After that transition I thought the world had ended." Maybe she shouldn't be so quick to doubt him now.

He pressed his hand on her upper arm and she luxuriated in the mild roughness of his hands. "I loved your realistic sculptures of nudes."

"I didn't have the style I wanted. Now I'm relaxing and love watching clay take form. I've added a nude female figure, swimming around a cup." Celia rubbed her fingers together as though feeling the clay.

"Hmmm. If it looks like you, give me a cup of java."

"It will cost you." She smacked his chest lightly then grew thoughtful. "As I worked I kind of became an observer, watching the sculpture take on a life of its own, almost coming alive. That's the same thrill when I dance."

"Really?" He looked surprised. "How's that?"

"Maybe it's odd, but in sculpture, hands give form to a blob of earth or stone. In dancing, your own body's movements are a kinetic sculpture." She twirled her hand in the air like a graceful dance step. "I sound bonkers."

"Not at all. I'm fascinated." They stood face to face now. "Go on."

"When you finish a sculpture you see a whole new part of who you really are deep inside. Maybe that's why I stopped sculpting. I didn't want anyone to see the real me. But dancing stirred something. When I dance, it sends thrills down my spine. I feel alive and no longer fear anyone seeing my inner self. Whoever I am deep down is out in the open, and I own it." Celia wondered why she was blabbing to him and worried that he wouldn't understand her.

Stanton looked at her, entranced. "Wow. I'd like to feel like that. And I think you're on to something most people, including myself, can't see. We need to keep dancing together so I'll feel that too." He took her hand and squeezed it.

Celia's heart leaped. *He gets it! I underestimated him.*

He held her hand tight as they wandered around the exhibit and discussed how bronze sculptures were cast and how molds were used to repeat the form. Then they fell into a comfortable silence, continuing their slow pace.

"I touch sculptures when the guards aren't looking," she confided in a low voice. "Even when it's metal, it's as though I can feel the blood pumping in veins, feel warm skin, and hear a heartbeat. The timelessness of it makes me feel … bliss."

"I love it when you talk dirty." Stanton lightly touched the indentation at her throat.

"Celia, Stanton, hello." A familiar woman's voice rang out, interrupting what felt like their own private world.

Celia turned to face Vanessa, clinging to a large, balding man with apple cheeks and a pleasant smile. He wore a beautifully tailored blue shirt with pressed jeans and filled the space with his presence. She felt her heart jump in her chest.

Vanessa gave a beguiling smile. "Meet Brady Shirkson, CEO of Global," Vanessa said, batting her eyelashes at him. Brady looked enraptured.

Celia got the message—Vanessa had landed the big fish, Michael's boss. Brady had to be the person providing her with the luxuries.

"It's a pleasure meeting you," Celia said, shaking Brady's hand

and hoping her alarm hadn't been visible. "I've heard nice things about you from my daughter, Allison."

"Allison's your daughter? We love her. Efficient, qualified, and nice to boot," Brady said.

"I was in the healthcare business myself," Stanton said as he and Brady clasped hands. "But by the back door."

"And what aspect were you involved in?"

"Mostly computer forensics for court cases. A lot of them were for healthcare firms and start-up medical technology companies. I'm a consultant now."

Brady gave an approving nod. "Maybe I can call on you for help. We look for new and innovative programing." He puckered his mouth. "I currently have a situation in mind."

"My pleasure," Stanton said, handing Brady his business card. Stanton seemed to be avoiding Vanessa.

Vanessa tugged Brady's sleeve and gave Stanton an alluring glance. "He's brilliant."

"I've got a technical question," Brady said. He took Stanton's arm. "Excuse us for a moment, ladies." Stanton looked relieved as they stepped aside.

Celia bristled and didn't hide her anger.

Vanessa looked contritely at Celia. "You're mad at me." She spoke just above a whisper, but her eyes appeared bruised with pale purplish blotches under her bottom lids. "Yes, the police questioned me about Melvin, and I told them that I saw you, Marcy, and Deb wheeling someone the night he died. I'd be in jeopardy if I didn't tell the truth." She frowned.

Celia's stomach flip-flopped. "That was Deb in the wheelchair. She has severe arthritis. We covered her up with a blanket."

"I saw you that night coming out of Melvin's office wheeling someone bigger than her. I didn't tell Allison."

"Why did the police come to you?"

Vanessa shrugged. "Edith said I might know something. Just be careful. There are enemies all around." She looked at Brady, who was still engrossed in conversation. "What most bothers me is that Allison is a great friend. I feel terrible about what I told the police. But I had no choice."

"What you told them isn't … isn't … well, quite correct." Celia stuttered.

"We have to run along for a lunch date," Vanessa said with an exaggerated sweetness in her voice as Brady and Stanton walked back at a leisurely pace.

Brady looked at Celia. "Nice meeting you."

As soon as they walked away Celia whispered, "Damn her. It's like sand gets kicked in your eyes every time she's around."

"What happened?"

"She admitted being the one who reported us to the authorities."

"You mean about Melvin? What did she report?"

"I should have told you. Melvin died while he was … making love to Marcy. Marcy's had a few previous infractions for what they called, uh … indecency. To keep Marcy from being evicted, we moved his dead body back to his apartment so it'd look like he died there."

Stanton grasped her upper arms. "Jesus, Celia! That's a crime."

"I know. There's a message on my machine from the police that I've avoided returning."

"I want to help. And I have to admit that the image of the three of you moving a dead guy in a wheelchair is darkly funny. But it seems you are in trouble."

Celia wheeled around so she had her back to him. "I'm a complete screw-up. Everything I've done over the years was dumb and naïve." She heard him take a deep breath. "Are you on the first train out?"

He gently turned her around to face him. "Absolutely not. You made a bad judgment call, and it'll get squared away. You don't have a record, you're a law-abiding citizen."

"And what if Vanessa testifies against us?"

"Maybe they'll say it's a misdemeanor and slap you on the wrist. I'll help you get a lawyer."

"We also tampered with the scene, so who knows what else they could charge us with?"

Stanton looked at her with a stiff smile on his lips. Celia felt her stomach sinking with dread.

Chapter 38

Allison

"Allie." Celia's voice sounded disconcerted. "I have to ask …"

Allison felt the back of her neck ache. "What is it? What's wrong? Are you all right?"

It sounded like her mother was searching for the right words.

"Nothing's wrong, exactly. It's just that I was wondering about … what do you know about Vanessa? Like her past."

Anger burned in Allison's stomach. "You called me in the middle of a busy day to ask me to gossip about my friend?"

"I'm truly sorry to interrupt your work, but there's a gap in her history I just thought you might clear it up."

"Did you Google her? What information could you possibly need about her?" Allison heard her voice rising. "Get a hobby. I've got a ton of work to get back to. Goodbye, Mother." She slammed down the phone.

What on earth had gotten into her mother? Maybe Michael had told his mother about Vanessa's sordid past—and Deb jumped to reveal it. And now her mother wanted to gossip.

Allison shook her head, trying to clear it, and got back to the stack of papers Michael had given her, trying to decipher the spreadsheets concocted by June Hartner, the embezzler. She needed to clarify this piece of the Well Services puzzle.

A few minutes later, a knock interrupted her and she looked up to see Michael entering her office. He greeted her warmly and she smiled. She'd had to cancel their date once again because Brady had asked Vanessa to investigate a charge by an ill patient that a caregiver had poisoned her with drugs to try to kill her. She asked Allison for advice because of her early nursing background. Allison had warned her that some patients hallucinated or became paranoid as the result of their illnesses or medications. Not going out with Michael disappointed her but also relieved her somewhat because she still had misgivings about dating him. But seeing him now made her feel tingly all over.

Before Allison could say anything, Vanessa entered.

"Hi, Vanessa." Allison had been so busy with the embezzlement spreadsheets she'd put aside other accounting responsibilities. "How are your classes going?"

"So far, so good. I've gotten an assistant to help teach Activities of Daily Living and checking aides' driving records. Also, I'm beefing up the training program for state certification requirements and Medicare reimbursement. Thanks for those manuals from the state."

"Are you ready to stop patient care?"

"Hell no," Michael said, with a laugh in his voice. "We need her in the field still."

"Agreed." Vanessa's face brightened as she made excited sweeping hand gestures. "Poor Julia is so ill she's going into a nursing home so that leaves me with three patients. I could pick up one more because between class sessions it gets quiet and patient care picks up the slack."

"We'll work around your schedule," Michael said, sounding a bit grumpy.

"I get a hollow feeling whenever I lose a patient." Tears welled in Vanessa's eyes.

Allison watched her body movements for a sign of insincerity. Nothing. She trusted her friend, but the prison record raised her antennae a bit and made her realize she should be cautious.

"You've got to distance yourself from the patient," Michael said, in a controlled irritated voice. "You're a certified caregiver, and now teaching. Be professional."

Vanessa dabbed at her eyes with a tissue. "I can't help it."

Allison thought Michael was a bit harsh and felt sorry for her. "Will you be doing some office time?" Since Brady had assigned Vanessa to help Allison two weeks ago, she hadn't given it more than three hours.

"After I finish organizing this class, boss, I'll have some time. Got to get back to work."

Allison didn't mind since she had so little time to orient her. As soon as Vanessa closed the door, Michael leaned his hip against the desk and stared at her. She watched his delicate fingers tapping on her desk, inhaling the citrus soap fragrance of his skin. He smiled and looked like he was about to say something. Then his cell rang. He checked it and mouthed, "Sorry," as he waved and hurried out.

Allison tried to focus back on her spreadsheets but felt distracted by Michael's delicious scent that lingered in the air. She wondered why he was sometimes short and irritated with Vanessa. Clearly, he didn't doubt her work ethic—no one could. *Maybe he thinks she's using Brady, but then Brady's using her as well.*

Chapter 39

Celia

Celia, Marcy, and Deb had come to the outdoor flea market separately as each had errands to run afterward. Celia waited for them, pacing, and as soon as she saw them stroll in ran up to them.

She told them how she and Stanton bumped into Vanessa and Brady and how Vanessa admitted to telling the police she saw them wheeling Melvin out of his office. "In fact, she kind of apologized for confessing, but implied she'd be in deep trouble if she lied."

"I didn't trust that bitch from day one," Marcy said. "What are we going to do?"

"She had no choice," Deb said in a meek voice. She looked baffled.

"There's more. The police came to my door, but I didn't open it," Celia said, seeing in their expressions she might as well have detonated a bomb. "They're calling me too. They'll be back I'm sure. I'm scared."

"It can't get any worse," Marcy groaned.

"Now you got me scared." Deb held out her trembling hand.

"I can't even think about the implications right now," Celia said.

"Well, let's keep moving," Marcy said. "We all need to chill."

Celia concentrated on the outdoor stalls weighted down with household goods, clothing, electronics, and designer knock-off watches and purses. The bright colors seemed faded as Celia envisioned being taken out of her home in handcuffs and led to a gray prison cell.

Marcy picked up an imitation Gucci handbag, inspected it distractedly, and put it back. "I can't shop. That's how shook up I am." She pursed her lips.

"I asked Allison to get statistics on deaths at Boca Pelicano Palms and see how they compare to other villages nearby. She wasn't thrilled. Hopefully, she will do it."

A few hours after Allie had refused to answer Celia's questions about Vanessa's past, Celia had called her again with the request, and she recalled her daughter's response.

"Mother, that's ridiculous! You are getting on my last nerve with these requests." Then with a shuddering sigh, she'd added, "I'll see what I can do, if anything."

Celia mentally tallied the recent deaths again—they were up to eleven that she knew of and all of those eleven had been Vanessa's clients: Melvin, John Rappan, Mr. Angstrom, Sadie, Marcy's neighbor Olivia, Lila Donaldson, her husband, and, most recently, Julia, who died right before a scheduled move to a nursing home, plus three others she only knew casually. Lyle had a count of twenty. She didn't know if that included her numbers. All of this in a few weeks. What about Stanton's wife? He'd made it clear it wasn't a happy marriage. Could he and Vanessa have conspired to do her in? She shook her head to rid herself of ugly thoughts.

Marcy turned and groaned. "Oh no, here comes Edith—or am I suffering from post-traumatic stress disorder?"

"You mean post-traumatic sex disorder," Deb said and shook

her head. Marcy glared at her and Deb shrugged. "Just lightening the mood."

"Never mind, both of you." Celia sucked in a deep breath.

They turned a corner to avoid Edith, but Celia felt a tap on her shoulder. Edith must have hurried to catch up.

"Hello," Celia said, sugar coating her greeting.

Edith pointed a trembling finger in Celia's face. "The police have all the information they need about you three. You killed Julia and I'm going to get her children to demand an autopsy. I've got your numbers. You don't mingle because you are madwomen killers." She ripped a tissue out of her bag and blew her nose as tears ran down her face. She threw the tissue at Marcy who jumped back. "You lured my Melvin, fed him dope, and screwed him to death, you, you … slut. He would have come back to me."

Celia pressed her palm on her chest. "You are insane. We'd never …"

Edith jabbed her finger in Celia's face again. "I'll get you killers."

Celia's heart pounded. People had begun to gather around them. "You got the police to interrogate Vanessa for no reason."

"I had every reason. You moved Melvin's body to hide the evidence. You're criminals, not angels of death." Edith's bent fingers clawed the air. "You haven't heard the end of this."

"Hey, lady, don't you know that Florida is the train station where people get off just before they pass on?" Deb asked. "Nobody kills them."

"You people have no respect. You are all disgusting and deserve what you'll get." She stomped off.

"God, Edith is never going to let up," Celia said, squeezing her eyes shut as though to make it all go away.

"That's a lousy thing to say about Florida, you old hag," Marcy said to Deb.

"I told Stanton about moving Melvin. I had to," Celia blurted out.

"What?" Marcy shrieked. "You know he's friends with Edith! Why didn't you tell him a cockamamie story?"

"Edith would have told him anyway."

"Holy shit. We are in big time trouble," Marcy said.

Chapter 40

Allison

Michael put cream in his coffee and Allison watched the white swirls bleed into the black liquid. They were seated next to each other at a table in his office. Allison had a folder on her lap as she sipped from her cup. She bathed in the pleasure of being one-on-one with no distractions, but a tiny whisper in back of her mind warned of the risk of being vulnerable with a man again, especially her boss.

"Why aren't you giving me a new date for the trip up the coast?" He leaned forward, rubbing his forehead. "I'm dying here."

"Too much damned work. I'm quitting to clean houses for a living, it has to be easier," she joked. She leaned back in her chair as far as she could, escaping the draw of his magnetism, his musky cologne, his humor that drew her into a silky web.

"Won't my dynamic personality entice you to stay?" He smiled.

"I don't have time to date you or anyone else. Between moving into a new apartment and my work schedule, I have no free time."

"Vanessa has to be a help."

Allison snickered. "I love her as a friend, but when she's in the building it's mostly to see Shirkson. I don't mind, believe me."

He held his hands out. "By the way, she told me she gave you her history, but ..."

"That doesn't bother me. I think she's learned her lesson," Allison said.

"She better not mess it up."

"Why are you so hard on her?"

"Because I don't want her to think she has a free ride. Brady's her ticket to a good life. I want to keep her on her toes."

"Makes sense," she said, pausing to sip her coffee. "Now, let's get down to the reason for this meeting—the damage June Hartner did." Allison reached into her pocket, her muscles tensed, and withdrew some scrunched-up papers. "I found these stuck in the back of my desk drawer—looks like someone tried to hide them in a hurry and left them behind. They seem to link up to my findings." She pressed them flat on the tabletop with the heel of her hand.

He drummed his fingers on the table, examining the wrinkled receipts. "They're computer-generated invoices." Michael put them in his wallet.

"When I followed the numbers trail, here's what I found. June Hartner faked receipts for material never purchased. Then there were sham corporations that they owned, receiving payments from Well Services for imaginary goods. The phony companies were set up to look like they sold medicine, caregivers' uniforms, ambulance services, and medical equipment. Her husband's name, Richard Hartner, appears in some of those places as CEO running those sham companies."

Michael raised his eyebrows. "Wow. I didn't know that piece of it. I foolishly trusted her and it nearly got me canned." He raised his coffee cup. "If you pulled anything with the books I'd be forced to report you to your mother."

Allison smiled. "I'd worry about her reaction more than I'd worry about prison time." She wrapped her hands around her warm cup. "I need you to tell me what you know."

He wrinkled his brow. "Can't get much information from the FBI until they finish their investigation, which is ongoing. I get bits and pieces, and I think Brady knows more than he tells me."

"Why?"

He shrugged. "I know that the FBI tracked an account to Gibraltar that was opened in 2008 belonging to June's husband, Richard, with ten million in it, exactly the amount missing. It's hard to freeze accounts out of the country, and before we knew it the money had been moved to—we think—Costa Rica, but they don't know for sure. They haven't gotten enough to indict, but they are working on it." His face brightened. "What you found should be helpful. The Hartners swear they're innocent, and he's made threatening calls to employees. Then he showed up at the party." He rapped his fist on the table. "Let me know if he ever phones you."

Allison sipped her coffee. "They played everyone."

He reached over and patted her hand. "I'm glad you came on board. Not just for me, but for the company too."

"Happy to be here." She wagged her finger at him. "Not just for you, but for the fat paycheck."

"Are we overpaying you then?"

"Never you mind." She felt her smile dissipating. "What's next?"

"The board is pressing charges, and when the indictment comes down, I'll have to testify before the grand jury. Not fun." He looked away. "Those two lived simply so they must have shoved it all into offshore accounts. I had just been made CFO." The sun streaming through the window struck his face, and his blue eyes shimmered. "Then this scandal hit and I almost lost it all." Michael looked anxious.

Allison tried to phrase her next question delicately. It was something that had been nagging at her for a while. "There's an audit coming up and it's the second one in two months. Doesn't that strike you as a bit excessive?"

He puffed his cheeks, letting out a big whoosh of air. "That's a new procedure ordered by our dear CEO." He reached out and took one of her hands in both of his. His soft touch felt reassuring. "Your cost-cutting helped, but now we're in the red again. Costs for materials are up, as are salaries and employee benefits. So even with an increase in enrollment at Global, our profit margin dropped. Since the two companies are linked and we avoid lay-offs, we went into a hole again. Executives are taking a pay cut of ten percent."

"Sorry, but that doesn't pull on my heartstrings."

He slapped his cheek. "What are you saying? I'm about to get a second job."

"Like hell. Your incomes are public information. I know about your six-figure salary and stock options and bonuses. And Brady does even better at seven figures. His bonuses are off the charts." She gave him a chiding look. "It's like legal embezzling."

Michael gave her a crooked smile. "No sympathy, huh?"

"No way. I'm hoping to get your position. Why else do you think I take your nonsense?"

"Because of my charms and good looks." He scrunched his face.

Allison laughed and thought, why must you be so handsome, damned witty, and charming? *Irresistible.*

"We stopped renovations on the new office building till things get better, so we're stuck in this scruffy building for a while. And I'm getting food stamps."

"You're nowhere near qualifying, but I know you work your butt off."

He tapped his spoon against the edge of the cup. "I'm glad my butt is something you think about."

"Don't read too much into that."

He gave her a mischievous grin. "Let me just take you on a tour of the coastline, please." He pressed his palms against his chest and gave her an exaggerated angelic look. "No funny business. No business at all, in fact. You need some fun."

She pushed her spoon against the sides of the cup, swirling the coffee. "Maybe."

"Come on, admit it—you want to go because you're crazy about me."

"I think there's a difference between being attracted and crazy about you."

"I'll take it any way I can get it." He ran his fingers over her cheek. "Tonight?"

Allison felt her face flush and quickly stood. "I'm seeing my mom tonight." At her mother's insistence, she'd had Vanessa gather death statistics so she'd feel useful in the office. Vanessa seemed happy to have a task. She took time to explain that the higher incidence of deaths at Celia's retirement community compared to some others was due to a higher age average because Boca Pelicano Palms offered care ranging from well-elderly care to nursing home care, unlike many others. In Vanessa's search, she found that ninety percent of the residents' health insurance was with Global HMO.

Hopefully giving her mother this information would put her mind at rest and stop her nagging.

Michael smiled. "How about Saturday night?"

She thought of different ways to say no gracefully and came up empty. "Okay." As Allison left the office, she felt both nervous and elated. *It's a mistake, mistake, mistake. But let Saturday come quickly.*

Chapter 41

Celia

Celia sat on her sofa next to Allison, examining the sheets of statistics. She wanted to tell her daughter about her dilemma, but worried about overburdening her when she already had so much on her plate. "Thank you for bringing these over, Allie."

"I can't help but think you have a morbid curiosity, Mom."

"Indulge me. Tell me what you think this means." Celia lifted the papers.

"Don't jump to conclusions because statistics can be deceiving. In the last year, this community did have a jump in deaths compared to other gated developments." Allison rubbed her forehead. "The average age here is seventy-eight. Out of four hundred residents, there's been thirty-two deaths—eight percent. Other communities have around four percent."

Celia considered telling Allie how the deaths she'd known about had been Vanessa's patients. But she knew how questions about Vanessa annoyed Allie so she refrained from mentioning it. "That's high. I've got the heebie-jeebies. Something odd is going on."

Allison gave her a condescending sideways glance. "Other places have spikes, but maybe not as high per capita as this place. Remember that Boca Pelicano Palms offers better than average amenities like shows, movies, good meals, and transportation. Most residents have excellent coverage with Global HMO, our parent company, which even sends doctors on house calls. They do everything to keep people at home with better quality of life. All that appeals to an older, sicker population who is more likely to die." Allison sighed. "Look, we can check stats next month and see how they compare to other similar villages. Would you please relax?"

Celia's back stiffened. "Don't be condescending."

Allison looked skyward, as though a helicopter might drop a ladder down to rescue her. "You can't pick numbers out of left field to justify some unrealistic fear."

Celia gave her a dirty look, and Allison shot back a wry grin. "Is some old codger murdering folks with a walker or a cane? Where would they find the energy?"

"You'd be surprised." Celia immediately regretted the lilt in her voice.

Allison gave her a dubious glance. "I don't want to know."

Celia knew she was referring to Stanton. "You're right. I'm probably off the wall with my concerns. Thanks, Allie. I know you went to a lot of trouble."

"Do your friends feel the same way?"

Celia cleared her throat. "Marcy does. Deb is wavering."

"Well, Marcy is even more bonkers than you. I've heard she has quite a reputation as a troublemaker around here. And Deb is no picnic."

Celia forced her voice to stay even. "Marcy and Deb are wonderful friends. Sure they have flaws. But everyone does. Look, you went out with Deb's son, whom she raised. You like him?"

Allison jiggled her knee. Celia braced herself for an angry response, but to her surprise, her daughter's expression softened. "He's nice. I've been lonely."

"Are you okay?"

"Mom, please. I'm fine," Allison said, her voice softening. "Enough. I know you mean well."

Please talk to me. "Michael speaks highly of you to his mom."

Allison stood. "We like each other, but I'm wary of getting too involved right now. I'm still raw. And he's my boss." She gave Celia a sly smile. "How's your beau?"

"Sit, please." Celia wanted to stretch out this quiet moment with Allie and went to the kitchen to fetch a tray with two slices of chocolate cake and a pot of tea, placing it on a cocktail table. "Stanton and I are just two old fogies getting together."

"Nothing for me, thanks. Who is he?"

"I know Stanton from college. Lo and behold, I ran into him while he visiting here from a neighboring community." More like strategic planning, she thought. "He's a widower."

Allison eyed her mother closely. "You never talk about Dad. You seem happier without him."

"No ..." Celia focused on wrapping her hands firmly around her teacup. "It's not a matter of happier. I'm just trying to move on."

"You weren't there for him," Allison said tersely.

"That's not true, Allison. I always tried to make our relationship better."

"Sounds like you're rewriting history."

Celia put a lid on her anger. She didn't want to reveal Gabe's secret yet. The time didn't seem right to tell Allison, what with her issues. Instead she silently repeated one of the cha-cha rules to center herself: CREATE YOUR OWN INNER RECEPTIVE SPACE. IT

ALLOWS FOR HEALING. "I was a woman who took a back seat to everything just as your father wanted."

"Are you implying Daddy controlled you?"

"I went along with the program, willingly. I'm not blaming him."

"You liked him taking charge. Now you can't wait to jump into another man's arms."

Celia sighed. "I found a man I really care about." She wanted to add, a man who didn't cheat on his wife.

Allison's brow was furrowing deeper and deeper.

"I don't know how much time is left to me, but damn it, I'm going to live to the fullest." She had never talked to Allison like this. "You don't know ... everything."

"Yes I do. You think because you were once meek, you've earned the right to act like a ... a ..."

"Say it. I'm acting like ... a slut."

Allison covered her ears as if shocked at hearing the word coming from her strait-laced mother's mouth. "You're an older woman who's supposed to be dignified. Act your age, for crying out loud."

Celia bit the inside of her cheek, keeping herself in check. "It's companionship that I didn't have with your father. I do deserve that."

"He was there for you but you hid under the covers." Allison threw her hands up in the air in disgust. "When I was growing up you were rational sometimes, but always emotionally disconnected," she spat out. "I so wanted you to be a ... a mom." Allison covered her eyes with her hands. The words pouring out of her daughter's mouth distressed her. *Why am I doing this to her?* "I'm sorry, Mom. I need to be responsible for myself."

"In my heart I was so connected to you, but your father shut me out." Celia reined in her mounting agitation. "Please, let's end this conversation now."

Allison's face melted. "I wish you could see that Dad loved us, broke his neck working day and night so we could have a nice house and send me to college. Admit it, this guy can't replace Dad."

"Stanton is a man with integrity." Indignation squeezed Celia's throat shut.

Allison looked stunned. "Daddy had integrity." She picked up her jacket and headed for the door.

Something inside Celia cracked. "No, he didn't. Your father cheated on me for many years with a woman who worked for him. Our accountant found the proof."

Allison turned to face Celia, flipping her shoulders in a dismissive shrug. "You made that up to justify your behavior," she shouted. She bounded out and slammed the door.

Silence filled the living room, but the sound of the door slamming continued to pound in Celia's ears.

After only three hours of sleep, the sun woke Celia. Before heading to the kitchen, she held the midnight blue handblown glass vase she'd bought as a housewarming gift for Allison's new apartment. After their argument from the night before she wasn't sure her daughter would want to see her, but she knew she couldn't let things drag on.

"This isn't going to be pretty," Celia muttered, carefully putting the vase back into its box and getting ready to leave.

In her car Celia tried to think of how to talk to her daughter to keep tempers from flaring, but her mind went blank. She decided to let things go wherever they might and pulled into the parking lot.

After several knocks, Allison opened the door, clutching her red silk robe at her neck. "Mother, what the hell are you doing here so early?"

"I have a gift for your new place." Celia heard the flatness in her voice.

"That's not why you're here. Come in. Let's get this over with." Celia brushed past Allison.

Allison's lips formed an angry O that she quickly snapped shut. She wheeled on her heel and marched into the kitchen, where she put on a pot of coffee, then flipped on the radio to a Latin station and turned the volume low.

Celia put the gift box on the table and watched the coffee drip into the pot. Coffee brewing usually perked her up. Not today.

The apartment had the scent of new paint and the white walls sparkled. The apartment seemed sparse, with only a chair, a sofa, and bookcases, but the navy and pale butter yellow colors were serene. Celia stared out the window.

Allison poured the black liquid into two cups, marched back, and placed the mugs on the table. She plopped on the sofa.

Celia folded her arms over her chest. "So, you think I'm a liar and it's all about me?"

"Daddy would never do … what you accused him of." Allison looked away.

Celia smacked her open palm with her other fist. "Why would I lie?"

Allison jumped up and pointed a finger at Celia. "I think you want to get out of responsibility for not being there for me." Allison's voice sounded raw. "And I'm doing the same thing with you, blaming you for my problems." She turned her back.

Celia put her hands over her face. "I did desert you. I copped out because it was easier. I had so little faith in myself." She lowered her hands.

Allison turned, her expression wretched. "If he cheated it was wrong, but Dad gave me everything he could afford. I'm grateful."

"Did he send you to medical school?" Celia didn't flinch when Allison gave her the most exasperated stare.

"You don't know what you're talking about! He couldn't afford it."

"He spent the money for your medical school on Ms. Fisherbach, his mistress." Allison looked befuddled, but Celia pressed on. "He paid her maybe four times what he paid his top-level employee and for twenty years or more." Celia's nostrils flared as she felt a wave of fresh anger towards Gabe. "Broke? Ha! He cheated you out of becoming a doctor and spent our inheritance on Fisherbach."

Allison gave Celia a defiant glare. "You're just jealous of my relationship with Dad."

"Not for an instant." Celia reached into her purse and took out the accountant's business card. "Call him if you don't believe me."

Allison broke down sobbing. Celia made a move toward her, but Allison extended her arm to keep her mother at bay. A minute later Allison's sobs subsided. "How could he do that?"

"I'm so sorry."

"No more." After a moment, she gave a cynical smile. "Well, I guess we have something in common now—cheating husbands." Allison dropped into a chair.

"It hurts and makes me sad." Celia looked at the coffee growing cold on the table.

Allison face crumpled. "Funny, but it always upset me that Thomas wasn't like Daddy. Now I see he really was like him."

Celia took a few deep breaths to quell the pain in her stomach. "I shouldn't have done this. You have enough to deal with."

The lights in Allison's eyes shattered like splintering glass. "I guess you had to be straight, but God, it's hard to be socked with this ... kind of crap."

Celia's heart pounded in her throat. She'd caused her daughter to lose a fiercely guarded image of her father. She knew he did love her in his own way, even if his intent might have been to divide and conquer. She had to find a way to bridge the chasm she'd helped cause. "I love you more than my own life. Can we be friends?" Celia asked as she stood and hugged Allison, who didn't resist. In a few seconds she pulled away.

"I'm not sure about the friend thing. I need time." Tears streamed down Allison's cheeks.

"I've really changed, Allie. I'm not depressed and emotionally withdrawn like I was for so many years. I'll do whatever it takes to win your trust. I want that more than anything." Celia pressed her hands together prayer-like against her chest.

The quiet sound of cha-cha music skimmed the edge of her awareness and Celia crossed the room to turn up the volume. The rhythm seemed to flow right through her and without noticing, she did a few cha-cha steps. "Cha-cha-cha and a one-two, one-two-three."

Allison's eyes widened. "What the hell?"

"Do you want to learn the cha-cha?" she blurted out.

"Mom, where in the world did that come from?"

Celia blinked hard to fight back tears. "I feel nostalgic. We never finished our lesson we started so many years ago." Celia stopped for a second. "I love you and can never be truly happy unless you are."

Allison stared at her mother with a flat expression. "How will dancing prove anything?"

"Dancing gave new meaning to my life. It's how I found new friends and learned to tap into my feelings and feel free. The cha-cha rules work for everyday living." Celia did a few steps and held her arms out.

Allison sat down heavily on the sofa. "Please, no philosophical stuff at this hour. My brain is frazzled."

"Just give me a chance to be a good mother to you. That's all I ask."

Allison rose, gave her mother a peck on her check, and urged her towards the door. Celia opened it and looked back over her shoulder. Allison gave her a small, quick smile before closing the door.

Celia drove home, feeling somewhat lighter than before, and parked in the courtyard near her building. As she walked toward her apartment, she saw Dawkins and Johnson at her door. Her body raced with panic, but before she could turn around and head elsewhere, the officers spotted her.

Dawkins called out, "Ms. Ewing. We've been trying to get in touch with you."

Shit. Be calm. "What do you want?"

"You didn't answer my calls, Ms. Ewing."

"Oh. I've been … uh, having problems with my voicemail."

"Uh-huh. We're asking you to come down to headquarters for fingerprinting."

"Why, for God's sake?"

"We've been conducting an investigation into Melvin Onstader's death and found fingerprints on a bottle of Viagra in his apartment.

Since it was reported that you wheeled Mr. Onstader out of his office the night he died, we are asking for your fingerprints. Either you come willingly or we get a warrant. It won't be good for you if we have to come again, trust me."

Celia could feel her insides trembling. "Okay." Celia held her wrists out, but they hustled her into a patrol car without handcuffs.

At the station, she was assigned a number and asked to wait in a dreary room with damp, peeling sheetrock walls and rusty water spots on the drop-ceiling tiles. She sat next to two women wearing glittery black miniskirts with messy teased blonde hair, their arms and legs tattooed in neon colors. Both wore halter tops pulled so tight their breasts nearly popped out.

"Hey, lady. You in for solicitation too?" the shorter one asked Celia, clapping her hands and smirking.

Celia snorted with laughter. "Not this time."

The taller woman looked at Celia with a sarcastic expression. "Yo, Noraleen, she does the old grandpops. We hand 'em over to her, all the old farts." She puckered her lip. "You do round the world?"

This time Celia belly laughed. She knew it must be some kind of sexual position. "The old guys I'd *do* wouldn't remember that anyway."

"They maybe don't remember their names, but they sure do remember around the world."

The women laughed hysterically, then the taller one said, "You're okay. Whatcha in for? You don't look like a criminal."

Celia pursed her lips. She shrugged. "Murder."

They both slapped their thighs and giggled. "That's one hell of funny lady."

"I wish I were kidding," Celia said softly.

A policeman stepped into the room. "Number 11?" Celia took a deep breath and tried to steady herself as she stood. The policeman looked irritated. "Hurry up, lady. We don't have all day."

In the booking room, she allowed them to smear her fingers with ink and press them on an official-looking document. If her fingerprints matched the ones on Melvin's Viagra bottle, they would get an indictment and arrest her formally. She took deep breaths to keep herself from shaking. She knew she should have a lawyer, but if she resisted now it would look bad for her. Her muscles felt pulled tight as wire. All the air in the room seemed to seep out, making it feel like she was trapped in an ugly, dank vacuum. Her throat closed.

"Can I wait for the results?"

"Yeah, but it'll be a couple of hours."

"I'll wait." Celia sat down on a hard splintery bench, feeling little stings through the thin material of her skirt. She didn't flinch, but the room spun. Closing her eyes, she leaned her head against the wall and drifted into an agitated doze. A noise disturbed her and she realized she'd been asleep for an hour. She waited another hour.

A police officer walked in. "No match," he squawked. "You're free to go, but don't go too far. We still have questions for you."

When would all of this be over? What if it never was?

Chapter 42

Celia

Celia sat in Stanton's living room, staring out the floor-to-ceiling windows as the orange sunset peeked out from fingers of pink clouds. The beauty of it distracted her for a moment. The dread still roiled in her body from the afternoon at the police station.

Stanton looked at her with a raised eyebrow. "What's going on, Celia? You're so pale you seem to be disappearing."

"For one thing, I finally told my daughter that her father cheated on me. We had an argument at first but wound up nearly okay."

"It's tough for a child to handle. I know I don't have kids, but maybe she felt caught between the two of you."

Celia stared hard at Stanton. "No, you don't have children, so how can you understand?"

"I'm just going by human nature."

"I just need you to listen and not make judgments."

Stanton nodded. "I didn't mean to ... what else happened?"

"Gabe was good to her, but she has this impression he was flawless and can't let it go."

"Idealizing happens when a parent dies, or even others for that matter."

Celia's eyes narrowed. Allison was still reeling from her grueling divorce, adjusting to a stressful job and an unknown future. Of course she'd cling to memories of a happier time to keep her world from dissipating. Celia's heart went out to her, and she felt her face soften. "You're right."

"Is that all that happened?" Stanton pressed gently.

She looked down. "I was taken down to police headquarters to be fingerprinted." She looked up and saw his stunned expression.

He shook his head. "You caught me off guard with that one. Why?"

"They found prints on a medicine bottle in Melvin's apartment, but they weren't mine. But we're not off the hook yet." Her spine tightened.

She agonized whether to tell him about the death stats and her suspicions that it might be the work of a serial killer, but decided this was enough for one day. "I'll be honest. Arguing with my daughter unsettled me more than the police and the prints."

He poured each of them a glass of wine. "I get it."

Celia knew that the minute she stepped out of Stanton's apartment, she'd be forced to deal with reality. But for the moment she wanted to forget all the heart-wrenching events that threatened to completely unravel her life. She took a sip of her drink. "No more unpleasant talk. I'm sorry I dumped on you."

"No apologies. I'm glad you trust me enough to confide in me." Stanton dimmed the lights and closed the wooden slats on the window shades. Lit candles were scattered around the room. "I added candles."

"Nice touch." She gave him a soft smile and raised her glass in a toast. The wine slowly untied the knots in her stomach.

He looked at her askance. "I'm here for you. You know that don't you?"

Celia drank a little too quickly and coughed. "Yes, and I appreciate that so much." She tugged at her knee-length dress, which had ridden up to the middle of her thighs, and rested her head on the back of the sofa. For now the teeming, frightening world outside his door floated in the distance. She silently thanked Stanton. *And kudos to the wine.*

He leaned over and kissed her. "I love that pensive expression of yours." He stared in her eyes. "I really like the new Celia. She's so … open, if that's the right word."

She swirled the last of her wine. "I'm starting to stop worrying about what the world thinks of me."

She enjoyed how the wrinkles on his face disappeared in the pale light, reminding her of the old Stanton. Her lips brushed his cheek, his nose, his chin and mouth. Each time their lips touched it felt like being at a warm beach with waves lapping at her toes. She pressed herself against him. He cupped her breasts.

"Maybe we should …" she said, out of breath.

He stood. "I think you're the sexiest woman I've ever known."

"Really? When I was younger I wanted to be admired for my mind. Now sexy is better." Locked in an embrace they waltzed into his bedroom.

"At one time I'd have carried you into bed, but I don't test my old back anymore. It creaks." His grin went sheepish when he looked at her.

Celia sat on the bed. He stared at her for a long time then gently lay her back on the bed.

Stanton spooned against Celia's back and threw his arm around her waist. "Whew. Don't know if this used heart can take such fabulous lovemaking."

She loved when he teased her like he did back in college.

"If my socks weren't already off, you'd be knocking them off." He hummed tunelessly. "Talk to me," Stanton said, pressing closer. "My ears are still burning. How do you feel?"

"You blew the top of my head off." Her quickened breathing subsided. "Quiet. I just want to doze," she said, her voice fuzzy.

"And they say only men want to sleep after making love."

She reached back and tugged his hair. He kissed her shoulder.

Celia thought that he couldn't get her out of her awful situation, but this strong erotic pull could divert her a bit. Handling her predicament fell on her alone. After several sweet kisses on her neck and back, her fervor returned. The outside chaotic world was, once again, obscured. Old fogies my butt, she thought as she rolled over to his embrace.

The next day, as Celia neared the end of her routine morning walk, she felt as if she were dancing over the path, listening to the pleasant thwack of the soles of her sandals hitting the bricks. She still basked in the afterglow of the previous night and found herself humming "Let's Get Loud" by Jennifer Lopez, one of her favorite modern cha-chas. She kept the beat with each step.

As she neared her apartment, she saw two police officers at her door. She stopped in her tracks. Before they saw her she ducked into an alcove, her heart pounding in her chest, sweat beading on her forehead. She called Stanton on her cell phone. When he picked up, she spoke in a hoarse whisper: "The police are at my door. I'm terrified."

He was silent for a few seconds. "You'll have to face them sooner or later."

"I know. But here's the problem. You can believe it or not, but I think there's a serial killer on the loose."

The silence was so heavy she thought she'd scream. He finally spoke. "Geez. Are you sure? Is there proof?"

"Just a strong hunch. The autopsies being done are really unusual. They're looking at us now. I need a criminal attorney ASAP."

"This is bigger than I thought. I can recommend one, an old friend. But I feel somewhat at a loss." He gave her the name.

She had assumed that as long as they avoided actually hiring an attorney they'd kept the situation under control and nothing bad could happen to them. That had been foolish.

"Call me after they leave," Stanton told her.

She hung up and stepped from her hiding place, deciding to be super friendly. "Hello," she called. "C'mon in."

"We meet again," Officer Johnson said, stepping into Celia's living room. Detective Dawkins trailed behind, casting glances around the room.

Celia wiped her damp hands on the hem of her T-shirt and managed to compose herself. "How can I help you?" She pointed to two chairs with a trembling finger and sat on the sofa, stiff-backed. They looked serious.

Dawkins scanned the room, eyes roving, lighting upon pictures, chairs, bookcases. Celia bit the inside of her cheek to keep her expression unflappable.

Officer Johnson checked his notes. "As you know, we're investigating Melvin Onstader's death. What do you know about him?"

Oh shit. "I knew him only casually. What is this about?"

"Just tell me about Mr. Onstader. Didn't one of your friends date him?"

"Listen, I don't know what you're leading up to. Just spit it out." Her sweet demeanor ebbed.

Instead of answering, he asked, "What medications have been prescribed for you?"

"Don't worry," Dawkins piped up, still looking around the room. "We know a lot of people take medications. Heavens, I take them myself."

Was she playing the good cop? Celia began to sweat. "My medical history is my own business."

"Not necessarily."

"Stop beating around the bush, damn it." Steel bands tightened at her temples. She worried she was getting another migraine.

Officer Dawkins smiled too sweetly. "Don't get excited."

"I've already been fingerprinted and cleared."

"Mr. Onstader's autopsy raised questions," Johnson said.

Dawkins gave Celia a sobering look. "We just need you to tell us all you know about Mr. Onstader. We trust your judgment."

That's a big fat lie, she thought, *and I don't trust yours.* "If you don't get to the point then leave."

Dawkins continued walking around and looking in every nook and cranny then spoke without turning around, pointedly. "Were you ever intimate with Melvin Onstader?"

Celia snorted a harsh laugh. "He was involved with lots of women, but never me."

Johnson looked up. "Did that bother you? Were you mad at him?"

"As a matter of fact, I was relieved. He's not my type."

"Melvin Onstader's autopsy showed high levels of Viagra, antidepressants, and oxycodone, none prescribed by a doctor. It proved lethal."

"So what does that have to do with me? Viagra and oxycodone aren't hard to obtain on the internet or on the street."

Johnson smirked, then, seeming to catch himself, stuck out his bottom lip. "Did you give him any of those drugs—you know, just trying to help as a friend?"

Celia shook her head. "Absolutely not."

Johnson tapped his chin with his pen. "The label on the prescription bottle was written by hand and not traceable."

Dawkins kept looking around the room. "Is what you're telling us the truth, Ms. Ewing?"

"Yes," Celia spoke sharply. No one spoke for several seconds. "Can I show you out?"

"Not yet." He sniffed and checked his notes. "On the evening of January 5, at 4:30 a.m., did you, along with Marcy Worthmire and another woman, remove Melvin Onstader's dead body in a wheelchair from the board of directors' office?"

The dreaded question that she'd known was coming still blind-sided her. "No." Celia stared at him, forcing herself to make eye contact. Shit, she thought. If they prove I'm involved, I'm dead.

"You already know we have a witness attesting to seeing you and two other women transporting a large person in a wheelchair. She was certain it was Mr. Melvin Onstader. It was the night the man in question passed away."

Celia stuck out her chin. "This so-called witness is the caregiver, Vanessa Cordova. Why would you take her word over mine?"

"We have another witness who ran into you on the morning of Mr. Onstader's death and reported that you looked frazzled," he said. "Did you see anything suspicious?"

"That would be none other than Edith Onstader," Celia said. "I took an early morning walk, that's all, and your witness was also out at that time. She's a suspect, right?"

"We didn't say you were a suspect," Johnson said, gloating. "We're only interviewing."

Dawkins pointed to her cheek. "Do you mind if I put my gum in the wastebasket?"

Celia pointed to one beside her desk. Dawkins stooped over the basket and peeked in, then she fished around inside it. Celia heard paper crinkling. Why didn't she just throw her gum away?

"Can I help you, Detective Dawkins?" she asked, her voice sounding raspy.

Dawkins snapped on latex gloves. Celia sprang up to stop her. But in an instant, Dawkins's hand emerged from the basket with a scrap of paper.

Perspiration formed on Celia's temples. She wished her air conditioner worked better. Eying the door, she imagined flying out into the sunshine, free of all worries.

"We hoped for cooperation." Johnson rubbed the side of his pencil point on his check, leaving a small smudge.

Dawkins looked like she'd scored a goal in a soccer game and handed Johnson the slip of paper, now safe within a plastic envelope. Celia's pulse ratcheted up. Dawkins chewed hard on the gum still in her mouth.

He read the slip through the plastic then stared at Celia. "Label from a prescription for Elavil for you, prescribed by Dr. George Drudding." He half-grinned. "Very high doses of Elavil by itself can cause someone to die of a heart attack. You telling the truth?"

Celia almost screamed. "I never heard of a Dr. Drudding. That label has been planted." Chills ran down her spine as she realized that someone not only kept tabs on her activities, but also had invaded her apartment. Celia fisted her hands. "Someone's watching me, knows my habits, and planted that while I was out walking this morning."

"Any signs of a break-in?" Dawkins drawled out each word.

"These doors open with a credit card, and whoever planted that tipped you off! This is entrapment." The chills turned into a solid glacier. She knew most residents knew each other's habits. Surely Edith knew her morning walk routine. Had she told Vanessa?

"We're going to search your apartment. We have probable cause with this label."

"You don't have a warrant." Celia had a sudden urge to pee and squeezed her knees together.

Dawkins gave Johnson a pointed look. "Don't need one now. We're using a law called the plain view doctrine," Dawkins said. "Because we found something related to the case, we have the legal right to search your apartment." She spoke in a nonchalant manner as a friend might ask about her apartment decoration. "We suggest you cooperate."

Celia gritted her teeth.

Johnson produced latex gloves from his pockets, then each officer went in separate directions.

Dawkins walked right into the bathroom. After several minutes she walked back, grinning, holding a plastic bag with a dozen vials of pills, and called out to Johnson. Celia watched their movements, frozen to her chair.

"These meds are prescribed by the same Dr. Drudding and say Elavil and oxycodone. I found them taped to the drainpipe."

Celia's heart pounded so hard she thought it might break through her breastbone. "I've never seen those before and don't know Dr. Drudding. I've been set up, I told you!"

"We need to have these analyzed to make sure they are what they say."

Celia fastened her fists to the side of her thighs to keep from snatching the package away. "You can't prove those are mine." Her stoic appearance gone, her voice bordered on panic. "Check with that doctor. He'll tell you he doesn't know me."

"We did find them in your apartment, didn't we?" Dawkins asked.

"I'll have to ask you not to leave town," Johnson said.

"Am I a person of interest?" Celia asked.

He snorted a laugh. "You've been watching too many TV mysteries."

"But you act as though I'm under suspicion."

He gave her a gap-toothed, phony smile. "We will need to question you again."

Dawkins looked indifferent. "Thanks, Ms. Ewing."

The casual thanks sounded more like a death sentence to Celia.

"Wait. You have to believe me ..." But her voice reverberated against the closed door. She needed to call this Dr. Drudding.

First she called Marcy, but the call went to voicemail. "Call me right away. The police came to see me about moving Melvin's body.

They might be calling on you and Deb. We need a plan of attack. We need lawyers. It's bad."

She then called Deb, alerting her as well. She realized that they had to scour their apartments for planted medications or anything else that seemed odd. Apparently she'd scared someone who needed to stop her from going further with her amateur investigation.

A thought suddenly struck her. The police visit came on the heels of Allison pulling those death statistics. In obtaining the data, had her daughter disturbed someone with a vested interest in making Celia a scapegoat? Anyone could hack into computers. Was there an "angel of death" roaming their communities?

Had she been wrong to trust Stanton with so much information? Did he tell Edith?

Celia called Allison at her office. They hadn't spoken since she'd told her about Gabe. "Allie, do you have a minute? It's important."

"I'm really busy, Mom, but you sound stressed. Are you okay?"

"Did anyone know you gathered statistics for me?"

"That's a weird question. No big secret about statistics. I use them at work a lot."

"Please, Allie, just tell me." Celia sensed Allison's own agitation.

"I had Vanessa pull the initial stats from the accounting department, and my computer is hooked up to the top brass. They can access information from everyone's computer at any time. Not unusual." She exhaled. "What's going on?"

Celia avoided mentioning the police visit. Allison would find out soon enough.

"Some of the deaths are being investigated as possible homicides. Some autopsies ..."

Allison tsk-tsked. "People get overwrought when a person close to them dies. They rant and rave and want someone to blame. Sometimes they sue frivolously. Well Services has several of these suits." Celia could hear irritation in her voice. "No patient has ever complained about Vanessa and she does a great job. She's my friend. Stop listening to nonsense, Mom." Allison paused. "Have you told your beau?"

The implication in her daughter's tone cut Celia to the bone. "Some."

"He might think you're bonkers. Let this death statistics thing go!"

"I'm not bonkers, Allie."

Allison groaned. "If this rumor gets around, Vanessa's reputation could be ruined."

"You're right. I'll let you get back to work."

"Good. Behave yourself," Allison said with concern before hanging up.

Celia waited for a couple of minutes and tried to untangle all the weird connections that swirled around her before dialing Marcy again.

Marcy sat across from Celia in her living room. Celia had just told her everything about the police visit and had laid out some of her theories and suspicions.

"So, let's say Vanessa is guilty," Celia said. "Do you think she acted on her own?"

"She had access. If she's a nut who thinks people in distress have to die, it would be her alone."

"We just need some proof." Celia sighed. "I have to tell Allison about the police visit. She has a right to know."

"Put it off. We have work to do first."

"You're right. What should we do first? We need a list."

"Like a grocery list for finding a serial murderer, huh?"

Celia shivered. "I guess you could call it that. First, we scour yours and Deb's apartments in case the police show up soon. Next, we plan our defense and lie about moving Melvin. We have to investigate this Dr. Drudding and then find lawyers. Let's not forget that we need to dig up information on Vanessa."

Marcy clapped her hands together loudly. "It's a lot to do but we desperately need a plan. Let's get moving."

Chapter 43

After two weeks of putting it off, Allison went on her second date with Michael. He looked casually chic in pressed khaki pants and a white shirt with thin vertical blue stripes, open at the collar, his blue blazer slung over the backseat.

They picked up sandwiches at a roadside stand before heading up the coast, the sun setting in the radiant orange-striped sky. The worry lines that dogged Michael's face at work disappeared a few at a time with each mile they drove, his smile broadening, his body sinking more and more relaxed into his seat. "You know what Floridians like to do most?" he asked.

"What? Play golf? Tennis? Go to flea markets?"

"Wrong, wrong, and wrong again. It's watching the winter weather reports from up North. We gloat that we're basking in eighty-degree sunshine while Yankees are stuck in a blizzard."

"And do Northerners gloat in the summer when the Florida heat is suffocating?"

"Suppose so." He laughed.

"Does everyone have to feel they have it over someone else?"

He wiggled his eyebrows. "Sure. I'm your boss."

"Ha. Some boss. I tell you what to do."

"And I listen very closely." He cupped his hand behind his ear.

They both laughed. She appreciated that he was trying to put her at ease, but her stomach felt tight. To soothe her jitters, she shared bits of office gossip, speculating on who was possibly having an affair with whom. She mentioned that there was buzzing about Brady and Vanessa. "Let's hope they beat the odds of Brady's lousy romantic track record," she said. Michael nodded.

Driving past miles of gated communities, Allison observed that while they looked more or less upscale than her mother's place, they all seemed remarkably similar in their layouts. "Why do all the gated communities have that same spouting fountain?"

"It's a shtick. Be forewarned," Michael said. "Everyone will take you on a tour of their development, swearing their grounds, club-house, and condos are more beautiful than any others. There's a rumor that the occasional alligator sightings are planted by the con-do committees for the sake of authenticity and excitement."

"Wouldn't surprise me. But all in all, it's great lifestyle for older folks. It gives them a built-in group of peers, activities that keep their minds alert, and care when they need it."

"Spoken like a healthcare person at heart."

Allison sighed. "I wish my mother took advantage of all that. Even with this new beau of hers, she sometimes acts goofy. Just the other day …" She trailed off. "You know what? I don't want to talk about my mother. Not today."

"I'm all for that," Michael said with a grin. "It's just about us."

As they meandered up the coast, she enjoyed the briny scent in the air, beautiful flowers lit up along the outside edges of gated communities, and vast pinpoints of stars starting to appear in the sky as sunlight faded to dusk. To Allison, Florida was a sad tussle between nature's beauty and humanity's invention of concrete. Michael slowed the car and turned onto a dirt road and the ocean disappeared from view. She worried about how she'd respond to his advances if they happened, then worried about how she'd respond if they didn't.

After driving another fifteen minutes, Michael took another sharp turn and parked at what appeared to be a lagoon. A nearby marina spread pale lights over piers and anchored boats that swayed in the gentle waves. A warm breeze blew in through the open window, ruffling her long, curly auburn hair and caressing her cheeks. Pinpoints of light from faraway homes sparkled in the water's reflection like pearls as the sky darkened.

Michael cut the motor and left the headlights on. Drooping mangrove tree limbs created a privacy screen. Frogs croaked in the distance, and the muscled air had a thick swampy, earthy fragrance. Pale moonlight crisscrossed Michael's face, enhancing his strong features.

She loved the romantic atmosphere. "Is this where you take all of your dates?"

"Yes," he said, pursing his lips. "And I bet those women bring their new dates here after they dump me." He gave her a wry smile and moved closer, brushing a strand of hair from her forehead.

She swallowed hard, her heart pounding faster.

He retrieved a small cooler from the back seat and removed two craft beer bottles, unscrewing the caps and giving her a beer and a sandwich. He clinked his bottle on hers. "To your continued success at Well Services. And to us."

She felt her face flush and swallowed hard, the beer twisting into a knot on the way down her throat. His intent stare made her scalp prickle down to her neck. She knew that if he made a move, she wouldn't be able to resist him.

"My mom is really into this guy she's seeing." Allison said, breaking the silence.

Michael laughed. "I thought we weren't going to talk about your mother."

She clapped a hand over her mouth. "Damn. Sorry."

"It's all right. I hope when I reach her age, I'm still having fun. He gave her a knowing glance.

"Yikes. Spare me the details! How about you tell me what you were like as a kid," she said, taking a bite of her sandwich. "A devil, I'll bet."

He gave her a bemused look. "In high school, I thought I'd be lucky if I wound up sweeping streets." He unbuttoned his cuffs and rolled his sleeves up. "At fifteen I joined the football team to prove my manliness." He flexed the wiry muscles that pressed against the material of his shirt.

She patted his bicep, and let her hand slip down the taut, smooth skin of his arm. "Most men like to think they were bad boys, especially if they were introverted."

He gave her a soulful gaze. "The best I can offer is a shouting match with a high school coach and then getting kicked off the team. He gave his son my position of quarterback while I got benched. When I did play I outdid that creep." He gave wry smile. "One practice session, the coach's son tackled me over a concrete barrier and elbowed me hard. I had three broken ribs, so I was out of commission a couple of months."

"That's terrible! What a jerk."

"Yeah. Coach ruled it an accident." Michael finished his drink.

"Then my mother got herself involved and, at the homecoming game, got herself kicked off the field. I never played again. I guess that's where I get my feisty side."

"And do you behave yourself now?" She teased.

"My mother watches me like a hawk to make sure. But I'm worried her mind's starting to slip."

"I hope not."

Michael waved his hands in the air, as though wiping a slate clean. "Enough. I thought we'd agreed not to talk about our mothers. How about you? You're much more intriguing."

"To be honest, I'm still a little nervous about us," she said quietly, wrapping the remaining half sandwich, her stomach too jumpy to eat much.

"Me too. I want this to be right." Michael touched Allison's cheek and moved closer. She could feel the heat of his body through her thin blouse, seeming to sear her skin.

He took a deep breath and kissed the inside of her wrist, trailing his lips up her arm to the indentation at the base of her neck. She leaned into him, the warmth of his body heating her own. His mouth, firm, soft, and warm, sent currents zinging from her lips to her stomach. She gripped his shoulders and pulled closer. He cupped her face in his hands.

He leaned back to look into her eyes. "Are you sure you're okay with this?"

"No, but don't stop." She pulled him back and ran the tip of her tongue along his ear and down his neck.

"I want you so much," he whispered in her ear. "Let's go back to my place." He started the engine. "This car is good for show, but not for anything else."

They buzzed down the road, warm, sultry air stroking her hair, electric currents pulsing through her belly. Though still unsure, she lost any will to say no.

When they arrived at his townhouse, the fragrance of money hit her at once—the waxed-oiled smell of leather coming from a massive white sofa that dominated an entire wall, surrounded by three matching white leather chairs. She skimmed her fingertips across the supple arm of the sofa. "This is gorgeous Italian leather."

"Not as beautiful as you." Michael stood close. She blushed, then turned away from him to study pictures hanging on the wall, noting with surprise that they were original lithographs by Picasso, Chagall, and Miró.

Michael produced a bottle of cold Taittinger champagne and popped the cork. "Lithographs are much less expensive than oil paintings," he said, pouring the bubbly liquid into flutes. "Don't be impressed. I didn't have time to decorate so I hired an interior designer—and paid a walloping amount."

They clinked glasses. "To us," he said. He looked upbeat.

Allison forced a smile and yanked in shaky breaths.

Michael furrowed his brow, then stroked her cheek with the back of his hand. "I think I make you nervous."

"Less and less," she admitted.

He drew her to his chest. "This isn't just about sex, Allison. I care for you. I want to keep you in my life. I can hear your heart beating deep in my bones," he said softly.

His warm breath brushed her bare skin as he leaned his body into her. He kissed her hard and she met the pressure, her insides fluttering, her fingers digging into his back. The kiss lingered as his desire saturated into her skin.

Then he led her up the carpeted stairs, stopping on a large landing, pulling her in close for another kiss. When she started unbuttoning his shirt, he covered her hands and pulled, ripping the buttons loose. Pausing to lift her gauzy blue blouse over her head, he pointed his chin toward the bedrooms upstairs, but instead they fell to their knees and she knew they'd never make it.

Her body had never before responded so profoundly to a man. Michael's magnetism drew her in so deeply she became a part of him. He moved with her at a slow pace at first, picking up speed until she reached the precipice. She dug her fingernails into his back, and when he stroked her nipples she moaned. Her body splintered in ecstasy as he pressed into her.

When their rapid breathing slowed, they collapsed into each other's arms, neither of them moving or speaking for several minutes.

"God," she said. "Oh my God. I feel like a savage animal."

"Long live savagery," he said hoarsely. "I think we're at a point of no return." He sat up, holding on to her and looking right at her. "Even if I could jump back into my old life, I don't like where I'd land."

"Me either." She admonished herself for her inane response, but Michael's contented face told her something else.

"Come shower with me."

She nodded. He seized her hands, pulling her up. As they walked toward the bathroom, a phone on the hall table began to ring. He picked up the receiver and put it on speakerphone.

"No old girlfriends calling?"

"Nope," he said.

"Mr. Castor," a frantic voice yelled. "This is Ilene Junro."

She knew it was the receptionist at the office. She wouldn't call on a weekend night if it weren't an emergency.

"I just got the news that June Hartner was found dead in a motel. She killed herself."

"What the hell are you talking about?" He raked his hands through his hair, his face creasing with worry. "Why? I can't believe … did she leave a note?"

"There was a typed message that said she couldn't face going to jail."

"Shit. She didn't have to do that. Shit. Thank you, Ilene." He hung up and covered his face with his hands.

Allison clutched him in her arms, feeling his pain seeping into her, the bliss they'd shared just a few minutes ago now seeming a thousand miles away.

Chapter 44

Celia

For two hours, Celia and Marcy searched Marcy's apartment, emptying every drawer and closet. Lingerie piled up on the bed. Despite the urgency of their task, Celia took a moment to run her fingers over the silky fabrics. "There's enough underwear here to clothe a dozen strippers," she teased Marcy as she opened another drawer. It was filled with sex toys, and she couldn't help but laugh.

"Hey, I like to try new ones to see which is best. I'd get a job as a dildo tester if I could."

"I bet you would," Celia said.

Marcy lifted a large dildo with an odd small attachment on the end. "I'd say this one is the winner. It does double duty. See that little gizmo on the end? It kind of does anal …"

"Stop!" Celia grimaced. "Too much information. We should get rid of these in case the police search your place."

Marcy shrugged and dropped it back into the drawer. "I'm out of pot so that's a plus."

The women moved on to Marcy's medicine cabinet. Celia carefully checked her prescription bottles. Just medications for high blood pressure and cholesterol. They were all clear.

"Are you sure we've looked everywhere?" Celia asked.

"Well … we missed my hidden stash of Viagra that I keep for emergencies." Marcy opened an aspirin bottle and spilled a few blue pills on top of a pile of skirts.

Celia picked up the pills and stared in disbelief.

"Hot-blooded women are alert for an impulsive fling." Marcy shrugged. "The authorities can't use four little pills that anyone can get online against me."

"They can and they will. We're first in line of suspects. So far, I got away with my fingerprints, but Vanessa's story is being taken seriously. I'm flushing these." She went to the bathroom and dropped the pills in the toilet.

"They can't indict us on this flimsy stuff."

Celia squinted at Marcy. "Listen up. They're trying to pin Melvin's death on us, and we can be accused of more deaths. There may be more people exhumed for autopsies. Start using your head."

"Head is what got us into this trouble."

Celia groaned at Marcy's bad joke.

"I'm so scared most of the time I have to poke fun just to help me deal."

"I get it, but we've got to stay focused," Celia insisted. "Someone is doing us in." She huffed in frustration. "Don't let your hormones rule your brain."

"Okay, okay."

"Now we'll help Deb search her place," Celia said, refolding some shirts, "and we'll have to clue her in on how to answer the police if and when they show up." She hesitated. "I'm going to use Stanton's friend as a lawyer."

Marcy looked distressed as she piled a stack of towels back into the linen closet. "Getting lawyers is a punch to the stomach. It means we're in deep shit for real." She groaned.

On the way to Deb's apartment, Celia composed herself to keep from alarming her fragile friend. Deb looked dazed when she let them in. She had a pill in her hand that she popped in her mouth.

"What is that?" Celia asked, frowning.

"My son organizes all my daily pills in a special case so I don't have to worry about them."

Celia looked at a filled monthly pill organizer case on the kitchen countertop. Each compartment held a number of different pills. "How nice that he's looking out for you."

Navigating Deb's apartment was like a maze. She had numerous mismatched coffee and end tables, sofas, and floor lamps, as well as a roll-top desk and an armoire crammed into her living room, all of them looking worse for wear. Celia knew Deb never threw a piece of furniture away. She started opening the kitchen cabinets.

"An afternoon visit? A spot of pot?" Deb asked, grinning.

"No," Celia said, half-regretfully. "If you have any, flush it down the toilet." She watched a pouting Deb do just that. "We have to talk. The police came by my place and found pills in my bathroom. Someone broke in to plant evidence to make me look guilty. The cops are analyzing them to see if they match up to the meds they found in Melvin's body. We need to make sure your place is clean. Marcy's is okay."

"Michael counts out my pills for the month and puts them in that case for me."

Celia nodded. "Okay. We'll double check and be sure there aren't any bottles of anything mysterious floating around anywhere, just in case."

Deb's face creased with distress. "We're at the end of our rope. It's Michael I'm worried about now."

"He's an adult," Marcy said. "He can handle it."

"Oh, he can handle that his mother might be arrested as an accessory to murder?" Deb replied sarcastically as she perked up. "You kidding me? It'll look bad for him."

Celia pinched her lips together. "I hope I haven't gotten Allison mixed up in this. She got the death statistics, and then right after that, the drugs were planted. I can't help but wonder if there's a connection. Vanessa pulled the stats so maybe she's connected, or maybe that Hartner guy is hacking into the company computers." She didn't voice the rest of her thought that it could be Stanton doing it. She knew he had the know-how, and she'd confided so much in him. It wasn't outside the realm of possibility. But she didn't want to further alarm her friends.

Marcy pointed to the pill organizer on Deb's counter. "What are all these pills you're taking?"

Deb's shoulders drooped. "Michael handles them. He picks up all my prescriptions and counts them out so I won't miss a dose. They're for all my ailments. They calm me." Deb looked smaller and more fragile than ever, as though she might disappear like a leaf in a strong wind.

Celia and Marcy resumed their search mission, but found nothing. "Where do we go from here?" Marcy asked in shaky voice.

Celia consulted her list. "We start by Googling deaths in retirement communities and check for any that look suspicious in ours. And we have to be sure to erase our searches." Celia sighed heavily. "And I have to find out who this Dr. Drudding is."

On the way back to her apartment, Celia wondered what kinds of questions might come up in a future interrogation. She'd researched enough to know that she didn't have to go back to the police station unless they provided a warrant. But if they accused the women of moving Melvin, they could go further and also accuse them of murder for not calling 911.

Celia turned the corner of the fourth-floor outdoor corridor. Glancing down over the railing, she saw a man wearing tennis clothes. His wide shoulders and stance made him look like Stanton, but his back was to her so she couldn't be sure. She willed him to turn around.

Just then she heard an earth-shaking clatter and turned her head in time to see a large metal dolly hurtling down the handicapped ramp that connected the building's floors. She jumped forward and pressed herself against the wall as the dolly skimmed the backs of her ankles on its way to smashing into the corridor's wrought-iron railing.

She felt searing pain in her ankles and struggled to breathe. Bracing one hand against the wall, she carefully moved each foot to ensure nothing was broken. The backs of her ankles were skinned and bleeding but she was otherwise unhurt. When she looked around, she saw no one. If she hadn't gotten out of the way, the metal dolly would have crashed into her, seriously hurting her or knocking her over the railing.

Had someone carelessly left the dolly at the top of the ramp? Celia knew the community maintenance staff was vigilant. Even if it had been left on the top landing, why would it randomly roll down the ramp? When she glanced back over the railing, she noticed that no one was around, and the man she'd thought might be Stanton had disappeared.

As she limped home, taking deep breaths to try and still her pounding heart, she felt the squeezing sensation around her temples that meant a migraine was coming on. Did someone push that dolly? Who would want to hurt her—or kill her? And why?

At home, she winced as she cleaned and bandaged the cuts on her ankles. She sank onto the couch with a heating pad on her aching back. She was in danger now, she knew it. The worst part was that the police would never believe her. But she couldn't back down now. Follow the cha-cha rule: DON'T BE AFRAID OF RESISTANCE. IT OPENS NEW HORIZONS.

When the pain had subsided a bit, she returned to her list. She looked up Dr. Drudding's number and dialed. She needed to figure out what was going on with those phony prescriptions.

"Dr. Drudding here."

Celia found it odd that a receptionist didn't answer. "My name is Celia. There were prescriptions for oxycodone and other drugs written for me by you, Dr. Drudding. But I've never even seen you. Could you help me figure out who the person was?"

"Sorry, all medical records are confidential. You'll have to prove who you are with a picture ID to see if they were ordered for you."

"When can I come in?"

"Uh, I'll be going away for a month. Doing charity work in Ghana. No staff. Call later."

Celia heard a soft click as the line went dead. A sinking sensation gripped her. This didn't seem right at all. Things were veering out of her control and she felt as though she'd stepped into quicksand.

Chapter 45

Celia

Mid-afternoon, Celia, Marcy, and Deb sat at a crumb-littered table in a local deli. It was nearly empty at that hour before the early bird rush, and the damp air was laced with the scents of detergent and spiced meats. Celia had filled them in about the dolly incident and her unproductive call to Dr. Drudding.

"Let's see the damage," Marcy said, and Celia hiked up her slacks and displayed her wounds. Marcy's and Deb's eyes widened.

"Do you really think someone pushed that thing?" Deb finally asked. "It could've just been gravity."

Marcy crossed her arms across her chest and narrowed her eyes. "C'mon, Deb. Maintenance wouldn't leave a metal dolly in such a precarious place. How would it get down the ramp on its own?"

"Well, you should know how thorough the maintenance crew is," Deb quipped.

"Listen," Celia said, slapping her hand on the sticky table. "We need lawyers. Now. I keep repeating myself, but I'm at fault, too."

"I've gone ahead and gotten a public defender who looks and acts twelve. Both of you are next. Michael needs to get you a lawyer now," Marcy insisted, pointing a finger at Deb.

Deb's face creased with worry as she slipped several packets of sugar into her bag.

Marcy gnashed her teeth. "This whole mess is my fault. I'm so sorry I got you all involved."

Sunlight poured through the large front window, and Celia shaded her eyes. Her headache wouldn't go away. Celia knew these women were her safety net. "You'd have done the same for either of us." She sighed.

Celia let out a big breath and repeated a cha-cha rule aloud: "EMBRACE YOUR MISSTEPS. THEY ARE THE KEY TO DISCOVERING YOUR INNER SOUL. That's kind of ironic right now."

Marcy looked stricken. "I hate my missteps, and I not only have lost my inner soul, I've also put you both in danger."

"There's something else." Celia had debated whether to share this with her friends, but she knew she needed to tell them everything now. "When I woke up from a nap earlier today, I found a voicemail from Detective Dawkins, telling me that the police analysis of the containers in my apartment proved they contained Elavil, oxycodone, and Viagra—the stuff that killed Melvin." She grimaced. "Between the drugs at my place and a confirmation from Vanessa about moving Melvin, I'm betting there's enough evidence to seek an indictment from the DA. I'm the killer and you're accessories. Dawkins demanded I come down to headquarters, but I had to tell you both first."

"This can't be happening," Deb said in a loud whisper.

Marcy rubbed her temples. "We can only trust each other. Except for Allison. Right?" Marcy pursed her lips. "Um, as for Stanton, you don't know enough about him now to fully trust him yet, do you?"

Celia rested her chin in her hand. "He's been very open and supportive. I think I can trust him," Celia said. *I hope I can.*

"Who could have planted those drugs?" Marcy asked. "Edith visits the sicker residents and has a master key because of her position on the board. I thought her shut-in visits were man-hunting, but now who knows. And Vanessa ..."

"We visit the sick, too," Deb said, fluttering her fingers at Marcy.

"But we don't have keys," Marcy shot back.

"I checked. People have been convicted for murder with less evidence," Celia said.

Deb's face sobered. "So, what do we do? Michael will go crazy."

"If we get ..." Celia gulped, "indicted we say you weren't with us."

"I won't let you do that. All for one," Deb declared, raising a butter knife from the table like a sword. Celia felt her heart swell as she and Marcy also lifted their knives and clinked them together with Deb's.

"Allison claims the statistics about deaths in Boca Pelicano Palms aren't relevant. But I say we need more proof there's a serial killer on the loose. I'll start by looking into deaths for a few years back. I want to see if Vanessa was involved or connected in some way with more of them."

Marcy gave Celia a skeptical look. "I think we're screwed." She stirred her coffee so hard it spilled over the rim of the cup. "Why don't we just cha-cha until we're buried?"

"We'll beat this," Celia said, trying to convince herself. She looked up and saw Stanton approaching their table. Marcy and Deb rose right away, said their goodbyes, and greeted Stanton on their way out. Stanton sat next to her, giving her a kiss on the cheek.

"I know I came uninvited," he said. "Edith said you guys would be at this deli and that you all seemed quite upset."

"Geez, how did she know?"

Stanton looked befuddled. "You know how gossips are. Don't worry, she's harmless."

"Why are you defending her?"

"Look, I am not Edith's keeper. Who cares?"

"Well, I do. How would she know where I am? That's stalking." Celia cleared her throat. "The police found oxycodone, Elavil, and Viagra in my apartment that didn't belong to me. Someone planted them."

He winced. "Who do you think did it?"

"Wish I knew. Melvin's autopsy showed he died from overdosing on meds like those. I'm implicated for sure." Celia felt blood pounding in her head, making the pain barely bearable. "Vanessa ..."

He knitted his brows. "Come on. What would be her motivation?"

"For one thing she's volatile. Maybe she believes in mercy killings, or she hated her father, or she hears voices telling her to kill. Or she steals their money." Her voice bristled as she turned her ankles toward him. "Someone hurled a metal rack down a ramp right at me. I moved away in time before it seriously hurt me. Or even killed me."

Stanton grimaced then jumped up. "Holy mother of God. Let me take you to the ER."

She pulled him back down. "No, it's okay. They're clean and I wasn't seriously hurt. But someone was clearly tracking me and knew that corridor was isolated enough that they could get away with it. So much points to Vanessa."

"Vanessa treated my wife with compassion her entire illness." He sounded defensive.

"All I know is that once Allison had Vanessa pull those death stats I requested, all hell broke loose. Doesn't that count for something?"

Stanton frowned. "It's public information. Anyone can get it."

Celia pressed her fingers into the aching muscles of her neck, trying hard to stay civil. "I've done some research. Antidepressants or Viagra could be put into food, dissolved into a jar of jam or a drink. And Viagra is effective with food and alcohol. Put in fatty foods it slows the process, but it still works. I know Melvin ate a lot of fatty foods."

"Hey, do you think someone slipped me Viagra? I eat strawberry jam every day," he teased.

"It's clear you don't need it." She gently poked him in the ribs with her knuckles, but was determined not to let his humor detour her train of thought. "I've got to find out who gave those pills to Melvin. That's key. Have you ever heard of a Dr. Drudding?"

"No. Why?"

"His name was on the labels of the prescriptions found in my apartment. I called and got nowhere."

"I'll ask around, but I believe you're being set up." He wrinkled his nose. "Maybe it's just one death. Do you really think it could be serial killings?"

"I know it sounds ridiculous, but it's got some substance." She made a shooing motion. "Run while you can. No good deed goes unpunished, and you might wind up in trouble too, since you're associated with me now."

"I'm not going away. This is serious." Stanton rubbed his bristly chin.

She hesitated to ask the next question but gathered the courage. "Where were you yesterday morning?"

"In my community playing tennis. I got asked to join an early game before the heat of the afternoon." His jaw set. "Why are you even asking? Are you trying to implicate me?"

"This whole thing has me jumpy."

He looked at her sideways. "Not trusting me is insulting."

"Can you blame me for being cautious? I'm being implicated in murder."

Stanton grabbed her hand. "I'm your friend. Let me help."

Celia wanted to trust him. He'd never done anything to make her suspicious, really. Her life depended on it. "I do trust you," she said finally, and Stanton squeezed her hand.

That evening, Celia's doorbell rang, and when she opened it Allison pushed past her into the apartment.

"Something wrong?" Celia asked, her heart fluttering. They stood face to face in the living room. *She knows.*

Allison's hands were on her hips and her face pale as she squinted at Celia. "Who *are* you?"

"What do you mean?"

"Michael got a call from a reporter at the *Centennial* with questions about a murder investigation that involved you and your friends. They found out he's Deb's son and that made better news."

"Oh, the media is always overly dramatic. And not always accurate." Celia's eyelid twitched. It surprised her that the big county newspaper got on it so fast, but then Edith had to be the culprit for letting the news leak. Even the smaller community newsletter that covered five gated communities had contacted her.

Of course she'd declined to comment. Before this brouhaha, the most exciting news concerned an old person driving into a reflecting pool.

"Then why does Michael's mother want a criminal attorney? She claims you're under surveillance, a target or whatever. Is it true?" Allison smacked her fist into her open palm.

"Well ... yes ... in a way."

Allison huffed as though out of breath. "Have the police questioned you?"

"Yes, but I didn't have anything to do with the death of Melvin Onstader."

"You have to fill me in on every single detail and not leave one thing out." Allison steered Celia to the sofa.

So Celia told her everything. When she finished, there was a moment of silence. She almost felt a sense of relief getting it out.

Allison exhaled forcefully. "You are aware that it's illegal to move a dead body." Allison tapped her forehead. "What were you thinking? Helping a friend is no excuse, especially someone who is ... a troublemaker, getting into, uh, compromising situations."

Celia bristled. "How my friends conduct themselves is their business as long as they don't hurt anyone."

"What do you call murder?" Allison shot back. "Seems that's hurtful, wouldn't you say?"

"We didn't murder anyone, just moved his dead body. I did it to help a friend."

"Just moved a dead body? My God, would you rob a bank to help a friend?"

Celia said nothing, but considered that she might.

"What if they prove the man was murdered? You and your friends look guilty." Allison threw her hands up in the air. She seemed to be viewing her mother for the first time. "You wanted a new life and adventures, but for God's sake ..."

"It wasn't what I had in mind either." Celia wheezed, trying to catch her breath. "Maybe he committed suicide."

Allison heaved a huge sigh. "Don't count on it. Maybe you're getting depressed again, or starting to lose your marbles. You should see a shrink." She rubbed her temples. "Chances are Florida jurors will be older. They might be more sympathetic to someone with senility."

"Stop it." Celia shook her head vigorously.

"You all might be senile."

"Allison, stop! We all make mistakes."

Allison's face turned a deep red as she crossed her arms over her chest. "You didn't call 911! At least that would have put you on record of trying to revive him."

"He was very dead. Okay. That's enough. I'll handle this by myself."

Allison looked a bit contrite. "I'll never desert you. But you need the best criminal lawyer you can find. I have one. He handled the theft at Well Services."

"Stanton recommended a friend ..."

"You use this lawyer. He's the best there is. Call him right away."

"All right." Celia was unsure about using Stanton's recommendation anyway, and this gave her the perfect out. The thought of finally talking to a criminal attorney gave her chills. "I'm more worried about your safety," Celia said.

"Like you embarrassing me to death?" Allison glowered at her mother. "I'm convinced it might be possible."

"This thing exploded after Vanessa pulled the data for you. Right after that, someone planted bottles of meds here, the same kind that killed Melvin. Then they tipped off the police, who came and found them." Celia wrung her hands as she spoke. "I worry that I've implicated you somehow."

"That's ridiculous." Allison stood. "I've got to get out of here before I explode." She handed Celia a slip of paper. "The attorney's name is Albert Jackman."

Celia put the paper in her pocket. "You look tired."

"It's from trying to think of ways to save you. Call Jackman ASAP."

"I will, but … how will I … never mind."

"I know you're worried about paying him. Michael got him to cut his fee big time because of the work the company gives him. He'll also let you pay it out each month." Allison fisted her hands. "I insist on going with you. Michael is getting a different attorney for his mother." Allison walked to the door and gripped the knob. "You know, Michael thinks his mother might be losing it."

"I've noticed little lapses here and there but I think she's okay," Celia fibbed, but she knew her friend was slowly slipping. Celia crossed the room and gave her daughter a quick hug. Allison quickly hugged her mother back before opening the door. "I'm hoping it all works out. I am in your corner."

Celia stood in the doorway watching until Allison got in the elevator.

Celia always saw Gabe and Allison as mirror images of each other and herself as the outsider. Now she saw how much she and her daughter were alike. Both tended to sweep trouble under the table until it exploded in their faces, and both had clung to bad marriages for far too long.

The phone rang. Celia hurried to answer it, expecting to hear Stanton's voice.

"Ms. Celia Ewing? I'm Samuel Littleton from the *Centennial*. I just want to ask you a few questions to get your side of things for an article that's appearing in a few days."

"I won't give an interview," Celia shouted then slammed the phone down.

Celia took out the paper with Jackman's number on it. She would call him first thing the next morning, and opened a drawer to put it in for safe keeping. There she saw the paper with the cha-cha rules on it. Reflecting on applying those rules to real life made her aware that life could be messier than the exhilaration of dancing.

Her eyes lingered on one rule: IT IS DANGEROUS TO FEAR RISK. WE MAY NEVER KNOW JOY. *That's it.* She knew the time had come to take a risk, regardless of whether there was to be any joy.

Chapter 46

Celia

When Celia called Albert Jackman the next day, he barked a gruff hello.

Celia sank into her chair. "I'm Celia Ewing. I got your number from my daughter, Allison, from Well Services."

"Oh yes. Michael called." His voice warmed. "I don't have a lot of details. Fill me in."

"I could be charged with obstructing justice at the least and murder at the worst." Celia shared the details about moving Melvin. "He was already dead, I swear, but a witness saw us wheel him back to his apartment." She explained the autopsy results and numerous other deaths then cleared her throat. "I ... I think there might be a serial murder on the loose."

"Really? Ahem. That would be highly unlikely ..."

"I know it sounds unlikely, but listen." Celia relayed all that had happened.

"Come in tomorrow at four. I'll make time for you. In the meantime, don't talk to anyone and that includes the police. Call me first."

"Got it." Finally, a shred of good news in the swirling storm of her life. She silently thanked Michael for coming through.

Later that evening, Celia picked up the most recent copy of the

Centennial. When she glanced at the front page, she threw it down on her kitchen table as though she'd put her hand through fire.

MYSTERIOUS DEATHS BEING INVESTIGATED IN GATED COMMUNITY

"I can't read this." A profound urge to dance struck her, and she immediately called Marcy and Deb. They would meet in the community room and dance the cha-cha. She didn't care if Edith didn't want them using that room. She needed some dance therapy, and her friends agreed.

They met at the door and entered, keeping the lights off. Deb carried a flashlight and put a CD of Latin music in the player, a song Celia didn't know, but she liked the rhythm.

Light from a full moon streamed through the windows, providing enough light to dance by once Celia's eyes adjusted to the dimness. Snappy music spun out a fast cha-cha, and they lined up in a row instead of facing each other. As their bodies moved, Celia's distress rose out of her body and soared through the ceiling, through the windows, and through every crack in the walls and floor.

Celia saw the ecstatic expressions on the faces of her friends. She clapped in time to the music until her hands ached, but still they danced. Stopping now would have thrown her to the floor in a heap, but as long as the music played and her legs moved, there could be no other reason for existence. At this moment, she lived for the dance, and it resonated in her head and body. She raised her hands overhead, wriggled her fingers as though playing castanets, and abandoned herself to the passion roaring through her.

The next day Celia and Allison sat in Albert Jackman's office. The sun shone through the windows and glinted off the numerous brass accents on the furniture. Celia wanted to put on sunglasses. She'd come in feeling somewhat refreshed from the first good night's sleep in weeks. They'd danced for two hours, blissfully free of intruders. But now, she hated the bold, gleaming objects surrounding her, solid, secure, and indifferent to her plight.

Jackman's folded hands were on top of the gleaming glass-topped desk. He sat in a tall, rocket-like brass triangle that topped the back of his chair. He looked ready to launch into space.

"Ladies, Melvin Onstader's death is considered a homicide by the police—no ifs, ands, or buts. They might have called it a suicide had he died at home due to the large amounts of toxic drugs in his system. But because they believe his body was moved, they're calling it homicide. There is a witness who claims to have Celia and two other women moving Onstader's body. We'll try to discredit the witness because she didn't really see Mr. Onstader's face, only the bulk of a body. But because of the drugs found in your mother's home, Allison, she is their main target. But again," he turned to Celia, "you could have been taking those drugs yourself and forgotten. You know, age and ..." He leaned back in the chair.

Celia swallowed hard and gripped the arms of her chair. "I didn't use anything."

"The police are investigating whether Onstader's death is part of a succession of suspicious deaths. Did you socialize with any of the people who died?"

"Just a friendly hello to some," Celia said. "Once in a great while I'd briefly visit in their homes."

He cleared his throat and looked at the wall. "In that case, connecting you to Onstader's death is weak. It's circumstantial evidence."

"But is there any way they can link her to the other deaths?" Allison asked.

Jackman sniffed. "I have to see what witnesses say. For instance, will someone say they saw your mother going into the homes of those suspected of being murdered around the time of their deaths?"

Celia's throat constricted, knowing Deb and Marcy visited the infirm regularly and that some of them had recently died.

"Let's concentrate on the most pressing aspect. Worst-case scenario: charges can range from first-degree murder to involuntary manslaughter. The good news is that they haven't yet convinced the district attorney that there's enough probable cause for a warrant to charge Ms. Ewing—no fingerprints, DNA, things like that. The Boca police need a stronger case. I'm preparing for any and all possible outcomes." He wrinkled his brow. "If any others are indicted, I'll be asking for separate trials."

Celia squeezed her eyes shut, trying to still her pounding heart.

"If by some chance the DA's office brings an indictment against you, Ms. Ewing, there will be a preliminary hearing where they'll make formal charges. There are still the lesser charges of obstruction of justice for moving a dead body and lying to the police." His face remained staunch. "For now, sit tight."

Celia sat on the edge of her chair, thinking that this whole thing sounded worse spelled out in legalese.

"I know my mother is innocent," Allison said, glancing briefly at Celia. "I'm not sure about the other two women."

Celia's blood went cold. "They're innocent too."

"What if my mother forgot that the evidence they found in her bathroom was really for her own personal use? A woman with a boyfriend might have Viagra." Allison's voice turned to ice as she grimaced. "She has a history of depression that could strike again at any time. That could be why she had Elavil and oxycodone."

Celia stiffened her back. "I won't go that route. Those drugs weren't mine."

"Mom, we're here to consider every aspect for you, and you alone."

"Perhaps there has been a lapse in your mother's memory," Jackman suggested as he rubbed his chin.

"I won't do it." She hated that he spoke as though she weren't in the room. She grasped the shiny glass edge of the desk and said, "Don't put words in my mouth. Someone planted those drugs in my bathroom. I intend to get to the bottom of it." When she removed her hand, the glass was smudged. Mr. Jackman took a handkerchief from his pocket, reached over, and wiped the smudge away.

Allison gave her mother a caustic glance. "Please continue, Mr. Jackman."

"A warning to you both—don't do anything on your own. One step at a time. For now, we wait until charges are made, if they're made," he said.

"My mother's been getting calls from the press. Maybe she should she give her side."

Jackman put up his hand. "Don't talk to the media. They'll twist everything. They can only speak to me. I'll get you through this," he said. "One other thing." He leaned forward. "Don't let the police take your mom to the station unless they have a warrant. The strategy is to get her downtown, even though she's not obligated to go, then browbeat and bamboozle her to confess."

"What are my mother's chances of getting out of this if she happens to be indicted?"

Jackman shrugged, then sighed. "I can't tell just yet, but I'm always hopeful, especially in a case of no previous record. But we *are* talking murder here ..."

Celia wondered if she should jump off a bridge now or later.

Chapter 47

Celia

Celia had barely walked into Marcy's apartment when Marcy pulled out a joint.

"Everyone in this damned place is watching. One sniff coming from your apartment means trouble." Celia pulled a bottle of Pinot Grigio from a paper bag, uncorked it, and poured the pale liquid into three stemmed glasses. "This will do."

The three women settled around the table with their glasses, then Celia pulled some papers from her bag. "Nick at the front gate didn't want to give me the data from his computer. He said I'd have to get written permission from the president of the board—which is Edith, of course. So, with a hundred dollars and a bottle of eighteen-year-old single-malt scotch, I got information about everyone who died here over the last couple of years."

"Boy, he's cheap," Deb complained. "He gives confidential information out too easily."

"Be grateful," Marcy snapped. "This is vital stuff. What did you find out, Celia?"

Celia explained how the printout contained next-of-kin information for all the deceased residents, as well as the names of any caregivers or other healthcare workers who had visited each of them. "I eked out twenty-eight names in the last year. Vanessa was the caregiver for all but one of the patients. I made calls to each one's next of kin; children, siblings, friends, and all of them responded." Celia looked sheepish. "I told them I was from Well Services and doing a survey on the caregivers' abilities."

"A good cover," Marcy said, snapping her fingers.

"They all said their sick relatives got the best care and praised Vanessa's thoughtfulness to the skies. A few of them even mentioned how Vanessa brought special food treats to her patients to cheer them up." Celia tapped the papers. "They all died in short order after Vanessa started working with them, but they were all very sick to begin with.

"I found common threads. Each had nuclear families living out of the area who didn't visit often. All the patients needed complex therapies—oxygen, dialysis, insulin, intense physical therapy after strokes, X-rays, MRIs—you name it, along with lots of medications. All of them were enrolled in Global HMO, the umbrella company for Well Services. And it turns out that five of the departed were suing Global, including Melvin, for malpractice."

Marcy let out a low whistle. "What do you make of it, Celia?"

"I'm not quite sure, but here's the kicker. At least three quarters of the families I connected with said that their relative had a Dr. Drudding prescribing their medications."

Marcy's eyebrows shot up. "Maybe Vanessa was in cahoots with him."

"Let's not jump to conclusions," said Deb.

Celia stared outside the window, trying to gather her thoughts. "Allie mentioned that Vanessa's friendly with the head pharmacist at Global's mail-in prescription service."

Marcy got up and paced. "It's a needle in a haystack. Do we have enough evidence against Vanessa to bring in the police?"

"Dawkins and Johnson said they're checking on everyone, but we're the targets so far," Celia said. The air in the room felt tight and heavy, and Celia felt like it was hard to breathe.

Marcy jabbed her fist in the air. "Vanessa and Edith are in on it. They have to be."

"We need evidence," Celia said emphasizing each word. "More than this printout. It's a start, but not enough. Deb, has Michael said anything?"

Deb's knotty hands were clenched together on the table. Her eyes were glazed over, and she looked down. Celia put a hand gently on her friend's wrist. "Deb, did you hear me?" Deb looked at her with an unfocused gaze, so Celia shook her arm gently. "Deb! Has Michael said anything?"

Deb shook her head, the daze seeming to dissipate. "Yes, sorry. Michael. He mentioned that all this media attention has led to gossip in the office and upset his boss, Brady Shirkson, who is an idiot." Her bloodshot eyes glistened with tears. "I'd just die if this causes him to lose his job."

"Don't worry. He'll be all right," Celia said.

Marcy gently rubbed Deb's shoulders to calm her. "We should tell newspapers our side of it. Show them we're innocent."

"No interviews. That's final." Celia looked at her sternly.

"You'll be looking to tell your side of it from prison," Deb said. She started rising slowly from her seat, but seemed to be having trouble standing. "I'm tired. I can't talk about this anymore. I'm going home to bed."

Celia and Marcy each put a hand under Deb's arms and helped

her up. Celia noticed with alarm that Deb seemed weightless, her papery skin stretched over thin bones. "Can I walk you?"

"No, I'm not an invalid yet." Deb gave her a feeble smile. "I just need rest."

Deb hobbled out the door, and Celia stood in the doorway staring silently after her for a while. She turned back to Marcy. "I'm worried. Have you noticed that Deb's becoming more distracted and distant lately?"

"I've seen it. Maybe it's because we're in a pressure cooker," Marcy said, pouring them both more wine. "I can't sleep."

Celia shrugged. "I look over my shoulder wherever I go." A vision of prison life from movies flashed through her mind; women bullying each other, toilets in cells out in the open, disgusting food, rapes, scuzzy beds, and orders for everything. They'd die in there.

She shuddered and pushed the image out of her mind. She thought instead about practicing new cha-cha steps, sideways or in a circular pattern. That would be lovely.

Chapter 48

Allison

Paying the bills and payroll had become more of a tenuous balancing act of late, and Allison looked for yet more ways to cut expenses. No more parties, no new office furniture, and reduced expense accounts for executives. Allison smiled, as she knew Michael would come whining to her in a joking way. But why were the profit margins of Well Services slipping despite an uptick in membership and serious economizing?

Before she could look into it further, Vanessa walked in, carrying a post office bin full of mail. She wore a designer mid-thigh black leather skirt and a fitted green V-neck shirt, looking stylish and coiffed as always. It made Allison self-conscious, and she swiped a lock of hair off her forehead. Her work schedule kept her from paying attention to her appearance, and it definitely showed when Vanessa was around. But she didn't begrudge her after all she had gone through.

"Look at all this mail!" Vanessa dropped the bin on the desk and sighed exaggeratedly. "I'm not here for four days and chaos reigns. You do need me."

"True. I've been swamped." Allison thumbed through the pile.

"Michael seems to be in a bad mood," Vanessa said, her face dour. "He's been on my back, barking orders about doing a good job for you and the patients." She smacked her fist on Allison's desk. "I damn well do that."

Allison reached over and squeezed Vanessa's hand. "You are very good. He's under a lot of pressure. We have to make more cuts and we've got thin pickings. It upsets him to have to cut staff."

"Are you sure he's not just pissed that I'm taking up his boss's time?"

"I doubt it," she said lightly, pretending to be engrossed by something on her computer screen.

Vanessa snorted. "I'm sure he's not thrilled about having to take a pay cut."

"Well, it's like being forced to buy fine aged steak instead of the top of the line Kobe beef." Allison leaned back in her chair. "I don't think he will suffer."

Vanessa grinned. "Regardless, he *is* crazy about you."

Lately, Allison and Michael had spent little quality time together. Michael had been upset and distracted by June Hartner's suicide and other work issues. Missing him felt like she hadn't eaten for a month. Were things between them over before they'd even begun?

Vanessa made an impatient sound. "Hell, girl. Michael knows you're a rare catch of beauty and brains."

That made Allison feel better. She couldn't believe her mother suspected her friend of being involved in serial murders of elderly patients. Why would she put her promising future on the line that way? It made no sense.

She looked up when she heard Vanessa giggle. Vanessa was thumbing through a Victoria's Secret catalogue. "Did you have to send that here?" Allison's voice barely hid her irritation.

"Yes!" Vanessa said gleefully. "I leave it open to items I like and put it on Brady's desk." Her cell rang and she looked at the screen. "Speak of the devil, it's Brady. I'll be back."

Allison swiveled her chair and watched Vanessa's retreating back. She wasn't so sure Vanessa actually would be back. She needed to concentrate on the accounts in any case.

Well Services had only been in business twelve years and now grossed twenty-four million dollars a year. Allison wanted to get clear on what they were paying out and started a list.

Research and Development, workshops for healthcare workers, and more efficient systems in general came in at two million. Administration, salaries, and benefits reached nine million; travel, corporate sales, and operating expenses topped out at two and a half million. Building rent, maintenance, and staff supplies totaled three and a half. That came to seventeen million. Allison started with expenses at twenty-one million. Costs were down by four million. So why were they in the red?

Something caught her eye. There were vendors' names she didn't recognize on the spreadsheets. Substantial payments had been made to them. She found no authorization for the outlay and she hadn't seen them before. Was this still part of the Hartner's scam? Had someone in accounting usurped her authority? She tried calling Michael but he didn't answer. She left a message to call as soon as he could and went back to her spreadsheet.

The phone rang, startling her. "Michael?"

Instead, a gravel-voiced whisper asked, "Allison?"

"Yes, who is this?"

After a long hesitation she heard, "This is Richard Hartner."

She gripped the phone, pressing it hard against her ear. She recalled the office party that Hartner crashed. Her heart beat faster. "Are you looking for Mr. Castor?"

"No. I want to speak to you." His heavy breathing made her stomach tighten.

With a trembling hand, Allison pressed the intercom that sent a signal to Michael's office. He'd surely pick up when he saw Hartner's number. *Please be in, Michael.* "It's not appropriate for you to speak to me."

"To hell with appropriate. If you value your life you won't hang up."

Her ear numbed from the pressure of the phone against it. "Are you threatening me?"

"No, but we're in danger. My wife wasn't so lucky. You don't believe for one second that she committed suicide, do you? She fought those bastards over their trumped-up allegations and look what happened."

Allison wanted to hang up, but her hand froze. "What are you talking about?"

"My wife was fucking murdered. Can I be any clearer?"

"I'm so sorry about your wife, but, Mr. Hartner, the authorities have to handle …"

He exhaled loudly. "Fuck them, fuck your organization. Someone set her up, and when she had proof to exonerate herself, that same person killed her. I'm going to find out who did this, and they'll pay. If you're not tied up with those gangsters, get out fast."

He paused. Allison took a gasping breath, trying to steady herself. "No one here would do such a thing." She pressed the intercom button again. Where was Michael?

"The account in Gibraltar was faked, planted in our names,"

Hartner continued. "If we stole that much, do you think we'd stick around? Lady, get out while you can."

"Mr. Hartner, give yourself up. It'll go easier for you."

He snorted. "I can see I'm wasting my time. Just keep looking over your shoulder."

Without another word, he hung up. Allison could feel her body shaking. She tried calling Michael's office and then his cell, but he still wasn't answering.

She got up and went searching for him. She found him standing in a corridor huddled deep in quiet conversation with Brady. As she got closer, Michael looked up and Brady turned and hurried away. Wordlessly, Michael led her into his office, his face pale.

As soon as he'd shut the door, Allison said, "Michael, I tried to get you on your phone. Richard Hartner called. I tried to keep him on the line, praying you'd pick up."

"What nerve." He looked distracted, his brow furrowed.

"He said June was murdered."

He snapped to attention. "He's a pathological liar and will say anything to get out from under all this." He gestured for her to sit. "Never mind him. We have to discuss something very serious."

A chill went through her, like the icy feeling when she had found out that Thomas emptied their accounts.

"The auditors believe you and Richard Harter are in cahoots to hack into our computers to embezzle. He's a computer whiz and you have access."

Allison laughed, thinking Michael was joking. When she saw that he wasn't, she wanted to run. "What the hell are they talking about? I'd never heard of the Hartners until I started working here."

"The auditors told Brady they believe that you and the Hartners were embezzling even before you came to work here. It stopped with June leaving and started up again when you arrived. It's that scheme of defrauding us by using shell corporations as fake vendors." He lowered his head, chin on his chest.

Allison clenched her jaw as her body trembled. "I brought that scam to your attention with receipts I found stuffed in a drawer. Why would I do that if I were guilty?"

He took a deep breath. "They found an offshore account with your name on it in Costa Rica with substantial monies, but I don't know how much. They're looking to prosecute." He raised his hands helplessly. "I know they have it all wrong."

"It's insane," Allison shouted, jumping up and pacing. Sweat dotted her temples and forehead. "I couldn't possibly … I didn't even know if I'd get this job."

"Brady claims you figured yourself to be a shoo-in because of your experience. He thinks you picked up where June left off."

"How could he believe this nonsense? How could he?"

Michael pressed his lips together. "Brady says you two laundered stolen money by shifting it through a series of sham corporations until the money reached an offshore bank."

"How dare he? I've never stolen a cent in my entire life. Even if I could concoct such an elaborate scheme, I'd never know how to do it electronically."

Michael sat on the edge of his desk and shook his head. "One guess is you're Hartner's scapegoat because he never stopped embezzling from us."

"Dear God. What happens now?"

"Brady ordered all programs changed. He said I should tell you there's a minor glitch and that the computers will be down for a week.

He doesn't want you to know what's going on until they get foolproof evidence." He made a disgusted sound. "I know this is a horrendous mistake."

Allison sensed the futility of the situation. Her mother had given inklings of danger, and she admonished herself for not listening. Now it seemed clear that both of them had been framed. Could it be a coincidence? She'd never survive this.

She thought again of her mother's suspicions about Vanessa and her checkered past. "Could Vanessa have been working in cahoots with Hartner?"

Michael shook his head. "She didn't have access to the books." He sucked in his breath and let it out slowly. "Right now there's not enough to indict you. But if the auditors prove computer hacking, well ... it goes before the board of directors. We're a public company and will be forced to press charges. We have to figure out what really happened, and fast. I'm here for you."

"Why didn't they tell me to my face?"

"Until all the results are in, they didn't want to give you an opportunity to skip town. And they worried that if they were wrong you had a legitimate defamation suit. I'll do my best to back you up and defend you."

Allison walked to the window, envying the pedestrians who looked calm and untroubled. Her world had just blown apart. How could Michael be there for her? He would be loyal to the company and saving his own ass no matter how he felt about her. He hardly knew her. Allison held her fists to her chest as though protecting herself from some unknown force.

Michael tapped a finger on his desk. "What exactly did Hartner say to you?"

Allison relayed her conversation with him, watching Michael's clear blue eyes darken. "I wish you'd been able to pick up. I kept signaling for you on the intercom."

He sighed. "I know, but Brady held me up."

"The thing is, why would I talk to a coconspirator on a business phone line if I were guilty of conspiring with him?"

"You wouldn't, of course. It's certainly curious why Brady is so anxious to make you the scapegoat. He had access to the books too, although he has a right to that."

Allison was quiet for a long time. "Am I going to prison?" she asked quietly, not turning around from the window.

He came and stood beside her, gently touching her arm. "Not if I can help it. And this goes without saying, but Brady can't know I'm helping you. I'd be out of here in a minute."

"It's best for you to stop seeing me." It pained her to say it.

Anger flashed in his eyes. "Never. Look, I have access to a computer expert with a big staff and connections to professional hackers and all kinds of banks. He owes me. I hired his brother at a good salary, so he'll discount his fees."

"But hacking isn't legal."

"It's his line of work. It's crucial to find the real owner of that account for both our sakes any way we can." Michael hugged her and then stepped back. "From here on out, come to work every day and act like nothing is wrong. I know that'll be hard, but just leave everything to me."

She scrutinized his face. "Do you really believe I'm innocent?"

"Why else would I jeopardize my position? But we need to find proof soon. We have only about one week before this goes public. I'll get you a lawyer. The best money can buy."

She stared at him. "Why are you doing this for me?"

"Because I'm crazy about you. Isn't that obvious?" He pulled her close.

She resisted for a moment before collapsing against his chest. She wanted to trust him—she had to. There was no other choice.

"We're going to figure this out." His chest heaved. "Keep in mind no one can know I'm helping, not the office staff, and not even cleaning crews. They have instructions to report any suspicious activity by you."

"Oh shit. Everyone knows. Everyone is watching me." She stepped back and looked up at him. "What if you can't do this?"

"Don't say that." Michael pulled her back against his chest. But he wouldn't meet her eyes.

Chapter 49

Celia

Marcy and Celia sat at Celia's kitchen table sipping coffee in silence. Her lawyer had informed management that protestors gathering outside Celia's window adhere to the law and stay thirty feet away. Yesterday Edith and her crew had walked around outside with signs calling for the undesirables to move out. Today none of them had appeared and Celia figured it was due to bingo day.

A knock on the door startled her out of her reverie, and she opened it to find a tall older woman with short gray hair in a navy business suit. She carried a computer satchel and smiled at Celia as she crossed her arms. "Can I help you?"

"I'm a reporter from the *Retirement Newsletter* that goes to the five surrounding gated communities."

"Can't help you. Find a person whose car went through a store window to report on." Celia pursed her lips and started to close the door.

The woman put out her hand. "Please. I'll just take a moment. I'd like to interview you and your friends so you can tell your side of the story. There's time for an article before the newsletter goes online this evening." She tried to shake Celia's hand. "I'm Rose Gamble."

"I'm sorry, but you have to leave." Celia tried again to shut the door.

"Hold on there," Marcy said, coming up behind Celia and holding the door open. "I'm Marcy Worthmire and in charge of media affairs for our group."

"Marcy," Celia said through clenched teeth, "no interviews."

"You're going to be on our side, right?" Marcy asked the reporter, ignoring Celia.

"My job is to be objective. May I come in?"

"No, you may not," Celia said. "Marcy, come back inside."

"My apartment is close by," Marcy said, stepping outside. "We can go there."

Celia's stomach sank as she watched Marcy hustle the reporter away. Almost as soon as she closed the door there was another knock. Celia was tempted to nail her door shut. But she opened it.

"Hello, Ms. Ewing," Detective Dawkins said quietly.

Celia's heart sank. She remembered what Jackman had warned her—not to talk to the police without him present.

"Excuse me. I have an important errand." Celia grabbed her keys and stepped out, locking the door behind her.

Dawkins held up her hand. "Hear me out. This is serious."

"I won't talk to you without my lawyer," Celia said.

"In that case, I'll just give you information, no response necessary." Celia braced herself for more bad news. "You don't seem to be the kind of person who would get involved in criminal activity," Dawkins said. "Are you sure you won't come downtown with me so we can talk privately?"

"No," Celia said firmly.

"Ms. Ewing, we spoke with Dr. Drudding by phone and he

confirmed that a patient by the name of Celia Ewing came in, complaining of depression and of back pain. He prescribed Elavil for depression and oxycodone for pain."

"Not possible. I never heard of him. I'm not his patient." Celia bit her tongue. She wasn't supposed to be talking to the police. Damn, they were tricky. She chided herself for not being more careful.

"He didn't remember what the woman looked like. She wasn't a regular patient. So just know that you're still on the hook. The meds from your place match what killed Mr. Onstader."

Celia gripped her keys more tightly, the metal biting into her palm.

Dawkins pushed her cheek out with her tongue. "Don't forget that you obstructed justice and now there's a possible murder. We've got convincing evidence that we're about to give to the DA. We believe there'll be indictments."

Celia kept silent this time.

"I thought that you might want to talk to me." Dawkins leaned in. "Woman to woman. If you have anything you want to tell me, it would help your case. I'd put in a good word to the DA about how cooperative you've been. I can't promise a deal, but what I recommend is meaningful."

Celia gave her a cynical half-smile. "I have nothing to say. Call my attorney. Good day."

Dawkins turned to leave then said over her shoulder, "By the way, we have more families calling for exhuming their relatives. The families are willing to pay just to get to the bottom of things. That might go badly for you." She looked at Celia expectantly.

Celia went back inside and slammed the door. She pressed her back against it and slid to the floor. "Oh shit, shit, shit." A headache clawed from the base of her neck to the top of her head.

She saw the voicemail light flashing and listened to the message. Allison's voice, sounding tight: "Mom, I've got to talk to you."

Romantic woes? Trouble with her ex? Issues at work? With the exception of Allie wanting to talk about her situation, Celia welcomed any distraction from the constant barrage of troubles that hurtled at her one after another like a meteor shower. She needed to call Jackman and tell him about her latest interaction with Dawkins first before that got out of hand.

Scrolling through her e-mail, Celia found the latest issue of the retirement community newsletter, *Retirement Newsletter*, in her inbox.

WOMAN OF INTEREST IN THE MELVIN ONSTADER CASE SPEAKS!

In an exclusive interview with Marcy Worthmire of Boca Pelicano Palms Retirement Village, she stated that she and her friends, Celia Ewing and Deborah Castor, were innocent of any involvement in Melvin Onstader's mysterious death. "Police need to investigate others who might have perverted reasons for such an act."

Worthmire is one of three women targeted by the police in this case. She said, "We are simply three good-looking, single, intelligent, ethical, charitable, and environmentally aware women." Worthmire further stated that, "The police are too lazy to go out and find the real culprits. The investigators are retired and were rehired. They should go back to their favorite donut shop and just hang out."

This reporter found Worthmire, age 56, engaging and outspoken. When asked about her whereabouts on the night Melvin

Onstader died, she said, "Celia, Deb, and I got together to discuss classic books. Oh, and we might have wheeled Deb to the kitchen for milk and then to her apartment because she has bad arthritis. That's about it."

Worthmire said that because of her beauty and youthful looks, some residents of Boca Pelicano Palms are jealous and implicated her. Worthmire will respond to comments. Her e-mail address is at the end of the article.

Celia rolled her eyes. Including Marcy's e-mail address made the article tantamount to a personal ad. She worried that Marcy's criticism of fellow residents and the older police force might backfire, but at least she hadn't given any information away.

If Marcy applied the same efforts to solving their dilemma as she did to attracting men, there was no doubt in Celia's mind they'd win their case.

When the phone rang, Celia's saw Jackman's number on the ID and answered. "Hello Mr. Jackman. I was just going to call you."

"Ms. Ewing. Someone just e-mailed me a newsletter."

"I'm so sorry. My friend got out of hand. I told her not to do it but she wouldn't listen."

"You can't let this happen again."

Celia told him about Dawkins's surprise visit.

"You did the right thing. Don't let the police, under any circumstances, entice you to go with them to the station or to come into your home unless they have a warrant. Without it, they'll try to sweet talk you or, if that doesn't work, threaten you. If they have a warrant, don't say anything to them and call me immediately. Good night." He hung up.

The silence in the room rang in Celia's ears. She left a message on Allison's cell phone asking her to come to dinner that evening. When she glanced out her front window, she saw that Edith hadn't returned to her protesting, but she spotted Stanton talking to Brady and Vanessa in the courtyard. Celia's heart beat faster and she jerked the blinds shut.

Celia resisted calling Stanton. What was he doing with Brady and Vanessa? Maybe he'd been in the neighborhood and just happened to bump into them. But why would he be here? Was he visiting Edith?

She needed to distract herself. In the kitchen she preheated her oven then started scrubbing her kitchen counters. Then she rolled out dough she'd prepared earlier, added canned cherry filling, and popped the pie in the oven. Even the delightful scent of sweet cherries baking didn't stop the image of Stanton in the courtyard from flashing in her mind.

The phone rang and she picked up right away.

"Hi," Stanton said. "How about we go out for dinner tonight?"

"What's with you cozying up to Brady and Vanessa?" she demanded, her voice sounding sharper than she'd intended.

"Celia, what on earth ..."

"I saw you with them outside just a short while ago."

She heard a slight sigh. "Brady wants to hire me for a consulting job. We had lunch at Toby's Café and Vanessa showed up at the last minute. Then we walked her back to her client's apartment."

"Really?"

"Really! Anyway, I turned him down for the job."

Celia closed her eyes. "Sorry."

"I was going to tell you, but you jumped the gun." His voice sounded taut, like a dog pulling tightly on a leash.

"Allison is coming for dinner. I'd invite you, but I think she has something personal to discuss," Celia said in a quieter voice. "But I'll save you a piece of cherry pie."

When he responded, Stanton's voice was warmer. "I love any kind of pie. Especially if you made it. I'd like to meet her one of these days."

"You will."

"By the way, the article in the gossip sheet was funny. There's no way you three come off as dangerous characters. It looked more like a classified ad for Marcy."

"It was. My lawyer had a fit. By the way, Allison insisted I use the criminal attorney from Well Services. He kept his fees low."

"Hey, that's fine. I'm sure he's quite capable."

"Glad you don't mind."

When they hung up, she called Marcy, but her voicemail picked up. "Marcy," she practically yelled into the phone, "I'll break your knees if you do another interview."

After setting the pie out to cool, Celia prepared a dinner of comfort food, meat loaf with mac and cheese. Cooking often calmed her, but now it didn't seem to be helping. The stakes had jumped higher. The police had zeroed in and sunk their teeth into them with a vengeance. She'd never even had a speeding ticket, yet now faced prison.

Soon, the air in the apartment filled with a gently spicy scent. Meat loaf was Allison's favorite. The phone rang again. She dusted crumbs from her hands into the sink. "Allison?"

"This is Detective Dawkins. I'm outside with a warrant. I didn't want it to have to come to this, but this is what happens when you don't cooperate. We know you're at home, so open the door."

Celia hung up then froze, recalling that Jackman told her she'd have to cooperate with a warrant. Her heart squeezed painfully in her chest. With measured steps Celia walked to the door. Detective Dawkins held up the warrant and Johnson stood just behind her.

"Are you going to take me in?"

"We're confiscating your computer. We won't take long." They pushed in and located it on the desk. Assured it was Celia's, they did a cursory search of the drawers and the bathroom then marched out. Celia's head spun and her body trembled, trying to guess what they were looking for now. She quickly called Jackson.

"Is there something in the computer you wouldn't want them to see?"

"Nothing I'd call incriminating."

"Good. Try to relax tonight, Ms. Ewing. I'll call Dawkins tomorrow, although I'm sure she won't tell me much. I'll keep you posted."

"Right." He might as well have asked her to climb the Alps. It would have been easier than trying to relax.

Celia took a hot shower to ease her pounding head, then dressed quickly in jeans and her favorite red blouse. Promptly at seven she heard a knock on the door. Celia took a last look in the mirror and hoped Allison didn't notice dark circles under her eyes, neatly hidden with makeup.

Allison came in looking distressed—hair disheveled, eyes wide with a look of fear.

Celia's stomach twisted. "Sweetheart, what's wrong?"

Allison's face fell. "I didn't do it." She squeezed her eyes shut.

Celia took Allison's shoulders. "Do what? What do you mean?"

"Mom, I'm sorry, so sorry."

Celia's pounding heart throbbed in her throat. "What is it? Tell me."

"I've been accused of colluding with the Hartners to steal money from Well Services."

Celia shook her head. "No. The Hartners embezzled, not you. How could they even suspect you?"

Allison clenched her hands. "Michael told me and is trying to exonerate me. Someone trumped up documents and set up offshore accounts with my name."

Celia felt her breathing grow shallow. "Sweetheart, you are the most honest person I know. You'd never do that, ever! They have to see that you're innocent."

"Brady Shirkson is on a tear to name me." Allison sank onto the couch, looking more despondent than Celia had ever seen her look.

It struck Celia she had somehow caused this dilemma. She gathered her last shred of inner strength and clung tightly to it. "What exactly happened?"

Allison took a deep breath and told Celia what Michael had told her and how he intended to help.

Celia felt her jaw drop. "You've got to call the police." Even as she said it, she knew if the cops assigned to her case were anything like Dawkins and Johnson, Allie was doomed.

"Mom," Allison moaned. "I have one week to prove I didn't do it. Right now all the evidence is against me. Somehow we've both been framed."

"Could there be a connection? I'd go crazy if anyone harmed you.

Thank goodness for Michael." Celia held tight to Allison's arm as though she'd disappear.

"Michael thinks Hartner is trying to frame me. I can't see how we can get the truth in one week. Michael's workload is overwhelming by itself. He's doing this behind Brady's back."

Celia felt the pulse of anger beat in her throat. "Michael must take every minute of time for you this week."

"He's trying."

"Someone knows what they're doing." Celia counted on her fingers. "It could be Shirkson, Michael, Vanessa, a Boca Pelicano Palms resident named Edith, or any combination of people. Then throw Hartner into the mix." Celia bit her lip. "The big question is why."

"If Michael did it, he'd have turned his back on me, but he even offered to pay for my lawyer." Allison voice sounded flinty. "Maybe it's someone we don't know. Or maybe it's Stanton. Didn't you say he was a computer expert?"

Celia's heart sank, hearing her daughter voice her own nagging suspicions. "Anything is possible," she said. "But for now, let's look at the overall picture." She sat up straighter. "First, there appears to be a connection between what's happened to both of us."

"It might be a wild coincidence. Sorry I didn't believe you sooner." Allison looked contrite.

"Never mind. Let's look for a link and see if it's connected or not." Celia thought hard. "This Edith. She has access to people's condos. Maybe she had Vanessa's help. That would make them both crazy, but they *are* both oddballs."

Allison shook her head. "The person needs high-tech smarts. Vanessa admitted she doesn't have those skills." She hesitated. "This is supposed to be a secret, but all bets are off. Vanessa told me she went to prison for embezzling when she was in her twenties, but she was trained as an accountant."

Celia felt a chill run through her. "I didn't find anything online about prison. I suspected there was something shady in that woman's past."

"Her records are sealed, but she was upfront with me about it."

"Why did Michael hire her?"

"Company policy allows hiring of some ex-cons if their crimes are nonviolent, a first offense, things like that. It helps give them another chance."

"Finding answers is like shadow boxing. There's not a solid surface on which to land a blow. We have to figure this out."

"I checked more recent statistics on Boca Pelicano Palms, like I promised. There was a big uptick over last month's death rate. It's clear this community had a disproportionate share out of four other communities, although three others are on the high side too."

Celia gasped.

"It's looking like there is a serial killer preying on the very sick and very elderly—just like you thought."

"And we're the patsies," Celia said. "I did a little digging of my own and found out that there were one hundred and two deaths in the last three years."

Allison's mouth twisted into a sardonic smile. "Vanessa said upgraded services in your community attract an older and sicker population. That accounts for the higher incidence of deaths. Foolishly I bought it."

"It really is a good explanation, but the numbers are proving things are not as they seem." Celia stood and started pacing. "Can we get into the computers in your office building?"

"Nothing's off limits now. My only shot is to figure out the pattern of theft, which might not be possible, then find the person who put my name on an offshore account, which is definitely possible. But I have no qualms about breaking into the office after hours," Allison said, sounding stronger.

"It's illegal." Celia wanted Allison to be absolutely sure. "This could end your relationship with Michael if he finds out. Or it could get us in more serious trouble."

"I'm already the walking dead, so I'm willing to try anything."

Celia hugged her daughter. "I'm driving you there. How will it work?"

"I'm guessing that they didn't change the alarm code to the office yet." Allison looked skyward as though invoking good spirits. "You wait in the car and drive off if someone comes."

Celia shook her head. "Never. Show me the office window where you'll be and if I see anyone, I'll flash a light, warning you to get out." Celia's knees went weak, but she straightened and put on a brave face. She had to save her daughter.

Chapter 50

Allison

"Head to Boynton on 95," Allison said, as she snapped her seatbelt in place.

Celia adjusted her rearview mirror one last time before accelerating out of the parking lot.

Except for Allison's driving instructions, the two women were silent, the air in the car terse and heavy.

When they arrived, Allison directed Celia to park in front of a deserted movie theater thirty feet away from the entrance of her office building.

"Allie, what's the drill?" Celia asked.

Allison pointed through the windshield at the building. "See the entrance in front, the one with the columns on either side of those big white double doors? That's the staff entrance. Top execs use the back so they don't bump into employees." Allison gasped for air. "Shit, my heart is racing right now."

Celia put a hand on her shoulder. "Take a breath, Allie. I'm here with you."

"Okay." Allison took a long deep breath, then squinted at the building. "You can see the side of the building straight ahead. I'll be on the second floor above the delivery entrance." She pointed to a sagging platform made of metal grating. "When you see a blinking light at that window—let's say three flashes—go to the back behind Elm Street to pick me up."

"Got it."

"If you see people go into the building with buckets and brooms, it's the cleaning crew. Don't worry. I know their schedule from working overtime."

Celia nodded, then pulled a flashlight out of her backpack. Allison got out of the car.

Allison stayed close to the wall of the movie theater, then hurried up the three marble steps to the large white doors of her office. She punched the passcode into a keypad, praying under her breath that it still worked. The door buzzed open, and she let out a breath she'd been holding. She stepped into the entrance lobby, unsteady and queasy.

Leaving now was not an option. They could change the door code tomorrow. She had fifteen minutes until the cleaning crew arrived and twenty-five till the cleaners got to Michael's office. She had to hurry.

Allison hurried down the corridor and found Michael's door open as usual. On his desk, she noticed a folder labeled "Mom." When she opened it, she read the top letter dated two weeks prior from an Adrian Hallowell, MD. She shone her light on it.

Dear Mr. Castor,

Thank you for referring your mother, Deborah Ruth Castor, for physical and mental assessments. In the physical examination, and in accordance with previous medical records, we concur that your mother has diabetes, heart disease, and severe rheumatoid arthritis. The diseases are difficult to treat because of medication interaction.

Extensive testing and evaluation for cognition and comprehension were administered. We concluded that the patient has moderate to severe dementia or perhaps Alzheimer's disease. In order to determine a definitive diagnosis, we would need further testing and a PET scan, which have all been scheduled.

We understand that this can be difficult information about a family member. We highly recommend that the patient follow our prescription plan, which includes daily doses of Aricept, a drug used to help retain memory. If you see no clear signs of improvement within a month, please contact the office. At that point we can add Namenda XR, which has been shown to enhance Aricept. We recommend a comprehensive follow-up and a treatment plan. Regular visits to our office should be scheduled monthly.

Sincerely,
Adrian Hallowell, MD

Allison sat back in her chair, feeling winded. If the diagnosis was accurate, in time, Deb would succumb to a snarl of mental tangles and disrupted brain cells. She knew how devastating the news would be for her mother.

Drop it for now, she told herself. She rummaged through his drawers, rooting through staplers and pens until she found two flash drives. She lifted each gingerly between her thumb and forefinger as though they might burn her. Spying on the man she was crazy about pushed her over the edge.

She flicked on the computer and inserted one flash drive. Blue light from the screen bathed her face in an eerie glow as she looked through the list of documents on the drive. On it was a copy of the death statistics report Vanessa had gathered for her. Michael had never told her he'd seen them, and she wondered if Vanessa had given him a copy and whether she'd explained why she'd pulled them.

She hesitated for only a moment before opening Michael's work performance evaluation. In it, Brady praised Michael for his ability to cut to the heart of a problem, solving issues that few others grasped. "Hands-on executive in all areas of the business, even attentive to janitorial services. Communicates well with employees on all levels." Allison knew that to be true.

As she read on, her eyes opened wide. The same report cited Michael for having an office romance. Allison read and reread the next paragraph in disbelief. Michael had had an affair with … June Hartner? "He's a damned liar," Allison said in a hoarse whisper.

Suddenly she heard footsteps in the hall. There was a clang of buckets and the swirling noise of a floor polisher. It was ten after nine. She knew the cleaners would be in Michael's office at nine-forty. Her heart pounding, she pulled out her own flash drive and jammed it into the computer, copying all the data from both of Michael's flash drives. She then put his flash drives back in the drawer and scattered the pens on top of them. A door opened and closed in the hall.

Allison cracked the door then eased it shut. Brady and Vanessa were heading in her direction! What were they doing here? He hardly ever seemed to work, let alone at night. She looked around in a panic and spotted the large closet that housed a file cabinet. She opened the doors and squeezed into the small space, moving several boxes to the back so she'd fit.

The office door creaked open and the lights turned on. Allison looked down and saw a three-inch gap under the closet door. She was certain her feet could be seen, so she forced herself back a few inches.

"Let's go, darling. I saw the cleaners down the hall. We don't want to do this now," Vanessa said.

"Where the hell does he keep those flash drives, Vanessa? Do you know?"

Vanessa giggled. "Damned if I know. I'll find them when he's out of the office. Don't you bother about it now. Come on, baby."

Allison bent down and saw shuffling feet. It appeared Vanessa was tugging Brady toward the closet. She bolted upright and crowded herself back into her small space.

"Good," Brady snorted. "We have better things to do right now."

Brady's large black shoes stopped in front of the closet door and Allison held her breath. A woman's five-inch red stiletto heels shuffled in front of Brady, facing him.

"Sweetie," Vanessa said, "I love you." Allison heard their lips smacking and her stomach twisted.

After a long silence Vanessa groaned, "Oh baby." Her back rammed against the door and Allison watched in fear as it started opening. She was about to be exposed.

"Baby, you're hurting my back," Vanessa complained. They shuffled away, but the door remained ajar.

Allison heard Brady's heavy breathing. "Let's go to my office and finish what we started."

"What about the car?"

"Don't worry about it. The chauffeur knows to wait for us. Come on." Vanessa giggled as the lights went out and the door to Michael's office closed.

Allison's heart sank. She knew the cleaning crew parked in front and had a man who swept the pavement and washed the steps right around the entrance. Brady's driver parked out back. That meant both the front and back entrances were now blocked. How would she get out? Everyone had been alerted to report seeing her.

Slipping out of the closet, she crossed to the window facing the side alley above the loading dock. She opened it and flicked her flashlight three times. Within seconds, Celia flashed her light back.

Allison looked down and saw her mother approaching. "Psst. Both entrances are blocked," she said in a loud whisper. "There's a ladder near the dock on the right."

Celia retrieved the ladder and struggled to pull the ropes to unfold each section, and Allison thought she might faint with fear, certain someone would hear the racket or that the cleaning crew would come into Michael's office early and find her.

Finally the ladder was fully extended, and Allison held tightly to the windowsill as she eased down the first three rungs of the ladder. Her foot slipped. "Oh my God, oh my God. I … no, I can't go any further. I'm terrified of heights," she moaned.

Celia climbed the ladder and clamped herself to Allison's back. "Keep moving. You can do it. I'll help you." Allison took a deep breath and listened to her mother's soothing, even voice.

"Do you remember when you were six and climbed a tree at the park? You were just as afraid then to come down, but I came up and we got down together. We'll do the same thing now."

Celia guided Allison down rung by rung like a firefighter. Once they both reached the bottom, they quickly brought the ladder down and carried it back to the loading dock. Then they rushed to the car and as carefully as they could, rolled out of their parking spot and sped onto the road.

Allison took deep breaths until her body stopped shaking. "Mom, you're strong. It must be all the tennis you play. And you stayed so calm under pressure. I was just frozen." She awkwardly touched her mother's knee. "Thank you."

"A mother always finds miraculous strength for her children. I think I'd be able to lift a truck to free you," Celia chuckled.

Allison wanted to hug her mother, but niggling thoughts about Michael's lies swirled in her mind. Of all the people to have an affair with—June Hartner. "Brady came into Michael's office looking for his flash drives. I hid in the closet. I wonder if he's trying to find out if Michael is helping me."

"Everything is out of whack." Celia's voice quivered.

They drove in silence. Suddenly, Allison's body shook as she sobbed, gasping with each intake of breath. Celia pulled the car over on the road, then threw her arms around her. "Shhh, Allie. It's going to be fine. We'll find a way out of this."

"Michael lied to me. I found out he dated the embezzler, June Hartner. Jesus. Why do I pick the wrong men? What's wrong with me?" Allison wailed.

"Damn it. Maybe it's a mistake. We'll slog through it all." Celia's face hardened as she offered Allison a tissue.

"I love you, Mom, but you're in big trouble yourself. You have to take care of yourself."

Celia snorted a laugh. "You come first."

"Mom, I have to tell you something else. I read a report a doctor sent to Michael about Deb. She has serious dementia. Maybe even Alzheimer's."

"Oh no," Celia said between clenched teeth. "I suspected it, but hearing it …" Celia pulled in ragged breaths, reaching for a tissue herself. "Oh God, I'm going to lose her."

The two women drove along without talking, tears sliding down their cheeks.

Chapter 51

Allison

After Celia dropped her off at her apartment, Allison inserted the flash drive with Michael's files into her computer. It was late, but she felt like she'd never be able to sleep again, agonizing over Michael's secrets. She scanned through the files looking for more clues, but the rest of the files were mostly correspondence back and forth between Well Services and the State of Florida over inadequate training programs. One file contained research on offshore bank locations in Costa Rica, dated and timestamped just after he told her about her predicament. At least he was telling the truth about helping her.

It was midnight, but she felt compelled to drive to Michael's place. She had no idea if he'd want to keep helping her when she told him what she'd discovered on his computer, but she knew she had to take that chance and confront him.

The lights were out but his car was in the driveway, so she knew he was home. When he didn't answer her initial knocks, she banged on the oak door harder until he finally opened it, wearing a black terry robe she knew from a brief but happier time.

"You scared the hell out of me." He stepped aside and tightened the belt. That action told her he knew this would not be pleasant. "What's the matter?"

She walked inside. "You had an affair with June Hartner."

Michael's body seemed to deflate. "Where did you hear that?"

"Never mind. Talk to me."

He rubbed his forehead. "It's not what you think. Look. I took the flak for Brady. *He* had an affair with June. Just before the embezzlement news broke open, he begged me to lie for him so he could keep his job. If I did, he promised I wouldn't be fired. I agreed to be his shill, and he kept his word."

Allison's body flooded with relief and shame. Why had she accused him without first giving him a chance to explain?

He looked at her, and with a pang she noticed the dark circles under his eyes. "I really fell for you, and I'm doing whatever I can to help you. Please trust me."

Allison wrung her hands. "I want to. Are you truly being honest with me?"

"I'm not Brady. He's a womanizing prick. He'll probably break Vanessa's heart sooner than later."

Allison felt her body sagging with exhaustion. She leaned against the wall.

Michael's face softened. "I realize you're desperate and reaching for straws. Let's put this behind us." He held his arms out. "I'm on your side."

She could feel herself pulled to him and wanted nothing more than to rest her head against his chest, but she held firm. "Did you know Vanessa pulled death statistics for me?"

He cocked his head. "Sure. We know everything, but I assumed she was doing research to identify communities with sicker residents to better be served by our company. I didn't know you ordered it."

She watched him closely to see if any fidgety expressions or gestures would give away that he was lying, but he seemed completely unfazed. She had to believe him.

"Brady asked me about that."

He led her over to his couch, where she sank gratefully into the thick cushions.

Sitting beside her, he grasped her hand. "But Brady wanting every little detail of this embezzling makes me wonder what's up with him. And he's dead set to blame you."

"You mean …"

"I don't know what I mean." He waved his hand. "Forget I said that."

"Are you saying he might be involved with the Hartners? If so, that would make him a suspect in her death—that is, if she didn't commit suicide," Allison blurted out.

He shook his head. "God, I don't know. It's gotten harrowing. I don't know what to believe anymore." He rubbed his eyes, looking weary.

"And what happens now that you're having an affair with the newest embezzler?"

"It's curtains for both of us." He pronounced it "coitins" like an old-time movie gangster and gave her a tight-lipped smile. "But remember, I'm dedicated to proving your innocence."

Her anger dissipated as she stared at her hands in her lap. "I'm scared. I feel like my life is in danger."

"You can't listen to a psychopathic liar like Hartner." He swallowed hard. "I wonder if the conspiracy is against me. Brady is looking for proof I'm helping you, I'm sure of it."

She looked up at him. It was just what she thought about Brady and Vanessa looking around in his office. "If you have anything in your office about my situation, get rid of it."

Michael slammed his fist on the coffee table in front of him. "Damn him! I'm sure he's looking for proof that I told you something. Good idea. I'll do it first thing in the morning. He's been on my back and I just deny, deny." He looked straight at her, his eyes boring into hers. "I have to get you out of this. I'm nuts about you."

Allison felt her heart melting. "I swear I appreciate what you're doing for me. It means everything, whether it works or not."

"It's going to work." He rose and pulled her up into his arms, hugging her so tightly she gasped. She'd avoid telling him about the break-in or how she and her mom suspected the two trumped-up charges against both of them were connected.

"Don't kill me with love," she teased. The laugh was cathartic, and she raised her head to meet his kiss. In his arms, she was filled with the sensation that she'd arrived home safe and sound. How she'd missed Michael, her refuge. She was sorry she'd ever doubted him.

Gently he kissed along her jawline and neck, and her body felt as though it had caught on fire. When he kissed the hollow at the base of her throat, she knew if she let him get any further, there was no way she'd be able to leave.

She forced herself to pull away. "It just isn't a good time. I only wish … Good night, Michael." She walked to the door.

"Understood." He sighed wistfully but made no move to stop her.

By seven-thirty the next morning, Allison had showered and dressed and headed to the office, trying to arrive early to avoid facing people. They all knew too much.

When she got there, she found a security guard posted in the corridor near her office. She turned on her heel, went back out to her car, and drove home, leaving a voicemail for Michael from her cell. "I can't face anyone today. Tell everyone I'm sick."

Next she called her mother and told her she was on her way over. When she arrived, Celia had coffee and Danish pastries waiting.

"If states had a symbolic cake representing them, Florida's would be Danish," Celia said, sounding awkward in her attempt at humor.

Allison sank into the sofa. As she sipped her coffee, she noticed the pile of unfolded laundry on a chair and was startled. Her mother was a meticulous housekeeper.

Allison began folding the clothes and filled her mother in on what she'd learned during her midnight visit to Michael and that he was innocent of dating June Hartner.

Celia stopped her from folding. "Are you sure you can trust him?"

"Yes. He's spending time and money to get to the real culprit and exonerate me, and he's putting his own job on the line to boot. I saw proof of that on his computer," Allison said firmly, her tone of voice shutting down anymore discussion.

Celia nodded. "Okay. So if Michael's off our list of suspects, who else? I know Vanessa seems likely because she was in prison for a similar crime before, but when I did my own digging, not one of her deceased clients' next of kin complained about anything suspicious or illegal." Celia refilled their coffee mugs. "Most of her patients died, but she seems to take on a sicker population. If she's the one, the only explanation is insanity."

"I'm not sure about Vanessa anymore," Allison sighed, wrapping her hands around her mug. "She was with Brady last night when I was hiding in his office and told him she'd look for Michael's flash drives when he wasn't around. I'm not sure whose side she's on." She shook her head. "This is too complicated. Have you heard from the police or your lawyer?"

"Nothing yet. No reports of finding anything incriminating on my computer—so far."

"Well, that's one small bit of good news. We certainly need it."

"It's too bad our break-in didn't get us more information." Celia half-smiled. "I guess I'm too old to be climbing ladders anyway."

Chapter 52

Celia

Allison had left and Celia was trying to put her apartment back in order. She finished folding the rest of the clothes, wiped down the kitchen counter, then began dusting when the phone rang. Hearing Stanton's warm hello on the other end should have made her feel better, but instead she felt her hackles rise. Catching him talking with Brady Shirkson and Vanessa still troubled her. She hated being suspicious, but she had no choice right now. Her loyalty belonged to Allison, Marcy, and Deb.

"Celia, how are you? How was your dinner with your daughter?"

"Fine," she said tightly.

"I wanted to see if you were free tomorrow evening."

An expectant silence filled the phone line, but Celia couldn't bring herself to reply. Thoughts of dates with Stanton—of their nights together in his bed—seemed a thousand years away.

"Celia?" he asked uncertainly.

"Yes?"

"Are you all right?"

After another awkward silence she said, "I can't see you for a while."

"What do you mean by a while? Is that a day, a month, a year?"

"I just don't know."

His voice rose slightly. "Why are you shutting me out?"

Celia felt her stomach sinking. "Nothing in my life is resolved, Stanton. In fact, everything just seems to be getting worse."

"Then I beg you, let me help. Confide in me. I care about you, Celia. I want to help you."

His voice sounded so earnest and sincere, but Celia's mind muddled as she wavered about believing him. "There's nothing … there's nothing you can do." Her voice cracked.

He hung up without saying goodbye.

It was the ugliest sound Celia had ever heard.

In her mind, Celia examined each word with Stanton multiple times. She knew she'd insulted him, but a murderous maniac stalked her. Allison's problems came first. She tried to discuss it with Marcy on the phone, but when Marcy asked questions, Celia's voice failed her and she promised to call back later.

As Celia moved uneasily around her apartment, she realized with a start that she hadn't had her usual morning call from Deb. She'd been so distracted she hadn't noticed it till now. When she tried calling there was no answer.

Celia hurried out of her apartment, arriving at Deb's door slightly out of breath and sweaty. She raised her fist to knock but stopped when she heard loud voices arguing inside. One voice was Deb's, the other was an angry male voice. Celia couldn't make out what they were saying. She pounded on the door.

"Who is it?" Deb called, sounding tense.

"It's Celia."

A moment later the door opened. "Are you all right?" Celia asked. "Who's here with you? Why all the shouting?"

Deb sat down in a chair and wrapped her arms around herself. Celia looked around and spotted Michael in the kitchen entrance.

"I'm glad you're here, Celia. Maybe you can help." There was no sign of distress in his voice and he seemed calm, so unlike how his voice had sounded just a minute ago. "My mother is giving me a hard time about overusing Elavil."

Celia's heart quickened. She'd had no idea Deb took Elavil— one of the medications Melvin's autopsy had revealed. This might be why Deb seemed to be losing it. Michael took good care of Deb and seemed to be giving Allison enormous help, too. She didn't want to lecture him about yelling at older women in fragile health, so instead she nodded at him.

"It makes me feel better," Deb said. "I'm not worried about addiction at my age."

"Michael is right. It might be making you foggy," Celia said.

"She told the doctor she's depressed but doesn't know how many she takes a day," Michael said.

"Haven't you been helping your mother with her medications, monitoring what she's on?" Celia blurted out.

"Of course I have. I found a few vials of medication she'd gotten on her own in the pocket of her slacks." Michael said in a tight voice. Celia's eyes widened. In an instant his expression went from angry to anxious. "I'm sorry I snapped. I'll admit that this past year I've been a little too preoccupied to pay enough attention." His arms hung at his sides and he looked despondent. "There's been so much chaos at work, and I've been holding onto my job by a thread. Most important is helping Allison. You know what I mean." His look told her not to mention anything in front of Deb about their shared concerns.

"We're all on edge," Celia said.

His shoulders slumped. "My mother's behavior has become erratic, and I have to believe that it's in part because of the medicine. And the other part of it is that she's been diagnosed with the beginnings of dementia."

Celia felt relieved that it was finally out in the open. "Maybe if she got off the meds … is it for sure?"

"Yes. She's accused Brady Shirkson of being a killer. That's textbook paranoia."

"You talk like I'm not here. I'm not crazy. I don't hurt anyone," Deb protested. She seemed like she was only partially following the conversation.

"Why did you say Brady Shirkson is a killer?" Celia asked, trying to keep her voice calm.

"He's mean to Michael and wants to fire him."

"He's not going to fire me, Mom," Michael said patiently.

"I still have my mind, Michael," Deb said, yet her eyes looked out of focus. "Once …"

"I'm getting Mom a caregiver." Michael looked pityingly at his mother.

Oh Gßod, not Vanessa!

"In the meantime, would you mind taking her to stay with you for a couple of nights, Celia? I'm sure she'd rather be with friends than in respite care right now. I'll be out of town a few days, and I don't want her alone."

"Of course. Anytime." Celia squeezed Deb's shoulder.

"Thanks," Michael said, looking relieved. "I packed an overnight bag, and her meds are in there with directions. I didn't have time to organize them. She's to take only Aricept for her memory and Motrin for arthritis." He handed the bag to Celia. "No other drugs. I'll call to check on her."

"I'm not loony," Deb insisted as Celia helped her slowly to her feet.

"I know you're not, honey," Celia said softly, leading her friend out the door, Michael following behind. With a final understanding look at Michael, Celia put her arm around Deb, took the bag from Michael, and led her slowly to her own apartment.

When the women got to Celia's apartment, Celia helped Deb into her nightgown and eased her into the bed in the guest room, urging her to get some rest. Then she called Marcy.

Marcy arrived in five minutes. Celia sat her down and told her about Deb's diagnosis, the fight with Michael, and Allison's information. "Deb's going to stay with me for a few days. Frankly I'm relieved. This way I can keep an eye on her."

"Oh God. This is getting worse by the minute." Marcy wrung her hands. "But she still cracks jokes at our expense so much of the time. It's hard to imagine that her mind is going." She shook her head sadly. "Once she gets off the drugs she'll be fine, won't she?"

"Fingers crossed," Celia held up her hand. "Let's look at her meds. I didn't want to do it alone."

"Okay."

Marcy rummaged through the overnight bag and found several vials of medicine. She examined the labels. "Yeow," Marcy yelled. "This Aricept is prescribed by Dr. ..."

"Drudding?" Celia felt a prickle up her spine as Marcy nodded.

"That's what I was afraid of. Deb might not be able to tell us how she got to him. Oh God. Why can't we just go back to dancing? I'll have to check and make sure she isn't hiding any Elavil pills."

Marcy looked sheepish. "Do you have anything to eat? When I'm stressed I get hungry."

"I can heat up some leftover meat loaf." Celia walked into the kitchen, glad for something to do. She put a plate of food in the microwave.

Marcy placed the plate on the table and dug in with a fork. "Mmm. Delicious. You're a damn good cook. This takes me out of my misery for a minute." Marcy took another bite and chewed, then jumped up and headed to the liquor cabinet, grabbing the bottle of peach schnapps. "Since it's not the time to dance, I think we both need this." Marcy took two glasses from the cabinet and poured a healthy slug into each one.

The two women drank, then Marcy looked at Celia with tears in her eyes. "If Deb's really taking all those medications ..." She threw her arms in the air. "It can't possibly be Deb poisoning all those people. Can it?"

Celia swallowed a lump in her throat. "I don't know anything anymore."

Marcy poured two more glasses of schnapps while Celia filled her in on all the details about Allison's terrifying situation. Celia shared her last conversation with Stanton but stopped when Marcy rolled her eyes.

"Why not let him in?" Marcy asked, sipping from her glass.

Celia sighed. "I'm afraid to. I messed up. But I'm also angry that he wasn't more sympathetic to what's going on in my life. He isn't the focus right now, maybe that's his problem."

Marcy opened her mouth to reply but was interrupted by an urgent knock at the door. Celia cautiously opened the door and found Detective Dawkins and Officer Johnson on her doorstep. Her heart sank. What now?

"Well, if it isn't the dynamic duo," Celia snorted. "I don't have to let you in."

Detective Dawkins smirked at her. "We're just here with a little update you might find interesting. We found big orders on your computer for Viagra, Elavil, and oxycodone, some of them coming from illegal sources. The orders went to an address in Del Ray. We searched that house and found it deserted."

"That info gives us enough probable cause to present to the DA to get a grand jury convened," Johnson piped up.

"Whoever planted the drugs used my computer to write those orders." Celia wanted to scream but held her composure.

Dawkins leaned against the doorjamb. "Make it easy. Just tell us the truth." She cocked her head. "We know you've been addicted to tranquilizers before."

"How ..." Marcy and Celia stared at each other for several seconds.

"Now you people listen up. This is another frame-up," Marcy yelled. "Can't you see?"

Dawkins ignored Marcy. "We want to talk to your friend Deborah Castor but can't find her. Just a friendly chat."

Friendly? Ha. Celia's threw her head back. "Deb is ill. She has dementia."

"She can't speak to you jerks," Marcy said defiantly.

Officer Johnson narrowed his eyes at Marcy. "I'd be careful, Ms.

Worthingmire. We saw your interview in the *Retirement Newsletter*. Would you happen to have any donuts?" He slapped his thigh and guffawed like a horse neighing. Then he stared Marcy down. "We do our work conscientiously, for your information."

Marcy pointed a finger at Johnson. "For your information the name is Worthmire."

"Look, Ms. Worthmirer, this is an unusual, high-profile case." He rubbed his hands together. "And we mean to solve it."

"We have more information from toxicology reports that we can't discuss, but it doesn't look good for you." Dawkins planted a fist on her hip "Do you or your do-gooder friends visit sick or bedridden people?" Dawkins furrowed her brow.

"I know where this is going. Knock it off." Celia knew they were frothing at the mouth over a big case like this. She wrapped her arms tightly around herself, trying to still her thundering heartbeat.

"Now see here …" Marcy started, but Dawkins turned sharply to face her.

"What about you, Ms. Worthmire? You visit shut-ins as well. Perhaps the three of you have your own little murderous circle, off-ing sick old people for kicks. There are some around here who believe that."

Celia's skin was crawling. They were out for blood.

"Gray hairs were found during the autopsies," Dawkins continued. "We need a sample of Ms. Castor's hair. And samples of both of yours while we're at it. Although neither of you is gray." She looked down her nose at them. "Not that your hair couldn't be the result of a dye job."

"I'll have you know this is my natural color!" Marcy said indignantly. Celia pinched her arm hard to stop her, but she kept going.

"There are loads of other people you should be investigating in this case. Edith, Vanessa Cordova—they have more motive than we do. It's Vanessa's patients who keep dying; how could she not have a hand in this?" She held up a trembling finger and pointed it in their faces. "So get your retired asses out there, find the guilty person, and leave us alone. Then get back to your rocking chairs!"

Celia could swear she saw steam coming from Dawkins's nose. She tried to swallow past the tight knot in her throat. "We're done here. You have no warrant, so please leave. If you have anything further to ask, talk to our lawyers."

She pulled Marcy into the apartment and slammed the door shut. She listened to the officers' footsteps walk away down the corridor.

"The nerve of them, trying to accuse us of serial murders." Marcy staggered into a chair.

Celia walked into the guest room door and looked in. Deb was sound asleep. She searched Deb's clothing to see if she'd sneaked in Elavil pills. Nothing. She joined Marcy in the living room. "She's out like a light. I'm worried about them trying to talk to her—for her sake and ours."

"I almost threw up when they asked about her," Marcy admitted. "How about another?" she asked, pointing at the schnapps bottle.

Chapter 53

Allison

"Michael," Allison said, pressing the phone close to her face as though that could bring him into her apartment. They had decided not to meet in person, but right now he provided the oxygen that gave her a chance of survival. She and her mother had discovered information she needed to confront him about. "Look. I did some digging and discovered that Brady hired Vanessa four years earlier than I'd previously thought. What is that about?"

"Oh, that." Michael sounded as though she'd asked him what he had for breakfast. "Vanessa took an online caregiver course while in prison to get certified, and just before her parole, wrote to several organizations looking for a job. She included pictures of herself, a smart move. Brady's affair with June was over, but he needs a woman in his life. Vanessa's beauty intrigued him." He sniffed.

"So he hired her while she was still in prison?"

"He visited her in prison and believed her charges were trumped up. He strong-armed me into pitching the parole board with a promise to hire her and he got her an attorney to seal her records." He cleared his throat. "Of course, it's … confidential. I had to do Brady's bidding, and it was totally legal. After I met her, I believed she deserved a second chance since her crimes were nonviolent. You have to admit she's smart and a good worker."

"I agree," Allison said. "And I like her as a friend too, but there's so much about her past that seems ... murky."

"Never mind that. Here's some potentially good news. First the bad news." Michael paused momentarily. "My techie investigator discovered different levels of this puzzle. He's got bank insiders and some are in Costa Rica. One of his connections did some digging in bank records and found an account with your name on it. I know it's a forgery."

"What the hell is that about?" Allison's toes curled.

"Well, it's a money laundering scheme. Someone sets up a fake corporation to dump illegal monies into. This one was set up by a Richard's Investment, Inc. with you as the CEO. The money from this sham corporation is next transferred to an account in an offshore bank, like the one in Costa Rica that is numbered so the US government can't trace it. It's near impossible to track unless you have connections like this investigator does. Whoever stole the money from our company wound up parking it all in Costa Rica International Finance and pinned it on you."

"Damn it. My name is really on a money laundering scheme?"

"Offshore banks rarely question or verify identities. I kicked in some bucks and my techie got a bank's assistant manager to trace it back the last transaction. It has your name on it."

"How do I prove it's not me?"

"We don't have PINs or passwords yet, but he's working on it." He paused and sighed, seeming to carefully consider his next words. "This information hasn't reached Brady's desk yet. My guy thinks Well Services will have what he found in about two days. It's the evidence Brady needs to take to the board and press charges against you."

She shuddered as though a winter blast had shocked her body. "What are the chances of getting to the truth before they meet?"

"It's looking better. He told me the giveaway is people who do this don't give real names. They list fake names for company officers. Given that, why would you use your real name? I'm working on the premise that Brady's behind it all because, with your smarts, he knew you'd figure out he embezzled from us."

"If he engineered this, I have to believe Vanessa is involved too." Allison's head spun.

"I doubt it. She doesn't want her sealed records opened up, which they can do if she's in trouble again. And her next sentence would be more severe."

"Brady could bamboozle her," she muttered.

"We need to concentrate on finding the real name or names of who set up the account. It requires sophisticated hacking. There's a chance Richard Hartner's name will turn up."

Allison's heart went into overdrive. "I could never have gotten this far without you. Thank you, Michael. I'm indebted to you."

"It's for both of us," he said soothingly. "We've got something special going. We're not going down without a fight. Once this is all over, we'll start fresh."

Allison wondered if she should tell him about what she and Celia had been discussing—that a series of murders seemed tied to the embezzling—but stopped because she'd promised her mother not to tell anyone. Who knew who might be watching or listening? She would take no chances of tipping off the wrong person. "I'm hoping for a new start."

After she hung up, she considered calling her mother with an update but decided to go see her in person instead. She grabbed her purse and keys and headed out to her car.

As she hurried through the underground garage of her apartment building, she noticed a man approaching her. He wore a red-hooded sweatshirt that partially concealed his features, but she caught a glimpse of a round face and long nose. He was short and built like a fireplug. Her heart started pounding as she hurried towards her car, just a few spots away, but the man caught up to her. Her body went numb when his hand closed around her arm.

"Let me go," she said in a shaky voice.

"Allison, I'm Richard Hartner. I won't hurt you. Please listen to me."

She tried to break loose from his grip but couldn't. "Leave me alone." She looked around, but the garage was deserted. Her vision blurred with panic as he tightened his hold.

"I heard they accused you of colluding with me before you got the job. We have to help each other."

"How did you know that?" she demanded, her voice still quivering.

"Never mind. Look, we're not safe. I'm good on the computer, but I need you to get me Shirkson's password. Then I can help us both."

Is he insane, she thought. "I don't know it. I can't help you." She stepped back, trying again to twist her arm out of his hand.

Just then there was the scrape of a door opening. Another resident was coming into the garage. Hartner looked over his shoulder. "If you value your life, come to my house later. We have to talk." He stuffed a piece of paper in Allison's hand then released her and ran away. Allison crushed the paper into her pocket and tried to fit her keys into her car door with a shaking hand. When she finally opened the door, she slumped over the steering wheel.

Chapter 54

Celia

Even though Celia was angry at Stanton's silent treatment, she still missed him. She missed his warmth, his touch on her bare skin, his deep voice calming her, and his curiosity about art and relationships. She missed dancing the cha-cha with him. She wanted to touch his cheek, be in his arms, inhale the citrus scent of him.

When she examined her response to him, she knew she'd never explained Allison's predicament. *I couldn't. Now I have to fast-track for answers if I have any hope of saving Allie and myself and salvaging this relationship.* Allie was running out of time to prove her innocence before the charges would be pressed against her as the embezzler. So far, it seemed like Michael's promises meant nothing without actual proof—a bitter pill to swallow.

Celia tiptoed into her guest room and looked in on Deb, who was sleeping on her back, the blanket up to her chin. Celia smiled to herself. When she was asleep, Deb looked sweet and gentle and not at all like someone with an acerbic tongue. Sleeping so much, she thought, must be from weaning off the drugs.

Michael had called several times, checking on Deb's condition and making sure she got the right doses of Aricept. She hadn't told him that she'd found the bottles of Elavil and oxycodone in Deb's bag.

She didn't want him to get angry with Deb and put her in a nursing home because of mental incompetence. Celia had looked up dosing instructions on Elavil online and started lowering them to wean her off it slowly. Deb slept a great deal, but when she was awake, she seemed a bit more alert than usual—one good piece of news.

There was a knock at the door, and Celia's stomach sank. What if Dawkins and Johnson were back to arrest her? She was relieved to look through the peephole and see that it was Allison.

When she opened the door Allison pushed into the room. "Richard Hartner stopped me in my garage to warn me. He wants me to come to his house tonight." Allison held up her hand stopping Celia from speaking. "To answer your next question, he didn't hurt me."

Celia's scalp prickled at the image of a man accosting her daughter. "No! Don't go. God only knows what he wants. It's too dangerous."

"I have to see this through."

"In that case, I'm coming with you."

"Mom, there's more." Allison recounted her conversation with Michael about Vanessa's employment and the money laundering.

Celia started pacing. "I should never have given her the benefit of doubt."

"What are we going to do?" Allison moaned, putting her head in her hands.

Celia put her arm around her daughter's shoulders. "We're going to that man's house to find out what he knows. I'll call Marcy to come take care of Deb."

"God, I can't stop shaking," Allison said, drawing in a deep breath. "I'll drive."

Allison sat in the passenger seat and directed Celia to Hartner's house with her GPS. Celia couldn't believe that not that long ago she'd been feeling good about life, enjoying her friends and dating a wonderful man who had made her feel alive again. How had it all fallen apart so fast? Everything about Florida seemed menacing now; the swaying palm trees, pastel stucco buildings, flowers, and salty ocean air.

"This might be a trap." Celia kept her voice calm, but nervously bit her lip.

"I'm going to prison without passing go. I have nothing to lose by seeing Hartner."

Celia bit her lip harder. "Just in case, I brought this." She pointed to the canister of pepper spray tucked into the car's center console.

They arrived at their destination, a semi-detached concrete rancher with faded yellow stucco walls streaked with rust. The lawn was a tangled mass of brown weeds. "Doesn't look like wealthy people live here," Allison said. Both women gathered their nerve and stepped out of the car.

They walked up the rickety wooden steps onto a porch with uneven boards. Celia peered into the dark front window and tucked her pepper spray back in her pocket. "Looks like no one's here."

Allison knocked on the front door, which was ajar, and it swung open by itself.

"This is like a scary movie," Celia said, a strained smile on her lips. A car screeching by the curb stopped abruptly. Allison turned, grabbed Celia wrist, and dragged her back toward the car. "We're out of here."

A man stood on the curb about thirty feet away under a cone

of light from a streetlight. "Is that Hartner?" Celia asked as she and Allison jumped into the car.

"No, Hartner was shorter and stocky and he was wearing a red sweatshirt. This man is taller and thinner, and his sweatshirt is gray." The hood was pulled up so they couldn't see his face. He seemed to be looking closely at their car, then reached into his pocket and pulled out a dark object. A cell phone? Whatever it was glinted in the streetlight, and Celia realized with a start that it was a gun, pointed right at them!

"He has a gun!" Celia screamed.

"Move out of here, fast!"

The car bucked but wouldn't start. Celia grimaced and tried again. A bullet whizzed over the roof of the car. He sprinted toward them.

"Floor it!" Allison screamed.

The motor started. Celia stomped the accelerator again, and the car screeched away from the curb. "Duck down!" she shouted. Two more shots came from behind them but missed. Celia glanced in the rearview mirror and saw the man jump into his car and speed off in the opposite direction. At least he wasn't following them.

It took a while before Allison managed to stutter, "That bastard Hartner, he … he set me up. Oh God, I'm … so sorry I brought you into this, Mom. Are you okay?"

"I'm fine. Lucky for us, whoever that was is a bad shot." Celia wheezed as she kept her eyes on the road. "Did you recognize the car?"

"Hell no. We just about escaped with our lives." Allison pulled her cell from her pocket with difficulty. "I'm calling the police."

"Hold on." Celia pressed a fist to her forehead. "We're in enough trouble with the police. They'll want to know why we're lurking around Hartner's house, especially you."

"You're right." Allison put her phone down. She looked behind them again. "No one's following us. You can slow down."

Celia eased up on the accelerator. "God. Terror's become as routine as breathing. I never should have moved that man ..." She trailed off. "Anyway. Listen. Don't go home alone."

"I have security in the lobby twenty-four/seven."

Celia glanced at Allison from the corner of her eye. "You are in danger, Allie. I can't lose you." Her shoulders hunched forward as she suddenly realized how close they'd just come to death.

"I'll be fine, really."

Allison didn't sound convincing.

Celia admitted that with the front door security in Allison's building, she was safer at home. She dropped her off before driving back to her condo.

When she opened the door, she dropped her keys and purse noisily before yanking the window shades down.

Marcy had dozed off on the couch while watching TV and now sat up, alarmed. "What the ..."

"Stay away from the windows." Celia's breathing caught in her chest and burned. She clicked the off button on the TV remote and stood over Marcy, glaring at her.

"What the hell is going on?" Marcy asked, rubbing her eyes. "Why are you staring at me like that?"

"You caused this damned trouble, getting us to move Melvin. Now my daughter is accused of embezzling," Celia wailed.

"Shhh, Celia. Deb was up for a long time and got exhausted. She's finally asleep. Calm down. What does the embezzling have to do with Melvin?"

"Allison and I were nearly killed tonight. We went to the so-called embezzler's house, and someone fired a gun at us."

"A gun! What?" Marcy lunged off the sofa and tried to hug Celia. "Are you all right?"

Celia shrugged her away. "Do I look all right? He missed, if that's what you're asking."

Marcy started pacing. "Talk to me sensibly."

"You're one to talk about being sensible," Celia snapped. "You with your rooftops, gardeners, and whatever."

"Hey! Stop slinging crap at me," Marcy said, glaring at Celia. "Just tell me what just happened."

"Since that SOB Brady Shirkson claimed my daughter's in on the embezzlement, someone is trying to kill us! Allie's life is in danger."

"Wait. Back up and give me details. I want to help." Marcy pressed her hands, prayer-like, against her chin.

The enormity of it all crashed through Celia, her anger flickering like florescent lights. "My poor baby." A shuddering sob rose through her body. "You and your goddamn sex life got us into this. Chasing after men and blabbing to the media. What were you thinking?"

Marcy reached for Celia's hand. "Sweetie, I admit I got us into the mess with Melvin, but I have *nothing* to do with what's happening to Allison right now!" She helped Celia to the sofa. "Why would you let Allison go to such a dangerous place? You put yourselves at risk."

"I went to protect Allison and help her." Celia's arms flailed. "You talk about risk, having sex in the board of director's office, knowing you could be evicted!"

Marcy shook her finger in Celia's face. "At least I didn't put my child in danger."

"Why would you? They're not in your life."

Marcy's face turned white and Celia knew she'd gone too far, instantly regretting her words. "Oh Marcy … I didn't mean …"

Her friend's eyes filled with tears. "That was a low blow. I didn't force you to move Melvin. You could have called the police."

"And you'd be at risk of eviction." As she said it, she knew she'd do it all over again in a heartbeat

"I love my kids. There isn't a single day that the loss of them doesn't tear me apart."

"I know," Celia said, her own eyes filling with tears. "I shouldn't have said that, I don't doubt for a second your love for them. I'm sorry, I'm so sorry."

"I thought you'd be the last person to judge me. I guess I was wrong."

Celia's shoulders slumped. "My daughter's life is at stake and I'm freaking out. I've got to get Allie out of this—get all of us out of it."

Marcy huffed. "I offered help from day one, but you're such a control freak and a martyr that you have to do it all by yourself."

"There are hunches I have to work out on my own." Celia rose.

"Take your hunch and stick it you know where."

"You have no idea the pressure I've been under."

"That I understand. But I don't get how you can be so mean." Marcy put her forearm against her forehead. "I'm exhausted. I can barely stay upright."

"When are you ever upright anyway?" Celia snickered.

Marcy plopped down on the sofa and pulled a blanket over herself.

"Not funny after what you said. Don't worry. I'll be out of your hair soon." She closed her eyes.

"Marcy, you know you can stay here as long as you want to." Celia stepped closer.

Marcy waved her away. "I might have acted irresponsibly, but I'd never deliberately hurt you or Allison."

"I know," Celia said, weary down to her bones. "We can work together."

Marcy said nothing in response, and Celia was unsure if she was even still awake. She turned off the living room light.

She lay in bed watching the slats of moonlight move across her ceiling. She was exhausted but not sleepy, and alert to the softest sound that could mean someone lurking outside or breaking in.

How could she have said such mean things? She rubbed her dry eyes, worried she'd turned into an angry grouch like Gabe. It wasn't fair to take her fears out on her friend.

She stretched her back, trying to relax her muscles, but she knew sleep wouldn't come, so she got out of bed and picked up a thick manila folder full of HMO documents that Allison had left behind on one of her visits. In the hustle of the last few days, she'd forgotten to return them. Now she opened the folder and spread the documents across her bed. She wanted to better understand exactly the kind of mess Allison was in.

She carefully examined the figures under the columns marked Gross Income and Net Income after expenses were paid for payroll, travel, and advertising. Month after month, the business had sustained larger losses than profits. Why would losses continue after Allison put in cost-cutting measures and while demand for caregivers and HMO enrollments had risen?

She studied the numbers on a spreadsheet titled Account Receivable and Accounts Payable. She found it odd that so many payments—supplies, payroll, travel expenses, car rentals, and on and on—went to just four companies.

She knew it was late but she was desperate. After texting Allison to make sure she was awake, she called her. "Honey, I'm going through a folder you left here, and I see there's something suspicious."

"What? Where did you get that?"

"You left a few bookkeeping papers here. I'm looking through them. I want to understand what's going on better. What about these four companies that were paid huge sums over time?"

"Mom, those were fraudulent purchases made by the Hartners. Shirkson accused me of being in cahoots with the Hartners because the purchases continued after I arrived. But he could have continued hacking into our system. I don't know."

"Please explain to me how that worked exactly."

Allison sighed. "The Hartners used shell corporations with business names but they secretly owned them. No products were delivered and the companies were fake. The Hartners funneled money from the company to themselves through the shell corporations. June did a good job covering up." Allison sighed again. "Mommy, things are rough enough. You don't need to do this."

Celia's heart leapt at hearing her daughter call her Mommy. Allison hadn't used that word in ages and it felt like a beam of light in a pitch-dark world. "Don't worry about me, Allie," Celia said, hoping her voice sounded reassuring. "You're good at explaining. I understand."

"Thanks for being there." Celia heard Allison stifle a yawn. "I'm too anxious to sleep so I've been going through some numbers myself. One of the things I found is that several patients who took high doses of several medications, like Melvin, were suing our company in what were frivolous suits. But all those patients ended up dead."

Celia gripped the phone tighter. "Really, Allie? What do you think it means?"

Allison's voice sounded deeply weary. "I might be seeing connections that aren't there because time is running out. I'm scared."

"I know, Allie, but I'll keep racking my brain to try and help you piece this together."

"Thanks, Mom, I can't think straight anymore. Get some rest and call me in the morning." She hung up.

Celia's eyelids fluttered as she tried to concentrate on the documents scattered across the bed to find a clue to the mystery. She leaned her head against the pillow and fell asleep.

Early the next morning, Celia found Marcy turning on the coffee maker and felt a glimmer of hope that they could make up.

"Up early?" Like her, Marcy still wore the same clothes she'd had on the night before. Celia smoothed her rumpled blouse. She noticed, with a twinge of envy, that Marcy's smooth, clear complexion betrayed no signs of lack of sleep.

"Mmm hmm," Marcy muttered. "Figured I'd make a little coffee then make a quick exit."

"Don't leave. Deb's been sleeping on and off for like a day and a half. I've brought meals, but she's hardly eaten. She asked for you."

"Really? She slept through all of last evening," Marcy said, giving Celia a snide glance. "You look like death warmed over."

Celia gripped the edge of the kitchen table. "I'm sorry. I understand if you never talk to me again."

Marcy sighed. "I get it. You're over the top with worry about Allison."

"It's true. I'm not myself."

"We both said terrible things to each other and we didn't mean them. I'm sorry, too." Marcy walked over to Celia and wrapped her in a tight hug. Celia felt so relieved she burst into tears.

"Crying?" Marcy teased. When she pulled back, Celia saw tears in her eyes as well. She hugged Marcy again. Without a word, they both broke into a cha-cha. Marcy spun and nearly fell, but caught herself, and they burst into laughter.

Celia poured a mug of coffee for each of them as Marcy went to check on Deb, who was still sleeping. "At least one of us is getting enough sleep right now," Marcy quipped, settling down at the table across from Celia.

Propping her chin in one hand, Celia filled Marcy in on what she had discovered. "Well Services is leaking money and Allie is being accused of continuing the scam June Hartner had going. I'm beginning to think that if the Hartners really did it, they had help. Then again, it might be someone else. If Richard Hartner put Allie's name on an offshore account we need to find that out."

Marcy clicked her tongue and nodded. "You're pretty sharp on the high-tech. What do you think?"

Celia hesitated before continuing. "It's too sophisticated for me at the moment, but I'm looking into it."

Marcy raised her eyebrows. "It all boggles the mind."

Celia's phone rang. When she answered, Allison sounded frantic. "Oh Jesus, Mom, something horrible happened!"

Celia felt a prickle of fear go up the back of her neck. "What is it? Tell me."

Allison's voice shook. "Richard Hartner's body was found in the trunk of a black Lincoln Continental outside of Miami this morning."

"Oh my God!" Celia's heart pounded.

"He was shot in the back of the head." Allison took a breath. "Get this. The time of his death coincides with when we were at his house yesterday."

Celia gasped. "Who shot at us? No one else knew where we went, unless we were followed."

"I think it had nothing to do with Hartner."

"Allie. Don't leave your apartment. Don't let anyone in."

"I won't."

She had to do something right away with this new development, push harder no matter what the consequences might be. One rule came to her that steeled her against the fear. DON'T BE AFRAID OF RESISTANCE. LET IT WORK FOR YOU. "I'm on it."

Chapter 55

Celia

"I've got to find Dr. Drudding," Celia mumbled to Marcy, who sipped coffee at Celia's kitchen table.

Allison had lent her mother a computer after Celia's had been taken. Now she looked up Drudding's address. His office was across the city from the retirement communities, in a sad, run-down part of town.

She wrote down the address and grabbed her purse. "Can you stay here and keep an eye on Deb?"

Marcy put a hand on Celia's shoulder. "Of course I can, but where are you going? Remember, I want to help. At least tell me what's up."

"I'm going to find Drudding and talk to him. I'm convinced he's a key to some of this craziness. Call my cell if you need me, and only answer the house phone if it's my name or Allie's on the caller ID, got it?" Without waiting for a reply, Celia dashed out of the apartment.

On her way to her car, she saw other residents walking toward the clubhouse for breakfast, and many of them stopped to stare at her. She knew the gossip about their impending arrests, coupled with the articles, elevated them to pariah status. *To hell with you all.* But their stares still hurt.

Celia was so distracted thinking about the profits and losses statements, the speeding dolly, the bullets flying at her car, that she didn't realize she had accelerated to eighty miles an hour until she heard her car's engine whining. She eased her foot off the accelerator. I've got to calm down, she thought, because I'll be of no use to Allie if I end up in a hospital bed or at the police station.

As she drove, she turned over the details she knew in her mind. The guilty person had to have easy access to the residents at Boca Pelicano Palms and other retirement communities to be able to make it past the security guards at the entrance to each one. That meant it could be another resident, friends or family of a resident, a caregiver, or a professional like a lawyer or doctor—maybe Dr. Drudding?

In the rearview mirror, she noticed a black sedan following her. She caught her breath and made a sharp turn onto a quiet residential street and the car followed. Sweat beaded on her temples. When she got to the corner, she checked the intersection then hit the accelerator so hard the car bucked as it raced across. By the time she'd sped halfway down the block, the car had disappeared. Had it really been following her? Was she just imagining things? She pulled over and tried to steady herself.

What if all her efforts were hopeless? What if something happened to Allie?

For a moment she found herself wishing she had a vial of Elavil with her. She'd take a precious pill and wait for the all-encompassing numbness. She wanted to stop feeling.

She shook her head, hard. No, she'd never go back to antidepressants. Taking them for years had kept her flatlined, unable to feel good things—love and laughter and pleasure. Now she clung to the thinnest bit of hope, if not for herself then for her daughter and her two best friends.

When she reached Drudding's neighborhood, she saw boarded-up storefronts, abandoned cars on crates, and streets marked with potholes. The building with Drudding's address was a squalid, squat, green building, chunks of stucco missing from its façade. Smashed beer bottles and crushed cans littered the sidewalk in front of it. The run-down neighborhood surprised her. She double checked the address and found it to be correct. Yet he serviced so many people in her community on the other side of town. It seemed odd.

When she got out of the car, she stepped gingerly over the cracked concrete sidewalk. The front door opened easily and she walked down a dark corridor. She found Dr. Drudding's name on a door with a messy pile of envelopes strewn on the floor in front of it, nudging them aside with her foot. She knocked several times, increasingly loudly, but no one answered. A prickle of unease raised the hairs on the back of her neck. Using a credit card from her wallet, she hoped that his lock was as flimsy as the one on her front door.

A final flick of her wrist and the door swung open. A strong odor of mildew, oil, and rust pervaded and filled a space not much larger than a walk-in closet. A battered metal desk took up most of the room. More piles of mail had come through the door slot. She flipped through the envelopes addressed to Dr. Drudding; they appeared to be checks from government and insurance agencies. The red light on the phone flashed with waiting messages. It was clear no doctor practiced medicine and saw patients here. Was Drudding even a real doctor? On the desk she noticed a piece of stationery with Dr. Drudding's name and address. Above the heading, in the center, was an embossed logo that she recognized—a stethoscope and microscope.

It struck her. When she'd visited a sick, nearly blind acquaintance months ago, she'd noticed this on a stack of papers on her bedside table. It hadn't registered at the time, but the logo had caught her attention. She picked up the paper and stuck it into her shoulder bag. Then she took many close shots of the envelopes with her smartphone before hurrying outside. Someone had to pick up the checks. She'd stake out his office for a while to see if anyone came by.

After moving her car across the street, she found an old baseball cap in the glove compartment. She crammed it on her head and pulled the brim low on her forehead. Using her smartphone, she researched frauds in the medical field. One scam caught her attention. Anyone could obtain phony law degrees, doctorates, PhDs, MDs, MBAs—anything one wanted. Armed with a fake MD, a "doctor" could process forms and become eligible for government and insurance payments. They only needed an address to receive checks. Often they depended on patients who wanted opioids in exchange for giving the fake docs their Medicaid or insurance numbers. The so-called offices could merely be a mailbox posted outside a house. She settled down to wait, the humid air enveloping her in a hot bubble.

An hour later, a black Continental pulled up to the curb across the street. She slunk down in her seat, clutching her phone. A figure in a dark hooded sweatshirt stepped out and went inside the office. She couldn't tell if it was a man or a woman.

After a while the person came out carrying a large pouch and pasted something on the door. She couldn't make out the face under the hood but snapped several pictures. She tried to photograph the license plate as the car drove off, but some of the numbers were obscured with mud.

She waited fifteen minutes before slipping out of her car to examine what had been pasted to the office door. It said the office had moved and a new address would be sent to patients through the mail. Celia took a photo of the flyer. Her research had mentioned that these illegal offices moved often, especially if they thought the authorities might be on to them.

Back in her car, she examined the photos of the hooded person on her phone. It was hard to make out a face, but a vague idea occurred to her. She put the key in the ignition and prayed that she could work the idea into a plan. She'd have to eat humble pie to pull it off.

Celia parked at the station and noticed police cars neatly lined up like soldiers at attention. She entered the building and went up to the desk where a bored-looking officer sat.

"Can I help you?" the officer asked, sounding not at all like he wanted to help.

"I'm Celia Ewing. I'd like to see Detective Dawkins."

He picked up a phone, got the okay, pressed a buzzer, and pointed to the unlocked door. She shivered and hoped this would work.

"Second door on the right."

Celia moved quickly down a narrow corridor, her footsteps echoing on the tile floor, and entered Dawkins's office.

"Hello, Ms. Ewing. Please sit down." Dawkins's voice rang with sweetness as she gestured for Celia to take a seat across from her. "What can I do for you?"

Celia clasped her hands together to keep them from shaking. "I'd like to talk to you."

Dawkins looked skeptical. "You haven't talked to me much,

have you? Where's your lawyer?" She pretended to look behind Celia, smirking.

"It's just me. I need a favor that will benefit both of us."

Her smirk disappeared. "Why would I help you?"

Celia took a deep breath. "I respect you, Detective, but I believe you are way off track in the investigation."

"Backhanded compliment?" Dawkins smirked again, then leaned back in her chair. "Let's hear it then. What do you need from me?"

Celia took out her smartphone. "I have proof that Dr. Drudding, whose name was on those pill bottles that were planted in my apartment, is a fake. His office is just a glorified closet with a mailing address attached, and as of today, they're moving locations. I have photos of the person that picks up the mail there, as well as the relocation sign they pasted on the door. If you enlarge the photos, you'll get the answers you need."

Dawkins narrowed her eyes at Celia. "How can I be sure you didn't just fake these photos? You haven't exactly been upfront with us."

Celia rooted through her bag and pulled out the piece of paper with Drudding's address. "His name is all over the place. Here. Go to this office and see for yourself. Will you look at the photos or not?"

Dawkins puckered her lips, then sighed. "All right. Fine." Celia held out her phone and Dawkins quickly scrolled through the photos.

"It's hard to tell anything from these," she said. "We'd need to have them blown up and enhanced by the photo lab. And running only partial plates can be a wild goose chase." She looked more closely at Celia. "How can I be sure this isn't a ruse to get us off your back and onto false leads?"

"I swear to you, it's worth your time," Celia said, trying to keep the desperation from her voice. "Send someone to that office and you'll see it's a sham. Take a closer look at these photos. The envelopes I found there addressed to Drudding were government and insurance checks. You know that routine. Drudding must be raking it in hand over fist selling phony prescriptions—opioids to be exact. Look into this more deeply. Please. You have to believe me." Her voice faltered.

Dawkins picked up the paper with the address on it. "You may be on to something," she finally said, sounding guarded. She pushed a business card across the desk at her. "Here. Send the photos to my e-mail address and I'll have the photo lab get to work on them. May as well cruise out to this location and have a look."

Celia felt weak with relief as she took Dawkins's card and nodded.

"But don't think you're off the hook here, Ms. Ewing," Dawkins went on, shaking a finger at her. "Things still aren't looking great for you. Is there anything else you want to tell me?"

Celia considered telling Dawkins about the person who'd shot at them the night before, how that person had also been wearing a dark hoodie and perhaps was the same person. But she decided to keep that to herself for now. "No. I just wanted the photos to be examined."

Dawkins kept looking at her expectantly, as if waiting for her to backtrack and admit to something—anything. Celia stayed silent. Finally Dawkins dismissed her with a wave of her hand. "Let us know if you think of anything else."

Celia hurried out to her car. She had one more humble pie to eat.

Celia pulled into Stanton's development, her heart thumping in her chest. Now came the hardest part. What would Stanton say? Would he even agree to see her? A vein in her temple throbbed. For a moment she considered turning the car right around and heading straight home. She fought the urge to leave. She'd spotted his car parked across the lot and knew he was home. This had to do done.

As she headed toward his apartment, she wondered how to explain her sudden appearance. She just happened to be driving by— No! Stupid and he'd see right through it. *Just have to tell him straight out that I need his help!*

With his forensic expertise he might be able to help Allie untangle the origins of the bank accounts that were falsely under her name. Celia had no idea if he would or could help her, and she still wasn't sure if she could trust him, but she and Allison were almost out of time. Michael had yet to produce actual proof and she needed action.

When she rang his doorbell, she tried hard to calm the knot of panic in her stomach. It didn't help that when the door flew open a moment later, she found herself face to face with Edith.

"What the hell do you want?" Edith demanded.

"I'm looking for Stanton," Celia said through clenched teeth.

"I'll bet you are. I told him what a terrible person you are."

Go to hell. Just then, Stanton appeared behind Edith.

His face tightened. "Hello, Celia," he said in a neutral voice, as though he'd been expecting her. "Please come in."

Edith held the door open partway, and Celia squeezed past her. "I need to talk to you alone," she said, looking pointedly at Edith. Edith planted her balled fists into her hips.

"Edith, please excuse us," Stanton said.

"I see no reason why I can't stay," she said shrilly. "Anything she has to say to you she can say in front of me."

"Edith, please," Stanton said wearily. He took her by the elbow and turned her toward the door. "I'll call you later."

"Remember who your real friend is," Edith wailed. "It's not her."

"Thanks for coming by." He escorted Edith out the door, and despite herself, Celia felt a tiny surge of triumph. When Stanton turned back to Celia, the corners of his mouth edged up in a clipped smile. "How are you?"

"Why is she here? She's a damned troublemaker."

"Do you have the right to ask?" He frowned, then cleared his throat. "Why are *you* here?"

A chill overtook Celia as she scanned the familiar furniture and paintings. This room, which had once been so welcoming, now felt icy cold. It hit with a crushing blow that she'd become an outsider in a place that had once comforted her. "I'm sorry."

"You cut me off like some stranger. I thought we meant something to each other." His voice pricked her like a bee sting. She wanted to shout that he still meant so much to her, but instead she bowed her head and waited for more to follow.

"Isn't a relationship where two people work out problems together? What about trust?"

Celia's face grew hot. "When I asked you to wait till I was ready to call you back, my daughter had just been accused of pilfering company funds. Falsely, I might add. She's facing major jail time."

His face blanched. "How the hell was I supposed to know? I'm not a mind reader."

"The news hit me like a freight train. I wasn't in the right frame of mind. I'm sorry that I seemed abrupt and like I was cutting you off, but things have become dangerous for us."

"The dolly incident?"

"There's much more, but we're in trouble and drowning fast."

"I'm so sorry." Stanton's standoffish demeanor dissolved as his stiff posture softened and compassion filled his eyes. "You're here now. Start in the middle, the end ... wherever."

"Murder." The word hung in the air, tightening like a noose

around her neck. "We were shot at and Allison's life is in tatters. She is innocent."

"Holy Christ. What do you mean murder? Embezzling? Back up a bit." He steered her towards the couch and pushed her gently onto it, sitting next to her.

She took a breath and, as succinctly as possible, she told him about her and Allie's trip to Hartner's house, his subsequent murder, and how she'd discovered that Dr. Drudding was a fraud. "This Drudding has to be connected to these murders. It's too coincidental his name shows up on prescriptions for patients who died."

Stanton's face creased in concentration. "If you're right, I've exposed scams like Drudding's before." He rubbed his temples. "You know, I can't tell you names, but there was a so-called doctor at a hospital in the Midwest .... ah, never mind. It's crazy and complicated."

"Please tell me," Celia's eyes beseeched him. "It might help."

He pressed his fingers on the bridge of his nose. "Sometimes they don't needs a phony degree, but it helps. So, to qualify for receiving medical fees and the ability to write prescriptions, a person can simply get information from state medical licensing websites, then fill out a short application on the CMS website, and they're in. These frauds will often use a UPS addresses to receive checks for medical services they never provided. They get people to give them either private insurance or government insurance cards in exchange for controlled substance prescriptions.

"A government agency called the Center for Medicare and Medicaid Services, or CMS, will send checks to those addresses. It makes the program ripe for rip-offs. These real or fake doctors prey on people who are desperate for opioids. They trade scripts for submitting insurance claims of exams and diagnostic tests that never happened."

"It's a world I never knew existed."

"You and millions of others. When Feds get close to these fake doctors, they move to another site."

"That's exactly what I think this Drudding did."

She told him about the autopsies of residents without heart issues who died of what everyone assumed to be heart attacks. But toxicology reports revealed overdoses of controlled substances that hinted at serial murders.

"It's so hard to believe there is a serial murderer lurking in retirement communities," he said in disbelief. "Why?"

"Do you think there's a connection between my daughter's problem and mine?"

He frowned in confusion. "Why do you think that?"

Her throat was parched and she yearned for water, but she couldn't stop now. "Allison got me data on deaths in retirement communities and it showed a higher incidence of deaths in Boca Pelicano Palms."

He cocked his head, looking worried. "Celia, this is getting out of hand. You've got to go to the police now. Don't waste another second talking to me."

She threw her hands up in frustration and huffed. "Oh, the damn police are bumbling around, accusing me and my friends." She clasped her hands in front of her. "They're *maybe* going to consider a lead I presented to them. We'll see."

He looked away. "You seem to be proactive, and in a smart way. I don't know what good talking to me will do."

Celia pressed on. "June Hartner, the one who embezzled before Allison worked there, supposedly killed herself, and today, her husband was found shot to death. What if residents of Boca Pelicano Palms are being murdered by the same person who's responsible for killing the Hartners?"

"Jesus." He raked his hands through his hair. "You really think someone killed them to shut them up?"

"It's not out of the realm of possibility, is it?" Celia shuffled her feet. "Stanton. I'm desperate. I need a favor."

He raised his hands in the air and exhaled noisily. "You barge in after being rude and cutting me off with no explanation and ask for a favor?"

"I should have known better." She headed for the door.

"Celia, wait." He put a hand on her shoulder.

She stopped and bit her bottom lip to keep from crying. Spinning around to face him, she searched his eyes and saw concern but no sign of forgiveness. *I'm wasting my time.* "I don't know what's real and what's not." She clasped her hands against her chest. "Or who to believe."

He steered her gently back to the sofa. "I understand. I hope you can trust me. I only want what's best for you."

She nodded. "Okay. Can you tell me what it is that Brady wanted to hire you for?"

"Just some work on offshore accounts. I didn't like the sound of it so I cut him off." Stanton frowned. "You think Brady's the bad guy. Maybe I've said too much."

That Shirkson would even ask him to do such a thing shook her to her very core. "Listen carefully. Richard Hartner warned Allison to fear for her life, and considering what happened to him, and what almost happened to us …" Celia wrapped her arms around herself and shuddered. "I have these awful images of Allison being hurt. This is not a frivolous request. This is a matter of life or death."

Stanton ran his hands through his hair again. "Do you have an inkling who's behind it?"

"What Shirkson asked you about banks shakes me up. It sounds related to Allie's problem, and we only have till late tomorrow before it's over for her. And I'll be next." She clasped her hands together. "I beg you. I have the name of the offshore bank where Allison's name turned up. Would you try to find the real owner?"

He let out a short, harsh laugh. "Seriously? You're asking me to hack a computer in a few hours?" He shook his head. "Putting aside the legal issues, doing it right requires months and a team of computer experts. Not to mention bribing inside people at the bank like tellers or middle management. There's costly equipment, and sometimes even getting your own people to pretend to be tradespeople to get inside jobs so they can steal information." He squinted at her. "That's only the beginning. It's very complicated. It's far-fetched at this juncture."

She leaned back against the sofa and squeezed her eyes shut against a flash of light that signaled the start of a migraine. Pain ripped across the top of her head.

When he spoke again, his voice was softer. "I know it's scary but calm down. Give me more details. Where are the big guns in all this? Shirkson and Castor?"

"Brady Shirkson is the one who accused Allison. Michael's trying to track down the real owner of the account by using his investigator who has inside people at the bank, like you mentioned." She closed her eyes. "But there's no actual proof yet. He says his loyalties are with her, but who knows?" She looked straight at him and felt her fists tightening like claws. "I have an idea that might work. It's tricky, so will you help me or not?"

His cocked his head. "It's better not to get in Michael's way. His people have a better chance than I do of turning up something useful." Despite his confident words, Stanton didn't sound all that hopeful.

"Nothing is for sure until it happens." She felt her world flatten. For a moment, she recalled sitting beside him on this sofa not long ago laughing, then dancing the cha-cha. It felt like it had happened on another planet. *I'll get out of your life for good, but before I do ...*

She reached into her purse and pulled out a piece of paper, smoothing it with her hand before placing it on his coffee table. "Here's my plan B," she said. On the ride to Stanton's home, she'd stopped and furiously scribbled down the idea that had come to her. "This is my last ace in the hole. It needs to be done now, simultaneously with Michael's attempts."

He examined the paper and bit his lip. "Really? You kidding! I don't know ..."

She stood and walked to the door.

Just as she closed her hand around the knob, Stanton cleared his throat. "You've done a ton of thinking. I've got some real hesitations, but I'll do it."

Chapter 56

Celia

The next morning Celia blinked her eyes open, heart pounding, recalling what she'd asked Stanton to do. Did she do the right thing? Dammit, she had no choice. A rustling in the hallway got her out of bed. She threw on her robe and hurried into the kitchen barefoot, the tiles cool under her feet.

Deb stood in the kitchen, in a dress with a yellow and red rose print, looking alert. Seeing the spark in her friend's eyes uplifted Celia's mood. Just yesterday she'd tried to get her to eat a bowl of oatmeal that she'd refused. She wanted to ask Deb about Drudding, but held back.

"Are you hungry?" Celia asked.

"Not really," Deb said with a small smile. "But I'll keep you company." Holding on to the table, she lowered herself slowly into a chair.

Celia had taken over-the-counter migraine pills for her headache, but it still thumped some last jabs of pain. She dropped bread in the toaster, the idea of Deb's possible involvement in the criminal goings-on niggling once again. Deb's strong defense of Vanessa all along had been odd. Although it was very hard to believe, the past few weeks had shown Celia anything was possible. She let out a small sigh, rubbing her aching temples.

"Hey, Celia, join me." Deb stood up, moving to imaginary music, shifting her shoulders up and down. "Two-three and cha-cha-cha and three-four."

"Who needs music? It's in our hearts." Celia pranced into Deb's outstretched arms, remembering the rushing, warm feeling that flowed through her body when she danced, when life soared with promise.

But Celia thoughts tumbled helter-skelter, and mostly she couldn't imagine her wonderful, acerbic friend in decline; her memory dimming, her expressive face dulled, losing control of her bodily functions. Celia wanted to cry, but she didn't want to ruin this beautiful, carefree moment, so instead she fought back tears and smiled broadly, swaying to the imaginary music.

Deb's cell phone rang, breaking the spell. She jerked it out of her pocket, said hello, then listened in silence before hanging up.

"That was Michael." Deb slouched and scuffled her feet in place. "He wants to meet me at my place."

"How nice." Celia cupped Deb's chin and lifted her head.

"Can you believe they want me to have a caregiver? Shirkson's on his way, too. Michael wanted him there to convince me about using Vanessa." Deb pouted. "Marcy put the bug in my head that there's something not right about that woman."

"I won't let that happen." She put her arms around Deb, shielding her.

"There's nothing's wrong with me, right?" Deb stepped back, flexing her bony arms. "See, I'm still strong." She smoothed the bodice of her dress. "I'm going to give Michael grief." She sighed. "I should go."

"Listen," Celia said. "You can pretend to agree with them. But don't take any more meds that are prescribed to you. We're going to figure it out together with a new doctor."

Celia went into the guest room and returned with Deb's bag. She offered to walk Deb back to her place, but her friend firmly refused.

As Deb left, Celia could no longer keep her tears from spilling out. Her headache intensified and rattled her teeth. Shaking out two headache pills, she took them with water. After ten minutes, glimmers of relief blunted the throbbing, as though ropes tightly binding her whole body were loosening little by little.

She was bothered by doubts about involving Stanton. She considered calling him and telling him forget her plan, but it was the last chance she and Allie had. Instead, she called Marcy, gave her a quick update on Deb, then asked her to come over.

As soon as Marcy arrived, she settled herself on the sofa. Celia told her about the meeting with Dawkins.

Marcy clapped her hands. "Great work. It's got to help our case, if they follow through."

"I haven't heard back from Dawkins yet, but if she's any good, they'll blow up that photo."

Marcy snorted. "I'm not sure they're good at much of anything to be honest."

"We need to look out for Deb," Celia said. "Can you believe she was doing the cha-cha this morning?"

"Let's cha-cha in her honor. I just smoked a joint. I'm gung-ho."

Celia stood and put on a CD, straightened her back, and took her position. Marcy stood and faced her.

"This is for you, Deb. I hope we can help you escape Vanessa and Shirkson." The syncopated beat rose in the air and along with it the pull of a pulsing rhythm, accompanied by singer Celia Cruz.

My namesake, thought Celia. *I honor you, Ms. Cruz.* The music sedated the last shocks of pain from her migraine.

They smiled at each other and began the routine. Celia surprised Marcy with a double twirl without missing a beat. Marcy answered with a double twirl of her own. For fifteen minutes they danced and everything disappeared except pure pleasure.

Then Celia glanced at the time. "I should have insisted on walking Deb home. I haven't heard anything from Michael. I'm afraid they might convince her to use Vanessa."

"Hell to that. Over my dead body."

"Over both of ours. We'll fight them tooth and nail on that one. Let's go over."

Celia raised her fist to knock on Deb's door when three loud bangs erupted from inside.

"What the hell? Let us in," Marcy shouted, joining Celia in pounding on the door with both fists. No answer. Celia tried the knob, but the door was locked, so she pulled her key ring from her pocket, which included a spare set to Deb's apartment. Her hands were sweaty and shaking, but she managed to fit the key in the lock.

"Oh Lord, what's happening?" Marcy moaned, looking around. Several neighbors down the corridor had stuck their heads out their doors. Celia got the door unlocked and pulled Marcy into the apartment, slamming the door behind her. She saw a distressed Deb standing there, bent over something.

"I did it. I did it," Deb said, then started moaning. The sound was reminiscent of a mournful, echoing chant. As Celia took in the entire scene, she gasped and reeled back, hearing Marcy utter, "Oh shit," behind her. The object Deb was clutching was a gun, and across from her, Brady Shirkson lay dead on the floor. By now, Celia recognized what dead looked like.

"Oh God." Celia looked up, startled, at the male voice and saw Michael standing across the room, wide-eyed and open-mouthed and so still he seemed carved out of stone.

Celia sprang forward and helped ease the gun out of Deb's hand onto a table, holding her friend up as her knees started to buckle. Marcy rushed to her side and helped lower Deb into a chair. Celia felt her skin go icy as she looked up at Michael's parchment-pale face. He blinked his eyes rapidly, seemingly in disbelief.

"Oh God. I … Mother … what did you do? Oh my God, Brady's shot. He looks …" Michael groaned.

"What in the world happened?" Celia shouted.

Michael raked his hands through his hair. "It's crazy. We were waiting for Brady, and … and when he walked in he yelled that I was a crook. Mother got this look of pure rage. She started shaking and yelling at him not to talk to me that way. Then she turned away, reached into a drawer, and the next thing I knew, she'd pulled out a gun and shot him." He dropped suddenly into a chair and put his head in his hands. "This can't be happening."

Celia bent over Brady's body. He was motionless, eyes open in an expression of mild surprise. Blood poured from the wounds in his chest over his black silk suit, creating dark, wet stains. She looked at Michael. "Call 911."

"I'll do it," Marcy offered.

As Celia listened to Marcy talk to the dispatcher, she looked over at Deb, who sat motionless. How could she have done this? She crossed to her friend and crouched down in front of her, putting a hand gently on her knee. "Deb, why?"

Deb's eyes went hazy. "He was ruining my son, lying about him, trying to send him to jail. Do you believe he said Michael robbed the company? Not my son." Deb wagged a finger.

Celia looked at Brady again, his blood pooling on the floor. She swallowed hard through the knot of nausea in her throat. "How did you get a gun?"

With a slack face, she slowly said, "A man at a shop sold it to me. He showed me how to use it."

Michael pressed his hands against his forehead. "Mother, for God's sake. Your thinking is all wrong." His voice cracked.

"I needed to protect you, Michael," Deb said. "You trust people too much." Deb pointed to Brady's lifeless body nearby and spat. "That Vanessa too ... she's with Brady."

Celia massaged Deb's gnarled, swollen hands as her friend muttered incomprehensible words. "Psaw, lasaw agon it netting."

Marcy crossed the room and rubbed Deb's shoulder briefly, sharing a worried look with Celia. "I'll wait outside for the paramedics," she said, and slipped out. Sirens sounded in the distance, and Celia prayed they were on their way.

"Michael, before the police get here, tell me what happened," Celia said.

"I can't think straight." He pressed his knuckles to his forehead. "Brady came in and accused me of embezzling. But I told Allison I'd have my investigator dig deep into who owned the offshore account, and it turned out to be Brady. That would make him the embezzler, but before I could say what I'd found out my mother jumped into the fray."

Celia felt a twinge of relief. Was Allison off the radar?

"Brady kept flipping things on me, accusing me. And then Mother went berserk." Michael got up and started pacing the small room as though searching for an escape route.

She shook her head at the impossibility of it all. Embezzler or not, Brady didn't deserve to be murdered. Poor deluded Deb. "Do you have written proof about Brady embezzling?"

"My guy is this close to positive proof." Michael held two fingers close together. "We won't let Allison take the blame now that we know which direction to go in."

"We have to help your mother now," Celia interrupted, feeling guilty about the good news about Allison.

Michael moved to his mother's side, grabbing her hand. "I'll take care of you."

"There's nothing wrong with me," Deb yelled. She broke down sobbing. "Nothing."

Michael pressed his cheek on top of his mother's head. He opened his mouth to speak, but no words came out except for a grunt. His face took on a greenish pallor, and Celia worried he might be sick.

"He was coming after all of us." Deb went into a coughing fit.

Celia squeezed her hand. "You don't have to talk."

"I looked into his eyes and saw a killer, saw Allison in danger. Brady and Vanessa are murderers."

Michael threw his hands up. "Mother, stop that insane talk. They tried to ruin me, not kill me. Let's worry about getting you out of this awful mess."

Deb wheezed. Celia rubbed her back, realizing Michael didn't know what Deb meant.

Michael squatted in front of his mother. "Listen to me, the police will take you away, but I'll get you out." He furrowed his forehead. "I swear."

"Don't let them take me away, please, Michael." Deb dug her fingers into Michael's upper arms. "I did a good thing. I protected you. I protected my friends." Deb looked at Celia with puffy red eyes, tears streaming down her face. "Don't send me away."

"Try to relax, Mom." Still on his haunches, Michael lowered his head. "God help us."

Celia's heart wrenched, seeing her dear friend's blank stare, terrified of what they would do to her. Would their joyful cha-cha sessions ever resume?

The sirens were loud now, and Celia heard tires squealing to a stop just outside. A minute later, the door flew open and police and paramedics swarmed the small room, guns drawn.

"All right, folks," said one of the officers. "Everybody just come on outside with me and let's let the paramedics do their job."

Celia helped Deb limp to the door. "I'm okay, Michael," Deb said in a rusty voice. "I'm sorry I caused you pain. I love you." Deb raised her hands. "I did it for you, son. Mothers would do anything for their children." She turned to look at Celia. "Haven't you done the same for your daughter?"

"Don't say anything more," Celia murmured to her friend, as Michael came to her side and kissed her forehead. She saw Marcy standing by, her arms held behind her back by a policeman.

"No matter what, we'll get you out," Marcy shouted between sobs.

Outside the apartment another paramedic rushed past them, wheeling a gurney.

Celia saw Dawkins and Johnson milling around with other officers and groaned inwardly. She'd not heard back from Dawkins about the photos. She turned when she heard Michael talking insistently with one of the officers. "My mother was the lone shooter. I was there, I witnessed it all. The gun is on the table. She has Alzheimer's, she isn't right in her mind." He put his hands to his temples.

"We'll straighten it out downtown, sir," the officer said.

More and more of the residents had come out, trying to see what was happening around the yellow police tape. Celia's heart sank, and in spite of the compassion she felt for Deb, her forehead prickled with embarrassment.

"We'll need all of you to come downtown for questioning." Celia whirled around at the familiar voice and found Officer Johnson standing next to her. He let out a low whistle as he looked over Marcy and Celia. "You gals sure do attract trouble."

Deb and Michael were escorted into a police car together, and Marcy and Celia were escorted into another one. Celia's mind raced. She had to get a hold of Allison, and Jackman.

Celia and Marcy were in Dawkins and Johnson's car. Dawkins got in and sped out of the development, siren blaring.

"We are innocent," Marcy shouted to Dawkins.

In the rearview mirror Celia saw a lazy smile cross Dawkins's face.

"What happened to the photos?" Marcy asked in a snide tone.

"Marcy, we don't have to say a word to them without our lawyers," Celia said.

"You might want to listen to your friend," Johnson drawled. "We have to book you. But we'd be willing to be lenient if …"

"Did you just say lenient? We're innocent," Marcy squealed.

Celia tried to shush her.

Dawkins chimed in, "We're still talking to the DA about the contents of Ms. Ewing's computer. So we'll see if you talk then."

Marcy leaned her head back and sighed. "Damn, this is a friggin' nightmare."

"Don't talk. This isn't a newspaper interview," Celia rasped.

"Could you at least turn that damn siren off? It's giving me a migraine," Celia snapped.

Dawkins shot her a dirty look in the mirror but acquiesced. In the sudden silence that followed, Celia leaned her head back gratefully and closed her eyes.

Chapter 57

Celia

Inside the station, they were taken to the booking officer, a heavyset man who seemed to perk up at all the commotion. The sparse gray holding cell behind the desk was empty. The officer took their names and addresses and basic information. Another officer asked for their personal property. It would be returned when they left. Neither woman had walked out with anything except their cell phones and keys.

"We have to do a pat-down," he said in a monotone. Leading them to a small stuffy room, he told Celia to go in first. A middle-aged female police officer, chunky and weary-looking, snapped on latex gloves. She told Celia to hold her hands above her head and spread her feet apart. Then she ran her hands down Celia's sides, thighs, back, under her breasts, and down her arms.

"Finished."

"Was this necessary?" Celia demanded. Although she knew it would happen sooner or later, she hadn't imagined being treated like criminals. But it hit like a punch to her stomach.

"Lucky they didn't strip search you, lady." The officer dismissed her and Marcy went in.

The women were fingerprinted and photographed, and Celia

shuddered when she heard Deb yelling from another room, "It was me, acting alone! I did it! Me!" Poor Deb. She sounded like she was in hell.

Dawkins appeared "Are we finished?" Celia asked.

"You have to wait until we check the FBI database to see if there are any outstanding warrants before we release you. And then get your statement," Dawkins said.

"Statements only with our lawyers present. I'm allowed that call," Celia demanded. Dawkins led her to a phone where she called Jackman, who said he'd come right away. Then Marcy called her lawyer, who she described as "adolescent."

Michael strode over, his face flushed red. "My mother's attorney is on his way, but I'm not allowed to stay with her until he gets here, even though I keep telling them she's unwell. I assured them that she acted alone. I'm still in a fog." He shook his head. "The upside is your lovely daughter will be free," he told Celia. "We just have to get the paperwork finished. It's tricky."

"Thank you, Michael. I hate being a pest, but how soon can we expect this?"

"I've got my fingers crossed it'll be very soon. None of this is easy. With Brady gone I'll push for a bit more time, but the board of directors turned hardnosed since Brady made Allison the scapegoat. It's chaos now. I'm interim CEO until they hopefully decide to make it permanent."

Celia squeezed his hand. "Good luck. You know, you have my heartfelt thanks for everything you've done for my daughter." She paused then took a deep breath. "Do you think Brady was behind the Hartners' deaths as well?"

"If they found out Brady was the one and were about to turn him in, my guess would be yes." He rubbed his chin. "Celia, let's talk." He nudged her to a quiet corner. Marcy threw Celia a puzzled look from her seat nearby, and Celia shrugged.

"Celia. Something strange came up. My mother's illness can cause delusions. She says Brady and Vanessa killed a lot of old sick people. What is that about?"

Celia knew she should proceed delicately. "I realize her, um, mental faculties are impaired, but I don't believe she's off base. There's been an awful lot of suspicious autopsies."

Michael's mouth stretched to a pencil-thin line. "A few deaths in a retirement community occur and you concoct a serial murder theory? Why is this the first I'm hearing about this?"

"The police actually have been on my case about it. Your mother didn't quite believe it until recently so I guess she didn't tell you."

"Celia," Michael said harshly, "old sick people die. I can't believe an intelligent woman like you would go along with that idea. I thought of you as the most rational one."

"Police have been gathering proof that many members of Global HMO were murdered. Their deaths are all similar and appear to be connected. They all had high levels of the same medications in their systems."

Michael exhaled impatiently. "The Boca Beach Patrol is investigating? Give me a break. Elderly people are often confused and take the wrong doses of meds all the time. And you turned that into a murder theory. You've put this half-assed idea into a sick woman's head and fed into her paranoia. When Brady accused me, it pushed her over the edge." He shook his head. "Now she's killed a man."

Stunned, Celia sputtered, "I, I ..." *I'd die if I were responsible for Brady's death.*

Just then Dawkins came over, handing Celia her phone and keys. "No outstanding warrants. As soon as your lawyer gets here, we'll expect that statement."

Celia nodded. "Where's the ladies' room?"

The humid restroom smelled of disinfectant, urine, and mildew. Celia called Allison but got her voicemail. When the beep sounded, she blurted out, "Deb murdered Brady Shirkson thinking she was protecting Michael. Michael says Shirkson is the embezzler and just needs written proof, which is soon to come. We're almost there."

After hanging up she called Stanton. When he picked up, the words came tumbling out as she gave him details of what Michael had related, but she found that the words to tell him about Brady's death stuck in her throat.

"Man, this guy has incredible connections. That's great news for Allison. Looks like we can hold off on plan B."

It seemed clear to Celia that Dawkins had no plans to enlarge those photos. Her last-ditch plan had to be put into place. "Please, no. We have no hard proof yet." Her breath came in short, painful bursts. "Something awful happened. I'm at the police station." She struggled to make a coherent sentence. "Deb killed Shirkson, thinking he wanted to destroy Michael by blaming him for the embezzling."

"What? Good God. She murdered Brady Shirkson? How?"

"She bought a gun and shot him. They think Alzheimer's pushed her over the edge."

"Nice women in retirement communities don't go around shooting people. Dear Lord."

She lowered her voice. "If Shirkson isn't the killer, then some maniac is still on the loose. The Keystone Cops here at the station see me as that person. They're like sharks. They won't let go."

"Damn." A long pause followed. "We have to make sure you and Allison are safe."

"Yes, and that's why we have to move fast on plan B. There's no guarantee Michael will succeed. As you said, this is not an easy thing to do." She didn't want to give a hint of what the plan entailed. Who knew what rooms were bugged.

Stanton cleared his throat. "I think …"

"We don't have time to think anymore, Stanton." Her voice cracked. "We have to act. You're not doing anything illegal. Your part is innocent. I'll cover you." She held her breath.

He sighed. "Okay. I'll contact you as soon as I set it up."

"Thanks so much."

Just then Dawkins knocked on the door and poked her head in. "You done in here?"

Celia hung up. "Yes."

"Let's go then. Your lawyer is here and we need your statement."

Celia emerged to find Jackman, his face beet red, arguing with Johnson. "My innocent client withstood excessive force in an unacceptable manner. You booked and fingerprinted her when it was clear she was not in any way at fault and was, in fact, an innocent bystander. I call that police brutality."

"Innocent bystander in this instance is not exactly correct."

"Stop right there. You haven't an iota of evidence about anything."

Dawkins hooked her fingers into her belt and leaned against a desk.

Out of the corner of her eye, Celia saw Marcy standing with her young lawyer, Warner Appleton. He had black spiked hair and a weak, acned-dotted chin, and he wore a green T-shirt under his black and white plaid jacket. He looked so young Celia wondered if he had any idea what he was doing.

"We need her statement, and she waited until you got here," Dawkins drawled. She raised a clipboard. "Tell me what happened, Ms. Ewing."

Celia looked at Jackman, who frowned but nodded. Celia wrote down on the report exactly what transpired.

"There's not enough information here. Fill in the bottom question."

"That's enough. My client is suffering extreme emotional distress. Legally, she can finish her statement within the next two days when, I hope, she'll be in a better frame of mind. There are no charges. Release her immediately."

"For now. But no leaving the state," Dawkins said, stiff-backed. "We'll need to talk further, especially when we hear back from the DA's office."

Marcy's lawyer strode over. "Ah, yes. Uh, my client already gave you her statement. She's also free to go."

On their way out, they passed Michael, who paced near the door waiting for Deb's lawyer. Celia gave him a tight-lipped smile and wished with all her heart she could be with Deb, folding her friend safely in her arms.

A tall man wearing a cream-colored Italian silk suit with a crisp red dress shirt underneath strode toward them. He had a brown leather messenger bag slung over his shoulder and wore shiny, vanilla-white shoes the same color as his suit. Michael introduced him as Percival Jones, Deb's lawyer, before ushering him inside.

"Ms. Ewing, Ms. Worthingshire, as I said, don't leave town," Johnson called out.

"Yeah, heard that refrain before," Celia grumbled as they walked out with their lawyers chatting behind them. "Dawkins and Johnson are celebrities in their own minds."

"Yuck. They are the most undeserving comeback kids," Marcy grunted.

"We've got to free Deb ASAP."

"You bet your little tush." Marcy nodded with vigor. "We'll get right on it."

Jackman told Celia to call him, then Marcy's lawyer offered them a ride home. Marcy batted her eyes at him and thanked him with a giggle.

As they walked to where he'd parked his car, Celia heard the fronds of the palm trees blowing in the breeze, making a gentle swishing sound. It was a sound that had once soothed her, but today it didn't seem like anything would ever make her feel better again.

Chapter 58

Celia

Celia walked in circles around her apartment as time dragged by. That morning, she'd talked to Allison, who'd already heard from Michael that the investigator had figured out that Brady was the guilty party. The board of directors had granted Michael an extra twenty-four hours. All good so far, but not good enough for Celia.

She researched on the computer how Deb's illness impacted her circumstances and found she still had to be detained and interrogated. One site said: "If criminally insane, a patient can be kept indefinitely institutionalized; or if incompetent to stand trial, each year the patient must have a hearing to judge whether they are sane or not. If judged sane, they then stand trial." Then she saw something about a mercy release if an expert requested it. A pleading e-mail to Jackman got an immediate response. He recommended a forensic psychologist, Dr. Vilois, who could possibly help. She forwarded the e-mail to Michael.

She shuddered. It was terrible to think of Deb having to be judged insane, but in this case, she knew her friend's terrible diagnosis would benefit her. She wanted to call Stanton since she hadn't heard from him yet, but she knew he needed to get everything in order in a short time. Instead, to distract herself, she decided to polish what little silver she owned. The act of removing tarnish pleased her. It needed to become precious again.

When the phone rang in the midst of her task, her heart leaped in her chest. She answered on the second ring, trying to keep the tremor from her voice. It was Michael.

"Celia, I only have a minute …"

Celia interrupted him. "How's your mother? Did you get my e-mail?"

"I did. You're doing a great job." His voice sounded buoyant. "I presented my mother's case to the DA, a guy I know from college. He promised to rush court proceedings, including mandatory state psychiatric testing and a hearing with a judge and two psychiatrists, one being Dr. Vilois. I called him and he said from what documenta-tion I gave him, he'll fight to declare her incompetent to stand trial."

Celia guessed that as the new CEO of Global HMO, it helped expedite things. "Great."

"It'll take a couple of weeks. If his examination goes as expected, Vilois will push for a mercy release after some institutional time."

"She'll be held in a mental hospital in the meantime?" *No way.* She heard his breathing as he waited for a response. Her throat closed.

"Look, I've already got her lawyer pleading for a mercy release due to illnesses and age. Dr. Vilois says she stands an excellent chance of winning, but Celia, you have to know she'll have to stay in an institution for at least …" he paused. "One year till everything is in place."

Celia's forehead prickled. "We have to get her out now. Even a couple of months can kill her. She's so frail."

The door opened and Marcy staggered in, carrying a heavy box of papers. She dropped it with a resounding thump on the table before collapsing into a chair.

"Where are they sending her?"

He cleared his throat. "Hashford Institute for Life Improvement and Rehabilitation. It's a decent place, despite its reputation. The courts usually send neurologically impaired people there for treatment." He sighed. "It's the best option right now."

Celia's stomach twisted. She knew about Hashford and knew it was supposed to be one of the worst institutions in the area. How could Michael be okay with that? "I have some research on that institution and a bunch of other documents that might help. Can I deliver them to you?"

Michael hesitated. "Sure. Please do."

"They might convince the DA to keep her out of any institutions."

"Great. Now hold on. My investigator thinks he'll have the documents proving Brady's guilt by late tomorrow. I'd say he's ninety-nine percent sure. We'll make it in the nick of time."

She started pacing, pressing the phone harder to her ear. "Oh Michael, I hope that it happens."

"I'll be back in touch as soon as I get something." He hung up.

Celia turned to Marcy and hung her head. "That was Michael," she said, filling Marcy in on Deb. When she came to Hashford, she stuttered and spat it out. "I read reports of patients getting violent and attacking each other as well as staff."

Marcy winced. "What can we do?"

"We have to expedite a mercy release. Character witnesses can help."

Marcy pulled out her cell phone. "I'm on it," she said, dialing and pressing the phone to her ear. "Lyle, hello! I'm so glad you're there.

Listen, would you be a dear and write a letter about Deb Castor's many wonderful character qualities? You know, an excellent neighbor, good friend, how she helped all the shut-ins. Oh, never mind the personality part, just do it. You will? Thanks." After a long pause, "Well, that's flattering, but I'm too busy to go out now. Try me again in a couple of weeks."

She looked at Celia, her cheeks flushed. "I can also try three of our bridge partners and her neighbor down the hall."

Celia smiled. "That's excellent. We can do this." She sighed. "I'm so worried about her."

"I miss that wicked mouth of hers." Marcy grinned.

Celia checked her e-mail again and found one from Stanton. Her heart pounded as she opened it. She still hadn't told Marcy that she'd asked for his help, and she needed to keep it mum for now. She quickly read his message: "Scenario: Michael and I going to lunch today at noon where I make pitch. Deliver papers about Deb's case to his office. Stanton."

Her heart revved up. "Marcy, get to work on those character witnesses. I've got to deliver our research for Deb's case to Michael pronto."

"Good luck." Marcy was already dialing her phone.

Celia grabbed a box from her desk. "Be back in a couple of hours."

"What's in that box?" Marcy asked, looking up at Celia, holding the phone to her ear.

"Gotta run!" Celia hurried out before Marcy could ask anything else.

It was a short drive to the Well Services building. As she walked towards the entrance, Celia spotted Allie walking down the steps. Had Allie felt safe enough to go back to work? A moment before she called her daughter's name, Vanessa came out of the building and Allison put her arm around her shoulders. Celia ducked into the doorway, staying out of sight until the two women disappeared. Vanessa was sobbing, her body shaking. The embezzlement might have involved Vanessa. Celia hoped Allie didn't trust her.

When Allie and Vanessa had gone, she went straight to Michael's office with documents in hand. The administrative assistant was hustling out to lunch and told Celia to leave the expected papers on Michael's desk.

Chapter 59

Allison

"What am I going to do?" Vanessa wailed as she sat across from Allison in a coffee shop. "I miss Brady so much."

"I'm so sorry." Allison thought her friend's pain sincere but had reservations. Vanessa's name never came up in Michael's investigation. If Allison were honest with herself, Brady's death—while horrible to think about—was a relief. After all, he had implicated her in the theft and he was possibly responsible for the deaths of the Hartners. She gently patted Vanessa's arm.

Vanessa took a deep breath. "I got a call from a detective. Because I dated Brady they want to question me. I'm so scared. They could trick me into saying something that will make me look bad. I didn't know what Brady did!" Vanessa slapped her palm on the tabletop.

Allison considered her words carefully, wanting to pacify her. "They probably want to know what you might have seen or heard, who he talked to, where he went, things like that. I'm sure they don't suspect you."

"This might give them cause to open my court records. They could charge me with something—an accessory or some such crap. That will do me in. I won't go in without a warrant. I don't have to. I have to get a lawyer and I don't know how I'll pay for one." She wiped her face with a tissue and delicately blew her nose. "Embezzlement is one thing, but murder? Brady wouldn't do that."

"One thing going against you is that quite a few of the patients you helped care for died and were found to have high levels of drugs in their systems. I think they want to figure out if there's a link. You'll prove you're innocent, I'm sure." *Not perfectly sure.*

Vanessa sniffled. "I know a lot of my patients got their prescriptions from Dr. Drudding."

Allison felt a chill down her spine. Drudding's name had been on the pills planted at her mother's place. Her mother had told her recently how she found out he was a fraud. She kept her voice calm. "Did you ever talk to him?"

"Sure, I spoke to him on the phone a lot. Mostly I had questions on doses he prescribed. Sometimes I worried that they seemed a bit high, but he was the doctor and always reassured me it was all okay."

This time the icy chill shot through her entire body. "Is there any way these patients could have accidentally taken too high of a dose?"

Vanessa shook her head vehemently. "Not on my watch. I was always careful when I was with them. I doled out the right pills at the right times. I even cooked special meals for those on restricted diets." She sniffed. "Of course, visitors brought treats for them, a jelly donut, candy. It was out of my control, and I looked the other way. How bad can a little sugar be for someone near the end?"

Allison rooted through her purse and handed Vanessa another tissue. "What happened to these patients' medications after they died?"

Vanessa looked taken aback. "I put them in those special bags for disposing of prescription pills. Dr. Drudding always sent some kid to pick them up pretty soon after a patient died. It was a relief because in the wrong hands they'd get sold on the street." She shook her head and looked desperately at Allison. "I was always so careful. You believe me, don't you?"

"Of course. Did you trust Dr. Drudding?"

"I had no reason not to. He took care of so many people."

Was Shirkson Dr. Drudding? The situation for Vanessa sounded dire. But seeing her sitting there, looking so broken and vulnerable, Allison realized that her friend had to be innocent.

Chapter 60

Celia

After Celia finished at Michael's office, she headed home and tried hard not to speculate about what Vanessa wanted from Allison. She was tempted to call her daughter and ask what was going on, but she didn't want her to know she'd spied on her. She found Marcy still at her apartment.

Marcy grunted a hello. "Let's take a break," Marcy said, interrupting Celia's train of thought.

"Can't. I'm researching a US Supreme Court decision about detaining incompetent people for only a reasonable period of time, especially when it's proved they won't get better."

"I'm going home. I'm beat. Maybe I'll run into Lyle."

Celia stayed at her computer for the next hour. Suddenly, she pursed her mouth and gasped. "Oh my God," she exclaimed, her hands shaking as she quickly read the information she'd found. She jumped up, grabbed her purse and laptop, and hurried out to her car. She had to get to the police station fast.

She'd found new information that might concern this Dr. Drudding. Dawkins had to take this seriously, although she'd never heard a word about the photos. Though Brady Shirkson was dead, she now had an inkling that someone was still out there who might want to harm them. Perhaps it was an accomplice?

Dear Lord, she prayed as she kept the accelerator near the floor. She needed to get to the police station as soon as possible. *Please let Dawkins believe me.*

Chapter 61

Celia

A gunshot woke Celia from a sound sleep, and she rolled to the floor, ears ringing, heart hammering. She waited for a moment before lifting her head, her eyes darting around the room. Had it been a dream? A car backfiring? It sounded again, and she realized with relief that it was only thunder.

She went to the window and looked out at the dark clouds billowing in the sky, the rain pelting her window. Even though the clock said six a.m. she'd been too wired to sleep. Allison and Michael were coming for dinner at seven to celebrate the evidence that he finally received, which he'd promised to bring.

The storm clouds outside seemed to envelop Celia. She hoped everything would work out according to plan—whichever plan worked. If the one she'd worked on came to fruition, it only held grim consequences. She put it out of her head immediately and got to work.

Marcy had promised to come over early to help her prepare dinner but that was hours away. Celia had to keep herself occupied and unthinking until the time came to prepare the food. She decided a good cleaning might do the trick.

As she pulled out her broom, mop, bucket, and bottles of cleaning products, she reflected on how her life resembled a broken string of pearls, each pearl rolling away, out of reach. Allie's future. Her future with Stanton. The three musketeers who'd once danced the cha-cha with abandon. What evidence would Michael produce? Her heart ached as she scrubbed and thoughts of wanting to fly away overwhelmed her. Deb would be stuck in an institution as she slowly lost her mind, Marcy would continue to fill the void left by her estranged children with younger and younger men. It seemed to Celia that Marcy clung to youth, so that she might go back in time to redress the damage she'd done to her children. If only she could find a way to contact Marcy's kids and explain things, try to help them patch things up.

She opened the window to air things out, the humid post-storm air filling the apartment. Then she went back to the tub and scrubbed it a second time.

When Marcy came over later, Celia heard her call her name.

"I'm here. In the bathroom."

Marcy came to the bathroom door and found Celia in a heap, slouched against the bathtub. The room smelled of disinfectant and Marcy wrinkled her nose. "God's sake, woman, what on earth have you been doing all day?" She took Celia's arm, helping her up.

"Cleaning," Celia managed weakly.

Marcy snorted. "As if this place didn't already sparkle. Celia. It's four. You look like shit. Take a hot shower and revive yourself."

Celia didn't move. Despite the warm air, she felt a chill that sank deep into her bones.

"I know you're worried Michael doesn't have the right documents, aren't you?" Marcy didn't wait for an answer. "Have faith. He'll have them. Now take a shower so we can get to work whipping up dinner. You smell like Mr. Clean. He'd marry you in a heartbeat." Marcy dipped her head. "He is a cutie with those muscles."

Celia gave a half smile. "We wouldn't have to worry about moving his body. He'd disappear in a cloud of cleanser."

After a long hot shower, Celia blow-dried her hair and put on a black ruffled skirt and green silk blouse. She joined Marcy in the kitchen.

"Now that's my Celia, looking much better and festive like a real cha-cha dancer."

Celia looked in the oven and saw a fat turkey with green herbs scattered on top in a roasting pan, its cavity sealed with small skewers and its breast just starting to brown. The scent of parsley and thyme wafted past her, and she closed the oven door. "Nice job."

"I found everything in the refrigerator just about ready to go." Marcy cocked her head. "Maybe I was wrong on the festive part. You still look troubled. Talk to me."

"For one thing, I keep picturing Deb being attacked or neglected at that terrible institution." Celia huffed as though she'd taken a long hike. "And I feel like I can't breathe until Allie's in the clear for sure."

"You're expecting to save everyone by yourself." Marcy washed her hands and dried them carefully. "It's like you're half talking to me and half to yourself. Try this on for Allison." With her thumbs, Marcy raised the corners of Celia's mouth, forcing a smile. "This has been no picnic for anyone. I loved Melvin and now I'm sure who killed him—Shirkson."

"The real owner of those offshore accounts is connected to the serial killings."

Marcy grabbed Celia's hand and squeezed it. "You're still shaking.

I know it's been tough for you, being scared to death for Allie. Even though I haven't talked to my own kids in ages, I'd feel the same way if it were my kid." Marcy scanned Celia's face as though seeking answers.

Once again Celia felt a surge of determination to help Marcy reconcile with her kids.

"Just in case we go to prison, tell Allie to smuggle in hash brownies." Marcy winked.

"We'll need it." Celia let out a short laugh. "I'm making cherry pie, Allie loves it. And thanks for helping."

"You kidding? I say I'm a fabulous cook in my personal ads. Would I lie?"

"No, not for doing the turkey, I mean thank you for everything," she said, looking her straight in the eye. "Especially for being my friend."

Marcy tsked. "It's what best friends do. You sound like you're saying goodbye and going to jail right now." The two women hugged. "Now let's get this dinner finished."

Chapter 62

Allison

The front door swung open and Allison stepped in carrying a large paper bag. Marcy ran over and raised Allison's free arm in the air. "To the victor go the spoils, which in this case is a turkey dinner." She took the bag into the kitchen.

Allison followed her and found Celia basting the stuffed turkey. Celia wiped her hands on a towel and wrapped her arms around Allie's waist. "You've lost weight, you poor darling."

Allison sniffed the air. "I'll make up for it tonight." The comforting scent of onions and gravy wafted over Allison as her mother squeezed her hard. "Ouch, let go!" She laughed, stepping back and squeezing Celia's shoulder. "You look as tired as I feel."

"I've been so worried. It's been grueling for all of us." Celia tilted her head. "But you have color back in your cheeks. It's nice to see that."

"I'm feeling much better." Allison yawned. "You know, when your world seems to be coming to an end for so long it's exhausting." She held out her hands. "When it's over, it takes a while for relief to set in. I keep looking over my shoulder to see if trouble is still there."

"You need a delicious meal, some wine, and lots of rest," Marcy said. "We all do."

"I'm definitely looking forward to home cooking." Allison eyed the golden lattice-crusted cherry pie on the wire rack. Collapsing in a kitchen chair, her arms drooped over the sides, and she let out a shaky sigh. "So in addition to my being cleared, I heard you three are close to being off the hook yourselves. Even Deb."

"Hallelujah!" Marcy shouted, jabbing the air with a potato masher. She held it near Allison's mouth like a microphone. "Tell us everything."

"Let her rest." Celia tugged Marcy's arm. "She'll tell us in her own time."

"No, I'm okay, really." Allison felt like she could sleep for a week, but it hardly seemed fair not to tell what she'd learned.

"So, you know those offshore accounts? Michael's investigator found out Brady owned them. He's got notarized documents."

Celia clapped her hands. "Hallelujah!"

Allison blinked rapidly. "I can't believe the drive and stamina of that man. After two days and nights with hardly any sleep, Michael worked straight through, studying what I gave him, all the company records. He worked with his investigator and found that Brady stole from right under their noses all along. It was never the Hartners." Allison cleared her throat. "Those poor people were innocent. And this is nuts. Not only was Vanessa in Brady's life long before Michael hired her, Brady made purchases for her, using company money, four years before she officially went to work for Well Services."

"I knew that woman was a liar," Marcy said. "What else?"

"I saw Vanessa recently and believed she was innocent. How dumb am I?"

At this, Celia whipped around and started to say something but stopped. She turned away.

"Mom, I don't blame you if you think I was foolish to trust Vanessa. Turns out Vanessa used a company credit card Brady gave her to buy diamond rings, a ruby brooch, a Rolex watch, and the list goes on. Unbelievable. What's craziest is that he could have afforded to get her all of that with his own big fat salary." Allison shook her head.

"This just keeps getting juicier. Keep going," Marcy said eagerly.

"How about a condo with company money?" She let out a whoosh of air. "Brady made most of the items look like gifts to clients—Swarovski and Bulgari jewelry, large Versace and Gucci handbags, and more. Tens of thousands of dollars."

"That stupid bastard." Marcy shook her head. "Did Michael happen to find any of those diamond rings?"

Celia poked her in the ribs. "Now you want to fence stolen goods? You're in enough trouble."

"I meant for Allison, not me."

"Don't pay attention to her, Allie. Stop if it goes over the edge."

Allison's face sank. "I don't get it. Michael's sure Vanessa is involved. Even though she swore to me she wasn't. I feel betrayed."

Marcy pressed the masher into the potatoes. It clanged each time it hit the sides of the bowl. "I hope she's going down."

Celia shot Marcy a look.

Allison traipsed to the counter and dipped a finger into the bowl of mashed potatoes. "I'm so hungry, but I don't know whether to eat or cry."

Celia opened the fridge and pulled out a tray of cut vegetables and dill dip, Allie's favorite.

"Yum." Allison took a string bean from the platter, plunged it into the creamy dip, and munched. "I feel so strange, kind of in limbo. Anyway, this next one you'll like. Michael brought all the statements to Detective Dawkins. He hauled over a stack of papers and dumped them on her desk. They were in there for over two hours while he walked her through each purchase, page by page. They'd already been trying to talk to Vanessa, but with all this proof in front of Dawkins, they called her and demanded that she come down or else they'd get a warrant. Michael told me she got to the station in twenty minutes."

Marcy snapped her fingers. "Just like that, huh? Ah, justice is sweet."

"I'm guessing she's desperate to strike a deal with the DA and ask for a lighter sentence in exchange for giving evidence on Brady. You know, with her record and all."

"Did you hear if she took the deal?" Celia asked.

"I have no idea. All I know is that Michael feels like she stuck a knife in his back since he gave her a second chance and this is how she repaid him."

Celia squeezed Allison's shoulder. "I know you feel let down by her too," she said gently.

Allison rested her chin in her hand. "I admired how she'd beaten the worst odds. There was something so savvy about her ability to read people so well. She helped me land that job."

"Your skills got you that job," Celia insisted. "As well as an impressive résumé."

"Give her some credit, Mother. She admitted she wanted a boyfriend who'd take care of her. I'm sure Brady must have controlled and manipulated her and made her an accomplice to his theft, to some extent. Still, she befriended me when I needed it." Allison shuddered. "Sadly, she had a lot of darkness in her life. She didn't leave her past behind." Sadness for Vanessa encased Allison. "I heard they kept her in a holding cell overnight."

"Ach," Celia said. "Those cages don't look fit for animals. Why are they holding her?"

"After Vanessa caved she waited over twenty-four hours for a lawyer so they kept her. She had no one to bail her out—not even Michael, who is furious with her. I pity her." Allison had seen the raw pain on Vanessa's face when she'd shared those ugly memories of childhood. It was hard to imagine that this same woman who'd befriended Allison knew all along she'd betray her. Or was Vanessa a scapegoat too?

Allison turned her face away and blinked hard to stop the tears that had gathered in her eyes. She took a carrot from the tray and waved it in the air before biting into it. "So here's the kicker. Michael showed the police the hard evidence that Brady cooked the books. They had probable cause to raid his house and confiscate his personal computer. And Michael is ninety-nine percent sure Vanessa will rat out Shirkson not just for embezzlement but as the serial killer as well."

"Does that mean what I think it means?" Celia looked puzzled.

"Yes. Michael does believe in the serial killer theory now."

"I'm surprised he came around to it," Celia said. "He never seemed convinced."

"Well, you can't blame him for doubting it at first," Allison said, reaching into the paper bag she'd brought and pulling out a bottle of Pinot Noir. Marcy took the wine from her and popped the cork while Celia fetched three wine glasses from the cabinet. "It's hard to believe anyone is killing sick and old people, but the evidence is overwhelming." Allison sipped from her wine glass, eager for the alcohol to calm her.

Marcy stirred butter into the whipped potatoes. "I knew it. Shirkson's the one and Vanessa is his partner in crime."

"What I keep asking myself is why would they do it?" Celia asked as she sipped her wine. "It just doesn't make sense."

"I don't know anymore." Allison looked up at the ceiling as though an answer might appear. She tossed back the last remnants of wine. "People sure have sinister inner lives."

"Yes, they do." Celia gave Allison an odd look. Marcy poured them all more wine.

"Michael has all the proof of Brady's method to steal money." Allison swirled the wine in her glass. "As a matter of fact, Mom, you were on to something without realizing it. Remember that night you questioned me about the financial statements?"

"After our conversation I tried to explain it to Marcy."

She looked at her mom and Marcy to make sure they were following her. "Brady manipulated sham corporations to get payments from Well Services for imaginary goods. As for the trail of stolen money, Michael found out Brady moved it among several banks to throw anyone investigating off track. It's hard to follow when they do that." She planted her fingertips on the table. "To make it easier, imagine each spot I touch is a US bank. That created an e-money trail until it reached his offshore accounts in Costa Rica. It's money laundering."

The women kept their eyes on her fingers. "Bottom line? At least eleven million or more was stolen, but only one million is left in Costa Rica."

"Whew," Celia said, wiping her forehead. "That's a huge amount."

"Here's the most incredible part," Allison continued. "After raiding Brady's computer, the police found what I call a death list. The documents contained names of patients, their ailments, medications, necessary medical equipment, and how much it cost to insure each patient each month. It also listed those suing the company, and Melvin's name was there.

"He'd sorted the names by who was sickest and whose families lived farthest away." She shuddered. "Many were already dead."

Celia and Marcy shook their heads in disgust.

"Oh honey. It's so heartless," Celia said, pressing her lips together. "How many do the police estimate died that way?"

"Detective Dawkins told Michael that the count is well over forty-five to fifty-five and most are from Boca Pelicano Palms." Her voice quieted. "Many were Vanessa's patients who died well before I got here." Allison saw her mother's face blanch. Marcy gasped and gripped Celia's wrist.

"It's still circumstantial that Brady is the serial murder," Allison said. "They can say a CEO of a health organization needs that kind of data. Nailing him definitively can only happen with Vanessa's testimony."

"Michael is bringing all this proof for you tonight?" Celia asked.

"Yes. You can see this for yourselves. I just figured I'd prepare you in advance."

Marcy brought her hands together. "Thank you, Jesus."

"More like thank you, Michael. He thinks he can connect Brady to breaking into your apartment to plant the meds and put fake evidence on your computer. He was able to get past the gates into any community because he was head honcho at a company that medically insured almost all the residents. Who'd suspect?"

"People would be happy to meet the CEO," Marcy said. "So, explain the purpose of murders."

"Killing people who cost Global a lot of money to insure saved big bucks. That allowed Shirkson a nice margin to steal. Vanessa tried to pin the overdoses on this Dr. Drudding. She claimed to be concerned about the prescriptions, but Brady was behind it all, thanks to those lists on his computer."

"Such an evil man," Marcy said in disgust. "And I hope they find this Dr. Drudding soon."

"Lucky for us, Michael is so damn smart." Allison poured more wine but looked somber. "I'm still having trouble wrapping my head around Vanessa's involvement."

Allison thought back to her friend's longing expression after a few drinks, her face crestfallen. "You're lucky you have a mother who loves you despite all the stuff that drives you crazy," she'd murmured. Vanessa had been right on that score.

Celia sighed. "But honey, as beautiful and smart as she is, and as much as she helped you out, the fact of the matter is that she used everyone she met without a second thought." Her voice was hesitant, as though she thought hard about what she wanted to say. "Vanessa knew that old people are easy prey. They're in fragile physical and mental health and can be too trusting."

"You're right." Allison sighed. "It's going to take some time to get over this."

"Of course," Celia said gently.

The women were silent for a minute. Allison felt exhausted but exhilarated. Michael had exonerated her, and they were close to getting her mother and her friends off the hook as well—so close she could taste it. Allison's heart swelled. Despite everything she'd just been through, she felt so fortunate.

Marcy was the first to break the silence. "Where's Michael? It's seven-thirty."

"He'll be here soon," Allison said. "He's probably caught up with something at the office. I can't tell you how hard he's been working."

Celia set out some cheese and crackers on a dish, and Marcy plopped two chunks of cheese on a cracker. "It's too warm in here," she said, chewing. "Could you turn up the air conditioner?"

"It's never worked very well," Celia said. "I'll call someone to come and fix it tomorrow."

Marcy fanned her face with a paper napkin, making a crinkling sound.

"I'll call for you." Allison squinted. "Are you all right, Mom?"

"Oh sure. It's a little worse tonight than usual." Celia waved dismissively and turned to baste the turkey again. "It's all this cooking. Turkey's done. I'll turn the oven off."

Allison couldn't help thinking that something else was going on. "You'll be nice to Michael tonight, right, Mother?" she asked, an edge to her voice. "He's gone above and beyond through all of this."

Celia wiped the sweat from her upper lip. "I'm always nice to him."

"Good. I really owe him. We all do."

Celia turned and gave her daughter a small smile. "You're right."

Chapter 63

Celia

It was eight o'clock, and the women had just finished the second bottle of wine when there was a knock at the door. Celia jumped up.

"Finally, Michael's here!" Allison said, excitement in her eyes as she got up from her chair to answer the door. Celia noticed the happy flush in her daughter's cheeks.

Michael strode in, carrying a bouquet of peach and white roses. He kissed Allison, then pecked Celia and Marcy on their cheeks. "I'm so sorry I'm late," he said with a charming smile. "It's been one hell of a day. You must all be starved."

"We've been nibbling," Celia murmured.

"It smells heavenly in here." He glanced at the empty wine bottles on the table and smiled more broadly. "Looks like you ladies have been celebrating in my absence. I'll have to catch up." Though his elegantly tailored ash-gray suit was rumpled and he had dark circles under his eyes, he still looked handsome.

"I'm so glad you're finally here," Allison said, slightly breathlessly. She hugged him. "You look fatigued."

"I'm fine now that I'm here with all of you."

Marcy stepped forward and took the bouquets from his arms.

"I hate to interrupt this kissy-poo stuff, but you're crushing those gorgeous roses." She turned to Allison and said in a loud whisper, "I might squeeze him too. Got yourself quite a hunk. Don't let it go to his head."

Michael covered his face with his hands and peered out between his fingers. "A hunk of baloney is more like it."

"She's right about you, boss. You are still my boss?" Allison dipped her head and glinted at him from her eyes.

He smoothed the lapels of his jacket. "Truth is, I can't do without you."

Allison looked relieved.

"I'm late because I waited to get the documents notarized. You're free."

Allison clapped her hands. "Oh, thank God! I knew you'd come through. Thank you."

Marcy put the roses in a vase filled with water. She turned to Celia. "Thank the man," she whispered through clenched teeth. "He freed your daughter."

Celia shook her head as though coming out of a daze. "Of course! Thank you for helping my daughter, Michael. I know you've gone above and beyond."

He bowed slightly. "It was my pleasure. Anything to help this ravishing woman." He reached into the leather bag hanging from his shoulder and produced a bottle of Veuve Clicquot. "Anyone for champagne? Lord knows I could use a drink right now, rather desperately." He let his eyes rove across the room to a small alcove where Celia kept her stash of spirits.

Celia waved her hand toward it. "Help yourself." She seemed to totter a bit.

Michael wiped his forehead with a white handkerchief. "It's warm in here."

"I apologize for the broken air conditioning," Celia said. "Take your jacket off, Michael, no need to be formal here. Make yourself comfortable." He slipped his jacket off and she held out her hand. "I'll hang that up for you." She took the jacket to the closet while he poured himself a glass of vodka.

"So the board of directors gave me a hard time about promoting me to CEO. They implied I was Brady's lackey. What they didn't know was how much I covered for the man, did his work and mine, how Brady used me as a foil for his—shall we say—bad judgments." His face tightened, then relaxed. "In the end they agreed I was the best candidate to pull them out of the morass."

"I'll testify for you in a heartbeat," Allison said.

His shoulders slumped and his face sobered. "I need to talk about my mom."

For a few moments, it felt like all the air had been suctioned out of the room. "I'm glad you brought it up." Celia wrapped her arms around herself despite the stuffy air. "Can you get her out of that place?"

Michael closed his eyes and rubbed his temples. "First I got the DA to agree to cut the mandatory amount of time to six months. And then, we hope, a mercy release." He inhaled. "Second, to avoid a murder trial, she's got to be incapable of understanding right from wrong. Dr. Vilois thinks she can't."

The corners of Celia's mouth fell. "I don't want to criticize your efforts, but she has to get out now. There are numerous documented accounts of assaults by patients. Your mother is so fragile. That place will destroy her."

Michael's brow furrowed and he rubbed the back of his neck. "I certainly don't want her in a place like that. It's a court order that I got knocked down as much as I can."

"Get her lawyer to plead a mercy release immediately. Discharge requires supervision. Marcy and I will do it." Celia thumped a fist into her palm.

Marcy was setting the table and put the pile of dishes down with a thud. "That goes without saying."

Michael tugged at his lower lip. "You gals have done a phenomenal job to help my mom. I'll push the DA even more." He polished off his drink and poured himself another, then turned to Celia and put a reassuring hand on her shoulder. "I promise you, we'll get her out soon."

She felt a knot in her throat and turned away. "Dinner will get cold. Let's eat." She came out of the kitchen balancing a plump and perfectly browned turkey on a platter.

Michael rushed to help her set it down. "Let me carve." He held up the knife and sliced neatly as the string beans and potatoes were passed around.

"Celia, I'm in heaven." He looked heavenward after taking the first bite. "Your gravy is perfect." He looked at Allison and winked. "Teach Allison to cook."

Celia pushed the food around the plate. "I'm a lousy teacher."

When they finished, Michael popped the champagne cork and poured the pale liquid into flutes. He held his glass aloft. "First to my mother's release. Then to all of us." He looked around. "And to Allison. I believed in her always. I'm promoting her to assistant vice president."

Allison sat up, her eyes wide. "What? Do you mean it?"

"Of course I do. We work so well together. You're the perfect candidate."

"I can't believe it. I'm so happy I could burst." She reached her glass into the center of the table, and Michael and Marcy clinked their glasses to hers. Celia felt Marcy kick her under the table and realized they were waiting for her.

She quickly snatched up her glass and clinked it with the others. "I'm sorry. My mind keeps wandering. This is great news. Congratulations." She smiled at Allison.

Allison frowned. "Mother, are you all right? You seem dazed."

"I think I'm just so distracted worrying about Deb. But I'm fine otherwise." She waved her hand around dismissively and took a sip of champagne.

Michael cleared his throat. "I'm told that Vanessa will confirm accusations about Brady and her own involvement." He turned to Celia. "Apologies for dismissing your theory. You proved smarter than I am."

"As long as we're celebrating, let's hear it for the *Retirement Newsletter*," laughed Marcy. "I got some single men responding to the article."

Celia raised an eyebrow.

"And to Michael's new position," Allison said, perking up. "No one is more deserving."

"I'm grateful to have you all in my life," Michael said. "Soon my mother will join us around this table. I'm sure of it."

Celia looked at Allison. Her face was flushed and her smile was wide. Celia's eyes blurred momentarily with tears, and she turned her head away.

Michael got up and rummaged through the files in his bag,

handing a large manila envelope to Allison. "Brady apparently used an OCR computer program to duplicate Allison's signature. Here are documents for the offshore accounts in Brady's name. As for clearing the three Musketeers, ladies, as soon as they accept the evidence against Brady, you're off the hook."

"Again, my heartfelt appreciation." Clear-eyed now, Celia raised her glass to him, her voice upbeat. "Will the information from Brady's computer hold up?"

"As soon as they finish analyzing Brady's hard drive and get Vanessa's statement it will."

"What a relief. Allie is free." Celia took a deep breath and started sobbing. Marcy draped her arm over Celia's shoulder. "Thank you," Celia said through gasps.

"We have to make sure Global and Well Services survives with our reputation intact. I know that with you by my side, we can do it." Michael held Allison close, then kissed her. "Who knows what the future holds, but … Celia," he glanced over at her, and she wiped her tears away with the back of her hand. Michael continued in a hoarse whisper, his face soft. "I love your daughter." Allison's smile left Celia breathless.

Michael glanced down at his watch. "I have to dash. I need to get back to the office. Celia, thank you so much for this delicious dinner. It was such a pleasure to celebrate with all of you."

"I'll get your jacket," Celia said, getting up and heading for the closet.

Michael slipped into his jacket, picked up his bag, and gave each of the women a hug before heading out into the muggy night air.

Chapter 64

Celia

After Michael left, Celia stood at the door unmoving. Should she send her daughter home? No. A secondhand version would never have the impact of a firsthand viewing if all went as she hoped it would. It promised to be a disaster if it went awry. Celia heard china clinking as Marcy cleared the remaining dishes and Allie wiped the table, humming.

Love comes in many forms, Celia thought: children, spouses, friends, lovers, neighbors, acquaintances—each layer offering bits of insight until the final reckoning opened, like a clear blue sky. She looked forward to the day when she, Deb, and Marcy danced the cha-cha together again. After tonight …

"Mother? Why are you hovering by the door? You look strange," Allison said. "Do you feel all right?"

Celia started and turned away from the door. "Yes, yes, I'm fine. I think it's just the heat and the strain of everything."

Allison picked up the folder. "I can't wait to have a look at these."

There was a knock at the door.

Celia threw it door open and Detective Dawkins walked in, followed by a tall, bony, red-faced young man carrying a large suitcase. Without a word, they placed a series of electronic boxes and a speaker on the dining room table and started plugging them into the wall.

Allison looked stunned. Marcy shook her head.

"What are they doing here? What's going on?" Marcy's voice cracked.

Switching off the lights, Celia took Allie and Marcy by the elbows and urged them over to the window.

"What the hell are you doing?" Allison asked.

A moment of doubt struck Celia. *Too late.* She stared through the window at a darkened night sky, dotted with pinpoint stars. Outside the complex's overhead path lights had switched on. It was nine-thirty and most people at Boca Pelicano Palms were settled down for an evening of TV or preparing for bed. Celia remained silent.

"Do you know anything, Marcy?" Allison twisted her head in Marcy's direction.

Marcy shrugged. "Geez, I'm as out of it as you are."

Allison, still clinging to the stack of papers, took a step back.

Behind them in the darkened room, a white light from a monitor eerily illuminated Dawkins's face.

"This is madness." Allison stared through the glass. "Is that Michael?" She reached over to raise the window.

Celia stopped her. They watched Michael walk toward the parking lot, then a moment later heard his footfalls on the brick path through a loudspeaker behind them.

"Did you and Michael plan something?" Allison asked. "A joke?"

Outside, a figure jumped from the shadows. Michael stumbled backward as though threatened by a mad dog. "Vanessa, what the hell are you doing here?" He looked over his shoulder.

Noises squawked through the speaker. The young man made adjustments. Michael shoved Vanessa away from the streetlight into semidarkness.

"You scared the hell out of me." His breathless voice came through the speaker.

Allison grabbed Celia's shoulder so hard she yelped. "You wired Michael's jacket when you put it in the closet. Why?"

Celia put a finger to her lips and pointed for Allison to keep looking out the window.

The three women now saw Michael bend as though to kiss Vanessa, but she pushed him away. He faltered. "What the fuck is the matter? You know how hard I worked on getting you out. It worked, didn't it?"

Allison gasped.

"Don't lie to me. You did nothing," Vanessa said, her tone harsh. "You turned me in to Dawkins, you bastard. I pawned everything Brady gave me and used my savings to make bail, the bail you promised to put up and didn't. You're a piece of shit."

"I can't make any dramatic moves or the cops will go after me, and that wouldn't be good for either of us." He broke out in a sarcastic cackle. "You're wired, aren't you? You made a deal to entrap me."

"I'm not wired."

Michael pushed Vanessa into a semi-lit grove of trees off the path and frisked her. Their shadows were distinct. He snaked his hands up both thighs, then down her arms and chest, into her bra, around her back, and over her butt cheeks. "You're clean, but I must say I enjoyed doing that. It's like old times, huh, babe?" Michael said, chuckling.

Celia glanced at her daughter and cringed. Allison's face looked set in stone.

"You're a fucking pig," Vanessa growled. "You said I could use the company credit cards then you turned it against me, threw me to the wolves. You want me to rot in jail."

Allison wheezed as though she were having trouble getting enough air into her body.

"Listen," he said in a conciliatory voice. "They can't know we're together. I hired a new lawyer for cash. Last one was a jerk."

"You want me to give a cockamamie story to get Brady? You stole his keys from my bag to break into his house."

"So I doctored proof, put it into his computer for the police to find. Clever, don't you think? Look, just say Brady confided in you that he killed those people to cut high-maintenance medical expenses. That way the company made more money for him to steal."

"I don't want to lie for you anymore. I trusted you. I loved you. Instead you framed him."

Allison groaned and Celia touched her arm. Allison shook loose. Marcy shifted closer and gripped Celia's wrist.

Michael held up his hands. "Hey, it's now a given about Brady. You're off the hook. Don't ruin things."

"You're the embezzler and the killer." She pointed at his face.

He grunted and looked behind him. "Shut the hell up." He shoved her.

"Admit it. I know it's you."

"Of course I was. Deep down, you knew what was going on from the get-go. Don't play naïve. You're just as hungry as I am."

"I'd never kill anyone. You're the one behind Dr. Drudding, giving all my patients those pills. I knew those doses were too high, I knew it! It was you, or some crony you hired."

Michael snorted. "Yeah, so?"

"You even tried to murder Celia!" Vanessa went on.

"That nosy bitch. She's been a thorn in my side ever since her fuckwit daughter ordered those stats for her."

Allison slapped her hand over her mouth and muffled a scream. Celia could barely stand to look at her. She glanced at Marcy who stood deathly still, her nostrils flaring. "Damn," she whispered.

"I did it for us, and you're an ungrateful shit," Michael went on. "I'm busting my ass to set up a deal for you with the DA, and you accuse me of bullshit." His grim laugh, like a barking dog, boomed through the loudspeaker. "I told Dawkins nothing, babe. She took a shot in the dark."

Allison swayed in place. Celia held her up.

"You're a damned liar, setting me up as an accessory to serial murders when you're the murderer." Vanessa slapped his chest. He knocked her hand away with a resounding smack. "You're the one who killed Brady and then set your mother up. I know that was your gun."

He snorted. "Yeah, prove it." He reached out. She jerked away. "Look, just hang in there until we get the deal for you. We can replicate this model at other branches of Global all over the country. We can do it better now, be more careful."

Allison pressed the file folder against her abdomen as though easing severe pain.

"I'm so sorry," Celia whispered. This was going well, but it was almost killing her daughter.

"Tell me, Michael. You killed the Hartners, didn't you?" Vanessa demanded.

"Collateral damage. They got too close." Michael snorted. "I saved your sorry ass by springing you from prison once I put the bug in Brady's ear about you. I gave him your picture, your sob story, and got him to seal your court records. Be grateful or you'll be wearing orange for a long time." Michael stepped closer and ran his hand over her cheek. She tried to pull away. "Let me remind you, you're nothing without me. I'll get you out in a matter of weeks. If not, you serve a little time and then come back, and it'll be like old times."

"You poisoned sick old folks with your fake Dr. Drudding prescriptions. You're a sick fuck."

He looked over his shoulder. "Let's get out of here. Come to my place."

"Why did she buy into his bull crap to begin with?" Marcy asked quietly. "Huh?"

"Shhh," Celia said.

Allison dropped the file folder. "They're forged. These documents are forged. Oh God." Her voice spiraled with pain.

"I'm staying right here," Vanessa went on. "I'm telling the cops how you threatened me and forced me to set Celia up."

Michael pinned Vanessa's arms against her sides. "Like hell you will. That setup would have worked, too, if Brady hadn't figured everything out. Damn him. I had to get rid of him."

Allison's jaw dropped open. Celia grasped her hand. Her daughter held on tightly.

Vanessa swung her arms loose and punched Michael's upper arm. He jumped back. "You're a monster. What you're doing to your mother … it's unbelievable. Feeding her drugs so she acts deluded and senile," Vanessa spat out. "She took whatever pills you told her to because she trusted you and thought you were doing the best for her. Instead you drugged her too."

Michael looked like he was faltering for the first time. "Those drugs won't hurt her, not in the long run. It's easier to get an old woman with Alzheimer's off on murder charges than me. I'll get her out. She'll be fine."

"You're an animal!" She struck him again with her fist.

A choked sob escaped from Allison. Celia bit her lip until she tasted blood.

Michael made an angry sound. "Enough of your shit." He grabbed her arms. "You were happy when I falsified a résumé and assessments of your job skills. And you didn't seem to have any problem using Brady to live the good life."

"Maybe I used him, but I didn't kill him. I didn't kill anyone. You're the embezzler. You're the murderer," Vanessa sneered.

He laughed like a file grating on metal. "You dumb bitch. It's stacked against you, you and Brady. You're dead meat unless you play nice with me. I can get you out." With one hand he held Vanessa behind her neck and with the other pressed his fist to her throat.

"Stop." Her voice sounded stifled. "Can't breathe."

Allison gasped. Celia held her hand more tightly.

"Tough shit. Decide right now how you'll play it. If by some odd chance they can't nail Brady, we'll blame my mother's creepy old-bag friends. I set it up for the cops to suspect them anyway."

"Old bags?" Marcy sounded indignant.

"Shush." Celia wanted to tuck Allison into her arms like she did when she was a baby, but feared they'd both break down. She still needed her wits about her.

"Go fuck yourself," Vanessa barely croaked out.

Michael pushed his fist harder and Vanessa gave a strangled groan.

"Oh God, isn't someone going to do something? He'll kill her!" Marcy said in a loud whisper.

"Yes, please …" Celia yelled.

Dawkins shouted into the microphone, "Go. We have enough." She bolted out the door.

Moments later, four police cars screeched to a halt nearby with whirling lights so bright Celia squinted. Eight police officers jumped out, guns drawn. Headlights illuminated the pair.

"You're under arrest, Michael Castor, for murder," Officer Johnson said. "You have the right to remain silent …"

"What the fuck is this? Get away from me. Do you know who I am?"

"We know all right." One officer held Michael as he struggled, while another handcuffed him. Johnson finished reading Michael his Miranda rights.

"I didn't do anything. Arrest that woman. She's a murderer." As they lifted him to a standing position, he jutted his chin in Vanessa's direction. "She killed old sick people."

Vanessa stood breathing heavily and rubbing her throat. Dawkins went over to Michael and removed the tiny microphone from inside his jacket breast pocket. His eyes bugged out. "I was trying to get that bitch to confess. I didn't do it, she did. How can you believe her word over mine?" When no one paid attention, he bent his head toward the microphone and spat out, "Celia, I'll get you if it's the last thing I do."

Celia ducked as though he'd entered the room with a knife, making a beeline towards her.

Dawkins patted Vanessa on the back and helped her into a police car without cuffs. The other officers led Michael away and shoved him into another car, the whirling lights highlighting Michael's face in ghostly red.

Turning on the light, Celia noticed Allison's gray, pale face and wobbly legs. She slowly dropped into a chair, her eyes glassy and unfocused.

Detective Dawkins returned to the apartment and helped the young man finish packing up the equipment. "Congrats, Ms. Ewing. You helped us solve this case. You're to be commended."

"Holy shit. So that's why you've been so jumpy," Marcy said, gently shaking Celia by the shoulder.

Celia cleared her throat. Her voice felt rusty with disuse. "I gave the photos I took at Drudding's office to the police. They enlarged the photo and didn't think the person looked like Michael, but had probable cause to go to the office because of the checks and the bizarre setup."

"We went there and dusted for prints," Dawkins broke in. "They were Michael's. All officers at his company are fingerprinted. But it wasn't until Ms. Ewing brought in Michael's account numbers to offshore banks that we were able to get a warrant to wiretap."

"Account numbers?" Marcy gawked at Celia. "How did you find the offshore accounts? Why did you even suspect Michael?"

Celia shook her head. "Tell you later," she whispered.

Allison's eyes closed slowly and she slumped her head till her chin rested on her chest. "I need to hear it all."

Dawkins stood after unplugging equipment. "We called Vanessa in and offered her a deal that we wouldn't go after her sealed prison records if she agreed to be wired. But Ms. Ewing here pointed out that Michael would expect Vanessa to be wired, so we decided to have her plant the mic in his jacket. The air conditioning cooperated just as Ms. Ewing thought, or arranged." Dawkins laughed. "Maybe you ladies should join the force."

Celia smiled as she saw Marcy give Dawkins the finger behind her back.

Dawkins and the young man picked up the cases and headed towards the door. "Sorry we harassed you gals." She saluted and they walked out.

Marcy narrowed her eyes at Celia. "Tonight I thought you were worried about not getting the proof on Brady Shirkson, poor soul," she whispered.

"I was really nervous. If it backfired Allie might never have talked to me again." Pain roiled in Celia's head. Allison let out a sob and Celia turned to her. "Allie, I'm so sorry. It was so hard for me to do this, but I felt you had to see it to believe it."

Allison pressed her arm against her abdomen. "Oh Mom. You did the right thing. It just hurts so much."

"Celia, what I don't understand is why you suspected Michael or how you got those account numbers," Marcy said.

Celia got a slight nod from Allison. "When Deb stayed with me, I saw her Elavil came in a childproof vial that I can hardly open myself. With her arthritic fingers, how could she pull the trigger of a gun? When you told me about her diagnosis, Allison, I started researching Alzheimer's. I learned that most signs of Alzheimer's appear years before the disease manifests. Deb didn't fit that profile. Hers came on too fast."

"I'll be damned. You *should* join the police force." Marcy stared, wide-eyed.

"There's more. After that, I ate humble pie and got Stanton to take Michael out to lunch and make an offer for a shady business deal. While they were out, I went to Michael's office on the pretext of bringing Deb's documents. I had read up on how to install a keystroke logger, a device that records everything a person types, and set it up to go to my computer. Michael liked Stanton's offer and went back to his office to withdraw money from his offshore accounts. The logger got the information with the account numbers, bank names, and whatever else I needed to give to the police to track them down."

"What ruse did you use?" Allison's voice sounded weak. She gripped the arms of her chair so tightly her knuckles turned white.

"Stanton offered a deal to buy a patented drug cheaply from a foreign country so they could sell it here at a jacked-up price. Stanton would do the work if Michael put up the money."

"I underestimated you," Allison uttered in a near whisper.

"Desperation makes you smarten up. Research from the internet doesn't hurt either."

Allison rubbed her cheek. "Michael didn't hesitate when Stanton made the offer?"

"He moved faster than I thought. He started removing cash from his bank right away, and thanks to the logger, I got it all."

Marcy's eyes teared up. "We can get Deb out now, get her off those terrible pills."

"Yes, thank God, but this might destroy her."

"How sad for her," Marcy said. "Her only child ..."

Celia winced.

Allison began gasping for air. "Michael killed Brady, the old people, and the Hartners in cold blood. I was a just foil for him."

"He should go to jail just for calling us old bags." Marcy pouted.

"My poor baby." Celia knelt in front of her daughter. "You need to rest."

Allison lifted her head. "I'm so angry I could throttle him. What I don't understand is why didn't he kill us?"

"Good question." Celia exhaled. "I'm guessing he tried to kill us, but when it didn't work, he backed off. Maybe killing us so soon after the Hartners would arouse too much suspicion."

Allison clutched at her temples. "Damn. I remember how I told Michael once that you took antidepressants for years. That probably gave him the idea to plant the Elavil on you, make you a target. I'm so sorry."

"How could you know?"

"I'm so tired my gums ache," Allison said, rubbing her eyes. Her expression changed to anguish, like a child who had done something wrong, and she looked up at Celia. "You saved my life."

"I will always protect you. Your happiness is the most important thing to me."

"You put your life on hold to help Allison. That's as brave as a mother gets," Marcy said.

"Would both my girls like to stay over?" Celia asked. Marcy and Allison nodded, and then the three of them burst into tears.

Later, after Celia had settled Allie into bed in the guest room, Allie had looked up at her, her eyes plaintive like a child. "What about charges against you two?"

"Dawkins promised that we're off the hook about moving Melvin, which was our only crime. We did solve the crime for her."

"Michael," Allison said, her voice barely audible. "How could I have trusted him, how?"

"My darling girl," Celia said, "you only wanted the same thing

I want, someone to love you and whom you can love back." She covered Allison, who closed her eyes and turned over on her side.

In the living room, Marcy had made up the sofa and was already sleeping.

Celia retreated to her bedroom with her computer, which Dawkins had finally returned to her. She went online. There was one more piece of research she needed to do, a final e-mail to send.

Next, she called Stanton. His voicemail picked up, and she found herself grateful that he hadn't answered or she might have broken down sobbing. "All went well tonight. I can't thank you enough. Let's talk soon." She hung up, feeling hopeless. She had a feeling she wouldn't hear from him again, not after all she'd put him through.

She lay back on her bed, remembering the thrill of dancing the cha-cha with him, their thighs brushing, sending electric thrills down her spine. She couldn't tell if the perspiration on their hands and cheeks came from being together or the excitement of the dance. She heard his soothing baritone voice, his wispy S's, felt the gray stubble of his five o'clock shadow, smelled his citrus cologne. She pictured the world in Technicolor again and hoped beyond hope that she could have that with him again. Could she?

Chapter 65

Celia

Sweating under the thin sheet covering her, Celia awoke to bright sunshine streaming through her window. The apartment felt steamy. Now there was no reason not to get the air conditioner fixed. She checked her cell phone and found a text from Detective Dawkins. Then she put on a light robe and stumbled out to the kitchen.

Allison was already dressed and had made coffee. Marcy was still asleep. Celia hugged Allison tightly.

"Geez, Mom. What do I do now?" Allison asked in a muffled voice to keep from waking Marcy. "Feels like I've been hit with a stun gun at full blast."

Celia stepped back but kept a grip on Allison's shoulders. "You are going to live your life and enjoy every minute of it. You have intelligence, beauty, and youth." Celia pushed back a curl of hair on her forehead, thinking that she didn't tell her daughter often enough how special she was.

"That's a compliment coming from the best detective in Florida."

"Speaking of detectives, Officer Dawkins left a text. Want to read it?"

For a moment panic seized Allison. Her eyes glazed over. "Am I still in trouble?"

"No way." Celia held up her smartphone. Dawkins had passed on an apology to Allison from Vanessa for her deception and a solemn oath she would never knowingly kill anyone.

Allison exhaled, her lips in a thin line.

"Seems you meant a lot to her."

"Oh really? While she schemed behind my back and helped Michael frame me?" Allison grunted. "Like she didn't suspect Michael. She sold herself for baubles."

"You were the only true friend she ever had. In the end, she ratted Michael out." Celia's voice softened.

"She also cut herself a deal by giving Michael up." Allison gave a skeptical smile.

"Turning state's evidence put her at risk. Nothing is for sure."

Allison's face tensed. "You're defending her?"

"No, I'm not, but without her cooperation Michael would be free, possibly gunning for us right now."

"I guess there's some good in her." Allison sniffled. "I know this sounds crazy, but I miss her. I seem to take in wounded birds, like Vanessa and Thomas. And Michael, who was abandoned by his father and had an overprotective mother. He needed money and power to prove his worth." She puffed up her cheeks and exhaled hard.

"Don't beat yourself up. Just be a better friend to yourself. You might want to read those cha-cha rules now, like the one that says TRUST YOURSELF. BE YOUR OWN BEST FRIEND."

"Oh, those cha-cha rules. Hmm, maybe they'll help me stop needing to rescue people. Maybe it's why I first became a nurse."

Celia swallowed hard. "I think they will. I abandoned you for a long time. But I promise you it's going to be better from now on. If you'll let me."

Allison smiled. "You nearly died saving my life. It's better already." Allison's face grew serious. "We'll still have issues. Everything between us isn't somehow magically fixed, but now I can listen. We'll work them out."

"I know we can. I promise to try my best."

Allison looked wistful. "I love you, Mom." She gave Celia a rueful smile. "I'm off to reinvent my life." She paused. "Once again."

"Are you sure you don't hate me?"

Allison gave an exaggerated sigh. "I don't hate you even though you're starting to get on my last nerve, babbling so much." She gathered her purse and took out her car keys, but stopped near the door and turned around. "I did learn not to depend on a man. I own my freedom. How I use it is what matters." She hesitated. "E-mail me a copy of those cha-cha rules."

Celia clasped her hands. "You bet."

"I've been thinking about it. Michael's problem is that he never learned the cha-cha." Allison gave Celia a sardonic grin, then kissed her on the cheek just before she hurried out.

Tears streamed from Celia's eyes. She pressed her hands against her face.

She and Allie too readily accepted when others told them, "Trust me," without waiting to make sure that person's behavior matched the promises made. She decided upon her new mantra: Dig into what makes me insecure and fearful, so I can grasp why and then come to a better place.

It reminded her of the cha-cha rule that said: JUDGMENTS IMMOBILIZE THE MIND. THEY LIMIT FREEDOM OF CHOICE. She vowed to stop judging what she saw as the injustices of her past. She and Allie had to lock into the present and build a relationship. Never mind the past. Squeeze all the sweet juices out of life they could, including the pulp. They'd make a renewable contract to discuss and redress issues, accept each other's differences, and keep going forward.

Celia heard Marcy coming out of the bathroom. "Good morning," Marcy said, pouring herself a cup of coffee. She yawned, cocked her head, and peered into Celia's face. "I see that old, sad look in your eye. What's up?"

Celia wiped her eyes with the sleeve of her robe. "Looking to fix things with Allie."

"I'm still marveling at how you figured it all out. Are you a genius or something?"

"I do detective work on other people. Just can't do it on myself."

"Well, we're both working on that. Now tell me." She patted the chair next to her. "What's going on with Stanton?"

Celia sat and closed her eyes, stifling the piercing ache in her chest. "I'm sure I won't hear from him again."

"That stinks," Marcy said. "He should be more understanding. But he came through. That has to count for something, don't you think?"

"I'll get over him, if I live that long. And I'll be honest, I'm worried about Allie and Deb too, not just Stanton," she admitted, sipping her coffee.

"Allie has it all. No doubt she'll land on her feet. As for Deb, when she gets out we should both go and pick her up," Marcy said. "It won't be pretty."

"That's an understatement." Celia said. "I put her son behind bars, maybe for life. I'm picking her up myself, I need to make amends."

Marcy refilled her mug. "Listen, you didn't destroy Michael, he destroyed himself." She pointed her mug of coffee at Celia. "Michael got what he deserved."

"But Deb doesn't deserve this. The woman gave her life to her son, and I took him down."

Marcy grasped Celia's hand. "You saved your daughter's life. Deb will find a way to forgive us."

Celia looked down sadly. "I'm not so sure."

The next afternoon, Celia and Marcy sat on an outdoor bench on a walking path near the clubhouse, drinking coffee from Styrofoam cups. Celia basked in the warmth of the eighty-degree day. She reached into her bag and handed Marcy a Valentine's Day card. "Just a couple of weeks late."

"Thanks." Marcy pecked Celia's cheek. "The perfect person to get a Valentine from."

Celia hadn't heard from Stanton yet, but no surprise. She figured he'd done her one last favor and that was the end of it.

"Feels strange to think life is back to normal, almost," Celia said.

"Yup." Marcy drank her coffee and looked coy.

Celia squinted at Marcy. "I can see there's something you're dying to tell me."

"You bet your tootsies," Marcy said. "A hottie who read the article in the *Retirement Newsletter* e-mailed me." Marcy shimmied her shoulders. "Hot damn."

"Who is this guy?"

"He's a lawyer with the ACLU and was excited to read about all the charity work I do. He said he was excited to meet a fifty-three-year-old liberal he could share his life passions with."

Celia nearly slid off the bench. "You do some charity work, but you're not involved in liberal causes, and you're not fifty-three. That's downright deceptive."

"I don't do numbers, and I'm about to become an activist. I signed up to read to kids and volunteered in a soup kitchen." She thumped her sternum. "I think it's my calling."

"You'd better check this guy's medical history before you go to bed with him," Celia teased. "Make sure he has a strong heart and don't go calling me if he dies on you."

"Very funny." Marcy scowled at Celia then tittered. "This is for real."

Celia rose and threw her cup in the trash. "Good for you. I have some charities on my list, too." She returned to her seat. "Besides continuing with the pottery class, I'm volunteering to bring art to prisoners, abused women and children in shelters, that kind of thing." She nodded her head for emphasis.

"Sounds great." Marcy sipped her coffee. "What's happening with Vanessa?"

"Allie visited her. They'll never be friends again, but Allie said she owed it to her. Vanessa cut a good deal. Three years of community service, and six years of probation for aiding and abetting Michael's embezzling. There's no proof she had anything to do with the murders."

"That sounds too lenient," Marcy huffed.

"Of course she got credit for turning state's evidence. The upside is no bail for him."

Marcy looked serious. "In all this hullabaloo I learned something." She looked Celia in the eye. "At first, I was really mad at you when you called me out for my irresponsibility with Melvin. But I realized you hit the nail on the head." She paused thoughtfully. "I used sex like a junkie, but the addiction was for male attention. If I really like a guy, I use him and wind up tossing him aside before he can reject me. Underneath, I think I hate myself." She looked down. "Maybe I didn't have enough self-respect to keep my kids. Honestly, it sounds trite, but I had no sense of self-worth."

Celia touched Marcy's shoulder as her façade of self-assurance dissolved. She'd always suspected Marcy wasn't as enamored with the act of sex as much as needing to be desired by men, and she was glad she was finding it out for herself. "You're a victim of abuse, but then we all have to learn to get out of our own way or the past rides herd over us."

"I found that out just a tad too late. Lord, how I miss my kids," Marcy said, her voice cracking. She looked up, blinking back tears.

Celia wondered if she should tell Marcy what she'd done two nights ago. She'd looked up her son's e-mail address online and sent him a note: "Your mother has never forgiven herself for losing her children. She loves you and wants to see you. She begs for your forgiveness. Please, please respond. Her friend, Celia Ewing."

She hadn't gotten a reply yet and didn't want to get Marcy's hopes up, so she decided to keep it to herself.

Marcy dabbed at her eyes and sat straight up. "Anyway, with all that's happened, I have to change. I'm not looking for Mr. Liberal to save me either."

Celia took a deep breath and let it out slowly. "Look, it was easier for me to give in to marriage, a house with a white picket fence, church on Sundays, and raising a child even if I was unqualified. I love my daughter, but by ignoring the real me I wound up damaging her. I'm not sure I can ever forgive myself for that."

"Well, you should. You've proved yourself. And we all have

our shit," Marcy said firmly. "Deb ignored her abusive marriage by overprotecting a sociopathic son, enabling him to cover up his crimes until he felt invincible. She thought that was love."

"Amen to that," Celia murmured. "Well, we're all out of the closet now."

"Is that like coming out gay? Well, if I were gay I'd marry you because you're a good cook."

"I'll cook for you the rest of my life." Celia smiled then grew somber. "I'm picking Deb up later this afternoon."

Marcy's pained face spoke to how Celia felt. "We'll help her through this. We can do it. And Stanton? Will you try again?"

It was like an arrow piercing Celia's heart. "I don't think so. I'm just grateful he came through when I needed him."

"Another amen to that."

Back in her apartment, Celia's mind kept drifting back over the past few weeks. Her body still felt tightly coiled. So many lives had been changed or lost. Brady Shirkson, a powerful man who got caught in the trap set up by a manipulative woman, his ego outweighing his rational thinking. Unconditional adoration and good sex could entrap anyone. Vanessa had learned early on to use her street smarts and her looks. What a waste that such a clever and vibrant young woman had thrown away so much for a terrible man, but Celia also knew desperation drove people to do things they'd never imagined.

And, in the midst of the quagmire, Michael suffered from living only for the accumulation of wealth. The need for a big financial portfolio, fancy cars, palatial homes, designer clothes became an obsession to prove his worth. When the thrill of his new toys wore off, another frantic search began, and on and on.

People were simply pawns in Michael's sadistic game as he put wealth above humanity. He disposed of human life as easily as eating a meal. He had even sacrificed his mother, who gave him nothing but unconditional love. Was this weakness or strength as a mother? Could the fact that Deb never said no to him and never meted out consequences for inappropriate behavior have led to something as awful as this? No, he was an adult and had to take full responsibility.

As for Allie, her heart ached. She prayed that Allison would one day heal and find a good, decent man whom she loved and would love and trust her the way she deserved in return.

When she thought of Stanton the knot in her stomach tightened. She had arrived in Florida, her true self hidden so far inside that upon surfacing it needed oxygen. Finding independence had topped her agenda, and she'd made inroads even before seeing Stanton again. He'd infused every part of her with sweetness, adding a dimension of contentment she had never felt before. But now he was gone, leaving a scorching hollow in his wake. She needed to sort out the past harrowing events, and then get on with life or else. She looked forward to getting back to her pottery class and volunteering, like she'd told Marcy.

In the end, there was an upside. Allison said she'd decided to stay in Florida because she hadn't seen Hemingway's house in Key West yet.

Chapter 66

Celia

On the drive to Hashford, Celia thought about the irony that the name of this place sounded so innocuous yet housed so many disturbed people. She couldn't wait to get her sweet friend out of there.

As she neared the tall, rectangular brick building with barred windows, she brimmed with anxiety for how Deb would react to the news about Michael.

She pulled up and parked the car, walking along a cracked concrete path into a dark, dingy lobby. When she told them why she was there, an aide asked her to wait while they got Deb. Minutes passed. Finally Celia spotted Deb coming slowly down the hall, escorted by aides on either side of her. One of them held her suitcase.

It shocked Celia to see how much Deb had aged in a couple of weeks. She was much thinner, and the lines on her face seemed more pronounced.

Celia ran up to Deb, worried how she'd make it. She hugged her, feeling the thin, delicate bones of her back and chest. She was struck by the sensation that she cupped a baby bird.

"My darling friend," Celia cooed, but Deb stood stock still, arms at her sides.

When Celia released her, Deb let the aides help her walk to the car. They buckled her in as Celia hurried to the driver's side.

"You're all right now." Celia nearly choked on her words as she steered the car down the long drive and off the grounds.

Deb looked at Celia with watery eyes. "How can I be?"

Her expression broke Celia's heart, and she looked away. "So you know. I don't know what to say."

The silence hung thick between them. Finally Celia said, "Please, Deb. What I did was awful, but I had no other option. Exposing Michael … I had to save my daughter. I had to save all those people. I am so sorry, I can't apologize enough. I beg your forgiveness."

Deb stared out the side window. "I forgive you. I don't forgive myself."

"You had nothing to do with it."

"Yes I did. I enabled my son. He did some awful things. He once beat up a coach's son within an inch of his life because the kid accidentally caused Michael to crack a rib. As a juvenile, they sealed his record and he wasn't jailed because it was his first offense. But he was always getting into terrible trouble. Once, at age sixteen, he was accused of raping a fifteen-year-old. I paid that one off. I always had his back. He got counseling, but he used what he learned to cover his tracks."

"He's responsible for himself. You did what you thought was right, and you can't take the blame."

Deb turned her head away. Torn between love for her friend and anger at Michael, Celia's jaw clamped tight. "You know that Michael drugged you, don't you?"

Deb spoke slowly, haltingly, in a monotone. "I know that now. All those pills made me act senile, but I believed he wanted me to help me get well. They weaned me off them in that disgusting place. I believed I had Alzheimer's, so I took the Aricept. He's my son. I trusted him. Why would I think he'd want to hurt me? He's my son. He's my son. He's my son." Deb slumped in the seat.

Celia didn't know how else to console her. "You can visit him a couple of times a month."

"I know. My lawyer told me," Deb said in a monotone.

"Marcy and I will take care of you. I'll drive you to visit Michael, if you want."

"No. I'm going to live near the prison, wherever he ends up. If he gets a death …" Deb swallowed hard, bobbling her Adam's apple, and couldn't go on.

Celia gripped the steering wheel until her hands tingled. "Michael has to face the punishment, and you have to get on with your life."

"What life? You want me to do tough love at my age?" Deb sounded angry.

"It's not a bad idea," Celia said. "You'll wind up killing yourself otherwise."

"My son is gone. I'm dead now." Deb let out a sob. "I can't see you anymore, or Marcy either."

Panic prickled the back of Celia's neck. "Oh my God, don't say that. We're the Three Musketeers, remember?"

Deb glanced at Celia with a vacant stare. "I know you had to do it, but every time I see you or Marcy, it will remind me of what happened. It makes me know I'm as guilty as Michael."

Tears poured down Celia's face, shattering what little composure she had left. She veered the car to the curb and turned off the engine. Pressing her forehead against the steering wheel, sobs rose from deep in her gut, wracking her body. With the lightest touch, Deb put her hand on Celia's back, then pulled it away.

When Celia regained her breath, she restarted the car and drove home. She silently walked Deb to her apartment. Words wouldn't repair the rupture between them. Deb gave her a final long look before closing her door. The lock fell into place with a resounding snap.

On the slow trek back home, Celia felt like a pallbearer at a funeral.

Back at her apartment, Celia paced for several minutes, unsure of what to do next. The tomblike quiet filled the room and made her want to scream. It felt like a vital organ had been cut out of her body, and she'd been thrown out into the wild to figure out how to live without it. How would she and Marcy go on without having Deb as part of the family they'd cobbled together?

She lumbered over to her desk and checked her e-mail for something to do. Her eyes widened as she found a message from Daniel, Marcy's son, in her inbox. The message was short, and joy surged through her. Without wasting a minute, she ran to the phone and called Marcy. "Marcy, you're not going to believe this. You have a three-year-old granddaughter!"

"What? What? Slow down. What?"

"I looked up your son online because I couldn't stand thinking of you being separated from your children anymore. I wrote him a note begging him to reconcile with you, and he responded. He said you can meet your granddaughter."

Marcy let out a harsh, garbled sound. "Are you … is this for real? If you're pulling my leg, it's not funny. My God. Is this real?"

"I wouldn't kid about this." Celia paused. "Marcy, what's wrong? What is it?"

"Ah, it's just that suddenly, I'm scared of what I wished for with all my heart."

"What do you mean? Scared of what?"

"I'm so ashamed of deserting them. I won't know what to do or say. It's so sudden."

"Look, just say you're sorry and show how much you love them. They are opening their hearts to you. It's hard for them too. My God. You've got a grandchild. I so envy that."

"You couldn't have given me a better gift." She was quiet. "Thank you, Celia. Thank you, thank you, and thank you."

"I'm so happy for you! I'm glad I had some good news to lead with." She swallowed hard. "The bad news is that Deb won't have anything to do with us." Celia bit her tongue to keep from crying again.

"I'm so sorry. It's hard to get over a son murdering someone in her apartment, among other things. That can shock the hell out of you," Marcy said, her voice sounding mired in mud. "She'll come around."

"She's pretty determined." Celia said.

"Give her time." Marcy paused. "I have a date with Mr. ACLU, but I'll cancel it. We can smoke a joint together."

Celia chuckled. "You go. Relax, and have a good time. Remember, just be yourself."

"Celia, thank you again, sincerely. You're the greatest friend I've ever had. I love you."

"I love you too, with all my heart." Celia hung up. Silence filled her apartment again.

She felt restless and changed into old jeans and a T-shirt. Pulling out a step stool in the kitchen, she took all her dishes out of the cabinets to wipe down the already immaculate shelves. Then she washed all the dishes, dusted the vents, scrubbed the counters, and started polishing the silver. The harsh scent of chemicals burned her nasal passages but pleased her in an odd way, like receiving a well-deserved punch.

As she wiped polish over the silver, she thought about who she'd become. She'd spent years living with fear and a sense of worthlessness while trapped in a bad marriage and battling terrible depression. She neglected her own emotional needs and her child's as a result. Her future included being on the lookout for depression rearing its ugly head again, always battling her old demons. There was no easy way out. This was forever. But now she thought she'd learned new ways of coping that would help see her through.

The phone rang. She dropped the spoon she was polishing and picked up right away, wishing Deb would change her mind. "Hello?"

A resonant male voice said, "Sorry for the delay. Been doing some thinking."

Stanton's deep baritone voice startled her. He sounded neither angry nor inviting. Her breathing quickened as she thought about hanging up, but she owed him at least one last conversation. Afterward, she intended to take a sleeping pill and find a night of solace in bed with the covers pulled over her head. "Let me guess," she finally managed. "You're engaged to Edith."

"Pshaw." He laughed. "News flash: Edith Onstader is dating Officer Johnson. Apparently, they hit it off when he interviewed her, and she called him back. I'm happy for her."

"I don't know which one I feel sorrier for," Celia quipped. Stanton laughed warmly.

"I'm indebted to Johnson. He gave me an easy out." He chortled.

"Here's another tidbit of news. I hear that Johnson got promoted to detective and Dawkins is now Chief Detective Dawkins. They both wound up taking full credit for solving the case, never mentioning Detective Celia Ewing."

"That's all right. I don't need recognition. Saving my daughter mattered most."

"Well, I still find it unfair."

An awkward silence filled the air, and Celia struggled for something to say. "Thanks again for distracting Michael."

"You wrote the script. I'm just a humble actor."

"But a good one."

He clicked his tongue. "You'd have thought of a way to get Michael out of the office if I didn't do it. You did great, Celia." He paused. "Tell me what happened after I took Michael to lunch and made my presentation. It's only fair, you know."

She pictured the way he winked whenever they'd shared a secret and felt a jolt. He now sounded warm and fuzzy. Good sign? Bad sign? "Are you sure you want to hear about the crime I committed? You don't like finagling."

"I have to admit I'm dying to know."

"While you diverted Michael at lunch I installed the keystroke logger. When he got back to his office, he withdrew money from his offshore accounts for the new scam you talked him into. With his PIN and password in hand, I asked the bank for a financial statement on that account. I took the information to the police, who got a warrant to wiretap him. They offered Vanessa a deal if she lured Michael into admitting guilt on tape. She agreed and did a good job. We got it all."

"I'm a computer expert, so why didn't I think of that?"

"You have to think like a criminal. I seem to be good at that. Oh, and after Michael was arrested, chaos hit the office with FBI suits and employees running every which way. It was easy to go back amidst the hubbub and remove the keystroke logger."

"I'll keep my credit cards under lock and key when you're around. I might even hire you to do a computer forensic job."

Did that mean he wanted to see her again? *Stop being ridiculous!* "Michael was arrested, but the real downside is that Allie loved Michael and he betrayed her in the worst possible way." She bit her lip. "And Deb is devastated. She wants me and Marcy out of her life." She felt a tightening in her stomach and forced herself to take a deep breath.

"Oh damn. I'm so sorry to hear that, Celia. You went into battle and won, but the sad reality is that friendly fire hits your compatriots. It's inevitable in a war."

Celia winced. "Is that the meaning of victory being a double-edged sword? I understand it now on a personal level."

She listened to Stanton breathing for several moments. "You are brilliant, my dear, sweet Celia," he said softly.

Clamping her mouth tight, she wondered if she heard him correctly. "Stanton, I have to tell you something. When I first saw you in Florida I couldn't believe my good luck. But I'm afraid that I screwed it up and I've lost you."

He sighed. "I was angry at first when you cut me off, but I realize now you were just protecting your daughter. I acted like a jackass." Neither said a word for a several seconds. "I miss you."

Celia felt light-headed. "I ... I miss you too." A closed steel door to her heart swung open, and warm summer breezes flowed through her. Maybe Stanton wouldn't be the cure to what ailed her.

She needed to learn to know and like herself for herself. Whatever else came her way she felt ready to handle it. Bring it on!

"So, we can go out again sometime?" he asked.

Her throat closed up. She took in a slow, long breath.

"Celia, are you still there?"

The last rule of cha-cha coasted into her head, accompanied by a Latin rhythm. BE A LITTLE BAD. THE KIND OF BAD THAT ENHANCES LIFE!

"Yes Stanton," she said at last. "I am definitely still here. And I think we should go dancing."

Acknowledgments

I'd like to thank those who were helpful and supportive of me during the writing of this book.

To my wonderful, loving children, Carla Lieske, Stephen Lieske, and Ross Metzman; and my outstanding, talented grandchildren, Alexander and Zachary Lieske. To those who believed in me and helped me shape my story: Joy Stocke, Kim Nagy, Raquel Pidal, Jess Rinker, Hamadi Mosbahi, Wendy Mosbahi, and my students at Temple University's OLLI, who teach me about life all the time. Essie Goldberg and Ellen Marks helped as well, and my friend Arlene Olson has been a great cheerleader throughout. Last, but certainly not least, is one of the most important: thank you to Jay Joseph, who has given me unending support and so much caring.

Frances Metzman

If you enjoyed reading this book,
please put a positive review on Amazon.com.
It would be very much appreciated.

Thanks,
Frances

About the Author

Frances Metzman is the author of the short story collection *The Hungry Heart Stories* (2012, Wilderness House Press) and was nominated for a Dzanc Books Best of the Web award in 2009. She is also coauthor of the novel *Ugly Cookies* (2000, Pella Press). In addition to appearing on panels at various writing conferences such as Philadelphia Stories and Marymount Manhattan College Conference, she has given workshops at Temple University, Bryn Mawr College, Penn State, and many others. At Rosemont College, she taught publishing/writing skills to grad students. She currently teaches creative writing/memoir workshops at Temple University's Osher Lifelong Learning Institute (OLLI). As fiction editor for the literary journal *Schuylkill Valley Journal*, she selects and edits submissions. Her website is www.FrancesMetzman.com

 Frances Metzman Written Work

@FranWrites